TE

D0486488

Advance Praise for *Black Dog*

"As dark as hell, *Black Dog* is one wild ride, and I loved every delicious, twisted moment. Caitlin Kittredge is an author at the top of her game. Urban fantasy doesn't get more kick-ass than this."
—Adam Christopher, author of *Empire State*

"Caitlin Kittredge's *Black Dog* reads like *The Sopranos* with all the forces of Heaven and Hell at stake. A riveting, fun, and dangerous ride with angels, demons, necromancers, and a badass heroine to root for!"
—Melissa de la Cruz, *New York Times* bestselling author of *Blue Bloods* and *Witches of East End*

"Some books steal your heart, but *Black Dog* will steal your soul. Caitlin Kittredge has given the urban fantasy genre a kick in the face—she gives the genre tropes a much-needed upgrade and slathers the whole thing in a heaping helping of horror, humor, and hard-hitting prose. I want more and I want it yesterday."
—Chuck Wendig, author of *Blackbirds*

"Mwahahaha . . . That was wicked! Couldn't put it down. *Black Dog* is off the chain and Kittredge is in top form in this dark, twisty trip down a gritty road to Hell."
—Kat Richardson, bestselling author of *Greywalker*

"Caitlin Kittredge at her ferocious best. *Black Dog* sinks its teeth and claws into you and doesn't let go. And you won't want it to."
—Richard Kadrey, *New York Times* bestselling author of the Sandman Slim series

BLACK DOG

Also by Caitlin Kittredge

Black London Series

Street Magic
Demon Bound
Bone Gods
Soul Trade
Devil's Business
Dark Days

Iron Codex Trilogy (for young adults)

The Iron Thorn
The Nightmare Garden
The Mirrored Shard

BLACK DOG

HELLHOUND CHRONICLES BOOK 1

CAITLIN KITTREDGE

HARPER Voyager

An Imprint of HarperCollins Publishers

3NECBS0093513Q

Harper Voyager and design is a trademark of HCP LLC.

FIRST EDITION

Library of Congress Cataloging-in-Publication Data has been applied for.

ISBN 978-0-06-231691-2

14 15 16 17 18 OV/RRD 10 9 8 7 6 5 4 3 2 1

For Sara, the best BFF anyone could ask for

Blues falling down like hail
Blues falling down like hail
And the day keeps on worryin' me
There's a hellhound on my trail

—ROBERT JOHNSON,
"Hellhound on My Trail"

ACKNOWLEDGMENTS

Thanks to Barry Goldblatt, Kelly O'Connor,
Diana Gill, Richard Kadrey, Melissa de la Cruz,
Adam Christopher, Kat Richardson,
Chuck Wendig, and Stephen Blackmoore.
And, of course, thanks to my family for putting up
with me.

BLACK DOG

CHAPTER

1

||||||||||||||||||||||||||||||||||||||||||||||||||||||||||||||||||||||||||||

Knowing that a person is marked for death is a strange feeling, one that crawls inside you and puts down roots. It's stranger still when you're the one meant to deliver their soul.

My mark's gut strained against the blue fabric of his Breakfast Barn shirt, and sweat beaded on the back of his neck. He checked out a waitress's ass as she walked by the cash register. His name was, by cruel circumstance, Bob Dobkins.

I sipped cold coffee from a chipped mug, feeling the acid swirl around in my stomach. I wondered if Bob Dobkins would do something different if he knew this was the last day of his life. Wake up and try not to be an asshole, at the very least.

I watched Bob Dobkins cash out two teenage girls, leering down the T-shirt of the one on the left.

Then again, his day probably would have gone exactly the same.

The girls left, oblivious of the pervert behind the register, and their car left the parking lot empty and mud-spattered, aside from my road bike. No other cars made their way past the silver hulk of the Breakfast Barn, and if they did, I doubted anyone else would stop at this small gap in the primeval Oregon forest that closed in on all sides.

"Goin' on break!" Bob hollered at his shift manager and pushed through the double doors to the kitchen. I waited through two more swallows of coffee, put down a five-dollar bill on my sticky table, and followed him.

Nobody so much as looked at me as I slipped between line cooks and dishwashers in the back, the scents of grease and steam and rotted food clogging up my nose. People had a way of not seeing me. Of not *wanting* to see me, more like, that let me stay pretty much off human radar.

Unless that human was Bob Dobkins.

He leaned against the cinder block wall next to the trash bins outside the back door, sucking on a cigarette. The smoke blended with the thin tendrils of mist that clung to the tops of the fir trees, daring the sun to burn it away.

"Those are bad for you, Bob," I said, and he jumped, the butt falling from his fingers to sizzle out in a puddle.

"Shit," he grumbled, looking me up and down. "Who the hell are you?"

"You should be asking who I work for."

It took a minute, but Bob Dobkins figured it out. His eyes got big and shiny, like an animal's, and his pulse rate climbed up into the red zone. I smelled his sweat, even though I wished I couldn't.

"You've made a mistake," he managed, sounding like somebody was choking him.

I held out my hand for his pack. "May I?"

He held it out, never blinking. I took a cigarette and lit it. The first hit in my lungs stung, and I exhaled toward the trees.

"I don't think I have, Bob."

"That's not my name," he said, and he finally took his eyes off me long enough to flick them toward the parking lot.

Shit. He was calculating how fast he'd have to run to get rid of me.

"Oh, I know that here, you're Jerry. Jerry Finch. But back in Chicago, your name is Robert Dobkins, and no matter what your name is, buddy, you owe a demon your soul."

His heartbeat was a racehorse now, and I watched the thick vein in his neck jump. I smiled and let more smoke trickle from my nostrils. "I don't make mistakes, Bob. Jerry. Whatever. You're the one who made the mistake in this situation."

The cigarette wasn't doing me any favors. I'd been up for three days, tracking Bob Dobkins from the outskirts of Chicago, where he'd left a crime scene in his suburban garage, through three more dead girls in Minnesota, Wyoming, and Idaho, and finally here.

"Let's stop all the bullshit." Bob had finally found his voice, and actually managed to surprise me. "You and I both know what's going on, so name your price." He swallowed. I wondered how that big lump of terror tasted.

I let one eyebrow go up. Normally I find the expressionless leg-breaker act is the way to go, but human beings can always surprise you.

"I'm not involved in that side of things." I waved him off. "I don't make deals."

"Then get your cute little ass in gear and get hold of the guy I signed off with in the first place," Bob Dobkins said. He'd stopped shaking, and I took that as a bad sign. A mark who tries to run is normal—it's down to that survival instinct all humans have. Not the most fine-tuned I've ever seen, or they wouldn't get involved with folks like my boss in the first place, but it's there.

A mark who's not afraid of you, though—that's dangerous.

I dragged. Felt the nicotine light up my nerve endings, my tired brain, my poor abused stomach. "Not going to happen, Bob."

"I don't think you know who you're dealing with," he snarled. "I command dark magic, bitch, and you don't want to get on my bad side."

Stinky as his sweat was, his breath was ten times as bad. I took a step back, and Bob Dobkins took that as a sign of weakness. He backed me up against the Dumpster, one hand on either side of my head. He had a good six inches and hundred pounds on me, plus the aforementioned dark magic. Bob Dobkins had gotten mixed up with some heavy juju in Chicago, and when his human sacrifices had drawn the attention of people who object to that sort of thing, he'd signed on with my boss. Gotten protection, power. Everything he wanted, and I was threatening to take it away.

Probably not the smartest thing I'd ever done.

"Get your boss down here now," he said. "And maybe I won't peel your skin back inch by inch and see what's underneath." He lowered his head and snorted a hit off my hair, which was more disgusting than I can say. "Then again, I might. I always did like a pretty girl on my altar."

I raised the cigarette and blew smoke in his face, so he coughed and blinked. Possibly also not the smartest thing I've ever done.

"Let me ask you something, Bob," I said. "If you're the bad motherfucker you claim to be, why would my boss send a pretty girl to collect from you? For that matter, what on this earth makes you think that when you sign on with a demon, you can run off to Oregon, get a different name on your shirt, and avoid the debt you owe? Is it just human hubris, Bob, or are you really that damn stupid?"

He didn't hit me or try to sling a spell, and that was something. That lizard brain of his was chewing over my words, trying to figure out how they could hurt or help his chances to walk away from this.

"I'll make a new deal," he said, but a lot of his sass was gone.

"Not with me," I said. "I don't bargain. I don't argue. Just collect." I dragged again, and Bob Dobkins drew back from the hot cherry of my cigarette. "You had the time you were allotted when you signed on," I said. "And now that my smoke is gone, your time is up."

I stood up straight, knocking his hands off me, and he stumbled back a step.

I dropped my butt and crushed it under my boot, and Bob Dobkins's heartbeat started up again. The fear was back. Good. Nothing scares the shit out of bottom-feeding predators like finding out they're really the prey.

"Oh, and Bob?" I said as he took another step back, and another.

"Get your boss down here!" he hollered, although his voice broke on the last word. "Make me a new fucking deal!"

"If you run," I said, feeling my fangs burst through my gums and tasting the old-penny tang of my own blood, "you're going to find out exactly what's underneath my skin."

Bob Dobkins let out a yelp at the sight of my fangs and ran. I sighed and ran after him.

For a fat guy, he could move. He had a good lead on me across the parking lot and into the ditch on the far side of the state highway. Fine. He could have his lead until I hit the tree line.

I cleared the ditch, my boots sinking into the moss and fir needles, raising the smell of rich loamy earth. Bob Dobkins's blue shirt flashed among the branches, and I heard his lungs making hacksaw sounds.

I poured on more speed, and as the trees became a blur of green and brown and silky blue-gray mist, I lifted my feet off the ground in a leap, gathered, and landed on all fours.

My paws got better traction on the forest floor and I saw the hulk of Bob Dobkins ahead of me as I ran, showing up white-hot through the gray spectrum of my vision.

He looked back, saw what was behind him, and let out a shriek. Then his foot hit a stump, and he tumbled, ass over heels. Ate some mud on the way down. I can't say that didn't bring me a little satisfaction.

"I told you running was a bad idea," I said, which just made Bob shriek louder and try to claw his way up the nearest tree like a scared tomcat. Unless you're a demon, some kind of lesser Hellspawn, or a werewolf, my words when I'm walking on all fours just sound like snarls. Hungry snarls, judging by Bob's reaction.

He managed to crawl over the mud and down to the bank of a stream whispering between moss-covered rocks. Old stories about creatures like me not crossing running water, I supposed. Desperate people will believe anything.

I padded into the water, feeling the shock of cold on the pads of my paws. Bob was only sobbing now, incoherent and reedy, like a broken speaker.

Close as I was, I could see the halo of the dark magic he cloaked himself in, like his soul was covered in soot and oil. He'd done a lot of damage to himself. But that wasn't my problem.

I opened my jaws and bit down, hard. When I did, Bob was silent at last. Now the one making the noise was me. I felt a shudder worm its way down my spine as his soul's energy left his corpse and poured into me. When I didn't have to shift, I used a blade consecrated by a reaper that acted like a magnet for the unique frequency of power put out by human souls.

With assholes like Bob Dobkins, though, it was all tooth and nail. When I finished, my jaws were bloody. The taste of metal and fear rested on my tongue.

I shut my eyes, and when I opened them, the trees were in color again. I just lay for a few minutes, listening to my heart pound. My face felt sticky when I put my hand up, and I splashed water from the stream over my lips and chin.

My skin tingled and my muscles tittered, as if I'd been struck by lightning. The rush of Bob Dobkins's soul settled in my chest like a hot coal.

Getting up was a little bit of slapstick that ended with me up to the wrists in river mud. Shifting didn't take it out of me like it did a lycanthrope, but stripping out a soul with no buffer was akin to biting a power line.

Fucking Bob Dobkins. I hoped that whatever Gary had in mind for him, it was painful and would last at least a century.

2

Gary wanted to meet at a diner in Seaside, and thick patches of rain and salt-scented fog blanketed the place when I pulled up, droplets pinging off my helmet and the tank of my Harley Softail.

I shook off the rain when I stepped inside the diner. A narrow place tacked on to the side of an arcade that beeped and whirred through the wall, one door in and out. A few wet tourists arguing over where to go for dinner, a trucker at the counter, one waitress, one cook.

Not an optimal setup if I had to make a messy exit. And Gary knew it, which was why he'd picked it in the first place, I was sure.

Gary raised a hand from the last booth. Wilson leaned against the wall next to him, and a snarl rumbled in his chest when I slid into the seat.

I met and held his eyes, animal gold even when he was on two legs. Wilson was ugly enough to scare babies and meaner than a grizzly in a bear trap, but as long as Gary was holding his leash, all he could do was talk.

We stared at each other until Gary snapped his fingers in my face. "You come here for the coffee, or do you have something for me?"

Wilson snorted, but he looked away first. He turned back to watching the tourists and the trucker. His shaved head gleamed under the naked fluorescent bulbs, skin road-mapped with scars. The heaviest had partially shut his right eye and continued down his cheek like somebody had tried to carve him a new mouth.

"Always so nice to have the whole family together," Gary said. Acid etched his words, and he didn't bother asking when he grabbed my wrist and rolled up the sleeve of my leather. "Where'd you find him?" he asked as he rummaged in his briefcase for the sterile needle.

"Clackamus," I said. "Changed his name."

Gary shook his head. He put the needle on the table and produced a pair of reading glasses, perching them on his nose before he withdrew his ledger and his Scythe.

I don't really know how the whole image of reapers in Batman capes toting farm implements got started, but Gary couldn't be further from it. He wore soft sport coats in muted colors. His skin was office-worker sallow, his hair was dark and wavy, and he looked like my boring single uncle, if I were the type of person who had an uncle. Or a family.

Make no mistake, though, Gary was a hard-ass. You don't last long as a reaper if you aren't one. The career stresses are similar to being a loan shark. In Hell.

"Where's your blade?" he asked. I shook my head. Wilson swung his thousand-pound gaze back to me. Hoping, no doubt, that Gary would blow his dog whistle and give him the order to break my face.

"You went four-legged on this one?" Gary whistled, and put the needle back in his briefcase. "Old school. You want to tell me why you risked a shift in broad daylight for some B-list warlock dumbass who can't read the fine print?"

I lifted one shoulder.

"I see," Gary said. He hefted his Scythe. Anything could be a conduit for a reaper's power—I'd seen jewelry, statuary, even a baseball bat once. Gary was posh, though, and he favored a small dagger with a ruby-set handle, designed to be concealed inside a sleeve.

"You never have a reason for why you do anything, do you, Ava?" he said, so quiet I had to strain to hear him even with my ears. "You simply act and never consider the consequences, like the animal you are."

Inside, I felt my guts crawl with an entirely new kind of pain. Forget Wilson. When Gary was pissed, you ran for the bunker and prayed Kansas would still be there when the tornado was over.

"He ran," I said.

Gary stared at me, still holding his Scythe, with an expression that stopped my heart. The fluorescents flickered, and one sparked out with a tinkling of glass. Even the sounds of the human world outside seemed to fade and slow down. Sweat broke out all over me, ice cold against my burning skin. Gary could pulverize me and not think twice. Worse, he could decide he was done letting me run free and send me downstairs to our boss. Hellhounds didn't fare well among demons. At best, we were pets. At worst, we died for the Hellspawn's amusement.

Gary laughed. He took off his glasses and chuckled, examining them in the light before tucking them into his pocket. "I do like you, Ava," he said. "You're almost refreshingly stupid."

Faster than my eye could follow, his knife hand flashed out and pinned my own hand to the table, blade going clean through and biting into the tabletop. "Don't disobey me again."

I couldn't say anything, not that I would have opened my mouth. I wasn't as stupid as Gary thought. But the pain was too much, the pull of the reaper's Scythe removing and storing the condemned soul I'd brought it.

It felt like choking, like drowning and being burned alive at the same time. Like all the parts of me that weren't the hound were burning up along with Bob Dobkins's soul.

I didn't scream—that would have been embarrassing, never mind just tick Gary off all over again. Pain was something I'd gotten used to a long time ago. It always stopped, eventually.

Wilson smirked as I struggled, pinned to the table like a science experiment. I decided as soon as I could move again I was going to kick him, just to vent some frustration.

Usually reapers shared blood with their hounds and transferred the soul through the resulting connection. It worked when I used my own knife on someone who owed, the small blade working as an extension of Gary's Scythe with a fraction of its power.

Not when I drank the soul whole, though. This was the only way.

Gary withdrew his Scythe, wiping it on a silk cloth before tucking it into his jacket. I fell back against the booth, the cords of pain cut. All I could do for the moment was breathe and concentrate on not throwing up.

Gary made a note in his ledger, raising his eyebrow. "Come on, now. It wasn't that bad."

I knew what I was supposed to say, and that anything else would just aggravate his clearly rotten mood, so I shook my head. "No, sir."

Gary turned over a couple of pages. "Wilson, go start the car."

Wilson grunted, his lip peeling back from his teeth. "But—"

"Did I ask you or tell you?"

I was just glad I wasn't the one on the receiving end of Gary's glare this time. Wilson huffed a little air, but he limped out of the diner, slamming the door so hard the bell echoed over everything else.

"Ugly bastard, isn't he?" Gary said. I blinked, genuinely surprised. Gary wasn't what you'd call the chatty type, at least not with his employees.

"I don't think he likes me very much," I ventured. That was a nice way of saying Wilson would snap my neck like a twig if he ever got the chance. The scars and the limp were bad enough, but to have a parade of other hounds, hounds who could still go out and perform the duty we were bred for, clearly cut him to the core. Why he reserved his actual aggression for me, I'd never know.

"He was stupid," Gary said. "He paid the price. Crying about it just makes him look weak. Sooner or later something is going to take him up on the offer and then I suppose I'll have to train a new driver."

This was downright strange. Not to mention wrong. Wilson had been jumped by a pack of shifters—mostly wolves, some dogs and big cats mixed in. All outlaws, castoffs from various clans. Trying to set up a protection racket on Gary's turf, promising human warlocks and other small-timers like vampires and deadheads that they'd keep the Hellspawn off their asses.

Gary hadn't liked that, and Wilson had been his big stick at the time, but one hound, no matter how big and bad, was no match for twenty pissed-off shifters.

Wilson had been mauled and left for dead, and he'd not only recovered, but enough to walk and talk again. He couldn't run, and even when he shifted he came up lame, but the fact that he was alive should be enough to spread his legend far and wide, as far as I was concerned. Too bad he was such a jackass.

"Am I supposed to be learning some valuable lesson from all this?" I said.

Gary spun the ledger around so I could read the name at the top of the blank page. "You're going to the desert," he said. His finger slid along the type, highlighting his fussy accountant's penmanship. Gary's hand was soft and pale as the rest of him. Hounds sometimes said that reapers didn't really look human, that they were something else under the skin just like us, but I could never imagine Gary as anything but a tweedy dude with a bad attitude.

I read the name—ALEX IVANOF. I nodded, because the only thing you could do was obey when a reaper gave you orders, no matter how tired or hungry or hurt you were. "He's past due?"

"No," Gary said. "You'll get the download when you get to the safe house, but the short version is there's been a swing in the deadhead activity around Ivanof's neck of the woods, and the boss would dearly love to know what's going on."

He shut the ledger and tucked it away. "And when I went to visit dear old Alex, he'd done a rabbit. So now, Ava, you get to go do what you do best."

"And what's that?" I asked, not at all sure I'd like the answer.

Gary stood and grinned at me, a perfect white grin like a blade against my throat.

"Fetch."

3

Storms rolled east with me as I pushed the Harley down I-10. My hand still ached every time I squeezed the throttle, and my chest got tight every time I thought about Gary. I watched lightning fork back and forth between the anvil-shaped clouds, even though the land had turned from forest to desert around me.

Las Vegas lit up the belly of the storm, casting the scaly thunderheads in sharp relief. The spotlight on top of the Luxor pierced the storm, and like the desert knew I was coming, thunder cracked and rain blanketed the highway.

I pulled into a service station off the interstate and took off my helmet, feeling the water stream through my hair. Where I came from this would be hurricane weather, the sky the color of a bruise while the earth shook in time with the rolling thunder.

The rain passed after a few minutes as the storm scudded on past Vegas and out into the Mojave. I took off my gloves and swiped the water off my face, wincing at the deep red mark the Scythe had left on me. It was my own fault—I should have run down Bob Dobkins and cut out his soul like I was supposed to, not gone after him as a hound. I knew Gary had a temper and that he liked to take it out on his hounds. So what had I been expecting, exactly? It was like I *wanted* to piss him off.

There had been a time when that was true. But Gary had broken me a long time ago. I was his hound, and I would be until my contract was up. Or way more likely, until I was ripped apart by something higher up the Hellspawn food chain. No hound I'd ever known had survived the full term of a reaper's contract and gotten out.

We all died, messy and violent and in pain. It was just a question of when.

I got back on the bike and kicked the starter, wondering what exactly about this Alex Ivanof was so bad that Gary would send me. My boss wasn't the type who kept people around if they couldn't handle a couple of extra deadheads on their turf.

I kept my helmet off, feeling the desert wind smooth the last of the rain off my face, and wondered exactly what type of shitstorm I was walking into blind as I raced toward Vegas.

When I pulled up, 1073 Buena Vista Drive didn't look like much. A blinking sign with half the neon gone sat in the parking lot. The cartoon atomic blast rising from the top of the low building was mostly bare plywood, paint gone and riddled with buckshot.

The Mushroom Cloud Motel had a vacancy, according to the sign. If I said I was shocked, I'd be lying.

I parked the Harley next to a Jeep with a pot leaf sticker on the fender. There were only two other cars in the lot—a Dodge Dakota that had a trash bag for a back window, and a new Lexus with the motor running. I watched the drug dealer that went with the Lexus jaunt out of room 114, jump in, and squeal out of the lot. After that, there was nothing but highway noise and coyotes yipping in the distance.

The guy in the front office looked me up and down when I came through the door, turning down the volume on his game show. He put the stench of fur and fresh blood into the musty air, and his top lip curled back to show teeth.

I don't like shifters. I think there's some natural lycanthrope/hellhound adversity bred into us, a survival instinct for both sides. Lycanthropes are pack animals, though, and this one was alone. Judging by the scars on his face, the gang tats, and the general stench, there was a reason for that. Shifters who go mad dog and hunt indiscriminately draw way too much attention from humans and Hellspawn alike. They end up either working for the Hellspawn they pissed off as a debt or serving as doggie chow for their pals when they're expelled from the pack, a fun little party where all your friends beat you until you shift and then chase down your wounded, exhausted ass and tear you to shreds.

"I'm Ava," I said. "Gary sent me."

The shifter sucked on his gums. "You're late."

I folded my arms. My leather jacket creaked over the buzzing of a half-dozen fans and the rusty beer fridge plugged in behind the desk. "And you are?" I might have to play nice with Gary, but if he expected me to smile pretty for some asshole he caught poaching homeless guys on the Strip, he could bite me.

"Santa Claus. You were supposed to be in Vegas by sunset."

"Sorry, but did you miss the animals floating two by two down the I-10?"

He showed his teeth again. He'd hunted recently, probably tonight, and his blood was still up. "I don't like excuses, bitch."

I didn't flinch. He didn't mean the insult the way humans understood the word anyway. He wasn't calling me an uppity woman, he was calling me a dog. To shifters who'd never seen one up close, that's what hounds were. Lapdogs of reapers and demons, no free will, no spine.

"I'm no more of a bitch right now than you," I said. "You're bigger than me, and I know you'd love to hurt me, but we both work for Gary, and if you touch me, he'll turn you into a floor stain. So why don't you tuck it back in your pants and tell your boss I'm here?"

The shifter started to laugh. He slapped the counter and then lowered his head, muscles under his wife beater rippling. His whole body changed, hair sprouting and gang tats vanishing, until he'd lost three inches and probably sixty pounds. When he looked up, rather than a bulky gangbanger, a skinny kid with pimples and straggly orange hair grinned at me.

"Man," the shifter said. "I've never seen a hound IRL. You're pretty intense."

I expected that a long time ago, my mouth probably would have hung open, but I'd learned how to stay impassive in the face of most anything violent, gory, or just plain weird.

The kid stuck out his hand. "Sorry about that. It's just easier to deal with the crackheads looking like a badass motherfucker than it is as myself."

I didn't take it. "I still don't like being called a bitch."

"Oh come on," he said. "I was just messin' with you. Have a sense of humor."

He came around the desk and clapped me on the shoulder. "I'm Martin. Martin Skelling."

"You like your fingers, Marty?" I asked. He moved the hand without needing any more encouragement.

"Anyway, I know you've got a lot of questions. Like, how I did that thing just now."

"I don't really . . ." I started, but there was no stopping Marty. He reminded me of one of those toys where you pulled a cord and just had to put up with it until it wound down, no matter how loud and obnoxious it was.

"I'm a metathrope," Marty announced. He shoved open the door marked OFFICE and gestured me inside. I heard the whir of dozens more fans and saw a bank of servers sitting against the far wall, hooked up to monitors on top of a desk littered with Coke cans, food wrappers, and something that smelled like it might have been a chimichanga in a previous life.

I pasted a smile on my face in an effort to keep from gagging, which Marty interpreted as "Please, keep talking until we both die of old age." I gritted my teeth under my smile.

"Metathropes can shift into any shape," Marty announced. "Even other people. See, lycanthropes are locked into one shape, and they have to take conservation of mass into account. My muscles are ten times denser than a lycanthrope, so I can express ten times as much mass. So I can be a grizzly bear, or I can shrink it down and be a ten-year-old girl."

"You do that often?" I said. "Go out in public as a ten-year-old girl?"

"Anyway, you're not here for that," Marty said. He pushed a stack of porn mags and chip bags off a spare chair and gestured. I would have rather stuck a hot poker straight into my thigh than sat in that thing, so I shook my head.

"Did you know that there are over ten thousand cameras on the Strip alone?" Marty said. "Casinos, mostly. I watch things for Gary. Vampires love this city—where else can you find twenty-four/seven everything and an all-you-can-eat tourist buffet?"

"Gary said something about deadheads," I said, sensing we might be in spitting distance of a point.

"I'm getting to that," Marty said. He punched up a grainy image. "Deadheads like the desert too—dry, they stay preserved. But Gary has a strict no-necromancer policy on his turf."

I knew Gary's hatred of warlocks in general, and particularly necromancers. If one of them was working in Vegas, he or she was one brave asshole.

Marty played the footage. I saw a drunk and a girl in a tight dress come out of a club—hardly notable for a city like this. What got my attention was the deadhead who surged out of the alley—just a pool of black on video—and jumped the guy, ripping into him like he was a Double-Double from In-N-Out Burger.

"Sucks to be him," I said. I still didn't see why this was so important to Gary.

"See, I thought so too," said Marty. "Never a good night when you get mauled by a free-range deadhead. But watch."

As fast as he'd come, the deadhead stopped and took off running.

I understood now why Gary had sent me. A deadhead who's raised by accident, or who starts as a vamp and goes feral from a mutated strain of the virus that makes vamps crave blood and fear tanning booths, will kill until their body gives out or until someone like me shows up, rips off their head, and turns their corpse into firewood. A deadhead raised on purpose, by a necromancer, can be controlled, used like a much more sophisticated and terrifying version of a tire iron. Blunt but effective when you wanted to fuck somebody up beyond repair.

"You think this Alex Ivanof has started dabbling in necromancy?" I said.

"Hell no," Marty said. "Alex was my blood guy. He did most of the trade with the vamps, interfaced with the hospitals, shit like that. I haven't heard from him since the day before this video."

He cued up more clips. "There's more like that," he said. "Dude walks outside, gets chewed into hamburger, and the deadhead takes off without feeding. Between Alex disappearing and this, I called Gary right away."

His hands trembled a little when he said Gary's name. He might be irritating as fuck, but Marty wasn't dumb. He'd been right to call in the cavalry.

"Okay," I said. "I'll look into it."

I pointed at the frozen screen. The girl in the tight dress was backed up against the wall, but she wasn't freaking out like anyone sensible would have when a guy tries to eat your date raw. "Where is that?"

"Uh . . ." Marty pushed a few buttons. "The Switchback Lounge. Strip joint out on Sahara. You want the address?"

My heart was already beating a little faster. I might not always like what I did, or for that matter what I was, but I was a hound. I was made to hunt. It was all I was meant to do, the only reason my heart beat and my lungs expanded and contracted.

I deliberately kicked over a stack of Marty's weirdo nerd porn on my way out. "I'll let you know what I find."

I walked out to the bike and put my helmet back on, pointing it toward the Strip. I didn't know why a necromancer had set up in Vegas, and I didn't care. That wasn't my part of things.

My part was to track him down and kill him. Always had been, always would be. I was a hound. That was all I was good for.

CHAPTER
4

I used to love the night. I loved lights, I loved the smell of warm earth meeting cool dark air. I loved the snatches of music that would spill out of gin joints and jazz clubs, the ring of heels on brick when you were alone, walking down a darkened street.

That was before. Now night was just a means to an end like anything else, a cover for shifting into a hound or an opportunity to slip in the back door of a crappy strip club.

I waited until a dancer came out wrapped in a robe, tapping her pack of cigarettes against the heel of her hand. She didn't even look at me, and I slipped inside. More dancers crossed my path, made up and dressed on their way to the stage or sweaty and smeared on the way off, glitter clinging to their tits and makeup running down their faces.

I passed a bouncer who also paid me no attention and through a slimy nylon curtain into the main club, nearly pitch-dark and encased in the throbbing bass beat of the club's sound system.

I liked dark places. I was even more invisible than usual. Low light didn't bother me—I could see just fine, better than I'd like in a place like this. The carpet was covered in burn marks, the main stage curtains were peppered with runs and holes, and the dancers working it weren't in much better shape. I'd seen fewer tracks in a rail yard.

Marty's video hadn't really been much help. I was looking for a tall blonde in a leopard skin dress, which described half the strippers in Vegas.

If she'd even stuck around. How many working girls would jump back in after they'd had a john turned into a chew toy?

A pack of fat guys in cheap suits and convention badges elbowed me out of the way, heading for the stage, and the dancers circling the tables converged on them like thong-wearing piranhas, all except for one.

She swayed in place, on the side stage, holding the pole like she really needed it to stay up. Her eyes were red and lifeless as the buzzing neon sign back at the motel. Vacancy.

I got closer, staying at the edge of the pool of light from her spot. She was the blonde, all right. And she was bombed out of her mind. I'd seen it before. She wasn't doped—there were no needle marks on her, and she didn't have the violent flush of a speed freak or the loopy, uneven pupils of an oxy popper. In fact, she was so pale that under the spot she was almost corpse-colored.

"Hey." I reached forward and tapped the toe of her shoe. She gave one long, slow blink, pupils uneven, and then crouched down.

"You want a dance?"

I shook my head. Getting a whiff of her confirmed what I thought—she was fucked up on vampire venom. A sucker had fed from her, and recently. That might explain why I saw a faded black eye under her makeup, when I hadn't seen any on a video taken barely twenty-four hours ago. Vamp venom helped speed up human's metabolism and cellular reproduction, which meant you'd be beautiful, skinny, and invincible right up until the venom either popped your heart like a balloon or you lost the dice roll and a carrier vamp fed on you, you got the virus, and turned.

"What, then?" Her eyes had a hard time focusing, and she'd stopped any pretense of swaying, kneeling before me in torn tights and a purple bra and panties that were too big for her.

"Where's the guy who did that to you?" I pointed at her eye. A sucker had slapped her around and fed on her, and a sucker would know where to find Ivanof. Blood dealers were a lot less hassle than finding willing human feeders. Or unwilling. A tiny splinter worked its way into my mind. Feeding on someone who didn't want it was a violation, the same as any other. I didn't like throwing down with vampires—they were smelly and they bit—but this time I'd be happy to make an exception. With so many people out there who'd willingly give their blood to chase the dragon with vamp venom, there was no excuse for taking it by force.

The blonde pointed to the VIP room. "In there."

I turned on my heel and started for the curtains under the pink neon sign.

"Hey," the blonde said. "What are you gonna do?"

"I don't know," I said. "I didn't exactly get an employee handbook when I died and signed my afterlife over to a reaper. Sorry."

Ivanof had disappeared when the deadheads had appeared. I figured if I found him, he'd tell me what he knew, which would probably include the name of the necromancer responsible.

I sped up as I passed the door guy in the VIP room, two Indian tourists getting a lap dance, and a waitress loaded down with empties and went straight for the booth on the far wall.

Suckers aren't hard to pick out. They stink like old women's underwear, and unless they've got a good hemoglobin-rich supply, they start looking like beat-up luggage within a couple of weeks.

I grabbed the vamp by the back of his shirt collar and dragged him from the booth, his drink and his stack of singles flying in opposite directions. He didn't weigh much—he'd been around long enough for his internal organs to dry out and the water to leach from his body.

His skull made a hollow sound against the wall as I lifted him off the ground, his skinny legs dancing. A snakeskin shoe caught me in the shin, but I ignored it. "Where's Alex Ivanof?"

The sucker stared at me, his yellowed eyeballs bugging out a little. Vamps don't need to breathe, but nobody wants to end their night getting their neck wrung by something that can tear into them like kindling.

"Hey! I'm calling the cops." The door guy was trying to get involved. Clearly he took his job in a shitty topless bar way too seriously if he thought that was any flavor of a good idea.

"Stay out of this." I let him see full fang-face: red eyes, hound teeth, the whole nightmare. He didn't even scream, he just ran.

I didn't blame him. Hell, *I* didn't want to look at me. Not at my real face, anyway.

I looked back at the sucker still dangling from my hand. "Where's Ivanof?"

"I don't know!" he wheezed. "I'd tell you if I did! Fuck!"

We were alone in the VIP room when I dropped him. He made a sound like somebody let the air out of a blow-up doll.

"He's been gone for a week," the vamp said. "Whole town's dry. I've had to go back to scavenging." He rubbed at his neck. "Believe me, nobody wants to find him more than I do. Hard to make a bitch put out when you're hungry."

"About that," I said, drew back my boot, and kicked him in the gut. He screamed, and I felt something give. A vamp who can't digest blood can't heal. If I was lucky, this asshole would just dry up and blow away.

I felt good about my night's work for about two heartbeats, until I realized that I wasn't any closer to Ivanof, and only had a sniveling vamp to show for my effort. Gary was going to kick my ass.

The Switchback Lounge had given me all it was going to. There wasn't anything here except bottom feeders, and one unlucky son of a bitch who'd been easy pickings for a deadhead.

Light flared all around me, harsh house lights rather than the dim stripper-friendly glow. I thought the door guy had come back for another round, but then a body slammed into me and carried me into the far wall, where I left an Ava-shaped dent before I hit the ground.

The deadhead snarled and dove at me, and I felt like the world's biggest moron as I rolled out of the way. I'd been so caught up in shit-kicking a worthless vamp I'd let a zombie turn me into a hood ornament.

Forget Gary. I was going to kick my *own* ass.

The deadhead snapped but got only a mouthful of my jacket. I grabbed my blade out of my boot with my free hand while I flipped us over, getting the deadhead on his stomach and strad-dling his back, pulling his neck to one side and jamming the blade against his jugular. Deadheads don't have enough soul energy for the knife's borrowed power to kick in, but that was fine. I hadn't met many critters that could stand up to being decapitated.

It was a solid plan until he threw me off and I lost the blade as he knocked me aside. This time I didn't bounce back. The wall was cinder block, and I'd cracked at least a couple of ribs. The dead-head didn't show any signs of slowing down—in fact, white foam flecked his chin as he skittered toward me like a scorpion.

As he loomed over me, I finally got a look at the bloated face surrounding his wide, blood-crusted mouth.

It was then I realized I was fucked, that I wasn't going to find the necromancer in Vegas, because the necromancer had already found me. The deadheads hadn't taken Ivanof.

The deadhead *was* Ivanof.

I let my head clunk against the sticky carpet. "Shit."

5

vanof snarled again. The skin of his gums had receded in death, and his teeth were stained with old blood. He held me on the ground, nostrils flaring and tongue flicking in and out like a snake. I debated whether it would be worse if he bit me or just drooled on me.

Outside, the music had cut off. That wasn't good. People had realized something was wrong, which meant somebody was calling the cops. I'd been picked up a few times when I hadn't been a hound long, and was still stupid enough to think I was invincible. Fortunately, those were the days before computers, and if my files still existed anywhere, logic dictated that I'd be pushing ninety.

Still, I didn't need my picture and prints in the system. Gary would have a fit, and I'd fucked this assignment up enough as it stood.

The deadhead who'd been Alex Ivanof still held me down. I'd never tangled with a deadhead juiced by a necromancer, and it was like trying to heave a compact car off your chest. If I was going to even this fight, I'd have to shift, and that wasn't an option. Once you turn into a giant dog with red eyes and fangs, people tend to stop ignoring you.

I shoved at Ivanof again, only managing to aggravate my ribs. I thought of Wilson, that bum leg, the way he stared at the hellhounds who could still fight like they'd stolen something from him.

Gary wouldn't keep me around out of pity. If I let Ivanof tear me up, that was it.

"Enough." All at once, Ivanof's weight lessened, though he still sat atop me panting, no doubt imagining what my liver tasted like.

A man crouched down in my line of sight. He narrowed dark eyes and didn't blink. "Here for my soul?" he asked.

I narrowed my eyes in return. "Are you offering?"

He smiled. It wasn't a good look on him. He was having fun watching Ivanof smack me around.

"I'm offering a time-out," he said. "I know what you are and what you can do. And you know what Alexi can do. I'd say that shaking hands and walking away is your only option right now."

"You really want to piss off a hellhound?" I growled. "Maybe your corpse bride here can take me, but you can't. You're human."

The necromancer shook his head. He looked more like an undertaker than a warlock, nice-looking dark suit, pristine white shirt, short dark hair that called back to my heyday as a human, when most guy's hairstyles could deflect bullets. Humans messing with black magic don't tend to be very put together, so I looked a little longer than I should, trying to find a flaw, but there was none. "The last thing I want is you against me," the necromancer said, "but I also can't have you ratting me out to a reaper. So what are we going to do?"

"Let me up so I can kick the shit out of you?" I suggested, but at that point I was just talking. Hellhounds are single-purpose. If I wasn't on a collection or doing Gary's heavy work, I wasn't much use, and this asshole knew it.

"How about I buy you coffee?" he said. "And we can talk. Ava. That's your name, isn't it?"

I decided to skip the part about how he knew. Any one of a hundred bottom feeders on Gary's payroll could have dimed me out. Didn't mean I wasn't going to enjoy tearing the throat out of whoever had.

"Good a name as any."

The necromancer pulled me to my feet. "Leonid Karpov," he said, still gripping my hand. After the deadhead, his strength and warmth were surprising. "Most people call me Leo."

"I bet that's not all they call you," I said. I was used to going in hard and ending things messily, but if this Leonid guy didn't want to square off, I could play along until I found out where he was keeping the rest of his deadheads. Maybe even why he'd started a dustup on Gary's turf in the first place. Then I could go back to breaking heads and taking souls—the comfortable stuff.

Leo snapped his fingers at Ivanof, who hissed but followed us out a back door hidden behind a cheap curtain and into the alley off Sahara. Once outside, he went running off, that crooked off-balance run endemic to the dead.

"You sure he can find his way home?" I said. "I mean, without stopping for a snack?"

"They feed when I say," Leo said. "My control over the dead is absolute."

"Oh, good," I said. "I might as well pack up and go, then."

Leo pointed me ahead of him to a boxy black car in the alley. "I don't know much of anything about hellhounds, beyond what they can do. I didn't expect a sense of humor."

I stayed put. If he thought I was turning my back on him, Leo was a lot dumber than he looked. He sighed and pulled a key chain out of his pocket. The car started with a hum when he pressed a button. "Ava, if I wanted to hurt you I would have let Alexi finish you off in there."

"Nothing personal," I said. "Sorry if I don't trust a complete stranger who used a deadhead to get my attention."

Leo shoved the key chain into his pocket. "Fine."

He moved faster than a man had any right to, the small black box out of his pocket and leveled at me in the space of half a heartbeat.

The stun gun leads bit into me just below my clavicle, and the electricity knocked me back onto my ass. Hellhound bodies are designed to take a lot of punishment, even as humans, so it didn't put me out, but it hurt like a drunken bastard on payday.

Leonid rolled me onto my back and slipped a pair of disposable cuffs onto my wrist, pulling them tight. "I really am sorry," he said as I retched from the jolt, trying to get myself back under control.

Trying to fight. This was all backward. I was faster and tougher than any warlock, juiced on black magic or not. It took a lot more than a stun gun to put me down.

Cracked ribs, a deadhead beatdown, and *then* a stun gun seemed to be working, though.

"Stop it," Leonid said. He slung me over his shoulder like I was luggage while I kicked and snarled. Everything hurt, but if I could just shift, I could shred this fucker. Forget the deadheads. Forget what Gary had sent me to do. I wanted to rip Leo's head off, plain and simple.

Leo popped the trunk and dumped me in. I landed on a blanket that smelled like motor oil and fake pine trees.

"If you're thinking about going four-legged, it's not an option," he said. "The trunk is warded against anything that expends magic. That includes you."

"I'm going to fucking kill you," I rasped. My voice sounded like I'd been screaming for hours.

"Scary," Leo said without expression, and slammed the trunk lid on me.

I got the handcuffs off in the first couple of minutes—I was still stronger than any human woman, even beaten to a pulp. Escaping the trunk was a different story. I kicked the lid, I screamed, I jiggled the emergency latch until my fingers were raw, but the trunk lock was strong and the latch was disconnected.

Panting, I looked up at the rough symbols painted on the trunk lid. Magic sigil bullshit all looks the same to me, unless it's demon language, but when I tried shifting, it was like I'd jumped into a dry swimming pool.

Lycanthropes literally change their shape, but with me, it's something else. I'm always the hound. That black dog is always there, creeping in my shadow. If I was the kind of person who nerded out about physics, like Marty back at the motel, I'd probably guess that I existed in both states, and the power given to me when the reaper took my soul and gave me a hound's allowed the switch. Call it a pocket dimension, call it a dual state, call it Shirley. I'd heard a lot of crackpot theories during my time as a hound, and that was as good as any.

But Gary didn't reward theories—kind of the opposite—so all I really knew for sure was that it took magic to shift, and it wasn't there.

Something I hadn't felt in a long time crept into me, starting low down in my abdomen and spreading like spiders crawling all over my skin. Leo had actually managed to get the drop on me. I'd always thought I'd go down fighting, finally run up against something bigger and badder than me, but this could be it. One necromancer too smart for his own good, and that would be the period on the sentence Gary had imposed on me.

Almost a century of bringing trash like Leo to the reaper, and I was going to die in his trunk.

I let myself have ten seconds of the panic and fear, something I thought I'd almost entirely lost when I became a hound, and then I made myself think as the car rumbled on, picking up speed.

It didn't matter what else was going on here—I could care less what Leo was up to at this point. Back me into a corner and I'll bite, simple as that.

Leo was going to wish he'd never had the bright idea to kidnap a hellhound. For about ten seconds, while he watched his own guts spill out before he died.

I lay still, trying to breathe shallow, until the car finally pulled to a stop. I heard it crunch over gravel and then the absolute silence that told me we were far outside Vegas in the desert.

Leo's feet crunched toward the back, and after a moment the trunk latch gave.

I didn't even give him a chance to open it. I exploded out of the trunk, ignoring all the parts of me that screamed for mercy, landing on the gravel on all fours.

The shift came on, but even as my vision started to slide into gray scale I realized there was one problem. Leo wasn't in front of me.

I got out one breath before he raised the dart gun and fired until the clip was empty. Five darts, a payload that would drop a three-hundred-pound lycanthrope.

A blue velvet sky full of stars spun across my vision, and then the stars blurred into white lines on the center of an endless highway before everything went black.

CHAPTER
6

was seventeen when I left Bear Hollow, Tennessee, for the last time. I had one dress, one pair of shoes, and two dollars that I'd saved working since I was barely fourteen mending and taking in washing with my mother.

I had never seen electric light or indoor plumbing, but I was no dummy. I worked my way to New Orleans, mending clothes for rich women and cleaning houses when I had to, watching children, anything that paid the bills and didn't involve putting my legs in the air for strange men. Prohibition was going strong, and my grandmother had made the best moonshine in Bear Hollow, so it wasn't hard to set up a little shack in the bayous of St. Bernard Parish and watch the money roll in.

She was the one who told me about haints, about the black dogs that prowled the swamps where she grew up, deep in Cajun country. About the *rougarou*, the beast with red eyes who'd consume you, body and soul.

I guessed it was only fitting I'd ended up back there. And I made a good life for myself until I died.

After I became a hound, I'd catch glimpses sometimes of that mirror-still bayou water, silvered by the moon. Of the things moving in the cypress swamps, ruffling the hanging moss with their passage. No matter where I went, from Anchorage to Juarez and most every back road in between, part of me was always back in that bayou. It wasn't strange to me. After all, it was where I'd left my soul.

Cold water smacked me in the face, and I choked, sucking in sour-tasting fabric.

Leo yanked a black cloth sack off my head. I hissed as harsh light abused my dark-adapted eyes, and bared my teeth at him.

"Calm down," he said. "You've been napping for a while, and I need to talk to you."

My head was still muzzy from the tranquilizers, but everything snapped into focus pretty quickly. I was in a chair, two-legged again, chained down hand and foot. Smells of oil and hot metal and the lack of any furniture besides my chair and a rusty metal table told me I was probably in one of the hundreds of abandoned gas stations that littered the Mojave.

"You keep saying that, and then you keep knocking me out," I told Leo. He disappeared from the pool of light and wheeled a ratty old rolling chair to face me. He sat, taking a flat silver flask from his pocket and sipping before tucking it away.

"It's hard to talk when all you want to do is shift and rip me apart."

He was right. I wanted to shift more than anything, the craving like claws in my brain. I was frightened and hurt, and the hound in me knew the right response. Shifting in these chains was going to be a bitch—I could easily snap all the bones in my arm, and then I'd be a three-legged dog. That wasn't much more use than a chained-up woman.

Leo got up and disappeared again. This time he brought back a mechanic's cart covered with a rag. "You're the third hellhound I've caught," he said. He tossed the rag on the ground, and metal instruments gleamed.

I felt my teeth start to grow, and my muscles rippled under my shirt. Leo flinched a little. Good. At least I knew there was something that could get to him. "This is a hobby for you?" I snarled. I could still be hurt, especially like this. Get hurt bad enough, and I wouldn't be able to shift anymore. I'd be fucked, even if I did somehow convince Leo to take the chains off.

"No," he said. "This is my job."

He switched on a soldering iron and laid it back on the cart next to the knives and the sharp, silver needle-nose pliers. "I'm hoping I won't need any of this," Leo said. "I'm hoping that you're not like the other hounds, and that you'll actually listen before you start foaming at the mouth. But if not, I can't have you running back to your reaper and telling him all about me."

"Gary already knows about you," I said.

Leo frowned, tapping the pliers against the palm of his hand. "Beg your pardon?"

"My reaper. His name is Gary."

He threw the pliers back on the tray, and I tried not to flinch at the clank. "That's kind of disappointing. I was expecting something like . . . I don't know, Balthazar or Raven or something. 'Gary' sounds like an insurance salesman."

"Yeah, he's a salesman," I muttered. "And he knows all about what you're doing here."

"Tell me, Ava." He sat down in the chair and rolled close, close enough that we could have touched. "What *am* I doing here?" He smelled hot, like desert wind, tinged with vodka and cigarettes and something else, that dusty stink that warlocks give off.

"Making deadheads," I said. "Fucking with the blood suppliers. Beyond that I really don't care."

"I hate to tell you, but raising the dead and annoying vampires is hardly a master plan." Leo snorted. "Gary sics you on someone and you just do as you're told." He tested the iron with the pad of his finger.

"Is this the part where you tell me how pathetic I am, being some Hellspawn's lapdog?" I said. "Because you can save your breath. I know."

Leo picked up a pair of rusty scissors and moved around me, cutting away my leather jacket. I growled. "I know a lot of leg breakers, Ava," he said. "Aside from the Hellspawn blood, you and I do a lot of the same work." He dropped the leather on the ground and leaned down into my face. His was thin and hard, the sort of face that I'm sure scared the piss out of anyone who got on his bad side. Those eyes, which I'd been stupid enough to think looked warm back in the strip club, were burning now, a dangerous heat that would peel the skin right off you. "Somehow, though, I get the feeling you'll be more receptive than the other two."

"Why?" I said. I wasn't one to try and talk my way out of things. I wasn't good at talking. That was a reaper's job, but my go-to options of violence and running away were both shot. "What could you possibly want from me?" I asked Leo. "I can't void contracts, and I'm not going to let you go on about your business here, so you might as well start cutting. I can't help you."

Leo picked up the iron and brought it over to me. The heat made my heart jump, my pulse pounding against my throat. You can get used to pain, but it never gets easier to take.

"I think you can," he said. "See, my soul is my own, and this Gary keeps you so in the dark you can't tell me what my business is, so I don't want either of those things from you, Ava."

I blinked at him. "Then what?" I said, hating the fine edge of desperation that had crept into my voice. Leonid Karpov was a scary motherfucker, human or not, and I didn't relish being vulnerable to him.

"I want to kill your reaper," Leo said. "And you're going to help me."

CHAPTER

7

started to laugh. It bubbled out of me unbidden, echoing off the metal walls of the garage. Almost like I was screaming. "You're funny," I managed. "Look at you, in your scary hit man suit and your creepy torture chamber. You must be delusional if you think this'll end any way but with you on a one-way ride to Hell."

Leo pressed the hot iron to my bicep and then I *was* screaming, so loud I felt it tear out of my throat.

He stopped as abruptly as he'd hurt me in the first place. "I'm not joking, Ava. Your reaper sent you here with no clue about what you'd be facing. Alexi almost killed you, and if I'd wanted ten more deadheads to rip you apart, you'd be pieces in black plastic bags by now. He doesn't give a shit about what happens to a creature like you, Ava, so why would you not jump at the chance to get rid of him?"

Shaking, I worked on not tossing my last meal all over my boots. I forced myself to meet Leo's eyes. "Because it's impossible."

"It's *not* impossible." Leo's snarl came close to mine. I could see I'd hit a nerve, so I flinched back.

"Maybe not for you, but I can't help you," I said. "Gary is my boss. He *owns* me. I'm not going to flip on him for some psychopath human that already tried to kill me once tonight."

The iron hit me again, on the collarbone, but this time I was prepared for it, and my scream came through gritted teeth.

"Don't be stupid," Leo snapped. "You're disposable to a reaper. There's always more where you came from. He doesn't care about you, Ava. How can you not see that?"

I breathed in, out. Slow and soft, feeling my heart beat and my blood pump. Reminding myself that I was alive. "I do see it," I whispered. "What *you* don't see is that I don't have a choice." I squeezed my eyes shut. Sweat and stress tears flooded down my cheeks. "You think this is bad? Even if I get out of here, what Gary does as punishment for not putting you down will be so much worse. It's not a matter of whether or not we have warm fuzzy feelings for each other."

The shaking now wasn't entirely from what Leo had done to me. I hated it when I had to think about this, about what I really was and how tight Gary's hold was. "It's about who I'm afraid of. And that's Gary."

It would always be Gary.

I watched Leo pick up a knife, and sighed. "Now, I was already tortured to death once, so if you're going to do it, just get it over with."

Leo stopped in midmotion, went completely still as if all his joints had locked up. "You remember dying?"

"Yeah," I said. "I mean, it's sort of hard to forget."

Leo set down the knife. Something had changed in his eyes. I didn't know what I'd said, but this was more like I'd imagined—hard and empty, the cruelty that I expected from warlocks with as much power as Leo had.

"That isn't right," he said. "Hellhounds have no memory of their human lives."

"I'm a hellhound," I said. "And I remember a lot more than I want to."

Leo narrowed his eyes. "The other two—in Brooklyn and St. Louis—remembered nothing of their human existence," he said. "Sure, they knew they'd died and made contracts with reapers to save themselves, but they had no memory of dying or anything leading up to it."

"I don't remember everything," I mumbled. I was oddly embarrassed. I'd never even thought to wonder if Gary's other hounds were like me. I thought for sure that Wilson at least had to be a miserable asshole in life to be such a jackass when I met him.

"That you remember anything at all is troubling," Leo said. I felt my lip twitch back over my teeth.

"I'm so sorry that the information you tortured out of me troubles you," I said.

"Not me," Leo said. "But if you do help me, I wouldn't let your boss know that you recall being a human."

I stayed still and tense as he reached for me, but there was no pain this time. Leo touched my uninjured arm. "Relax, Ava. I don't care that you're a freak. I'm one too. Imagine being the only kid in Brighton Beach who could bring their dead dog back to life."

"Imagine being the dead dog," I muttered. Leo laughed. It was kind of shocking, even through the hot pain of the burns on my flesh. He didn't look like a chuckler, and his laugh was clear and genuine, completely at odds with everything else about him.

He took out his flask and held it to my lips. "Drink. It'll take the edge off."

I didn't disagree with him, so I let the vodka slide down my throat, the chemical burn giving me a shiver.

"Good girl." He capped the flask and sat down, rolling back and forth so the chair squeaked.

"Is this part of the torture?" I said. Leo shook his head.

"You're a kick in the pants. I'm glad Gary sent you."

Maybe I could still salvage this. If I could bring something like information on the nut job necromancer plotting his death, I could convince Gary to go easy on me for not shredding the guy when I had the chance.

Maybe.

"So what's your beef with reapers?" I said. "And how exactly do you think you're going to kill one?"

"Reapers are parasites," Leo said, taking another drink himself. "Parasites with demon magic, but if humans stopped giving up their souls, where would they be then?"

I shrugged. "I'm not the brains of the operation."

"Clearly you're smart," Leo said. "Smarter than most hell-hounds I've run into."

I laughed, and it hurt, which was fitting. "That's not a very high bar, trust me."

"Warlocks can't seem to resist cutting deals with Hellspawn," Leo said. "I've seen more than one idiot dragged off screaming in the jaws of a hound."

"But not you," I said.

Leo's face went from pleasant to furious like a trap snapping shut on my foot. He slammed the flask down on the tray, making all the pointy objects rattle. "I'm nobody's bitch, Ava. Least of all a demon's."

"You're packing way too much voltage to not have a demon behind you," I said. "Warlocks who are strictly white don't raise the dead, just to start."

"Call me gray," Leo said. Given the chance to talk about himself, he was practically chatting my ear off. "There's a lot of stuff floating around out there. Books, other warlocks. The type who can be convinced to tell you what a demon told them."

That didn't play. Warlocks are worse than stage magicians—they never share the tricks up their sleeves. "I'm supposed to believe you tagged a guy like Ivanof and raised him based on some secondhand story?"

Leo's lips parted. "I can be persuasive."

I wriggled against the chains. Nope, still bone-crushing tight. "As persuasive as you were with me?"

"I have a skill set a certain kind of person finds valuable," Leo said. "I didn't enjoy hurting you, if that's what you're asking. I don't *enjoy* hurting anyone. But it doesn't bother me, either." He slipped out of his suit jacket and slung it on the back of his chair. His black shirt opened at the throat, and I caught ink creeping up above his collar, his wrists, everywhere there was a little bit of skin. Well, there was no rule a Russian gangster couldn't have a hobby.

"I knew your reaper would send someone if his blood dealer went belly up and deadheads started turning tourists into fast food," Leo said. "And turning Alexi into a deadhead was a bonus, really. Miserable fuck that he was. Did you know he used to dose women with vamp venom when business was slow and drain them while they were out of it? Making him attack but never feed, bend to my will—that I *did* enjoy."

"Can I ask you something?" I said. Leo nodded, fishing in his pockets and pulling out a squashed pack of smokes. He offered me one, but I shook my head.

"Did Marty the metathrope have anything to do with this?" I said. Leo's laughter sent a warm feeling up and down my spine. How fucked up was it that a Russian leg breaker who raised zombies on the side and had just finished spot-welding my skin was calming me down? It wasn't like I held the torture against him, I reasoned. For most Hellspawn, what he'd done to me would be foreplay.

"Marty's a lovable nut job, but he's way too chatty for my liking," he said. "If he knew me, your reaper would know me."

"Good," I said. "One less person I have to kill when I get out of here."

Leo leaned back and managed to look like he owned the room, even though it was a shitty garage and we were the only people in it. "So you'll help me?"

"I told you," I said. "Even if I wanted to, I can't."

"See, I think that's bullshit," Leo said. "You couldn't stop me from hurting you. I have all the power here. I could make you hurt so much you'd forget your own name, but I won't. I *choose* to try and persuade you."

"I hope you're better at cutting than talking," I said. "Because this is not changing my mind." Hounds didn't turn on reapers. Reapers made them, and we served them. Unconditionally. Turning on your reaper was a taboo that had only one outcome. Reapers were our masters. That was that.

"You can choose to fight back," Leo said. "You can choose to tell this Gary, this asshole who sent you here to be ripped apart by a deadhead without a second thought, that you're not a slave."

He tilted his head, his black eyes catching the light and reflecting my pale face back at me. "Tell me that you're fine with this. Tell me that you're truly happy being a hound, like the others, and this'll be over. Tell me being Gary's dog is everything you want."

I felt something like a rock land in my stomach. Usually I didn't think about anything except the job, the next contract to collect on. I didn't think about me and Gary, beyond what he'd do if I failed him.

I sure as fuck didn't think about how I'd ended up like this, how I'd gone from dying in the mud, broken and bloody, to a hellhound bound to Gary.

That was how Gary got me, after all. I was afraid, of dying, of crossing, of finding out what was waiting for me. I let him take my soul and turn me into his monster, together for a hundred years and a hundred more—the same deal every hound got with their reaper.

I was less than halfway through my sentence, and I was already skating so close to the edge of death I could see across the chasm to the day I'd spend eternity in the Pit.

All that stuff I didn't usually think about knotted up, squeezing a sound from me that was less than a whimper.

"Ava." Leo's fingers wrapped around my arm and squeezed. His hand was hot and hard and strong, and when I managed to meet his eyes, I felt wet, stinging tears slide down my face.

"I hate him," I whispered.

"I know," Leo said, reaching out and brushing away a tear with his thumb. "Believe me, Ava. I know what it is to be under someone's boot."

I choked on whatever was making my throat tight. I refused to call it fear or especially grief. I didn't feel anymore. I'd left all that with my broken body, there in the mud, when Gary took me in.

Nothing I could tell Gary was going to save me. I'd known that as soon as I'd showed up in Vegas. I was already on thin ice because of Bob Dobkins and this was the kill shot.

This was my life, had been for more lifetimes than any human got. And I couldn't do it anymore.

"Tell me what you need," I said to Leo.

He sat back, his expression so smug it practically dripped. "I don't care about Gary the reaper, for his own sake. He has something I want."

I waited, quiet. I don't like the conversational games humans play, feeling each other out while they listen to their own voices. I've never been any good at verbal fencing. Leo sighed. "Aren't you going to ask me what it is?"

"I kind of wish you could tell me while wiping that smug look off your face," I said. It was probably pointless to hope. Leo was the sort of guy for whom smugness was a chronic condition.

"His Scythe."

I stopped—breathing, blinking, I think even my heart stuttered on a beat.

"If you help me get it," Leo continued, "you can kill him with it. And your contract will be void, and you'll be free." He grazed his fingers down my cheek again, and I didn't even try to move. "Help me, and Gary will never hurt you again."

This was insane. I'd gotten knocked around and I'd taken temporary leave of my senses, but they were back now, and I had to get the fuck away from Leo Karpov. Colluding with a nut job necromancer to kill your asshole reaper boss was one thing. Stealing a Hellspawn weapon and using it was another. If I was lucky, I'd only spend eternity in the Pit as punishment for even listening to this.

"Don't back out on me now," Leo said. I'm sure my face was a five-car pileup of panic. "If you go crawling back, he'll kill you, and you'll never have this chance again."

He was right, even if I didn't want to hear it. The deep-down memories of when Gary had found me and turned me into a hound were supplanted by every memory of every time Gary had taken out his rage on me.

They piled up and crashed into the others, turning the inside of my head into a massacre. Fire and blood, fingers snapped, skin peeled off—he'd even shaved my head once when I'd taken too long to bring in a hoodoo witch hiding in the Georgia mountains, then kicked me out onto the winter street in bare feet, the nicks in my scalp still bleeding.

"Why do you need a reaper's Scythe?" I said softly.

Leo sat back, a crooked smile on his face. There was none of the warmth I'd glimpsed. We were back to the glass-eyed gangster who'd tortured me without a second thought. "I want to kill my father."

CHAPTER

8

I t had been so long since I'd even let myself think there might be a way out of my contract with Gary that it felt like I was falling, my stomach pressing up against my ribs, the rest of me just waiting for the impact with the ground.

"So why can't you kill your father the old-fashioned way?" I asked Leo. He'd agreed to drive me back to the Mushroom Cloud so I could make the call, and we were cruising through presunrise streets behind the UNLV campus, strip malls and off-brand casinos as far as the eye could see, blending into tract housing and then the desert.

Leo hadn't spoken much after he'd unchained me, and I hadn't felt like talking. Still, silence gets thick after a while, and I hadn't spent this much time with anyone who wasn't another hellhound or a collection job in a long time.

Leo's hand tightened on the steering wheel. His sleeve was rolled and showed the dagger tat on his forearm, ink popping off the lean muscle when he tensed. I wanted to see more of his ink, the stuff under his slick white shirt, but I figured asking would probably send him the wrong kind of message. Hounds didn't generally fool around with humans, and it was hard to remember how to even talk to a man, never mind ask him to take his shirt off without things getting weird. If I was more used to this, I'd probably also be telling myself that a guy who'd chain me up and threaten to torture me wasn't an appropriate lust object, but I couldn't bring myself to be that mad about it. Leo was doing what he had to do, just like I was.

"I want him to stay dead," he said. "Necromancers have a way of recovering from blades and bullet wounds."

I didn't ask why Leo wanted to kill his father. I'd wanted plenty of people dead in my time. "You think it'll be easy to get Gary's Scythe?" I said. "Because I don't."

Leo shrugged. "It's been pretty easy to take down three hellhounds. Usually the bodyguards are worse than the big boss."

I went back to staring out the window. I didn't want to be reminded of how I'd fucked up and let Leo drop me. It was embarrassing.

If Leo thought his plan was that foolproof, he was nuts. Gary was slippery as fresh blood on a blade, and he hadn't survived this long as a reaper by being an idiot. What was I thinking?

I wasn't even sure reapers could be killed. And if they could, what would happen to the pack? Not just me, but the loyal ones.

I was sure some of his other employees hated Gary as much as I did, but some really were lapdogs. They'd want a piece of me if Leo went through with this.

"You healed." Leo pointed at my bare arm and neck. I felt my eyes narrow.

"Yeah. You know what didn't heal? My fucking jacket."

"If this goes well, I'll be in a position to get you a lot more than a new jacket, sweetheart." He grinned at me as we pulled into the motel parking lot.

I snorted at the "sweetheart," but I didn't mind enough to tell him to back off. Truthfully, having someone pay attention to me who wasn't Gary or another hellhound was something I'd been missing for a long time.

I knew something was wrong the minute we pulled up to a parking spot. The neon sign was off, the lot was empty, and the air tasted metallic, like it did just after a lightning strike.

Leo peered out the windshield. "What a shitbox."

"Wait here." I didn't give him time to argue, just got out of the car and moved. Things had gone sideways, and I didn't need a warlock swaggering around getting in my way.

Marty looked up from his TV when I came through the door. He was back in his gangbanger guise, but he was so pale and shaky that any edge it might have given him was gone.

"In the office," he managed. "Waiting for you."

Fuck. There wasn't going to be any phone call to Gary. I could smell hound and Hellspawn from where I stood. Gary was already here.

Braced against the motel counter, I took three deep breaths. If this was it, I wasn't going to be quivering and crying when I went down. I also wasn't going to give Gary anything that I didn't have to. I'd never tried to lie to him before. Reapers have a way of seeing through you, like they can reach in and pluck out the truth like a weed out of dirt. And if you try to fight it, you get hurt.

There's a first time for everything, though. Dying, lying to your scary-as-fuck Hellspawn boss.

I shoved my hands into my jacket to hide them shaking and pushed past Marty, coming through the door like I had nothing to be afraid of. That was the biggest lie I'd tell today.

Gary looked up from behind Marty's rusty metal desk. Wilson stood behind him like some kind of butt-ugly mannequin left over from a haunted house.

"Have a seat, Ava," Gary said.

I did as I was told. The springs of the rolling chair squealed with my weight.

"Is there a problem?" I said. "I was going to call you when I had something."

"I know," Gary said. "Do you need to consult your notes, perhaps pull out some index cards? Did Leo Karpov give you a script?"

I was fucked. Gary knew about Leo. Of course he knew. Why had I ever thought I could get away from him?

Knowing that this was it actually calmed me down some. It had happened when I'd died too. Once I knew that I wasn't getting away, that the pain inflicted on me would eventually stop, and that I'd be gone, I stopped struggling. I was still terrified then, of course. But once I'd realized there was no hope, things went blank and cold rather than hot and panicked. It was the same now.

"Don't look so constipated, Ava," Gary said. "Leo's a smart man.

He knew exactly what information on a rat in my ranks would be worth to me. Someday, I'm going to cut him such a deal."

Gary's voice nauseated me. Leo had set me up. Gotten me to admit everything I'd buried so deep it might as well have been in a grave and then dimed me out to Gary.

He hadn't even had to torture me for very long. I should have figured it out—he'd set up the whole scenario with Alexi to lure Gary and me here in the first place, and now he was throwing me under the bus that Gary was driving.

I skipped wondering what Leo had gotten in return. Power. That was all men like Leo Karpov ever cared about. I'd been desperate, and I'd gotten sloppy. Any glimmer of a life other than this, and I was a starry-eyed idiot again, ripe for the plucking. The last time, it had just gotten me tortured and murdered. This time was going to be a lot worse.

"I'm glad you're not going to deny it," Gary said. "That makes this whole process much less embarrassing for both of us."

He stood up and came around the desk, leaning on it and tapping his fingers against the metal. I stayed put. He knew I wasn't going anywhere. "You know why I chose you, Ava?"

I was convenient, a pathetic dead girl who didn't know what she was agreeing to, freshly dead and terrified of what came after. No mystery there.

"I felt sorry for you," Gary said. My breath stopped. That was news to me.

"You were so small. So broken. I felt like I had to offer you a chance." Gary sighed, rubbing between his eyes with his index finger. "But I should have known better. You never offer someone a contract out of pity. That's the first thing they teach you when they hand this over."

He pulled out his Scythe. I could feel the crackle in the air as the blade drifted toward my face.

"So I think it's time I rectify my mistake," Gary said. "Cut my losses and move on." He closed his hand around my hair and yanked my head back, exposing my throat. Wilson made a small humming sound. I couldn't tell if he was excited or simply impatient.

"You were nothing special in life, Ava," Gary said. "And you were a pain in my ass as a hound. Good riddance." The tip of the Scythe pierced my skin, and I felt the bite of its connection searching for the thing that kept me running, the corrupted hellhound soul Gary had shoved into me in place of my human one.

"I remember."

I don't know why I said anything. I sure as shit wasn't going to change Gary's mind. I was tired, that much I knew. Tired of his talking, tired of his never letting me forget how pathetic I was. I was tired of being a dog.

Really, I just didn't want to die without giving Gary the finger.

The blade paused on its route into my major artery. Gary looked pissed as I'd ever seen him. "The fuck did you say?"

"I remember what I was when I was alive," I snarled. "And I was good, Gary. I was young and stupid and in love, but I was good. You took that from me, but you didn't take the memories. I remember that I used to have something good in me." I bared my teeth. The hound knew what to do, even if I didn't. "You *never* had that. You're a bottom-feeding piece of shit, and I hope when you die it's not fast. I hope you beg for the pain to stop, like every single one of your hounds did."

I relaxed into the Scythe and felt the cool slide of metal. Getting stabbed doesn't hurt at first, if the blade is sharp, and Hellspawn weapons always are. I'd said my piece. Before, dying had been the worst thing I could imagine. This time, it wasn't even close.

Gary, conversely, threw me away from him, out of the chair and onto the floor. I choked on dust and years-old crumbs.

"Did he send you?" Gary screamed. He pointed the Scythe at me, the tip dark with my blood.

I had no fucking idea what I'd said to set him off. I'd never seen Gary as anything less than the slick salesman Leo pegged him as, smiling and perfectly pressed while he bent you over and screwed you for everything you had.

"Boss," Wilson said. His eyes roved from me to the door to Gary. Seeing that Wilson was as freaked out as I was did not help.

"Shut up, gimp!" Gary bellowed. He grabbed me by the front of my shirt and lifted me one-handed.

That was the thing about Hellspawn. They look all nice and middle-American until you realize they can lift a car and light fires with their mind. By the time you do, of course, it's too late and you're fucked. Just like me.

"Have you been spying on me this whole time? Did he put you there in front of me like a fucking entrée because he thinks I'm *stupid*?"

If normal Gary was shit-your-pants terrifying, Gary when he'd lost it was making me think that if I survived, I was definitely getting fitted for a padded room and some Thorazine.

"I . . . I don't know what you're talking about," I said. "I just don't want you to kill me."

Gary rammed me backward into the desk so hard that the

metal bowed under my weight. More of my ribs decided to give up the ghost, but the pain barely registered as Gary's hand tightened around my throat, the Scythe hovering above my eye.

"You tell that motherfucker that if he thinks he's gonna rattle me with this amateur-hour shit," Gary snarled, "then fuck him and that pale horse he rode in on." His mouth flattened out into the Gary grin that I knew and hated. Gary only smiled when he was about to royally fuck up someone's day. "That is, if you run into him on your way to Hell, bitch."

"Boss!" Wilson had opened the door and was standing with Marty. Beyond, I saw the shadow of at least three more hounds. Gary had brought in the hard boys to deal with me. I'd have been flattered if I wasn't so fucking terrified.

"I'm a little goddamn busy!" Gary barked.

"Yeah, um, I think you need to see this," Marty piped up.

Gary whipped his head around, hand still clamped around my windpipe. Air become a precious commodity, and my vision went black and wavy.

"They just showed up out of nowhere," Wilson said. His voice sounded like it was coming down a long tunnel.

"What is this shit now?" Gary grumbled. "As if I don't have enough to deal with."

His weight pressed down on me again. "Let me deal with this and then we'll deal with them."

"There's a lot of them . . ." Wilson didn't sound thrilled.

"Do I ask you to think?" Gary shouted. "Do I ask you to do anything with that lump of shit between your ears besides let it keep you breathing? No! Shut the fuck up, Wilson!"

I felt his grip loosen a fraction, and I had the thought that I could get out of here, that this didn't have to be where I died. I might just prolong my life by a few minutes, but the hound wanted to survive even if I knew it was probably useless to fight back.

Shoving up with my knees, I knocked Gary away from me. His Scythe sliced through the meat of my arm when he fell off balance, and the shock felt like biting down on a power line.

I dropped to the ground, limbs twitching. My tongue contorted itself toward the back of my throat, but I scrabbled for purchase on the floor. If I was human, I'd already be dead, so that was something.

There was a lot of yelling, a lot of hounds snarling, but I'd stopped paying attention. I ran, shoving Wilson onto his bad leg so that he toppled and crashed into the motel desk. Marty got out of my way with a yelp, his eyes the size of quarters. Covered in blood and beat to shit, I probably looked a lot more dangerous than Gary, on the surface.

Temperatures had soared while I'd been inside, desert sun beating into the asphalt and sending waves of thick heat floating over my skin.

I skidded toward the black car across the lot. Getting the fuck out of there was my only priority.

For a second, I thought I'd actually made it. Then I slammed into a body solid as a concrete wall, and death stench filled up my nose.

I hit the pavement and saw a deadhead looking down at me like I was a five-dollar buffet at the Golden Nugget.

Not just one. Shadows crowded around me. It was like a deadhead convention out here. Behind me, Wilson and the other hounds snarled, forming a protective circle around the door of the motel office.

I could have told them they didn't need to worry—I was two feet away from the nearest zombie, covered in my own blood. I might as well have poured steak sauce over my head.

"Ava!" A hand yanked me backward as the deadhead lunged. Leo pulled me up and shoved me behind him. He had a gun in his other hand. I could have told him that this only works in movies, but I wasn't real invested in keeping him alive.

"You shithead!" I screamed, pushing him hard. He stumbled, almost going down.

"What did I do!" he shouted. "I'm trying to help!"

I pushed my claws out, which hurts like fuck when you're on two legs but can be handy when you're outnumbered and don't have a weapon. "I know you tipped off Gary!" I snarled. "Get the hell away from me before I give those deadheads sushi to munch on."

"Are you brain damaged?" Leo demanded. "Why the *fuck* would I let a reaper know what I was planning?"

"Should I care?" I shot back. "I see you even brought some company to clean up the evidence once I was dead!"

"Ava." Leo shoved the gun into his waistband and came toward me, grabbing my arms with a grip that surprised me, coming from a human. I growled, the growl that wasn't fucking around, from the lowest, meanest part of my hound side. He didn't let go, and he was squeezing my cut arm, but after a few seconds of pain his touch got me to relax.

"You're an asshole," I mumbled.

"I also didn't turn on you," he said. "Look. Are any of these deadheads interested in you?"

I looked, blinking sweat and old mascara out of my eyes, and saw that the deadheads were only interested in one thing—my fellow hounds. Two of the deadheads lay on the pavement ripped apart, and a hound had his arm nearly separated at the shoulder.

"It doesn't make any sense," Leo said. "You and I had a deal. Why would I convince you to help me only to turn around and get you shredded by a reaper?" He pointed behind me, and I saw some more guys in black suits and heavy ink standing by a couple of black SUVs. They all had small machine guns dangling from their hands the way rich women carry designer purses.

"I called my father," Leo said. "I knew things were fucked when the reaper was already here, so I called him and told him to bring the boys out for a snack, all right? That's all that's happening here. I swear."

Now that I wasn't being slammed repeatedly into hard surfaces, that did make a lot more sense. "You guys put your blood feud on hold to save little old me?"

"The devil you know," Leo muttered.

"Fine," I said. "I suggest you do something about Gary and his merry band of black dogs before they realize this is your doing."

The deadheads weren't faring well. One hound might have been in trouble, but against Gary's star heavies, they were basically just chew toys.

"I'm working on it," Leo said. A guy who I assumed had to be his father, since they looked pretty much alike, separated by about thirty years and one nasty scar across the guy's neck, shoved between us, looking me up and down.

"Who the hell is this?"

"Leave her alone," Leo said. "She doesn't have anything to do with anything."

Leo's father turned his head and spit on the ground, missing my boot by an inch. I was starting to see why Leo wanted to kill him.

"You call me out here to clean up your mess, there better be something for me besides your skinny whore, boy."

I saw Gary emerge from the office at the same time Leo's father did, saving him from my foot in his balls by way of explaining that I wasn't a sex worker. His jaw went slack and his eyes took on a gleam. "Fuck me," he said. "Is that a reaper?"

It was my turn to get in front of Leo as Gary drew his Scythe again and started across the parking lot, flanked by Wilson and a hound I didn't know, a big bruiser with a Mohawk the color of blue Kool-Aid.

"Deal with the hounds," Leo said in my ear. "I'll handle Gary."

I glanced back at him, but he seemed serious. Well, it was his funeral. He might not have sold me out, but I still didn't think he had more than an ice cube's chance floating in a hot chocolate made in Hell.

Blue leaped at me, shifting on the fly, and the time for thinking deep thoughts was over. I let him barrel by me, stepping aside and swiping his throat with my claws. Blood erupted, coating my palm and arm halfway to the elbow. Blue coughed once and collapsed, twitching. Arterial red turned black, just a slick shiny spot on the asphalt as he died.

Before I could celebrate, Wilson slammed into me from behind. He might not be graceful, but he had almost a hundred pounds on me, and that was enough.

"Always knew you'd turn someday," he grunted. "You think you're better than us."

"Wilson," I managed, even though he was slamming my head repeatedly into the pavement. "Why are you doing this?"

He stopped, chest heaving, staring at me. The white network of scars across his skull looked like fresh paint in the sunlight. The shifter pack had taken off half his face, and even hellhound healing wasn't perfect.

"Gary keeps you around as a joke," I said. In my peripheral vision, Leo accepted a black case from his father, taking out a flat bag full of red—a hospital blood pack. Alexi probably had an entire bank's worth on ice when Leo had capped him.

"Gary is my master," Wilson snarled. He shook me a little. It wouldn't take much more pressure to snap my neck.

"Your master did the same shit to you he just did to me," I said. "He sent you off to do his bidding and didn't give a shit when those lycanthropes almost made you hamburger. Why the fuck do you care about him, Wilson? To Gary, you might as well be a used tissue."

Leo poured the blood across the ground in a line as Gary came at him, and when the reaper hit the line he bounced back. The ozone taste of black magic hit my tongue, and all the small hairs on my neck lifted like lightning had fried the parking lot.

Gary shook off the impact, but I saw a thin line of black trickle from his nose. Hellspawn bleed black, nasty acid crap with fumes that smell like a mass grave. That Leo had made Gary bleed encouraged me a lot.

Wilson bared his teeth at me. "Gary saved me. That's what you never got. He made me. I owe him my life no matter what."

There's no point in arguing with thugs, especially happily brainless ones. I hit Wilson in the throat, the soft spot that makes a crunching sound if you do it right. He fell over, and I wriggled out from under him.

Gary still battered Leo's blood line, and it finally gave. Leo waited, watching Gary's Scythe as he advanced.

"Nice work," Gary said, swiping at his nose. "I'm still going to cut your balls off with this."

Seeing Leo pinned down and his useless father just standing there, I shifted without thinking about it. It hurt like hell, all my broken bones rearranging themselves into their four-legged configuration, Gary's cut making me favor my front right leg, but that didn't matter.

Leo poured out more blood, mumbling with his eyes closed, and red smoke started to rise as the stuff bubbled. Gary choked, his eyes watering, but he still came.

Until I hit him and wrapped my jaws around his throat.

Hellspawn blood tastes like sewage, and it burned, so bad that I almost let go. But I didn't. I wrestled Gary to the ground and bit down hard, feeling flesh and tendon and windpipe break under my teeth.

I may see in black and white, but my brain is almost sharper when I'm a hound. All that human fear and worry and indecision washes away, and I know exactly what I have to do. I whipped Gary back and forth, breaking his neck and choking off his scream.

Leo kept mumbling, and I could feel whatever he was conjuring with the blood creeping all over my skin. He opened his eyes at last, and I realized that some of Gary's blood had spattered across his face, fine black droplets like rain on his pale skin.

Before he could move, though, something hit me in the side, a small impact that quickly turned into wretched, burning pain. I went off my feet, and Leo's father pumped another spray of bullets into me for good measure.

He picked up Gary's Scythe and wiped it on the sleeve of his suit. Leo started to say something, but his father said a single word, something that landed on my senses like a hammer blow, and Leo went flying into the hood of his car, smashing it to shit.

I guessed Leo's plan wasn't as brilliant as he'd thought.

Leo's father and his men got back into their cars and drove away, leaving me in a pool of my own blood, surrounded by dead-head parts and bleeding hounds and the reaper I'd just betrayed.

Bullets don't slow Hellspawn down. If you're thinking about warding off a hellhound with some silver-tipped hollow points or a spray of buckshot dipped in holy water, kiss your gun hand good-bye now. All bullets do is piss us off. There are metals that can poison a hound, but usually only smart warlocks have weapons that pack the punch.

I was thanking everything I could think of that Leo's father wasn't one of those.

The bullets worked their way out of my side after a few minutes, sticky with my blood. I concentrated on breathing until they were all out, and then got myself up and padded over to Leo. I didn't really want him to see me fuzzy this early in our relationship, but shifting back would have knocked me out, and one of us needed to be conscious.

I nudged Leo with my nose until he muttered and started, coming awake with a groan. "Fuck me," he said.

I let out a whine to tell him he needed to get up and get moving. Gary wasn't stirring, but I had no way of telling if he was down for good. Between Leo's conjure and my mad-dog attack, we'd at least managed to dent him. Maybe later, if I survived, I'd celebrate.

Leo looked at me, eyes narrowing. "Ava?"

I bumped his hand again. Leo passed it hesitantly across my head, ruffling the hair. "Christ, that is freaky," he said. "You're a dog but you've still got your eyes."

I herded him toward the door of his car, and he stumbled. "Okay, okay," he said. "I'm only human, give me a break."

He winced every time he breathed, and I felt for him. I whined, scratching at the closed door, but Leo shook his head. "We gotta ditch the car," he said. "My father knows it."

I scanned the lot for anything else, since my beautiful bike was probably living in the Vegas impound lot by now, and saw the bulb of an enormous taillight protruding from behind the motel office. I let out a bark, one I hoped wouldn't make Leo pee himself. He started, but he kept it together.

"Okay," he said. "Keys?"

"Can't you jack it?" I said, but it just came out as a long snarl, and Leo recoiled. Shit. I really wished he could speak hellhound.

This was ridiculous. I wasn't going to get anywhere playing Hellspawn *Turner & Hooch* with Leo, so I gritted my teeth and shifted.

He caught me when I started to pitch over, even though I landed on his broken ribs. "Fuck," I said. "We're quite a pair."

"I'm sorry," Leo said. "I had no idea—"

"I completely understand why you want to shank your dad," I cut him off.

He nodded, still holding on to me. I wasn't sure if I was propping him up or the other way around. "Let's get the fuck out of here," Leo said. "We need keys for that thing."

"What kind of gangster can't wire a car?" I said. Leo's mouth crimped.

"Look, if you need someone to cook up a deadhead or drop some blood conjuring, I'm happy to help, but I never jacked cars. My skills run more to cleaning and disposal, if you get the drift."

I got it, and felt a little bit of my own smugness that I could do something a badass warlock couldn't, even if it was just petty theft.

The car was a monster, a candy-apple-red Buick Skylark from a time when there was enough metal in the fins alone to build a small aircraft. "I hope you weren't going for inconspicuous," I said to Leo, breaking the door lock with a sharp jerk. I slid onto the buttery white leather seat and pulled out the ignition wires.

"Something's bothering me," Leo said.

I stripped the ignition and the solenoid wires and started the delicate courtship of tapping them together until the motor coughed, then grumbled, then caught. "Getting blood out of white leather is your area, I'd think," I said. "But if it's really getting to you I can try to find a towel to sit on."

Leo shook his head. "Are you always this calm right after everything goes to shit?"

I wasn't calm. I was numb. But fuck if I was going to let Leo know that.

"It's that call," he said. "Gary said I called him, but I didn't. I'd say it was my father, but I think he was surprised as I was. Who'd pretend to be me just to get you iced by a reaper?"

I sat back, looking at the tchotchke dangling from the rearview mirror. A big fuzzy pink *M*, for *Marty*.

"You still have that gun?" I said to Leo. He pulled it from his waist and handed it over.

"Full mag, one in the pipe," he said. I flipped the safety off and stalked back toward the motel office, ignoring the dozen niggling pains that wanted to make me limp.

Marty had come out of hiding and was sweeping up broken glass from his front window, carefully skirting the pieces of deadhead that were scattered around like the world's most morbid store display.

"Why?" I said. He stopped sweeping and bugged his eyes at me.

"Did you really think Gary was going to pat you on the head and give you a corner office?" I said. "And don't you think you should have called him as yourself if you wanted to effectively kiss his ass?"

Leo had said Marty didn't know who he was, but I thought Marty was exactly the kind of prying jerkoff who liked knowing things he shouldn't. It probably got him good and stiff on nights when the Japanese zombie nurse porn just wasn't doing it.

"I don't give a crap about Leo Karpov," he said. "I just wanted Gary to fuck you up." He shrugged and went back to sweeping. "I'm a shifter. I hate hellhounds." Glass he'd collected clattered into his wastebasket. "Here's a tip: next time, be a little nicer. I respond to girls who have manners."

I shot him right between the eyes. It might not have been the tooth-and-nail death I wanted to give him, but I was tired. "Thanks for the tip."

Leo didn't say anything when I gave him back his gun, and I scooted over to the passenger side of the car. "You drive," I said. "My arm hurts like a bitch."

He pulled out of the lot, still silent, and I let the hum of the wheels even out my heartbeat. By the time Vegas had vanished into the shimmering Mojave, I'd managed to convince myself that I might not be fucked. Sure, Leo's father had the Scythe and we were bolting with a stolen car, no cash and dubious survival skills, but I was alive. I felt the air on my face, the drying blood on my skin, my heartbeat, and my breath more sharply than I had in decades.

Being alive was just going to have to be good enough for now.

10

Leo drove us as far as Elko, courtesy of a trucker in Henderson who left his wallet on the counter of a gas station.

Marty's car swilled gas like a wino with a gallon of Thunderbird, but nobody stopped us or even noticed, except a couple of guys who told Leo he had a sweet ride.

I concentrated on not passing out. I wasn't healing like I should. I didn't know if it was the cut from the Scythe or just being so beat to shit my body was giving up on me. Leo finally pulled into a motel at least ten times as crappy as the Mushroom Cloud, and turned off the car.

"You need to rest," he said.

"No," I said. "We should at least cross the state line."

"There's no magical fence keeping my dad out of Idaho," he

said. "And if you crap out, then you're not going to be very useful when he does catch up to us."

I flinched. I knew that Leo only went with me because I was good in a fight, extra protection against his father's gang of deadheads, but being reminded that I was only good for one thing didn't help me feel any better.

"Come on. At least let me take a look at that arm." Leo's voice was a lot softer. I had the thought maybe he'd realized he'd stung me, but that was silly. Guys who didn't care about hurting your kneecaps sure as hell didn't care about hurting your feelings.

The thought of a bed was appealing, even a bed in the sort of place where the working girls didn't bother to pretend they were just taking a trip to the ice machine.

"I'm pretty sure that trucker has canceled his cards by now," I said. "And he didn't have a whole lot of cash."

Leo helped me out of the car and pounded on the nearest door with the butt of his gun. He grabbed the shirtless guy who answered by the neck and tossed him into the parking lot. "Out."

"Hey!" the guy screamed. He had fewer teeth than he did prison tats, but he looked pretty pissed.

Leo pointed the gun at him while he held the door open for me. "Look at it this way—now you don't have to leave the maid a tip." He shut the door and put the chain on. The guy pounded for a minute, but he was gone by the time I'd cleaned up the burnt foil and glass straws on the bed and turned on the arthritic bathroom fan to air out the smell of crystal meth and cheap aftershave.

"Home sweet home," I said, tossing the filthy bedspread on the ground and sitting down.

"Just like my condo on Flamingo," Leo said. "Except this place has a painting of a sad clown to replace my flat screen."

He took off his jacket and rolled up his sleeves before he grabbed the ice bucket. "Sit tight," he said. "I'm going to grab some stuff to stitch up your cut."

"I don't need . . ." I started, but the door had already slammed.

I looked at the ceiling stains while I waited for Leo, listened to a hooker on the second floor curse out a john in English, Spanish, and what sounded like broken Cantonese—impressive—and tested the TV, which got a fuzzy porn channel and a shopping network selling me cubic zirconium jewelry that even Liberace would have said was a tad flashy.

Leo would learn that he didn't need to take care of me if he stuck around, but he wasn't going to. If playing nurse took his mind off things, then I wasn't going to pee on his parade. I liked him as much as I liked any human, but he'd learn soon enough why even warlocks didn't become best buddies with Hellspawn.

I pulled my knees up to my chest and listened to the helmet-headed bimbo on TV drone on about the brilliance index. I used to love the television—when they first started showing up everywhere, I always found a way to catch crap like *The Man from U.N.C.L.E.*, *Lost in Space*, and *Twilight Zone*. Humans were scared of all the wrong things, I realized when I started watching TV. Nuclear war, Communists, monsters out there in the dark.

The monsters weren't out there, though. They'd already come inside, infected the world like the zombie virus in *Night of the Living Dead*. Humans with a little power would always try to peer into the darkness, and things like Gary would always be there waiting, ready to cement Hell's foothold in their world another inch or two.

Really, I had more in common with them than I'd realized before I'd started watching those shows. We were both small things in a vast forest, and we could only walk so far before something higher up the food chain snatched us in its jaws.

All at once the room was too tight and too hot, feeling exactly like the filthy little box it was. I ran into the bathroom and spun the tap, orange rust water splashing over my shirt. I ripped it off, tossing it in the tub. It stank like stale sweat anyway, and was in even worse shape than me.

I ducked my head down and splashed water on my face until all the blood and salt crust was gone, and my hairline was damp. Black strands stuck to my skin when I came up for air, but I'd staved off the panic attack.

I wasn't used to being anchorless. I'd seen a thousand motel rooms just like this one, but I'd always been going somewhere on a collection or going back to Gary. Now there was nothing except this.

Vomit took the expressway up my throat and I dove for the toilet, which was a dubious choice at best. The grime-streaked bowl didn't help, and I retched until my abdomen cramped and my head was pounding.

"Take some deep breaths."

I shrieked and skidded backward on the slick tile until I hit the tub, where I managed to yank the curtain rod down and start an avalanche of tiny shampoo bottles.

The demon put down the toilet lid and sat, clicking her tongue. "You must be Ava. I'm Lilith. You're not at all what I expected, based on the things Gary said."

A weird thing happens when you see a demon in the flesh.

They're like a truck bearing down on you, even if they're just sitting there. You lose all logic and sense, and your hindbrain jumps in and sets up a litany of *ohfuckohfuckohfuckohfuck*. Which really is a perfectly normal reaction for a bunny rabbit running smack into a hungry wolf.

I'd managed to go my whole existence as a hound without running into Gary's boss. Clearly, I'd run through my luck when Leo and I made it out of Vegas, because here she was, tapping one foot on the tile and staring at me like I was supposed to do a trick.

"Sorry to just drop in on you like this," she said. "But I think you and I have something to discuss."

I pushed the shower curtain off me and tried to lever myself up, managing to sit on the edge of the tub. My fingers chipped divots out of the cheap fiberglass when I gripped it to hide my shaking.

"Gary was going to kill me," I said. I was whispering, but it still sounded unholy loud in the tiny bathroom.

"Ava, you're going to learn very quickly I don't like excuses," Lilith said. She stood, patting her hair in the cloudy mirror that still assured the entire world she was gorgeous. She was tall too, and had a round, angelic face and an adorably upturned nose. Her hair was swept back into a smooth bun, blond and glowing like somebody had cut her out of a magazine. Too perfect to be human, though I doubted anyone besides me would pick up on that before she ripped them apart.

"Not an excuse," I said. "If you want me to be sorry, I don't think I can do it right now."

"I also hate apologies," Lilith said. "They're weak. As for Gary, do you really think I'm happy that my employee let his own hellhound ventilate him?"

I stayed quiet, which made her turn back to me, white teeth bared. "Here's a hint: I'm not fucking happy."

"Please kill me," I blurted. "Please just do it here. Don't take me to the Pit." I was managing not to cry as I begged, so I only hated myself a little instead of to the core.

Lilith narrowed her eyes, and then she grabbed me and lifted me up so my head cracked the tiles when it hit. "I *really* hope that you're less of a pathetic whining waste of air than you come across," she said, "because if you don't get it together and do as I say, I *will* fuck up your day."

"Okay," I squeaked. I still wasn't sure why I wasn't already dead, but sometimes you just have to accept that the wolf isn't hungry and walk away.

Lilith dropped me and brushed off her skirt. She was wearing powder blue with a white blouse and pearls. Fucking pearls. I had the insane urge to laugh, but I turned it into choking instead.

"You do realize that a human warlock in possession of a Scythe is the worst thing that could possibly happen," she said. "Just be glad it wasn't your friend out there, because I'd rip him a new asshole where his balls used to be."

I started to talk, but she held up a finger. "I will handle Sergei Karpov. And you are going to get your ass back to work." She tossed a leather-bound notebook at my feet, and I realized with a start it was Gary's ledger.

"Gary's last outstanding collection is in Wyoming," she said. "He's been tracking him since the early seventies at least. I wasn't too happy that Gary never managed to collect from the prick, but now, if you want a chance in any realm of keeping flesh on that skinny ass of yours, you'll get him, reap him, and bring him to me."

She pointed to a name amid dozens of others. I wondered how many of those names I'd been responsible for. Gary's obsessive-compulsive handwriting spelled out *Clint Hicks*. I risked making eye contact with Lilith, which was like staring at a well-dressed bird of prey. "What's his deal?"

"I don't micromanage my employees," she snapped. "I don't know why meat sacks choose to sell any more than I know why Gary decided you were worth making part of his hound pack. Which is probably a good thing, because I would have told him to let you rot."

"I've been getting that a lot," I muttered.

"The last hound Gary sent got sent back on a ventilator," the demon said. "I understand this Clint Hicks surrounds himself with shifters, and when Gary came to me to track him personally, I found he had measures in place to keep Hellspawn out of the area."

"This hound," I said, feeling sickness that wasn't caused by Lilith grip my guts. "Was his name Wilson?"

"How the fuck do I know what his name was?" Lilith snapped. "For all I know, Gary calls you Sparky, Rover, and Spot. The countermeasures won't keep me out for long, but breaking them is more effort than I'm going to put into one damned soul who thinks he's smart, so go and fetch him."

There was that word again. *Fetch*. But since it was coming out of the mouth of a thousand-year-old demon, I pretended it didn't bother me.

I just nodded. Lilith opened the bathroom door and walked out, turning back only once.

"Ava, if you screw this up, do yourself a favor and walk into traffic before I find you. Because if I do, the Pit is going to be a vacation compared to what I have planned."

She left, and I was still curled up in the corner of the bathroom when Leo came back.

I managed to tell him the deal, in a fairly coherent manner, while he got me off the floor and carried me to the bed. I wasn't in the place to argue about that.

"Lilith?" he said as he uncapped a plastic bottle of gas station vodka and poured it over the cut on my arm. "Shit. *She's* Gary's head office?"

"Apparently," I said. "Gary never talked about her except to threaten us with being her purse dogs if we got out of line."

"Well, Lilith is a big fucking deal," Leo said. He got a needle and dental floss and positioned my arm flat. "This is going to hurt."

"What else is new?" I said.

Leo threaded the needle and started sewing, tattooed fingers moving without any hesitation. "You should probably do what she says," he said. "I don't think we have a lot of choice."

"The fuck is this 'we'?" I said. "You can do whatever you want. *You* don't have a shark-toothed bitch from Hell breathing down your neck."

"True," Leo said. "But one of the most powerful *vory v zakone* slash necromancers west of the Mississippi knows I'm gunning for him, so I'm thinking heading to some country that's inhospitable to both gangsters and deadheads might not be a bad idea."

"What's the deal with you and your dad anyway?" I said, gritting my teeth. I wasn't really interested in Leo's sad life story, but it was better than sitting in silence watching a needle slice in and out of my skin.

"Warlocks are supposed to pass on their skills to their legitimate kids," Leo said, eyes never moving from his work. "I'm not, but none of my fuckup half siblings got the blood. He wasn't happy about that, but he couldn't kill me, so he devoted himself to keeping me under his boot. Eventually we'll probably kill each other, but until then, I decided I was through being tied to his whipping post."

He bit through the floss and poured more vodka over my arm. "All done."

I examined the tight stitches. My arm already looked less like a flank steak. "You're pretty good at that."

Leo tossed the needle and the bloody pillowcase I'd lain on into the trash. "My wife was a nurse."

The past tense was enough to keep my mouth shut. If Leo wanted to talk about his dead wife, he'd be talking.

"In the morning we'll find a new set of wheels and go see what this Clint Hicks guy did to put a burr up Lilith's ass," Leo said. "In the meantime, I'm starving."

"I'll go get us some grease passing for food if I can find a shirt," I said. Leo's lips parted in a small smile.

"Yeah, I wasn't going to say anything." He unbuttoned his shirt and pulled off the black wife beater underneath, handing it to me. "Here."

I lost a few seconds staring at his chest, at the twin stars inked on his collarbones and the death's-head that took up the space from his heart to his abdomen. The hood and the scythe were a human's fantasy of Death, from someone who didn't know what really happened when you met a reaper. Cyrillic alphabet ran up his ribs, and his biceps were covered in roses, spiderwebs, and groupings of tiny crosses and skulls.

The daggers I'd glimpsed were pretty intricate and surrounded by red blood droplets, as if the ink had actually pierced him. Shirt off, I could see where he got his strength—he was all muscle on his thin frame, the kind of body designed by genetics for inflicting damage.

Leo put his shirt back on and buttoned it, not meeting my eyes. "Are you going to ask me what they mean? Because we could be here for a while."

"They mean the same thing as me having fangs and claws does," I said. " 'Stay the fuck out of my way.' "

Leo poured the last of the gasoline-smelling vodka into a dirty glass and drank it. "Close enough."

"You really don't have to stick with me," I said. "You don't owe me anything." Truthfully, I wanted Leo to stay more than I wanted anything, except maybe to have never met Lilith. But he wasn't going to, so why prolong things?

"I told you, it's not about owing," Leo said. "We're mutually beneficial. You could use a hand and I could use someone who can keep a deadhead off my ass if my father catches up to us."

I nodded. "Okay. But if you're gone when I get back with burgers, I won't hold it against you."

Leo shook his head. "Thieves like me believe in loyalty, Ava. I get that you probably haven't had a lot of that, but I'm not going to dump you after all this."

I backed out of the room and walked out to the county road without saying anything else. Leo was right. I'd never had somebody stick around when things weren't going their way. I'd sure as fuck never had my loyalty repaid by anything but more orders at best, and a knife in my back at worst.

I'd died because I was loyal. Loyalty was for stupid girls and brainless thugs, and I wasn't either of those things anymore.

Lilith had me by the throat, so I'd go to Wyoming. I'd do what she asked, but Gary was gone—Lilith showing up in his place proved it for my purposes—and as far as I was concerned my contract was void. Clint Hicks was my last roadblock, and I decided then that when I did find him, pet shifters or no, Clint Hicks was going to be one sorry son of a bitch for getting in my way.

CHAPTER 11

We crept out of the motel room predawn, before day-shift maids started their rounds. I figured not giving a fuck was a prerequisite for employment in a place like this, but Leo insisted.

"My father has a lot of people willing to do a lot of things," he said, shrugging back into his suit jacket. "Right now, his one and only priority is finding me and feeding me my own nuts. The fewer people see us, the better."

"Fine." I shrugged. My arm still twinged with every motion. I hadn't slept much, waking every few minutes whenever someone in the walkway stumbled to the ice machine or one of the happy customers in the upstairs room moaned.

Leo patted himself down for his crushed pack of Russian cigarettes and a lighter, sticking a smoke between his lips. He lit it while we surveyed the parking lot. "That one." He pointed at an orange Sprint that was more rust than paint.

I shook my head. The Sprint had left a glossy puddle on the pavement under the transmission, sported expired tags, and probably gulped gas like an end-stage drunk tackling a box of Franzia. "We wouldn't get fifty miles in that piece of shit," I said. Leo exhaled a cloud of rank blue smoke in frustration.

"We need something old, without an onboard computer," he muttered. "Don't need the electronics playing up if we tangle with more witches."

I crossed the lot to the far corner, examining an early seventies Volvo wagon parked underneath the one scrawny pine at the edge of the pavement. The back windows were piled with cardboard boxes and stuffed suitcases, a Michigan plate riding below the fat chrome bumper and bug-eyed headlights. It was clean, though, and had a current inspection sticker. Based on the number of stuffed animals and ultraviolent zombie video games I could see stacked in the back, I was guessing college students too poor or dumb to stay somewhere better.

I whistled at Leo, who wrinkled his nose at the sight of the car. "That thing? The Joad family will be coming back any second to claim it."

I ignored him, popping the driver's side lock and fishing out the wires from beneath the dash. I also popped the lift gate and gestured to Leo. "Leave their crap, will you?"

He sighed, grinding out his cigarette on the fender. "You kidding me?"

"Leo, they're just kids," I said. "We're stealing their car. We don't need their entire dorm room."

Grumbling, he went to the back and started tossing out boxes. "You know, for somebody in your line of work, you're pretty fucking saintly."

He slammed the back as I started the motor. It turned right over, grumbling in the snapping cold of the high desert. Leo slid into the passenger seat. "Let's get the hell out of here."

I put the Volvo in gear and drove for a couple of hours until we hit a faded truck stop on I-80, just over the Utah border near the singularly unremarkable town of Wendover. Leo had dozed off, and I nudged him awake.

"You better change your clothes," I said. His suit was looking crusty, never mind totally out of place in the land of padded vests, trucker hats, and Mormons decked out in mom jeans. I fished through one of the two remaining overstuffed suitcases on the backseat, pulling out a too-big peasant blouse to cover up the stitches in my arm. I found a fresh pair of jeans and socks while I was at it. The girl whose car this was had feet the size of Godzilla's, but the rest of her was close enough. I couldn't remember the last time I'd had new clothes, but all my spares were gone, along with my bike.

I checked myself out in the rearview mirror. I was a mess— greasy, pale, undereye circles that would do a junkie proud. No help for it. I'd have to make the crackhead look work for me.

Leo wriggled free of his bloodstained suit pants and coat, and I handed him a pair of baggy, frayed jeans with blue and red paint staining the knees and a faded Psychedelic Furs shirt. His boxers were white, little red and black card suits all over them. In spite of everything that had happened, I smiled a little. Enough bad stuff happens in a short enough time and you just go numb, things glossing over. If it wasn't for the throbbing, infected gash in my arm, I'd say this day wasn't going half bad.

I wriggled down my own bloodstained, filthy jeans, shooting Leo a glare. "Do you mind?"

He shrugged, a smile tugging at his lips in turn. "So you're allowed to ogle me but not the other way around?"

"Don't get excited," I muttered, balling up my jeans and shoving them under the seat. I yanked off the shirt Leo had lent me and thrust it back at him. "Humping you is less than the last thing on my mind right now."

Leo raised one eyebrow as he accepted the shirt. "Good to know." Cool morning air kissed the V of skin above my bra as he stared. I glared at him as I pulled the blouse over my head and zipped up the girl's worn-out hippie jeans. They slid down over my hip bones, barely clinging to my ass. Thieves couldn't be choosers. Leo grinned at me.

"You look cute. Like you're headed to the Lilith Fair."

"Fuck off," I growled, and shoved my car door open.

Leo climbed out after me, zipping up the pot-scented UNLV hoodie he'd found under the passenger seat, and ambled into the truck stop. Aside from the neck tattoos and the hit man stare, he could have been any other good-looking tourist stopping for coffee and a piss on his way to somewhere more interesting.

I gathered up all the cash we had left and followed him, grabbing a fresh pair of underwear and a bra from the little shop between the bleating arcade and the fast-food restaurant. I paid for a shower, bought some shampoo and soap from the dispenser, and stripped out of my stolen outfit. The tiles were slimy under my feet, but the shower was a strong jet, and I stood under it for a long time, letting the water droplets pound on the rooftop of my skull.

Clean for what felt like the first time in months, I felt some of the resolve to find and fuck up Clint Hicks as quickly as possible slipping away. I was only alive because Lilith thought I was useful, but once I found Hicks, then what?

Then I'd just be a stray dog, and a lot less useful.

I soaped my hair twice and let the water run clear, midnight strands sticking to my neck and shoulders like seaweed.

Who was to say I could even track down this Hicks? Gary hadn't been able to find him when he'd skipped out. Wilson had tracked him down and come back with half a face. Maybe this was just Lilith's little fuck you before she sent me to my death, an extra half twist of the knife in a wound that was already fatal.

I got out of the shower stall, standing now in a world of steam, and toweled off, putting my "new" clothes back on. Everything was baggy on me. I was on the small side to begin with and I hadn't eaten in a while. My stomach burbled in response, and I wished I hadn't spent all of our cash on being clean. Who was I trying to impress, anyway? A gangster who stashed dead bodies in fifty-gallon drums for a living?

I found Leo sitting on the hood of the Volvo, a wrapped breakfast burrito next to him letting off steam. He was paging through Gary's ledger, one side of his lower lip sucked into his mouth, teeth whiter than bleached bone pressing into the flesh until it turned crimson with concentration.

"Thought you'd be hungry," he greeted me, not looking up from the page.

I unwrapped the burrito and shoved it in my mouth, pointing

down at the Hellspawn scrawl against the ledger's pages. "You can read that?" A piece of jalapeño tumbled down my chin and I swallowed, embarrassed. You'd think after a century I'd have learned a few social graces, even if I did spend a good portion of it running on four legs.

"Yeah," Leo said. "It's not impossible for humans to understand Hellspawn writing. I mean, people spend all their free time learning Klingon, so why not this?"

I remembered a warlock in Arizona, the kind who spells *magic* with a *K*, real wannabe Ordo Templi Orientis fanboy, who came at me with some kind of replica *Star Trek* weapon when I showed up on the doorstep of his shitty condo outside Scottsdale.

Once he'd stabbed me with it in the shoulder and it had no discernible effect, the screaming started.

Leo snorted in amusement when I relayed the whole sad story, rifling the pages of the ledger. "Here it is—Louis Turnblatt, December fourth, 1992. Payment for . . ." He raised one thin eyebrow at the page. "Sexual potency and control over the lusts of others."

"Yeah," I said. "Some guys will literally sell their soul for magical roofies."

"I'm beginning to understand why your boss was so cranky," Leo muttered. He flipped the pages. "Your name is on a lot of these."

I crumpled the burrito wrapper in my fist, turning it into a hard little rock of paper and grease. "I was one of his best."

Leo shut the book. "Nothing before 1920, I noticed."

I fixed him with a stare. I needed to set some clear boundaries with this guy before he started thinking we were friends, or even friendly, and then put up an electrified fence around them.

"Just because I still remember what it was like to be human doesn't mean we're doing group therapy, Leo."

I opened the car door. "I don't care about anything before the last few days, and neither should you."

His face drooped, and I almost felt bad for a second before I reminded myself this was a guy who'd tied me to a chair and burned me with the exact same expression on his face.

"Suit yourself," he said, sitting beside me. "Are you at least interested in hearing what it says about Clint Hicks?"

I shrugged, pulling back onto the highway. "Other than that he has a stupid name from a cowboy movie?"

"His last address is in here," Leo said. "Although what are the odds of him still hanging around?"

"If it's all we got," I said. Whether he was part of a ploy to get me killed for good or not, at this very moment, Clint Hicks was the only thing keeping me alive. While most days I didn't exactly greet my continued existence with a parade, things felt different now. It was like I was unmoored, tossed from one wave to another on a stormy sea. All of Gary's tethers had been sliced, emphatically.

I should feel lucky—I was probably the only sorry hound in existence to cheat Death twice over. But I just felt a shiver on the back of my neck, from more than the wet hair plastered there. Why me? I was barely fit for one second chance, never mind two.

Leo turned on the radio, his thin fingers with their dark ink marks spinning the dial back and forth until he tuned in something other than static. Normally I would have objected to twangy guitars and twangier singers, but I let Merle Haggard's nasally whine fill up the car, glad I didn't have to talk.

Leo sang along softly under his breath, and I thought that if the rest of the trip to Wyoming went like this, I might actually exit the car with my sanity intact.

"See if there's a map in here," I told Leo. He'd ditched his cell phone back at the Mushroom Cloud and I had never had one in the first place. GPS wasn't in the college kids' budget, but there was a shiny new road atlas in the door compartment.

Leo read the map for a while, scribbling down turns in the margin, and I tried again to shake off that cold feeling, like Death had passed me by, but in doing so, he'd turned around and touched me on the shoulder.

"This place is a hike," Leo said at last. "Almost in South Dakota. Maybe Clint Hicks figures he'll stay hidden in the Black Hills long enough, your boss gets bored or forgets and he'll be free."

I snorted. The idea of Gary ever forgetting or forgiving was not one based in reality. "I don't think this Hicks is that stupid."

Leo sighed. "Me either." After another mile marker he put the seat back, lowering his head. "I just hope he's not too pissed off when we find him."

I gripped the wheel. "I guess we'll find out."

CHAPTER

12

|||||||||||||||||||||||||||||||||||||||||||||||||||||||||||||||||||||||||||||||||||||||||

We arrived at the Wyoming address a little after midnight. It was a flyspeck on the road between Hulett and Aladdin, once you'd gone past all the neat green Park Service signs pointing to Devil's Tower, past the false-fronted shops and galleries in Hulett, past everything except pavement, scrub pine, and a single lamppost floating up out of the darkness like a passing headlight.

Leo squinted out the windshield as I rolled to a stop. Gravel and broken beer bottles crunched under the Volvo's wheels. "Somehow I don't think this is home sweet home."

I looked past the pool of light at the building. It was weathered gray, silver in the illumination of the neon lights. Aside from a snarling coyote head painted across the roof peak, it could have come straight off the back lot of a western TV show. Replace the line of dusty road bikes lined up in front of the hitching post with horses and you'd have the complete picture. Underneath the coyote blocky letters almost as tall as I was spelled out ROAD DOGS.

"Depends on your definition of homey," I said, setting the brake and turning the car off. Once the clatter of the engine faded, I could hear hillbilly rock music, clanking beer bottles, shouting, and the sudden, explosive rattle of a Harley turning over. A big guy on a fat-tired bike roared out of the lot, spraying gravel that plinked against the Volvo's windshield. His leathers sported the same snarling coyote.

Leo grimaced. "I miss my gun."

I opened the door and swung my legs out, working the kinks from my shoulders and knees. "You afraid of a few outlaw bikers?"

"A few, no," he said. "Fifty, yeah. We don't get many One Percenters in Brighton Beach."

I wished I still had my jacket. I was going to stick out like a flower child thumb. "You're a long way from Brighton Beach," I told Leo.

"No shit," he muttered, lighting one of his cancerous-smelling cigarettes. I watched the figures move in and out of the clubhouse across the lot, wondering if Clint Hicks was among them. He was smart, hiding out with a shifter pack. They didn't like Hellspawn any more than we liked them. But when your ass was on the line, you'd make friends with the Devil if he'd keep you hidden. Look at me and Leo.

"Hey," he said as I started toward the clubhouse. I stopped, looking over my shoulder.

"Problem?"

"I know you're very good at your job and you probably don't need my advice . . ." Leo said.

"You're right," I said, staring him down. "I don't."

"I have done collections before," Leo said. "Back in New York. Clint Hicks has avoided Gary for what, twenty-five years and change? Guys who give this much trouble are either incredibly lucky or roll heavy."

"Guess it's good I've got you with me, then," I said. "Wait here, and if I'm not back in fifteen minutes, come in."

Leo sucked on his smoke until the ember glowed crimson, clearly not happy at this turn of events. I resumed my long walk, not trying to act like I belonged. I wasn't Wilson, throwing my weight around and getting mouthy until someone peeled my skin off, but they needed to know I wasn't afraid of them.

I paused for half a step on the sagging porch, the splintery barn door before me rolled open like a throat, exhaling darkness and smoke and earsplitting music. Another step and I'd be swallowed, churning along with the backlit shadow figures inside.

Was I afraid? It wouldn't matter if I was. Fleeting fear of the shifters inside the clubhouse was nothing compared to the very real possibility Lilith would taxidermy me if I didn't collect Clint Hicks.

I stepped inside. Music washed over me, turning into an insect drone over a shitty set of PA speakers, along with the chatter and body heat of a hundred drunks shoved into too-close quarters. Keeping my back to a wall, I let my eyes adjust to the dimness, little better than the night outside. Barn lights caked in dust hung randomly from the rafters, spilling irregular pools of light onto the bikers below. None of them noticed me, that frictionless invisibility I experienced going full force.

That, and everyone I could see was fucked-up beyond recognition, on their way to passing out if they hadn't made it already. I watched two burly guys, shirtless except for their club vests, roll a smaller guy's body off the pool table so one of them could rack up. By dawn, this place would look like Jonestown.

Moving away from the wall, I skirted the pool table, the bar that was really just a bunch of nailed-together crates and tubs full of ice and beer that went beyond cheap and verged on "glorified piss." Things crunched underfoot, bottle caps and peanut shells. More than once I felt the brittle crack of a disposable syringe. I breathed in the mixture of stale hops, sweat, and skunky pot that rolled over me like a gentle, pungent ocean current.

There was something else too, something tangy and sharp, like animal urine. Hot unwashed fur under a desert sun. The scent of something wild, something that wasn't content to stay within four walls, swilling beer until it passed out.

"Hey, baby." A hand swiped at my ass. I looked into the bleary eyes of a blond man who'd been all-right looking until somebody took a shovel to his nose. "Who'd you ride in with?" he said. The hand tightened its grip. I waited. I'd been around these types of places, with this type of man, way too long to lash out every time somebody helped himself to a handful of flesh.

"'Cause if you ain't riding with no one," the guy slurred, "you're gonna be riding with everyone. 'Less you and I go somewhere."

His accent was rounded and melodic, straight out of some shitty backwoods in the Alabama swamp. I considered asking him what his mama would think of this behavior, but just shrugged.

"There you go, baby," he said, grinning wide. His teeth were crooked, so many gaps his mouth looked like a hill of tombstones. "You don't need to be pulling no train, not with that face," he said. "You want a drink?" He brandished a fifth of no-name whiskey at me, and I grabbed it, cracking the brittle glass on the edge of one of the beer tubs and driving the jagged neck between his second and third knuckles, straight into the wall.

"Thanks," I said, and kept moving. He screamed, but he was so trashed and the music was so loud, nobody even looked in our direction.

I kept moving, scanning each face for either a shock of recognition or a guilty flinch. Being so close to so many shifters got my skin prickling and sweat working down my spine. Fortunately, these mutts couldn't do much beyond stare at me as I passed a sagging sofa holding a tangle of tits, bad Brazilians, and one hairy biker ass, all undulating in unison. Usually shifter packs were better organized, or less high, but they clearly felt safe here. They were the top of this particular food chain, and they knew it.

The clubhouse had been cut in half, a crude blockade of unfinished drywall covered in graffiti blocking my way. A girl in a leopard print top leaned against it, smoking a cigarette like it had done something to piss her off. She was smaller than I was, bad dye job radioactive under the barely there light. Fresh bruises tattooed what I could see of her rib cage, and her forearms had more lanes than the interstate.

She was the only one in the whole place who made eye contact with me. I stopped, waiting to see what she'd do.

After a long, vicious drag, she stomped the cigarette under her steel-toed boot and slipped through a pair of saloon doors marked with one of those naked girl cutouts. Someone had helpfully scrawled SLUTS across the cutout's ass, just in case I was confused about where to pee.

In the bathroom, the girl was sitting on the sink. Once upon a time, the place had had stalls, with doors, but they were long gone. Dim purple bulbs flickered in the single fixture above our heads. In the first stall, a skinny biker braced himself against the metal walls while a girl crouched on the stained tiles. He knotted one hand in her frizzy perm, eyes rolling back in his skull, as she bobbed her head like it was on springs. Neither of them paid any attention to me, so I returned the favor.

The girl I'd followed lit a fresh cigarette, exhaled, and looked me up and down. "You need something, dog?"

The animal-urine stink hung heavy around her. Not even the heavy coating of vomit and sex weighing down the bathroom air could hide it. I tilted my head. "You care if I do?"

"No, but they probably will." She jerked a thumb at the door. "Are you stupid or what?"

"I'm on the job." I figured I could leave out all that stuff about Gary being long gone, Leo's nut job father stealing his Scythe—all the information that would convey I had no boss, no real Hellspawn backing me up.

She blew smoke out her nose, a tiny, punk-rock freight train barreling down the tracks. "Come with me," she muttered finally.

We left the bathroom and cut through an opening in the wall. It was quiet here, no music, a warren of rooms built between the old board walls. The shifter girl walked fast, past a door that opened onto a patchwork of filthy mattresses, club members snoring like hibernating bears. I saw another room, lit by bright, harsh bulbs that hurt my eyes with their sudden brilliance. Two bikers in disposable face masks and black latex gloves weighed and sealed opalescent sandwich bags full of meth, stopping to stare at us without blinking as the girl strode by.

The Road Dog clubhouse, where the party never stopped. If Clint Hicks had washed up here, it'd be a miracle if he had any brains—or any molars—left at all. Though it did explain the feral undercurrent in the clubhouse, the feeling I'd come upon jackals surrounding a carcass and sinking their teeth in. Shapeshifter DNA and amphetamines weren't a winning mix.

The shifter girl stopped at the last door and hit it three times with her fist. "Billy," she said. I heard three or four dead bolts snapping, then a shifter in a black T-shirt cracked the door open. His forearm was almost as thick as my leg, and two scars slashed his bald head, like he'd been picked up by a giant bird of prey and dropped in front of me.

"Fuck off, Lolly," he said. The shifter girl gave him the finger.

"I found this wandering the clubhouse," she said. "And silly me, I figured Billy would want to know there was a hound in his crib. You'd think they'd learn."

The bald guy looked me over, his nostrils flaring. I think there was something about the smell of a hellhound that scared shifters on some elemental level. Sometimes you're just afraid of things. Your animal brain fought hard for thousands of years to pass the instincts on, the ones that kept you away from dark alleys and dogs that frothed at the mouth.

"You," he finally said, pointing at me. "You can come in. The skank stays outside."

Lolly sauntered back the way we'd come, casting one long look over her shoulder at me. It was the way you'd take a last look at a beloved pet you had to put down.

The mountain of shifter at the door pulled it wider, grinning as I edged past him. His two front teeth were rimmed in gold. "Billy," he said. "We got a visitor."

Billy stirred from his seat on an old daybed, piled with enough silk pillows and hippie print blankets to make Stevie Nicks orgasmic. "Seems we do," he said.

I looked to my left, catching a glimpse of two more shifters reclining on a swaybacked sofa. The vibe in here was more burnouts' dorm room than the crank-fueled orgy in the clubhouse, but these shifters weren't all fucked up and lazy. They were predators, and I was in their den. My only advantage was I wasn't part of the hive mind like the three bodyguards staring a hole through me. If I stayed calm and kept their bloodlust from cresting, I might walk out.

I'd guess that was the part Wilson had screwed up.

The two shifters on the sofa straightened up, their eyes shining the gold of coyote's in the dim light. "It's a little lost puppy," said one, black hair falling into his face, so I couldn't see much more than eyes and teeth and a sinewy body under black jeans and a Kevlar road jacket. "Should we eat her?"

The other, a woman, straightened up, uncurling legs clad in black leather to lean forward, one hand weighted down with silver rings digging into the dingy arm of the sofa. I shifted my weight a little. I'd been jumped enough to know when someone was considering the merits of beating my ass.

"Play with her first," she purred in a throaty growl that rightfully should belong to a black-and-white movie actress, not a strung-out hillbilly.

Billy raised his chin a little, nostrils flaring out. He swung his boots down to the ground and stood. I had to crane my neck to keep eye contact with him. He was at least six and a half feet tall, shirtless, jittery prison tats making his torso look like a stained shirt. Greasy blond hair brushed his neck, but his eyes were clear, and he moved to stand entirely too close to me.

"Leave her alone," he said. "I sure would like to know why she's here."

"I'm on the job," I said. Billy grinned. He had thin lips, almost bloodless, making his mouth all teeth.

"And your boyfriend outside, the meat suit with the greasy hair, he on the job too?" Billy smirked, reaching out and taking my chin between two fingers, turning my face side to side. "You're so small," he murmured. "You look so breakable."

"I don't want to do this with you," I said, pulling away from Billy. Time was, men like him would have sent me straight into his arms, and probably his bed. That was before I knew better, but I'd willingly spent enough time in places like this to know what made Billy tick.

"Do what?" His mouth twitched and he reached for me again. I caught his wrist. The smack echoed in the small, too-hot room. Instantly, the other three shifters jumped to their feet, crowding behind me like we were all in line to see their favorite band.

"If I was here on my own time, I'd be happy to have the dick-measuring contest you so desperately want," I said. "But unfortunately tonight I left it in my other pants. I'm here for someone, and beyond that, me and my company are none of your fucking business."

Okay, so I probably laid it on way too thick. The first rule of collections is stay calm. Let the guy you're after work himself into a lather, yell and threaten to cause trouble.

But I was tired, and this wasn't a normal job, where I had the power of a reaper behind me. Just me, and the me that had ridden thirteen exhausted hours to Wyoming wasn't in the mood for being felt up by any more shifters.

Billy detached his wrist from my fingers and waved his heavies off with a raised eyebrow, still smiling. He thought I was cute and amusing, rather than dangerous. Well, if it kept me out of the shit a little longer, I was fine with playing Shirley Temple. "Who's the son of a bitch unlucky and stupid enough to get you after him, darlin'?"

I took a breath. "Clint Hicks."

You could feel the mood of the room change, like a fast squall rolling over the Rockies and down into the valley, bringing cold wind and crushing rain. Thunderheads piled up in Billy's eyes, and he wasn't looking at me anymore, but at the other shifters. "Wait here," he said, brushing past me. The trio panted at his heels, and for such a big guy, Billy had vanished out the door in the blink of an eye.

The door lock clicked behind them, and I was pretty sure it wasn't for my protection.

I pressed my ear against the door, but all I heard was the vibration of the music from the front room.

I went back to the musty daybed Billy had been lounging on and pulled back the velvet curtains covering the windows. They dislodged clouds of dust that triggered a sneezing fit, and my eyes watered as I tugged on the window. It was painted shut, and I leaned into it with my shoulder, snapping the latch and pushing it open.

Voices and footsteps came back down the hall, only the voices were snarls and the footsteps sounded more like paws, claws clicking on the splintery wood.

I saw now the mistake Wilson had made was not trying to collect on Clint Hicks, but not running when he had the chance. Maybe I was fucking up by bolting, but better to be skittish than dead. I swung my legs over the sill and dropped the five feet to the ground.

I'd learned to tell when things had gone bad a long time ago. Even before Gary had found me, I'd had the instincts to know what streets in the French Quarter not to walk down, which of the mobsters I sold moonshine to could be trusted if we were alone, when it was time to stop being polite, turn around, and leave.

My instincts had only failed me once, and I figured since that time I'd ended up dead, I'd made my one big mistake.

Behind me inside the clubhouse, I heard the door slam open and shapes crowded the open window. I made it to the tree line, layers of pine needles muffling my footsteps.

"Puppy dog," Billy singsonged, leaning out the window and inhaling the chilly night air. "Where arreeee youuuuu?"

"Let her run," said a voice I recognized as the girl bodyguard. "Even if we don't catch her, she'll be back. We have the meat suit."

Shit. I felt my stomach flip uncomfortably, like I'd just stepped off an unseen stair into thin air. I made myself keep moving. I wasn't going to be any help to Leo if I let the shifters pulverize me.

I heard two soft thuds of feet landing on the ground, and I

peered around the rough bark of a pine tree, watching the girl stand with Billy's other heavy, who lifted his snout, pointed ears slicked against his skull as he scented for me.

He was big, maybe an eastern coyote or a young wolf, and when he caught my scent a low growl rumbled from his throat.

I took off, sprinting until my lungs burned and the pines and scrub turned into a blur. The clubhouse sat on the edge of unbroken woods, and the moon gave off just enough light to keep me from catching a fallen tree and breaking my leg.

The two shifters crashed through the brush behind me. I heard their high, vicious yips as they split up, flanking me through the night forest.

The ground sloped under me and I used the incline to push myself harder, feeling twin blades of pain from my lungs jab deep into my chest. It didn't matter. If they caught me, I was dead. Leo was dead. And even if I got away, Lilith would kill me anyway.

I crashed through a shallow stream, cutting up the rocky bed for a few hundred feet to confuse my scent before scrambling up the opposite banks. Rocks and roots cut at my hands. The coyotes snarled behind me, sliding down the bank into the stream.

Another sound joined their panting and yipping—the long, blood-chilling scream of a mountain lion. A swath of limestone cliffs, gleaming pure white in the moonlight, loomed up in front of me and I cut along the foot, shoving through the thick brush. Billy had joined the hunt.

I needed to gain high ground, get someplace where I could defend myself. Running from them would be easier if I was the hound, but my arm was still throbbing, and the last thing I needed was to pop my stitches and come up lame. If that happened, I might as well slap a $4.99 sticker on my forehead and call myself all-you-can-eat buffet for the shifters.

The coyotes picked up speed, close enough that I could see their low, slinking shapes against the forest. They were just playing with me, running me down until I was too tired and beat up to do anything but surrender.

I dug my boots into the soft dirt of the forest floor. I'd run for my life before, splashing through the bayou shallows, the hem of my dress weighted down with brackish black water.

The thick air coated my face and hair with damp, the kind of damp that rots everything it touches, sooner or later. My lungs burned, and choking sobs worked their way out of my throat no matter how hard I tried to stay quiet. I'd lost my shoes in the mud somewhere back near the old plantation house, the cane fields and grounds choked with kudzu and cypress. The swamp always reclaimed its own, and if I didn't run soon it would claim my bones.

Even though I was thousands of miles and close to a hundred years from the overgrown bayou now, running through a mountain forest and sucking down lungfuls of thin, clear air, the outcome would be the same. I'd run, but sooner or later I'd have to either kill or be killed.

The land dropped away, eroded down to the bones of pale limestone beneath, and I skidded to a stop. The coyotes burst out of the woods behind me and slowed, pacing back and forth to cut off any escape.

I tried to slow my heart down, really breathe and get my heart under control. The larger of the two, a black streak down her spine, stepped forward and bared her teeth. She barely gave me time to brace myself before she gathered her haunches and leaped.

Her weight hitting me felt like taking a Ford Pinto in the chest, but I managed to get an arm in between my jugular and her snapping jaws. I grabbed the fur between her shoulders with my other hand, digging my nails deep into her skin. She snarled and snapped, breath like a garbage furnace radiating against my face.

We stumbled to the edge of the ravine at my back, and instead of trying to stop my fall I leaned into it, the coyote and I still locked together. She yelped as we went over the edge, hitting the dirt and rolling, brush and dead trees snapping under my body. I bounced off a dead log and felt a spot under my lungs go tight, every breath hot and sharp as a punch in the ribs.

The coyote screeched as we tumbled down the almost sheer rock face, scrabbling with her paws to slow her descent. I could have told her it was useless, but a boulder filled my vision, sticking like a broken tooth from the loose gravel at the bottom of the ravine. The coyote unlocked her jaws from my forearm, slipping out of view as the rock came up at me. I curled into a ball, all I could do in the split second before I slammed into the rock and came to a dead stop.

Everything blurred gently, like ink running off a page. I saw the cold silver face of the moon, impossibly large, filling up my vision, before I blacked out.

My broken ribs brought me back a few seconds later, stabbing me with pain that would have made me vomit if there had been anything left in my stomach.

The coyote whimpered off to my left, scrambling up from where she'd landed and shaking herself off. She favored one of her hind legs, but she was in a lot better shape than I was. Both of my arms were cut up now, and one of my legs wouldn't hold weight when I tried to stand.

Above us on the ridge, Billy started to pick his way down, his blond coat sleek as a shark cutting through dark water under the moonlight.

The girl coyote let out a small yip, drawing her lips back. I'd swear she was laughing at me. And why shouldn't she? I'd basically laid out a free meal for the three of them.

My scrabbling fingers found a sharp rock within reach, and as she jumped at me I swung it and smacked her in the side of her skull. She yelped and snapped at me. I jammed my less injured arm between her jaws, feeling her teeth scraping my skin through my borrowed jacket. I grabbed her scruff with my other hand and jerked her head sharply to the left. There was a crack like a dry branch snapping, and she slumped on top of me.

For a moment, the ravine was eerily silent except for my own breath rasping in and out. The coyote's body was heavy, and I struggled to free myself. Billy let out a caterwaul, the sound Dopplering off the cliffs around us, and started bounding down the ravine, not caring when he stumbled and took a header on some gravel. The other coyote followed him. In thirty seconds they'd both be on me, and I doubted they'd be in a forgiving mood.

My arm was bleeding freely, black rivulets running over my fingers and coating the ground, turning the dust to mud under me. The edges of my vision started to blur and I realized the coyote had nicked a major vein. I'd killed her, but she'd killed me too.

This was familiar—my struggles getting weaker, skin going cold, the only warm spot the wound where the blood pumped out of me. Black dots spun in front of my eyes, and the weight of the coyote might as well have been a thousand pounds.

As I felt the ground shake under Billy's paws, a thunderclap rolled across the ravine. My skull vibrated, and Billy let out a scream. Not a thunderclap.

A gunshot.

Thunder rolled again and the rock next to Billy exploded, peppering him with chips of limestone. He and the male coyote turned tail and took off up the canyon, disappearing into the dark.

I lay alone, breath shallow, and saw a dark shape fade into view above me. It was walking on two legs, but that was about all I could say for sure.

"Are you alive?" a male voice asked. I tried to answer, but all that came out was a gasp. Staying conscious was officially way too much work, so I let the curtains come down and slipped under the cold waves.

CHAPTER
13

||||||||||||||||||||||||||||||||||||||||||||||||||||||||||||||||||||||||||||||||||

*B*ack on the bayou, I smelled smoke, and when I opened my eyes, dawn was creeping up on me, turning the cypress at the clearing's edge to black lines. The Spanish moss blended with the smoke from the dead fire and the fog clinging to the ground.

Cold slithered over my bare skin. I was naked, blood dried on my skin to the same shade as the mud coating my thighs and buttocks. The road map of cuts across my stomach and thighs, my breasts and forearms, radiating down to my feet had healed, the sticky residue all that remained of the hot, sharp pain that went to the core of me.

The fire had long since gone out, a jumbled mass of charred lumber scavenged off the plantation house. The white chalk paint of the *veve* was gone too, churned under a mass exodus of footprints *through the bloody mud. Caleb and the others had disappeared into the bayou. I was alone.*

"*You're not alone. You're dead.*"

I jolted awake, throwing the weight of the coyote off me. Not the coyote, I realized as something crashed to the ground. Blankets. And an enamel pitcher sitting on a nightstand, which was leaking water all over the braided rug next to a bed. I was indoors, in a small room little bigger than the bed, low ceiling of rough-hewn beams tilting overhead. An oil lamp hung from the rafters, calico curtains covered the only window. Decades of sun had bleached stripes into them, turning the weak light creeping through into a kaleidoscope.

I could have been back home in Bear Hollow, shoved into our too-small mountain cabin, able to hear the breathing of every other living soul within its walls, but the excruciating pain of being awake told me this was real life, not some memory flotsam that had bubbled to the surface, borne on my concussion.

There was no sound here, though. As far as I could tell, I was alone.

I braced myself and tried sitting up and swinging my feet over the edge of the bed. Bandages restricted my movements and my skull throbbed with a pain hangover, like every cut and bruise had its own heartbeat. My arm was wrapped in gauze spotted with rusty bloodstains. The spots were dry, and when I peeled the bandage back the bites had faded to red, puckered scars, joining the interstate of older injuries on my forearm. My ribs were wrapped, and I could actually breathe without wanting to scream, which was a nice change.

The cut from Gary's Scythe was still crimson and warm to the touch under Leo's stitches, but I'd take what I could get.

Leo. He was back at the clubhouse. If he hadn't cut and run when I didn't come back.

If Billy hadn't killed him outright.

I swung my legs over the edge of the bed and started looking for my clothes. I was wearing a nightgown covered in faded pink flowers, so old and thin it was practically transparent. At least whoever had put me here had let me keep my underwear. That pointed toward "Good Samaritan" rather than "cannibalistic sex offender." In situations like this, you had to be glad for the small things.

A neat stack of fresh clothes sat on a rough-hewn log chair by the bedroom door. Jeans, a man's T-shirt, an overshirt that smelled like it had been cozying up to somebody's grandfather for the last decade, even thick wool socks. I got changed fast, finding my boots sitting under the chair. They'd been cleaned up, free of the coating of road dust they usually sported.

Now I could run again if I had to. I left the nightgown draped over the bed and put my hand on the door, listening.

Nothing sounded from beyond the splintery wood except a faint thumping, arrhythmic and jarring. I eased the door open, finding myself in a dim, dusty room much like the one I'd woken up in. It was marginally larger, a stone fireplace taking up one wall and a small kitchen to my left. The cookstove was wood fired, and there was no sink, just a basin. It really was like being back home on the mountain. Outhouse and all most likely. I picked my way to the small front window and peered out.

A man stood in the clearing beyond the cabin, shirt off and

honey-gold skin glistening in the early sun. He hefted an ax and swung it down. Logs flew in either direction. He repeated the action twice more, then picked up the split wood and stacked it in a small, moss-covered lean-to.

I backed off, letting the curtain fall, and checked the other windows. An ancient pickup, composed mostly of rust and primer, was parked at the far end of the clearing. Otherwise, we were alone, just forest as far as I could see, crested by silver-peaked mountains beyond.

A hunting rifle hung above the front door, the kind with a carbon stock and a nightscope that cost more than a midsize used car, but I left it where it was. The kick alone would knock me on my ass, and it was bad manners to shoot the person who saved you from being lunch meat.

I backed away from the window and prowled the perimeter of the cabin. No photos, nothing on the walls except a couple of ancient taxidermy heads, nothing to tell me who the mystery man was.

A small oak desk was shoved into the corner next to the fireplace, and I sat down, trying the drawer. It was locked, but a few seconds with a letter opener popped it. Inside, an orderly stack of bills sat atop a yellowed permit from the National Park Service giving the owner of the cabin permission to maintain an access trail through federal land.

I froze, looking at the scribbled name on the first line, just below a date reading *June 27, 1962.*

Clint Hicks.

A split second later, I realized the noise from outside had stopped. I shoved the permit back into the drawer and stood up, knocking the desk chair over as I spun around.

I was too slow. The man from outside stood in the doorway, looking at me. "You're awake," he said, mopping sweat off his face with the tail of his shirt.

"Yeah," I said cautiously, planting my feet. There was no way he was Clint Hicks—if he'd made a deal with Gary that long ago, he'd be at least twice this guy's age—but the fact I'd ended up in his cabin was way too much good luck for me to trust it.

"They fit," the man said, and gestured to me when I frowned. "The clothes. I wasn't sure they would. You're small."

"I manage," I said. The guy's eyes darted from me to his kitchen, to the desk, and then back. Seeing what I'd touched, what I'd snooped into.

"Don't see many people this far into the woods," he said, running a hand through the damp black hair collected on the nape of his neck. "Then again, you're not people, are you?"

I stiffened. He smiled and held up his hand. His teeth were dazzling white in contrast to his dark hair and eyes. His eyes were black, so dark I couldn't pick out the pupil and iris. The smile didn't reach them. They remained still and cold, like the part of the ocean so deep no light can reach it.

"Let's skip the games," he said. "I'm in a good mood, so if you go out this door and tell your reaper you couldn't find me, I'll let you. Life and limb intact."

I sighed. "You are Clint Hicks." I skipped lying and telling him I didn't know what he was talking about. I also skipped wondering why a guy pushing eighty looked thirty. Bathed in the blood of unlucky hikers for all I knew, or just moisturized like crazy.

"What I've gone by lately," said the man. "I've been a lot of people." He stepped aside, pointing out the door. "It's about twenty miles to the highway. I suggest you start walking. Shifters will be out looking for you again as soon as the moon's up."

I stayed where I was. "I can't do that."

Clint Hicks sighed. "Don't be stupid. Whatever your reaper has threatened to do to you, trust me—it's nothing compared to what I'll do to not be found."

"Nothing stupid about it," I said, judging the distance between us. Less than five feet—I could smell the salty tang of sweat rolling off Clint's skin.

It would be over. After everything that had happened in the last week, this seemed distinctly anticlimatic.

That fit. I wasn't about big satisfying endings. I couldn't even die properly.

"I'm warning you," Clint said, dropping the shirt and shutting the door behind him. "I'm not somebody you want to mess with, no matter what your reaper told you."

"Gary didn't tell me anything," I said. "Gary didn't send me. He's dead."

Clint started to say something else, but I took a leap and landed, my claws digging into the splintery pine floor. I pushed off my back legs, landing on him with my full weight, and sank my teeth into the meat of his shoulder as we crashed to the ground.

Screams echoed, splitting my skull, and my vision bleached to white. It lit a fire behind my eyes like looking directly up at the sun, and whispers from a hundred voices skittered around the inside of my brain, never condensing into words, always just on the edge of hearing.

The pain got worse by the second, and I felt my heart thudding against my ribs so hard I was sure I'd broken them all over again.

In all of the hundreds of collections I'd made, I'd felt a lot of tainted, battered souls slither into my mind to rest until I turned them over to Gary. But not this. There was nothing here but agony, and finally, I had to let go or die.

When I was the hound, letting go was the last thing I wanted. Fortunately, the hound also wanted to live a lot more than I did, and I flew back from the blinding white void where voices cried and screamed.

Then it was just me, panting and whimpering, crumpled in the far corner of the cabin by the stove. Clint Hicks stood over me, just a black outline in the light from the door. Shadows played around him, enveloping us both, swirling like a black blizzard, overtaking my vision until it was down to a pinpoint.

"You bitch," Clint muttered, dabbing at the blood on his shoulder. He retreated, and the shadows with him, and after a moment the nausea subsided and I could draw a normal breath.

"What are you?" I croaked. Clint looked over his shoulder, wiping his wound clean at the basin. The bloody rags stood out like neon on a rainy night, the scent so rich and cloying my throat almost closed up.

"Somebody who doesn't want to be bothered," he said. That shut me up for a second. I hadn't met many men who understood hellhound talk.

The operative word there being *men,* which Clint Hicks clearly wasn't. At least not all the way. I'd turned over a lot of stones hiding nasty critters in my time, but never one who could repel a hellhound bite like an electric fence.

Clint examined the bite in a small hand mirror hung over the basin and winced. "Never do that again," he growled. "It hurts like hell and I think we've established it's useless."

I let myself shift back, sitting up slowly. I was dizzy, shaking, like I'd just taken a line of the hillbilly crank back at the shifters' clubhouse.

"You promise?" Clint Hicks demanded sternly, going to a squat chest of drawers and pulling out a clean shirt.

I pulled myself to my feet. "Yeah, it's useless." My throat was tight and hot, turning my voice to a whisper. "Because you don't have a soul."

Clint shook his head. "Nope. And now you've made things difficult for yourself. Now I'm going to have to set your reaper an example." He opened the cabinet farthest from the cookstove and took down a box of rifle shells.

"I told you I don't have a reaper," I snapped. "And if you were so worried in the first place, why didn't you let Billy kill me?"

He shrugged, taking his rifle down from the hook and starting to load the finger-length shells. "I needed to know who sent you. If I let the shifters rip you apart like they did that other hound, the reapers just send more."

"You could have just asked me," I muttered. Clint finished loading the shells and lowered the rifle so the barrel pointed at the floor. I felt sweat work its way down my back. The shot might not kill me, but at this range it would make life unpleasant for a good long while.

"No offense, but in my experience you all are a bite-first, ask-questions-never breed of thug," he said.

"It was Lilith," I said. I felt a flash of satisfaction when his face slackened, cut jaw and sharp cheekbones seeming to fall in on themselves.

"You're lying."

I folded my arms. "I'm not. I don't have any reason to. I just have a job to do."

Clint dropped the rifle and closed the space between us so fast I didn't even have time to make a sound before he shoved me against the stone fireplace, his fingers curling around my windpipe. His hands were thin, graceful, all bony knuckles and soft golden skin. Far from the calloused, knobby hands I would have expected a mountain man like him to be sporting.

They were plenty strong, though, and I choked as I struggled. My ribs starting throbbing again where he'd bashed me against the fireplace.

"Does she know where I am?" Clint snarled. "Right now. Does she know about this place?"

I clawed at his hands, but he hit me hard, knocking me to the ground. Blood erupted where my teeth cut into my cheek.

"No," I rasped, spitting it onto the floor. "She just told me to come find you when Gary bit it."

Clint turned on me again, pointing his finger inches from my nose. "Stop lying!" he bellowed. "Hounds don't exist without a reaper!"

"I do." I pulled myself to my feet, swiping at the blood on my chin. "I killed him, Lilith cornered me, and she told me to find you. So far I'm not having trouble understanding why she's got it in for you." I gingerly prodded my jaw, but my teeth seemed to have survived intact.

"You better not be messing with me . . ." Clint started. I pulled the twisted iron poker out of a dented metal trash can by the fire-place and pointed it at him.

"I swear if you come near me again, I will beat the shit out of you, soul or no soul," I said. A tic appeared in Clint's jaw, but he backed off, taking a deep breath.

"Lilith told you who I am?"

"She showed me Gary's ledger, told me to go collect, and she'd overlook the fact that I murdered my reaper. I didn't ask for your origin story."

Clint paced back and forth, stopping to peer out the front window, as if Lilith might materialize next to the woodshed. "So you're just following orders."

"I'm doing what I have to do to stay alive." I tossed the poker aside. "And now I'm going to go, and hope she's got bigger things happening than punishing one defective hellhound."

"How did you kill your reaper?" Clint's words stopped me at the edge of the porch.

"I saw my chance and I took it," I said. Clint grabbed up his rifle again and followed me, shutting the door.

"I can't say here," he said. "If Lilith found out what name I'm using there's a force-ten shit storm headed this way and I'd prefer not to be here when it hits." He headed for the truck. "Come on," he said.

I shook my head. "No. I have to go back to the shifter club-house."

Clint blinked at me. "Why the hell would you go back there? Billy almost ripped your throat out."

"My friend is there," I said. Clint heaved a sigh.

"I can't have you running around on your own. Lilith could

find you and pull this memory out of your head like you yank a weed out of your yard."

"Then I guess you're giving me a ride, because I'm not leaving him there," I said. Clint curled his lip.

"Oh, I get it. Your little boyfriend couldn't protect you, and Billy grabbed him."

"It's not like that," I snapped, getting in the passenger side of the truck. "Your choice. Drive me back or leave me for Lilith, who I will be happy to cooperate with when she lands her broomstick here."

Clint got into the truck, slamming the door and glaring at me as he started the engine. "What's your name anyway?"

I folded my arms. "Ava."

"Ava, anyone ever tell you you're a real pain in the ass?" Clint said.

I looked at the trees blurring around us as he accelerated down the pitted dirt track leading away from the cabin.

"Once or twice," I said. The clearing faded into the background until there was nothing around us but dark woods and under-growth, growing thick and wild and impenetrable. Usually, being away from humanity would have calmed me down, but today all I could think about was Leo. I slid down in the seat, trying to keep my ribs from hurting as the truck bounced and hoping I wasn't too late.

14

We were only about ten miles from the clubhouse once we hit the gravel logging road below Clint's cabin, and I watched for dark shapes in the forest, still wary of the shifter pack.

Finally, Clint spoke up. "We can talk, you know. Neither of us has taken a vow of silence."

I shifted my body away from him. "I don't want to talk to you."

He grimaced. "Is this about that love tap I gave you?"

"It couldn't be less about that," I said. "I'm not chatty. Deal with it."

"Strong silent type," said Clint, showing those matinee idol teeth again. "Prickly. I like it." The teeth were ridiculous, like somebody had come and adjusted each part of his face until all the dials were set to Maximum Handsomeness. Or until he had a perfect mask for a predator.

"Prickly would be me saying that's pretty big talk for a guy who pissed off a demon," I said. "What I am is unfriendly. There's a difference."

"Lilith and I are complicated," said Clint. "But trust me, what she and I have going is a lot more than some pissant reaper deal gone bad. I never met your reaper, and if I had, I would have saved you the trouble of offing him."

"I could care less," I said. "I just want to get Leo and be on my way."

"And you plan to run in there, boots stomping and guns blazing?" Clint asked.

"I plan to sneak up on them while they're passed out from last night and get as far away as I can before the moon comes up," I said. Clint snorted.

"Billy may be a hayseed, but he's not a dumb one," he said. "And you iced his best enforcer, so he's gonna have a good old hillbilly rage on if he sees you again."

"You talk like you know the guy," I grumbled.

"I dealt with the shifters when Billy's old man was in charge," Clint said. "This whole park is their territory, and even a demon would be insane to invade its borders. Billy's brain is rotted on meth, and the speed doesn't help any of his many and varied psychoses, so now I stay on the mountain and we keep out of each other's way."

"And this feud started when you were what, twelve?" I asked. Clint grinned.

"No fair me doing all the talking. Tell me something about you and I'll be happy to fill in my life story."

I glared at him. I was starting to hate his smile, so brilliant and smarmy. He was on the wrong side of a demon—what the fuck did he have to smile about? "I don't care about your life, Clint. I care if you're an asset or a liability when we get to the shifter clubhouse."

"You think diplomacy will solve this?" Clint snorted. "These are brutal creatures, sweetheart. They're not going to talk."

I folded my arms as we turned onto the highway. "Did I say anything about talking to them?" I'd come the same way only a day ago, but it felt like a century. As old as I was, weeks and months tended to blend into each other, and five years could pass before I knew it. I wasn't used to feeling every hour. It was almost like I was human again.

Clint pulled to the shoulder in view of the clubhouse. The Volvo was still there, poking out from behind the building. I could see they'd stripped it of the kid's luggage and probably the catalytic converters and anything else worth a few bucks.

"Dead calm," he said. "If your friend is still on the property, he's probably stuffed inside an oil drum by now."

"Leo's tougher than that," I grumbled, getting out of the trunk.

"You sure?" Clint called as I crossed the lot, staying in the shadow of the trees. Not that I needed to worry—the place was so still it might as well have been a boneyard. The bikes looked dusty and rattle-bang in the harsh sunlight, surrounded by a drift of beer bottles and Styrofoam containers that a rancid whiff told me had recently held barbecue.

"Yeah," I said quietly, skirting the porch and slipping along the side of the clubhouse. "I'm sure."

I didn't know why I was defending Leo. I didn't know him. He wasn't a good guy, or even a reasonably decent one. If our situation was reversed, he'd take off without a second thought and leave me at the mercy of the shifters.

Still, it wasn't like I was a virginal prom queen myself, and Leo had backed me up when we'd run into Gary. He could have bolted in Elko too, and he hadn't. I didn't know what he thought he'd get out of this—power, a pet hellhound, a night of getting sweaty—but if he hadn't hung me out when he could have, I didn't feel right about screwing him now.

Besides, he was a lot better company than Clint. If I had to spend any more time alone with him, one of us was going through the windshield of his shitty truck.

The windows at the back of the clubhouse were blacked out, or outright covered in sheet metal. A fat cluster of vents poked out of the roof, over what I guessed was the meth lab. Clint, who had followed me, frowned.

"I do not advise this plan."

"Good thing I'm not looking for your approval, then," I said, grabbing the windowsill and hoisting myself up. From there it was easy to grab the low lip of the roof. My stitches complained loudly as I pulled myself up, hooking a leg over the gutter and clambering to the vent, trying not to rattle the rusted tin under my feet.

The vent stack was quiet, no smoke wafting, so I ignored the overpowering smell of cat piss and pulled the cap off, lowering myself down. I dropped, hitting the frame of an extractor fan, trying to pull in on myself as much as possible. The vent was just large enough for me to wriggle out of. I kicked the fan blades until they clattered to the stained floor below and dropped, covering my face as fumes bit at my eyes and the back of my throat.

The lab had clearly been a walk-in cooler in one of the clubhouse's previous lives, and the big door creaked open like a spooky horror-movie tomb when I shoved it.

Nobody was in the warren of halls behind the clubhouse, and I could hear snoring and moaning from behind the wall separating us. Nothing like a little morning sex to cure your hangover. I wrinkled my nose and turned toward Billy's office.

The door was hanging open, and three half-naked women were curled up on the gaudy daybed. I was about to leave when I heard somebody sniffling in the corner and pulled aside a velvet curtain to see Lolly hunched on the floor.

"This is your fault," she hissed when she saw who it was. Her eye was black and her lip was split down the center, making her look like one of those pouty pinup girls you usually found sitting on the hoods of cars or posing with giant cardboard cutouts of fruit.

"Sorry," I said.

"All I have to do is scream," she muttered. "And Billy will come in here and rip you a new ass."

"You could do that," I agreed. None of the other shifters so much as stirred. Lolly looked like she'd never passed out in the first place. Her eyes were dark, and the cuts on her face couldn't disguise it was paler than a corpse. I crouched down and leaned in. "Or you could tell me where Billy's got the guy he dragged in here last night. Tall, dark hair, Russian?"

Lolly sneered, then winced in pain as her lip started bleeding anew. "Go fuck yourself. Billy beat me all to hell for bringing you in here, then he threw me to Mike and Esteban when they got back from chasin' you. I have a bruise for a face, I feel like I rode a mechanical bull backward, and I just wanna forget I ever saw you."

I leaned closer, so close I could see older bruises blooming on her shoulders and arms under her shirt, a black eye she'd tried to cover with faded, runny concealer and cakey eyeliner. "Tell me where they are, Lolly. Then take it from me—walk out the front door, do what you have to do to get a ride out of here, and don't come back."

She snorted, fishing in her pockets for a small bag of powder, and tried to tap it out with a shaking hand. "You really are a dumb bitch, you know? No wonder you're alone with nobody to look after you."

"It's hard at first, and no matter how bad things are, how hard they beat you or what they forced you to do, you think it can't be as bad as this. But then you learn to take care of yourself. And you might even realize life isn't a never-ending river of shit."

Okay, that last part was a lie, but I needed Lolly to stop crying and tell me where Leo was, already. She tapped out a bump and snorted it, quivering for a moment before she opened her eyes.

"That's exactly the kinda stupid crap I'd expect some ugly single bitch to be spouting."

"Yeah, because you, Mike, and Esteban have such a beautiful love," I said, snatching the crank from her and shoving the bag into my jeans pocket. She snarled. I snarled. We glared at each other.

"If you don't help me I'll still tell Billy that you did," I said. "And then every time he loses his temper he'll take it out on you. You'll spend the rest of your life wondering if this is the time where he beats you so badly he kills you."

She hesitated, sucking on her cut lip. "Lolly," I said. "I'm not talking in hypotheticals here. I've been exactly where you are." Sure, it was long before the advent of club drugs, fishnet stockings, and pushup bras, but I'd sat with my arms around my knees all the same, trying to cry silently and convince myself it didn't hurt all that bad.

"Billy uses the barn out back when he does business." She sighed. "He takes girls out there too—you know, human girls he meets on the road. It's private." She put her forehead on her knees. "I think he took the guy out there."

I stood up. "You should go," I said. "I mean it. This is probably the last chance you'll get."

"I don't need your help," Lolly grumbled. "My life is fucking fine, okay?"

I slipped out the door. "Whatever." I found a narrow hall that lead to an old freight platform at the back of the barn. A battered panel truck on blocks sat to one side, a welter of other stripped hulks spreading out from it into the woods like rusted, oil-streaked herpes.

The barn was probably a shearing shed for sheep farmers back when this was still the Wild West. The doors were shut up tight, but one of the shifters from last night stepped out of a smaller door at the side, wandering into the rusted cars and loosening his silver belt buckle.

I waited until he'd unzipped his fly, then picked up a concrete chunk fallen from the blocks holding up the panel truck and advanced through the weeds and broken glass. He whipped his head around at the last second and I hit him hard with the concrete. He let out a soft sigh and collapsed next to the burned-out body of a Chevelle, wafting the sour stink of coyote piss in my direction.

I dropped the block and eased open the side door of the barn, peering into dimness punctuated by sharp bars of light coming through jagged holes in the high ceiling. Something fluttered and squeaked high in the rafters above as I shut the door. "Leo?" I whispered.

I heard a cough from the shadows beyond the bars of light, and took another step into the dimness. "Leo," I said again.

"Ava?" he whispered. I felt something cold and tight uncurl inside my guts and slither back to where it had come from.

"Yeah," I said, picking my way around a broken tractor and a pile of dirty mattresses chewed through by rats. The remains of a conveyor belt were piled against one wall, and rusted hooks and saws hung from nails driven into the splintery wood, all that remained of the slaughter operation this had once been. Above me, a metal track creaked in its bolts, chains for hanging up carcasses dangling from rollers like the roots of some rusty tree high above us. The air smelled subterranean too, musty and dank with mold and old blood.

I let out a small breath when I saw Leo's face floating in the shadow. His wrists were tied with frayed, splintery rope, the loops caught over a rusty hook at the end of a chain. His shirt was torn open, revealing his tattoos down to his navel, and his head drooped as he tried to look at me.

"You came to rescue me," he said thickly. "I'm touched." His face was swollen on one side, his eye almost shut and crusted with blood. Droplets had dried on the floor around his feet, turning the dusty floor to mud under my boots.

"Don't thank me just yet," I said. I grabbed a rusty knife out of a wooden box of similar blades, things used for skinning and gutting and slicing. I kicked over the box to stand on and started sawing through the rope.

Leo sucked in a sharp breath, and I felt a rush of air on my face as the door flew open and a body smashed into mine, knocking the knife out of my grip.

"Hey, puppy dog," Billy said as he straddled me, grabbing me by the hair and pushing my face into the dirt. "I knew you'd come home when you were hungry."

Tears sprouted from my eyes as he yanked on my scalp, grunting. I tried to roll over and free my arm. One good hit to the throat and Billy wouldn't be so fucking smug. I struggled, my toes digging furrows in the dirt, but he was too heavy and he laid his torso on top of mine, his lips leaving spittle on my ear as he spoke.

"Keep doing that, puppy, and I just might keep you alive for a few days longer." He ground his pelvis hard into my ass, slamming me into the dirt again. His heavy pants cast sour breath against my cheek like a blast furnace, and I felt his fingers dig into the flesh of my hips as he yanked at my jeans.

I let myself go limp for a few seconds, so he'd think he was getting what he wanted. His panting went ragged, his thrusts more insistent, and when he tore the seam of my underwear I snapped my head back and cracked him in the nose. I felt the cartilage give with a pop like stepping on an aluminum can.

Billy screamed and reared back, clutching his face. "You fucking *bitch*!" he bellowed. Blood seeped from between his fingers, a lot of it, and I scrambled away from him as he swiped at me with one crimson-soaked hand.

"I'm gonna kill you," he ground out, his voice muffled from his smashed nose. "I was gonna be nice, but now I'm going to skin you inch by inch."

"Like you were nice to Lolly?" I panted. "I'll pass."

Billy went down on his hands and knees. His nose looked like something that had gotten run over by a semi on the highway, all blood and mangled flesh. I caught the white gleam of bone through the mess. The sight cheered me up a lot. "You're gonna pay for what you did to Tanya, and my fucking face," he snarled, his back arching so I could see all the individual knots of his vertebrae.

"That was her name?" I said. "I'd just been calling her Coyote Ugly, up until I snapped her neck."

Billy let out a roar, his flesh tearing and his muscles forming into the square-headed mountain lion that had chased me through the ravine. His fingers sprouted claws and his skull compressed and elongated.

I cast for anything to fight him off. If he shifted, I was fucked. I couldn't take him on as a hound—I'd be half his size. And as a human, I was basically a take-out gyro. My only hope was that shifting during the day would take enough out of him that I could get a shot in. Shifters weren't tied to moon phases, but the closer it was the easier their shift came, and to do it in broad daylight you had to be really strong or really pissed.

Billy tensed as his golden pelt sprouted from his skin. A shudder rippled through him as he locked eyes with me, lips peeling back from half-inch teeth. He gathered his legs and sprang, and I braced myself for the rib-cracking impact.

It didn't come. Billy's leap was arrested at the arc as Leo loomed behind him out of the shadows and jammed a rusty knife between his shoulder blades. Billy screamed as he thrashed in the dirt and snapped at Leo, who jumped out of the way of his jaws.

I grabbed up the knife he'd knocked out of my hand and drove it under Billy's rib cage hard, up and into his heart. He twitched once and died, head lolling in the dirt.

Leo spat blood. "Asshole." He held out his hand and pulled me to my feet. "You okay?"

I nodded. "Fucker ripped the only pair of jeans I own."

Leo gave me a smile that displayed his bloody teeth. "You're a lot tougher than you look, even on two legs."

"You too," I said, stepping over Billy's body. Inwardly, I was just glad I'd loosened Leo's ropes enough for him to jump in when he did. I might have seemed a lot less tough being ripped to shreds on the barn's dirt floor.

"Not the first crankhead who's tried to torture me," Leo said. "That guy hit like a drunken prom date."

Leo was limping as we pushed open the door and picked our way across the junkyard. My stomach knotted when I saw the shifter I'd clocked with the concrete was gone. "Leo . . ." I said, but the rest was drowned out when a shotgun blast ripped across the junkyard, taking out the windshield of a Pontiac over my left shoulder.

I ran, ducking between the rusted-out cars, Leo close behind me. Another spray of buckshot rattled against metal, and I felt flecks of rust bite into my cheek.

Leo panted a bit, pressing one hand into his ribs over the worst of his bruises. "Good thing he can't aim for shit." He craned his neck around the trunk of the Ford we were hiding behind. "Think we can make it to the trees before he reloads?"

"We're gonna have to," I said, standing up and running for it. We hit the tree line as a third shot rolled back from the mountains around us like distant thunder, warning that a storm was coming even though the morning was blindingly bright and clear.

"Please tell me you have a ride out of here," Leo said. We picked our way through the pines back to the parking lot, me keeping my ears turned toward the clubhouse. Not even a nodding crankhead could sleep through the O.K. Corral back in the junkyard.

I stopped short when I saw Clint's truck was gone. "Son of a . . ." I started, then settled for punching a tree. The bark scraped up my knuckles, but the pain didn't do much except piss me off even more.

Leo groaned. "I was really hoping this wouldn't turn into a nature hike."

The rattle of a bike engine drifted across the lot, and I watched a couple of half-dressed shifters jump on the starters, the girls gathering at the edge of the porch in a snarling knot. "Yeah, well," I said, "better to be alive and lost in the woods than back there."

"Amen to that," Leo grunted, then stumbled and collapsed against a tree, his face going pale. I started to help him, but he waved me off. "Just give me a second."

"No, you need a hospital," I said. I'd seen enough people die in the days before X-rays and modern hospitals to know what the deathly pale and the sudden pain meant. Not to mention if you did manage to get to a hospital, you could die from the ether surgeons used just as easily as from your injuries.

"That's not happening, so let's run instead of crying about it," Leo said between gritted teeth. When I still hesitated, he leaned forward and gave me a push. "Move your ass, Ava. I'll be behind you as fast as I can."

He swayed and I caught him. "We both know that's a lie," I said.

The shifters circled their bikes, spraying gravel, and aimed them toward the road.

I should leave Leo. That was the choice to make if I wanted to live past the next ten minutes. Leave him, feel bad later, and let him turn into just another bad memory that intruded when I couldn't sleep, which was most nights.

I couldn't seem to make myself move, though. I didn't usually have trouble making shitty decisions that would give me nightmares for decades. It was just part of the equally shitty hand I'd been dealt when Gary decided to pick me up off the muddy bayou ground. I couldn't now make myself let go of Leo. I couldn't shut off the small part of me that had existed before the hound.

"Why are you doing this!" Leo growled, trying to get free of me. "Don't be a fucking idiot."

"I guess I like you a little," I snapped, refusing to let go. We stared at each other, him panting in pain and covered in his own blood, me silenced by my own words, feeling his heartbeat reverberate through my hand.

It had been so long since I'd been honest with anyone, about anything, that I couldn't think of anything else to say. Ever since Gary had gone tits-up things had been leaking out around the edges of my mind—the nightmares, not leaving Leo, and now this. I hoped it stopped soon, if I lived. It was embarrassing as fuck.

"That'll be a real comfort when I'm torn limb from limb," Leo muttered, almost drowned out by the roar of bike engines.

As the shifters' bikes bore down on our hiding spot, Clint's truck roared up, slamming to a halt a few feet short of the trees. I slung Leo's arm over my shoulder and dragged him toward the passenger side. He tumbled onto the seat and I lost my balance and fell on top of him. Clint took off before I could even pull the door shut behind me, fishtailing onto the highway.

I yanked the door shut and propped Leo up. My pulse was pounding, but as I watched the clubhouse and the shifters' bikes retreat in the rearview mirror my breath finally smoothed out.

I reached across Leo and hit Clint hard on the shoulder. "Where the fuck were you!"

"Relax," he said, checking the rearview mirror. The shifters were still behind us, five or six of them, trailing the rattle-bang truck like a school of hungry piranhas.

"I'll relax when this shithole is five hundred miles behind us," I said. Leo let out a soft moan, shifting to look at Clint.

"Who the hell are you?"

"He's Clint Hicks," I said, still watching the shifters. They were gaining on us, the truck no match for the powerful Harley engines. "We need to lose them," I said to Clint.

"Won't be easy after you walked in there and humiliated their pack leader," Clint said.

"She did a little more than that," Leo muttered. Clint cut me a black look.

"Don't give me that," I said. "It was him or me."

Clint hit the steering wheel. "Do you have any idea what you've done? Before, they would have just ridden us to the edge of their territory and let it go unless you came back. Now they'll never stop." He looked at Leo and huffed. "Stupid."

"I don't see you stepping up, handsome," Leo said. His voice was a rusty creak and each word clearly caused him pain. "Maybe you should shut up and drive the truck. Seems to be what you're good at."

"If we can get to a city we can lose them," I said. Shifters hated cities. There were too many smells, too many humans and cars and other predators running around. Plus, cities tended to be home to vamp hives, and those were two groups who were definitely front-runners in the Asshole Olympics. One bite from a carrier vamp and a shifter was in for a slow, painful death that usually ended with your brain leaking out your ears.

"Easier said than done," Clint grumbled. Quieter, "I told you to leave him."

"You get us out of here or I'm going to call Lilith's particular brand of bitch down on your ass faster than you can spit out an apology," I said. "We clear?"

Clint's knuckles went white on the cracked vinyl covering the steering wheel, but finally he ground out an irritated breath. "If we get to 90 we can probably make it to Rapid City. The interstate is usually crawling with troopers."

I kept one eye on the shifters behind us. If not all of them knew Billy was dead, we might have a little time. There was undoubtedly somebody back there who was slamming back a celebratory shot, ready to step into Billy's skeezy leather pants as pack leader. I couldn't imagine the guy had made a ton of close friends in life.

Leo groaned, and I took off the overshirt Clint had given me and rolled it up to put under his head. "Try to rest," I said softly. He tried to smile through his swollen jaw, then grimaced.

"No argument. See you on the flip side."

Clint kicked the truck up to eighty miles an hour as the on-ramp to the interstate came into view, staring straight ahead at the road. "Going back for him better not screw me, Ava," he said as the black dots of the shifters appeared in a line across the white shimmer of the interstate. Arrayed like birds of prey, they kept just enough distance that they could close it and overtake us whenever they felt like it.

"It won't," I lied, and didn't look in the rearview mirror again.

CHAPTER

15

〿〿〿

Highways are anonymous. The horizon might rise and fall, the landscape might go from trees to scrub to desert, but the highway is always the same. For a long time, I'd found comfort in that. Rest stop after rest stop, mile marker after mile marker, never changing. Just like me.

Clint kept the truck fast through Spearfish and Sturgis, and the ink-blot trickle of towns leading up to Rapid City, barely dots on a map. By the time we started seeing signs for the city limits, though, the needle was on *E* and the engine began coughing.

Clint rolled to a stop on a side street lined with dilapidated ranches. "We're not far," he said. I got out and helped Leo, scanning the street for the shadow of the shifter pack, but for the moment they were behind us.

"Where are we going?" I said as Clint strode ahead. He'd zipped his rifle into a padded carrying case, and nobody on the broken-down block paid any attention.

"Somewhere safe," he snapped, and turned away from Leo and me. Leo grimaced.

The ranches turned to older frame homes, in even worse repair. Rusty bars guarded most of the windows, and half the yards were overgrown, listless, bleached FOR SALE signs leaning under weeds and drifts of trash. I heard the thump and blast of music from up the block, and a few old women stared at us from their porches as we passed.

At the end of the block sat a timber-frame church, twice as large as anything else in the neighborhood. A plywood sign was tacked to the siding. Part of it had broken off, reading SOUP KITC. Judging from the welter of flyers and leaflets on the door and the dusty grime-streaked windows looking out on a yard made of weeds and litter, the Soup Kitc hadn't been operating in a few decades.

A marquee next to the door was mostly covered with graffiti. The plastic letters were faded almost white, but I could just make them out as Clint tried the door.

AND I SAW AN ANGEL COME DOWN FROM HEAVEN

HAVING THE KEY TO THE BOTTOMLESS PIT

AND A GREAT CHAIN IN HIS HAND

It was no big surprise that Clint's friend didn't hold with the warm and fuzzy God. I wasn't sure that translated into a willingness to hide us from a pack of angry shifters, but who knew?

Clint cursed when a chain rattled from the other side of the door. "He should be here."

"I wouldn't be if I didn't have to," I muttered, but Clint ignored me other than an irritated shake of his head.

We slipped around the side of the building, through an alley choked with bursting trash bags and up a loading dock. Clint kicked at the rusted padlock on the sliding door, and managed to lift it a few feet.

"I hate you," Leo groaned as he crouched and crawled under the door, collapsing on the other side.

Clint found a light switch, and a swinging bulb lit the small van bay. "This way," he said. I helped Leo through the door into an industrial kitchen, which smelled like all church kitchens—bleach, stale coffee, and the faint whiff of rotting trash. During my low periods, church charities were a pretty reliable source of food and a place to sleep where I wouldn't end up with a hobo crawling into my cot or a bag lady helping herself to my only pair of shoes.

I'd always thought it was funny that I was something that lived in their nightmares, sitting on a dented metal chair, eating fourth-rate spaghetti off a paper plate while a grandmother with a chain on her cardigan asked me if I'd accepted Jesus. Long before that, my mother sometimes dragged me and my grandmother to the tent revivals that traveled up and down the hollers in Tennessee, men with hard eyes and sweat-stained white suits shouting into the night that we were all going to Hell.

I'd thought they were all full of shit when I'd been alive, but I guess that showed what I knew.

This place was a far cry from either of those. Everything was musty and closed up, and there was a strong rank odor drifting over the whole place, from the kitchen up the stairs into the vestibule and the church itself. Everything was rough and functional, from the boxy pulpit to the log pews that looked like they'd gladly plant a splinter in the ass of anyone foolish enough to sit down. A chalkboard hung to the left of the cross with hymns from two weeks ago written in crooked block letters.

I eased Leo onto the padded bench behind the pulpit and propped one of those weird little knee pillows behind his head. "Don't die," I whispered before I followed Clint.

"This friend of yours isn't great at hospitality," I told him. Clint pushed open the door behind the pulpit, flicking on another bare bulb that hummed and jittered.

"Father Colin runs this parish on a shoestring. He's always here, though. Colin!"

The floor under my boots was covered in a moist carpet, the boards underneath giving softly at each step. Everything was fake wood grain and harsh lighting, an update that had probably seemed like a good idea in 1972, but now just made me feel like I was on the set of a low-rent snuff movie.

The rankness tickled my nose with each step, strong now as a trash pile in the dead of summer. At the end of the hall, through a low arch, a metal desk crouched, watched over by a knockoff print of *The Last Supper* and a ragged cassock hanging from a hook.

Below the desk, a pair of feet in worn sneakers poked out, tilted sadly to the side like run-down windup toys.

"Colin!" Clint shouted, shoving past me and skidding to his knees next to the body. Father Colin was dressed in a gray sweat suit, one hand over his stomach like he'd fallen asleep. His face had a green, greasy cast and his eyes had glossed over with the pale cataracts death imparts. A fly poised on his parted lips, rubbing its legs together before tipping over the priest's teeth and into his mouth.

Clint pinched his forehead hard with his thumb and forefinger. "This can't be happening," he muttered. He slumped on his knees. "Colin didn't deserve this," he said, picking up one of the priest's hands. The fingers were squishy and bloated. I didn't make a habit of hanging around decomposing murder victims, but my guess was Colin had been there for at least three days.

"I'm sorry," I said quietly. Aside from his very dead, indescribably smelly condition, Colin looked like he'd simply lain down. There were no marks on him, nothing disturbed on his desk. A mug reading JESUS LOVES YOU—EVERYONE ELSE THINKS YOU'RE AN ASSHOLE sat half full of coffee next to a stack of check stubs and a paper ledger.

It went flying, along with everything else, when Clint stood up and knocked the desk over with a roar. I got out of the way as he turned on the file cabinet, smashing a Rolodex and knocking a picture of Father Colin standing in front of a small stone church to the ground. Glass tinkled, and he finally stopped, bent over, his shoulders shaking.

I knew myself well enough to know I wasn't a comforting presence—even if I'd run into a lot of grief-stricken types, I never knew what to say. There was nothing to soften the blow of death, especially when you knew what was waiting on the other side.

I eased forward and put a hand on Clint's back, feeling his lungs heave beneath my palm. He shoved me away and I stumbled, tripping over Father Colin's legs and falling to the ground.

"You just had to come looking for me, didn't you?" Clint ground out. "Just had to follow orders, like the pit bull you are. Clamp your jaws around something and hold on until it's dead."

"Pit bulls are loyal," I said, getting up and brushing black grit from my jeans. "They don't attack unless they're provoked. Or unless somebody turns them vicious on purpose." I glared at him. "If you think I had something to do with this, then you can fuck right off."

"*Lilith* did this," Clint ground out. "But you're with her. You're just waiting for me to let my guard down."

"I can't take your soul," I snapped. "You don't have one. So I've failed Lilith, and I am just as far up shit creek as you. If you'd pull your head out for a hot second you'd realize that." I spread my hands and saw that my palms were covered in sooty streaks. "I'm sorry about your friend. Are you sure it was Lilith?"

"You're wearing the proof," Clint said sullenly. He reached down and pulled up Father Colin's sweatshirt. There was a perfect circle burned into his pectoral, roughly the size of a fingertip. "She touched him," Clint said softly. "Burned the heart right out of him."

Suddenly, I would have given anything to scrub my hands until they were raw. "Why would she do this? I mean, I only met her once, but petty revenge murder didn't seem like her thing."

"To punish me," Clint said. "I avoided her for years by hiding with the shifters, but when I blew into this town in the fifties, Colin was the first human to help me. He was young, just over from Ireland. He joined the seminary after some trouble back there."

Clint sat in Colin's desk chair. The springs creaked under his weight. He looked utterly defeated, much paler than when I'd first seen him. "It was the middle of winter and I was sleeping rough. The cold will get to you, eventually, no matter what you are. Colin let me in to sleep in the vestry, even though the monsignor threw a fit when he found out. He gave me a job as a groundskeeper. We were friends. We talked about everything. When I told him what

I was, he put his hand on my arm and said he'd always known, that he would not forsake me, that I was always welcome under his roof." Clint swallowed. "He saved my life. I stayed on consecrated ground and for a while that was enough. Then Lilith got some thugs from the neighborhood to set the vestry on fire one night. Nobody was hurt, but I couldn't stay. I couldn't put innocent people in harm's way. I hadn't seen him in close to twenty years but I was hoping . . ."

I stayed quiet. Privately, I thought Father Colin was an idiot for believing that anything in this world could stop a Hellspawn. There was no sign, no church, no faith that could turn them back. They were implacable, unstoppable as a hurricane or an earthquake. All you could do was pray the storm passed you over and survey the damage afterward.

"I'll find some plastic to cover him up," I said finally. Clint didn't say anything, just sat staring at the far wall.

I searched the kitchen until I found a tarp amid some rusty paint cans in a supply cupboard. Clint and I rolled Colin into it and I duct-taped the ends. Another trip found me a handful of air fresheners. Replacing the stench of decay with the stench of Hawaiian Tropical Delight only improved things marginally, but it was a start.

"I should check on Leo," I said after we'd covered Colin's wrapped body with a sheet. Clint rubbed his hands over his face.

"He kept a first aid kit around here somewhere," Clint said, rummaging in the file cabinet.

I accepted the army surplus box and went back to the chapel. Clint needed to be alone and I wasn't going to help anything by hovering.

Leo was still on the bench, and my throat got tight until I touched his neck and found his pulse. It was slow but strong, and he muttered when I leaned over him. "This bench is hard as fuck."

"I think we're stuck for the time being," I said. "Lilith was here."

Leo scrubbed a hand over his eyes and sat up, the tic in his jaw twitching with pain. "What did we do to earn the big bad bitch's attention?"

"She killed Clint's friend," I said. "The priest here. She was sending a warning." I fished surgical scissors from the kit and clipped away the remains of Leo's bloody shirt. His torso was painted with bruises the size of blooming poppies, and his skin was so pallid it almost gleamed in the dim light filtering in through the cardboard-covered windows in the chapel. I got busy wrapping his ribs, and cleaning off the cuts on his face with peroxide. He inhaled sharply but never flinched or made a sound.

I didn't say anything either, just tried to be as gentle as possible.

Once I'd tossed the bloody gauze, I could see the extent of the swelling across Leo's jaw. One jagged cut bisected his eyebrow. I remembered the silver rings on Billy's knuckles and bit my lip in sympathy as I brushed Leo's hair out of the way so I could close up the gash.

"I'd do it all over again," Leo said as I put Steri-Strips on the cut, trying to be neat so his eyebrow would knit back together.

"Kill Billy?" I said. Leo nodded.

"Piece of shit."

He put his hand over mine, squeezing my fingers together, and I squeezed back. There was nothing keeping me from this now, not Gary and not my need to keep moving, keep drifting west and east and back again. I could let myself be still for five seconds, actually be grateful I had someone to watch my back, even if he was a professional killer and we were holed up in a church that smelled like decomp.

The bottom of the first aid kit had a Ziploc bag of pharmacy bottles, all in different names. I uncapped the Vicodin and shook out two tablets. I was glad Father Colin wasn't as squeaky clean as Clint had made him out to be.

Leo dry-swallowed the tablets and leaned back, eyes closing again. "I've had worse, Ava. You don't need to worry about me."

"I've seen worse, but most of those people died horribly," I muttered.

Leo ticked off his fingers. "I've been shot. I was stabbed twice, once by an Aryan in the shower at Riker's who melted down his comb and made a shiv."

"Damn," I said. "That's dedication."

Leo squirmed. He still didn't look good, but the pills were doing their work. He'd at least be able to breathe without excruciating pain. "His brother owed money to my father. I cut off his head and hands and left them in the guy's driveway." His voice was getting blurry, and I hoped soon he'd be out. Then I'd deal with the body, and Clint. "If you know where to cut, a reciprocating saw gets the job done. Got to do it someplace you can hose the blood off. We used the back of this deli in the neighborhood. Anyway, this guy jumped the, and I quote, 'murdering kike bastard' who took out his dead-beat brother. I have a scar on my back the size of the FDR . . ." He let out a long sigh, muttering something I couldn't make out.

I put my hand over his. "Get some sleep, Leo."

He grabbed me and I gasped. His grip was still like iron, even looking like he was about a half step from keeling over. "Is Lilith coming to kill us? I left the knife stuck in that asshole in Wyoming. And my cigarettes. I'd hate to get wasted without a smoke."

"No." I shook my head. "I think she made her point with the padre. We're probably safe for a while."

Leo didn't answer, and when I leaned over him his breathing had smoothed out, less ragged and rattling than it had been when we'd run from the shifters. I covered him with a blanket from a shelf of them tucked behind the pulpit, smoothing out the wrinkles so Leo would stay warm, even in the drafty South Dakota wind coming through every crack in the wall. He moaned but didn't open his eyes.

Padding back down the dank hall to Colin's office, I saw Clint bent over the priest's body. One hand on his forehead, he murmured gently in a whispery, acidic language that I didn't speak. He started when he saw me and looked around guiltily.

"I was just offering him last rites. He would have liked that."

I shrugged. "Some people want to be cremated and shot into orbit."

Clint sighed and stood up. "He has a little apartment through there. I don't know about you, but I need a few hours of sleep."

"Leo needs a hospital," I said. "He's bleeding internally, and I don't think he'll last if I don't get him help." I took a breath. "I'm going to stay with him, so we should probably stop here."

Clint shook his head, eyes narrowing. "No. You need to stay with *me*. Lilith . . ."

"Lilith was going to kill me no matter if I found you or not," I said. "She's just trying to clear off Gary's ledger. I'm not worried about Lilith." I had the strange thought that if I could just make sure Leo got through this, I didn't really care what happened to me. I'd been running on borrowed time since Gary kicked off, and deep down I'd known it when I wrapped my jaws around his throat. And that was okay, but I didn't need to drag anyone else down with me.

"She is *not* just tying up a dead reaper's accounts," Clint said, his voice so sharp it made my shoulders hunch involuntarily, waiting for a blow to follow the word. "Lilith is not stupid, Ava. She sent you to me knowing I don't have a soul."

"Yeah, and?" I shrugged. "Demons do a lot of unfathomable shit, Clint. Or whatever your name really is. Lilith will either find you or she won't. I'm going to take Leo to the ER, so I wish you luck on your quest." I stepped away from him when he reached for me, and I jerked my arm out of his range. "It's been real. Please don't be offended when I say I sincerely hope to never see you again."

I turned to go back to the chapel, but the bulb burned out in the hallway with a pop and a snowfall of pulverized glass. In the dark, Clint's voice felt like it was against my skin with actual weight, warm and hot as desert wind.

"You're right." He sighed. "My name isn't Clint Hicks. Or any of the other names I stole."

I waited, feeling my heartbeat pick up. I hadn't given Clint's species much thought once I'd decided he wasn't a threat to me. It wasn't any of my business. There were a lot of strange things creeping through the shadows at the edge of humanity, and I was one of them. Nothing Clint could say would particularly shock me.

"What is it, then?" I said into the silence.

Clint's voice was so soft he sounded like he was miles away. "It's Azrael."

I froze. I hadn't thought about my grandmother reading the

Bible to us in her measured voice for years, if not decades, but that name, I remembered. That name wasn't from the Bible, but from stories she'd tell me, about things older and darker than the good book, when she'd been drinking her own product and was in a bleak mood. "You expect me to believe you're a fucking angel?"

"Fallen angel," he said. I heard sounds of rummaging, and a weak flashlight beam flicked on, dazzling me. I threw up a hand, and Clint fumbled. "Sorry."

"Why should I believe you?" I said, although the denial was more me not wanting to deal with any more weird shit today than actually thinking Clint was lying.

"You know demons and Hell and reapers are facts, but you stumble on angel?" Clint muttered. "Typical."

"First off, your shitty tone isn't making me any more inclined to listen," I said, folding my arms. "Second, if you're more than a scary story in the Bible, then how come I've never run into an angel before?"

"Because we're not all that fucking common," Clint said. "The Fallen are dispossessed scavengers, and we survive by staying off everyone's radar, including Hell's. I hid from Lilith for centuries by finding warlocks who'd made deals with reapers and taking their place."

"You killed them, you mean," I said. Clint shrugged.

"Like you're shedding a tear for some anonymous warlock. No one expected me to be hiding so close to what was hunting me. It worked out. Until Clint Hicks."

"Because Clint was Gary's," I said. "And Gary was Lilith's."

"She's evil, Ava," he said softly. "All of the demons in Hell are inhuman monstrosities, but Lilith craves only the end of everything. She wants to taste the ash of the burning world on her tongue."

"Yeah, I got the vibe she was not humanity's biggest fan," I said. I turned my back on Clint, trying to weigh what would happen if I believed him for the time being. He wasn't any more a fan of Lilith than I was, but I'd never run up against the Fallen before, and I didn't like unknown quantities. I'd kept myself out of the Pit by being solitary and suspicious, not joining up with every loser who crossed my path.

"The Fallen are mainly a story," I said finally. "Even among Hellspawn. Just so you know what kind of a limb you're asking me to climb out on and how pissed I'll be if this is all a con."

"We were the first beings in Hell," Clint said. "When Lucifer rebelled, the Host sent him to the bottomless pit and every angel since who's stepped out of line has fallen after him." He flicked his beam up to illuminate Colin's cheap plastic cross. "The Host are the Gestapo of the Kingdom. The big swinging dicks. You don't want to see their bad side."

"Too bad you didn't figure that out before they tossed your ass out like a used diaper," I said. "And this doesn't change things. I'm still taking Leo to the hospital. If you won't let me use your truck, at least show me the phone so I can call a cab."

"I told you, Lilith will pulverize you if you leave my side," Clint snapped. "Don't you care about what she'll do to you?"

"I died a long time ago," I said. "As far as I'm concerned, the last hundred years have been a bonus round."

"So you'd die for a human you barely know, a human who would turn on you in a second?"

I narrowed my eyes at the puffed-up sanctimony in his tone. "Leo isn't the head case spouting nonsense about living on Cloud City and being on the run from demons."

"Leonid Mikhailovich Karpov is not a good man," Clint said. "I can see the truth of humans, Ava, and his soul is as black as the deepest part of Hell."

I folded my arms. "In the short time we've been together, maybe you didn't get that I don't really care much about the condition of a person's soul. They're either a job for me or they're not. Leo's not."

Clint went with the light through a makeshift door to the priest's apartment, and I was forced to follow him or be left in the dark with a corpse. He tried the light switch, and when more sparks showered us he sighed. "I told Colin to ask for donations to fix this place up. He always said the church didn't need any more money, it needed more faith."

"I'll be sure to drop an e-mail to the Vatican about his sainthood," I said. "Why does Lilith have such a hard-on for you?"

Clint found a cluster of half-burned saints' candles in a kitchen cabinet and lit them, making the miserable, mold-streaked kitchenette look much better than it had any right to. "The first demons were offspring of the Fallen, twisted images of ourselves. Eventually, there were more of them than us, and in the way of unruly mobs everywhere they kicked us out. Even after we gave them the divine gift of life."

"Demons are assholes like that," I said.

"The Fallen scattered to the four corners of the earth," Clint said. In the candlelight, I could easily imagine the angel's face as a vision of beauty and terror, inhuman as a shark gliding through cold, still waters.

"But you scattered to Wyoming," I said. "No offense, but if I had the chance to go anywhere, I would not pick Wyoming. Or anywhere Wyoming-adjacent."

"I've lived all over," Clint said. "Paris, Calcutta, San Francisco. I could tell you about it someday."

"You assume I'm some hillbilly who's never been anywhere but on a tour of America's more scenic truck stops?" I said. Clint shrugged, spreading his hands. Clearly, angels didn't give a shit about offending people.

"I'm starting to think Lilith was right about you," I grumbled.

Clint gave a grim smile that was more like a sneer. "She hates me. Always has, me and all the Fallen. Her mission in life is to collect us as trophies."

"If she collects the box set, does she get a prize?" I said. Clint checked out the narrow window, then pulled the greasy yellow and green curtains tight.

"She gets to work out her pent-up aggression on me for the next few thousand years." He paced the kitchen, but since it wasn't much bigger than a decent-size closet, he was limited to two steps in each direction, like a predator in a zoo. "Fallen used to be strong. Not compared to our brothers, but strong enough to take on someone like Lilith. But the longer we're out of the Kingdom, the weaker we get. And the longer Lilith has to think about how much she despises me . . ."

"I get it," I said. "You're not gonna stick your neck out for me. Are we gonna have a problem now, or are you going to let me and Leo go our own way?"

"You understand what it's like to be ground under someone's heel with no hope," Clint said. "I'm pissed as hell at you for leading Lilith right to me, but I think we can help each other. You're going to need me, now that your reaper is dead." He went into the small living area and lifted the cushions off the sofa. "We don't have a problem, but I could kill that Leo guy for putting you in that position."

"Leo's not so bad," I said. "He took care of Billy, and he hasn't left me, even though he doesn't owe me."

"Situations like Billy are exactly why you need to stick with me," Clint said, pulling out the sofa bed, along with the stench of mildew. "I stayed up all night making sure you two didn't die at Lilith's hand, so I'm beat. Want to catch some shut-eye?"

I hadn't hesitated to share the motel room with Leo, but I shook my head now. I didn't want to give Clint any ideas. If angels even got ideas. I didn't really want to think about angelic genitalia or lack thereof right then, or ever. "Somebody should keep an eye out."

"Suit yourself," Clint said, stretching out and pulling an afghan the color of old and new bruises over him.

I went back to the chapel and sat next to Leo on the floor, pulling my knees up to my chin. He moaned softly in his sleep, and I looked up at him, making sure he hadn't taken a turn for the worse. Before I died, I'd sat with my grandmother when she took a turn for the worse. The damp air of the bayou clamped down on her lungs, slowly suffocating the life out of her over the years. Now, of course, I could see that the foul cigarillos she smoked almost constantly for my entire life gave her emphysema, and with no oxygen tanks or inhalers to treat her, the decline was sharp and fast.

I wished more than anything there was something I could do, something to ease the terrible wheezing every time she drew breath, something to speed along the inevitable. In the end I just poured her doses of opium-laced cough syrup until she slipped off to sleep and never woke up.

Most days, I was glad she died before I did. If she had ever seen what had happened to me, her heart would have broken.

I leaned my head back against Leo's bench, staring up at the dusty rafters of Father Colin's crappy church. The sheen was wearing quickly on the whole "being free" thing. Even if I managed to convince Lilith not to pulverize me, I was still a woman who'd been dead for ninety years. I couldn't get a driver's license or a job. I'd be stuck drifting from one town to the next on the interstate, sleeping in a blur of motel rooms if I was lucky, parking lots and overpasses if I wasn't. I'd still be nothing to anyone. And every shifter, hound, or reaper I ran across would want to be the one to take me out.

Leo's breathing stayed shallow, and he was still so pale I could see every vein under his skin, but his forehead was cooler, and he was in a deep sleep. I stayed with him until the sun was fully up, then stepped out on the loading dock. The sunrise was brilliant orange and pink, rolling forward to touch the Black Hills. My breath frosted when I exhaled and my fingers prickled with cold. I stuffed them into the pockets of my jeans and watched a few snowflakes drift around me, landing and sticking on the cracked, dirty concrete.

The snow fell faster and faster, piling around my feet. The wind blew in clouds from the plains that swallowed up the sun, until everything was the eerie gray dark of a black-and-white movie.

I shivered and looked up at the sky as a dim streetlamp flickered to life. Squalls weren't unheard of in the fall up here, but this didn't feel right. The flakes landing on my skin froze to it, stinging like pinpricks all over my hands and cheeks.

There were demons who brought inclement weather. Thunderstorms, tornadoes, upheaval among animals and plants anywhere in their vicinity.

Sure, it was probably just a freak storm. Still, I spun and jogged inside, locking the door behind me.

I went straight to the now-pitch-black apartment behind the chapel, flicking on the light and shaking Clint's foot. "Wake up." He started awake, hand reaching for his rifle before he saw it was me.

"What is it?" he said, sitting up and reaching for his boots.

"We need to go," I said. "All of us. This place isn't a safe haven anymore."

Clint didn't question, just grabbed his jacket and bag and rifle and followed me into the chapel. He strode right past Leo to the door, turning in irritation when I didn't follow.

"Ava. Now is not the time to be a hero."

Leo sighed, shifting the blanket tighter around him. The temperature in the chapel had dropped at least twenty degrees in the last five minutes and I heard his teeth chatter.

"Either we take him or you can kiss my ass and any help it might provide you good-bye," I snapped.

Clint folded his arms. "This man is directly responsible for you being on a demon's hit list. Give me one good reason we should let him weigh us down."

Leo levered himself up on one elbow, scrubbing his hand across his eyes. "Because I can get you to an actual safe house."

16

Clint wasn't happy helping Leo out to his truck, but once we were inside, windshield wipers swiping furiously at the driving snow, he relaxed a hair.

"I'll call the police from a pay phone, tell them about Colin's body."

"Are you high?" Leo said. His voice was gravelly from pain. "Cops nowadays have software that can trace a call in thirty seconds. Not to mention voice prints, AFIS, and traffic cameras on every lamppost even in a place like this." He pointed at a four-way intersection coming up in the twin cones of the truck's headlights. "Turn right up here."

"Then what, I leave him there to rot?" Clint gripped the steering wheel hard enough that the plastic creaked.

"Yup," Leo said. "In the twenty-five years you've been on the mountain, the government has developed fifty new ways to spy on your every move. Sucks to be Father Colin."

"He'll be found on Sunday at the latest," I said, glad I was sitting between the two of them. Clint looked ready to break Leo's jaw. "Are your prints on file anywhere?"

Clint made the turn, the back wheels fishtailing on newly slick pavement. "I don't have fingerprints."

Leo snorted. "'Course you don't."

I nudged Leo. "Stop it," I muttered. Leo glared across the cab at Clint but went quiet except to call out turns. I'd have to keep them from killing each other until I could fill Leo in on Clint's real deal.

We were practically the only car on the road, passing a few four-wheel trucks and snowplows, but otherwise the storm had fallen over the Black Hills like someone had turned off the lights.

Clint stopped the truck across from a three-story brick town house sandwiched next to a closed-down movie theater and a convenience store, which was stubbornly still open, even though almost a foot of snow had drifted on the sidewalks in front.

"What is this place?" he said as we stood on the sidewalk in front, Leo leaning heavily on me.

Leo coughed, smiling even though I saw fine droplets of blood on his lips. "A whorehouse."

Clint didn't say anything, just pointed up the steps. "Get him inside," he told me. "I'll pull the truck into the alley so no one sees."

I didn't think hiding one ugly pickup would do much to keep Lilith from spotting us, but I helped Leo up the icy steps and leaned on the bell. After a minute, the door opened and a sliver of face peered through. "Password?"

Leo muttered something in Russian, and the guy opened the door wider. He was old, face like a leather handbag and a luxurious silver ponytail curling over his shoulder. His jeans and work vest looked distinctly out of place in the water-stained Victorian foyer we stepped into. A canvas camp chair sat just inside the door, next to a folding table holding a coffee cup and an overflowing ashtray. I spied a Winchester Model 30 propped in the corner, oiled to a silvery, snakeskin sheen.

"Evening, sir," he said. "I'm afraid the lady can't come in. House rules."

"She's my bodyguard," Leo said. The guy looked us over, clearly reconsidering his decision to allow us over the threshold. I spent the silence considering how best to drop Leo, relieve the door guy of his shotgun, and avoid anyone getting peppered with buckshot.

"Sorry," the door guy said again. "Maybe you should go home, pal. Sleep it off. Try again tomorrow. No use wasting your money on whiskey dick."

"Listen, asshole," Leo ground out. "Go find Veronica. She knows me."

"Lots of guys sayin' they know Veronica come in here." The door guy folded his arms across his lumpy vest. "Not a single one of 'em is telling the truth."

"Leonid is a lot of things, but not a liar." The silky voice drifted down the scuffed, sagging staircase, followed closely by its owner, a woman wrapped in a Chinese-style robe, which showcased both her impressively giant hairdo and impressively giant tits.

The door guy instantly straightened up, looking like he'd just been caught smacking around Veronica's favorite puppy. "You sure about that, Miss Ronnie?"

Veronica glided up to Leo, ignoring me entirely. She was about a head taller than I was, and twice as wide at both the boobs and the ass, the kind of hourglass figure that could not only stop traffic but also cause the pavement to spontaneously combust.

"Look at you," she said. "Blew in on a storm, as usual." She removed Leo from my grasp, helping him up the stairs. "Let Mama get a look at you," she crooned. The door guy and I shared an uncomfortable moment before Clint rang the bell.

"He's with us," I said. "I apologize in advance for any self-righteousness or strange rambling."

The door guy snorted. "We get more of that than you might think." He let Clint in and showed us to a set of rooms connected by a shared, cramped bathroom. The place wasn't exactly modern, but it was a hell of a lot less depressing than Father Colin's apartment. Clint showed his appreciation by glaring at the sounds of a girl's screaming orgasm coming through the wall. I didn't know if he was irritated by the sex or by her terrible acting. Maybe both.

"You need anything, I'm downstairs," the door guy said. "Veronica would want Leonid's friends taken care of."

"What's your name?" I said. Leo was in good hands—he clearly knew the girls here well enough to strut like he owned the place. Hell, for all I knew, he *did* own the place.

"Wallace Bear King," he said.

I held out my hand. "Ava." Wallace took it and shook it gently. A lot of men did, taking my slender fingers and small palms to mean I was more delicate than most.

"No last name?"

I shook my head. "Haven't needed one lately."

"I hear that," Wallace said. He pulled out a drawer in the banged-up dresser squatting in one corner of the small room and showed me a collection of odds-and-ends clothes any self-respecting hobo would reject. "Take a shower and change. You look like you need it."

The door shut, and I sat on the bed, listening to the moans, the creaking springs, and the breathing of a house full of too many people, every one crammed full of desperation. I tried not to worry about Leo. This was his territory, and I needed to follow his lead. Some cheap whiskey and cheap ass would probably help him a lot more in the long run than me hovering. It wasn't like *I* was going to help him in that department, even if I did wish he was the one in this depressing excuse for a bedroom with me instead of the angel. At least Leo would be more talkative.

Clint stood in the bathroom, staring at me like he was afraid to cross the threshold. "You okay?"

I nodded. "Fine."

Clint sighed, then stepped back into his own room. "I told you not to bring him."

"Thanks," I said as he shut the connecting door. "That's very helpful. Your contempt has solved all my complex feelings about this situation."

I slumped back on the bed, and when I couldn't take staring at a stain shaped like a Winnebago anymore, I changed out of my clothes into an oversize Timberwolves shirt. The blizzard had made the streetlamps come on even though it was day, bright and golden, and the flimsy, half-shredded blind didn't do much to keep the glow of the storm out. I wandered down the narrow hall, listening to ten variations on low-rent porno moans that seemed to be the gold standard in Veronica's place.

The door nearest the stairs opened and I jumped. Leo stepped out, a sheet wrapped around his lower half, and started when he saw me. "Ava. You need something?"

I shook my head. "Just didn't want to be cooped up." Beyond him in the bedroom I saw Veronica rise from the mattress, her auburn hair spilling down her back in a tidal wave. There was an elaborate tattoo on her back, of a weeping saint whose tears turned into black birds that took flight across both her shoulder blades.

Leo lit one of his noxious cigarettes with a gold lighter. "I figure we'll stay here until the roads are clear, figure out a more permanent solution."

Veronica wrapped the silk robe loosely around her and sauntered over to Leo, draping an arm over his shoulder. I looked at my feet, dirty, one bruised toenail sprouting off legs that could pass for fence posts. I felt stupid standing there, and ugly. I wasn't used to it, and it soured my stomach and made my throat clench. I wasn't used to being noticed by anyone, period, and Veronica was staring at me with what even the most confident of women would describe as a vagina-melting glare while she ran her red nails idly over Leo's ink. I could have told her she had nothing to worry about, but I didn't like her cheap nail polish and, I decided, I didn't like her all that much.

"She's a little more heroin junkie than you usually go for, Leo. You get a fetish for Goth girls while you've been away?"

Leo's mouth turned down. "I told you that's not how it is. And

just because Ava doesn't have an ass you could park a truck on is
no reason to run your mouth."

Veronica pulled away, her robe falling open to where I could see
a fresh handprint in the deep valley of her waist. "All signs point to
you enjoying my ass just like it is. Dickhead." She sauntered down
the hall to the bathroom and slammed the door.

I leaned against the wall, tilting my head into the rotting wallpaper and the crumbling plaster beneath it. At least I wouldn't do
too much damage to my skull if I beat my brains against it.

I didn't have anything against brothels or the people who ran
them. I'd spent plenty of time hiding in them, living in them. I
tried to avoid actually working, but life didn't always work out like
I wanted it to. It wasn't like I pulled down any kind of salary as a
hound, unless you counted my continued existence. Being alive
didn't exactly cut you checks to pay for food and clothes and a bed
that wasn't also a refrigerator box.

Leo went back to the bed and lay down, stubbing out his cigarette in a saucer next to the bed. "She gets a little territorial."

"She'd be less territorial if she pissed on you," I said. Leo flashed
me a grin.

"I'm not into that. If you wanted me in your bed, why didn't you
say something downstairs?"

I sat on the edge of Veronica's mattress. Everything smelled like
her, like them. Rose perfume and menthols mixed with sweat and
musk. The bedstead was iron, covered in white sheets and shams.
Everything in the room was white or pink or gold, satin and overstuffed. I felt like I was inside a very bright, very girlie coffin. "That
is not something I need complicating my life right now."

Leo stretched one arm behind his head, leaning back against

the avalanche of pillows. "Not now. But someday. You and I are too much alike not to at least try it on."

I dropped my gaze from his, noticing the bruises on his back and side had faded to at least five days old, and the swelling in his jaw was gone. "Veronica isn't just a friend," Leo said. "One of her sidelines is a blood seller."

I wrinkled my nose. "She looks pretty healthy to be laced with vamp venom."

"She sells to people like me," Leo said. He held up his free arm so I could inspect it. Woven amid the almost wall-to-wall tattoos was a patch of rusty dried blood from an IV needle. "All better," he said with a slow grin. "A little conjuring put me right as rain."

Now I knew why he was in such a good mood, and running his fingers up and down the bare, bruised skin of my thigh like he'd paid money for me and not Veronica. "Stop it," I said, moving his hand. "You're high." Leo shook his head.

"Just feeling right for the first time in a while. Willing human blood for healing and protection. Unwilling for black magic and cursing. The more you know." He offered me a cigarette from the pack on the nightstand, and this time I took it, dragging deep. The unfiltered Russian tobacco, undoubtedly sprayed with some hideous Soviet-era pesticide, burned all the way down. It felt about right for the shitty day I'd had so far.

"I'm glad you're all right," I said in a rush. Leo waved me off.

"Did the conjuring, had some vodka, fucked Veronica's brains out . . . I told you I'd survived worse."

I stood up. "I was going to say sorry for getting your liver or spleen or whatever busted in the first place, but it looks like Veronica took care of that."

"Hey." Leo grabbed my wrist, tilting his head. "Are you *jealous*?"

I glared down at him. "That's rich coming from the guy who's been following me since Las Vegas for no good reason other than he might get laid. For your information, the angel in there has a better chance." It was a shitty thing to say, but I was in a shitty mood.

Leo dropped his grip on me, his eyes going wide. "Back up. Survivor Man in there is *what*?"

"You heard me," I said. I *was* tired now and wished I could just curl up in Veronica's mind-destroying cupcake nightmare of a bed and pass out for a week or so. How had I gone from being the least favorite of Gary's hounds to the most wanted lapdog in all of Hell? Oh yeah, I thought, looking down at Leo. I let a human talk me into going against my fundamental nature, for him to dump me and get obliterated with his favorite whore the minute he got the chance.

"He's a Fallen angel," I amended. "Lilith and him have some big feud that's been going on lo these thousand years, or something. To be honest, I kind of blanked out on the more biblical aspects of his history lesson."

"Fuck, Ava." Leo grabbed an almost empty bottle from the floor and uncapped it, pouring it into a souvenir glass painted with a picture of Mount Rushmore. He killed it in one swallow and refilled the glass in a single smooth motion. "So does Captain America in there have a flaming sword and all that crap?"

"I dunno." I shrugged. "He just said his name was Azrael and Lilith had it in for him."

"Jesus," Leo muttered. He scrubbed a hand over his eyes. "You aren't freaking out about this. Why?"

"If we stick with him, maybe Lilith will think twice about punishing us for Gary," I said. "And vis-à-vis the angel thing—why not? I'm a hellhound and you raise monsters from the dead. Why can't Clint have come from the good side of the tracks rather than the shit side?"

"I guess if you're gonna hang with an angel, go big or go home," Leo said. When I didn't reply he frowned. "When was the last time you perused a Bible?"

"Seventy, eighty years," I said. By the time I landed in Louisiana I was more interested in a good time than in my eternal soul.

And even if I had believed, it wouldn't have done me a damn bit of good.

"I suffered through an Orthodox service every Saturday for fourteen years," Leo said. "They never actually mention him by name, but Azrael is one of the heavies in the Old Testament. There's this book called the Zohar that all the weird old guys at temple loved to talk about, the mystical shit. Azrael is a big deal to them."

"I'm not exactly a fangirl of religion," I said. "What's the big deal about him supposedly?"

Leo took the cigarette from my fingers and dragged on it. "He's the angel of death."

I dropped my chin to my chest, squeezing my eyes shut. A headache clamped down on my skull like a vise. "Of course he is."

Leo shrugged. "Could all be crap, but if he is who he says he is, he's not fuckin' around."

"And neither is Lilith," I said. "So I'd rather keep the Old Testament hit man close than piss him off."

"I don't know, Ava." Leo sighed. "The idea of a heavy like that breathing down my neck is killing my buzz with a fucking hammer, I'll tell you that much."

I spread my hands. "What's to know? He can help us out, so if it takes a few hundred awkward miles crammed into his truck, small price to pay."

"Or you could just tell Lilith where he is, and let the two of them duke it out," Leo said. "You're punching way above your weight with this guy, Ava. Sell him out and get Hell's very own bunny-boiling bitch off your tail, is my advice."

"And I need your advice, yeah, because I'm so weak and helpless," I snapped. Usually I was better at reining in my temper, or at least keeping my thoughts to myself. It was easier to avoid getting smacked if you were quiet.

Leo reached for me but I jerked my hand away, scrambling off the bed. The room was way too hot, and the stench of Veronica's perfume suddenly stank like an open sewer full of flowers. "I didn't mean it," he said quietly. "Calm down."

"Clint saved your life," I said. "And you *ruined* mine, so do me a favor: stick your dick back into your BFF Veronica and I'll handle keeping us alive."

"Your life can't have been that great," Leo drawled. Only his eyes gave away anything, and they were dark and hard as stone. "You agreed to help me liquidate Gary. I didn't even have to hurt you that much."

"Fuck you," I said. "I'm leaving in the morning. Free advice— quit pretending like you're my friend before I get disappointed enough to stick a blade in some part of you that's important."

I stormed back to my room, pushing past Veronica in the hall. Her full lips parted as she bumped into the wall, and I held up my hand. "He's all yours. You can pull your fangs back in."

I slammed the door behind me, threw the bolt, and curled up on the faded bed. It had been years—decades—since I'd cried more than a few tears. Pressing the musty feather pillow against my face, I sobbed until I thought my chest would crack open. It wasn't because of Veronica, or Clint, or even because of Lilith. I hadn't realized until this moment that I was alone, and I'd been stupid to ever think anything else.

The moment I'd closed my jaws around Gary's throat, I'd consigned myself to the loneliest existence I could imagine. Even hounds had other hounds, their reaper. There was order and structure, even if the flip side was punishment and a violent, pointless death when your luck finally trickled out the ass-end of the hourglass.

Now I was nothing. I'd let myself pretend that Leo would stick with me, that his disobeying his father was the same as my killing Gary. I'd let myself drop my guard around literally one human in a hundred years, and I was screwed. Leo wasn't in the same boat. He was safe on shore, watching me drown. He'd deserted me as soon as he'd remembered he belonged among humans. Not that I blamed him. I wouldn't pick me over Veronica.

He was right about Clint too. I should do what Lilith asked and be done with all of this. Get busy with the endless stretch of empty highway that was the rest of my unending life.

Finally, my throat was ragged and my eyes too swollen to cry anymore. I watched the snow and the streetlight blur as I drifted finally into the sort of sleep that only comes to the profoundly exhausted. The full weight of what I'd done was slowly crushing me, but that didn't mean I'd feed Clint to Lilith just to prolong my existence. My existence wasn't worth it. I might be a traitor, but I wasn't a coward. Lilith couldn't do anything to me that would be half as painful as the simple fact I was still alive.

CHAPTER

17

|||||||||||||||||||||||||||||||||||||||||||||||||||||||||||||||||||||||||||||||||||

Louisiana, 1919

There was no real land in the heart of the swamp, and no real water. We'd pushed the flat-bottomed boats until we found the slight rise of solid ground that Jasper told me was where the priestess and her acolytes had congregated in the slave days, when the plantation was full of people and surrounded by flat fields instead of the tangle of the bayou.

Caleb was the first one out of the boat, standing on the apex of the hillock with his hands on his hips. He nodded at the cypress roots and the ragged Spanish moss as if he'd personally constructed the swamp—stink, gators, and all.

Once this small dry place amid the mud had been secret,

a respite from the big white house, its porches and peaked roof crouching over the sugarcane fields like a gigantic mausoleum, the upstairs porch just high enough to catch a glimpse of the Mississippi.

Now the big house was rotting and full of possums and bats under the eaves. The ornate railings of those porches were pitted with rust, one felled altogether by a Union gunboat during the war. The bayou had crept in on the heels of the last owner, who took sick with TB and moved to Arizona in 1901. Native plants surged to orgiastic in the damp heat, choking out the carefully planted roses and magnolia trees. Kudzu vines strangled the live oaks into pale skeletons that lined the overgrown drive.

Jasper and the others had to hack a path up to the plantation house, and then tear boards off the fallen pile that was the slave quarters to cover the shattered windows and a gaping hole in the floor just inside the front door. The inside not only looked like a tomb, it smelled like one—rotting plaster lying in piles all over the floor, wallpaper drooping like peeling skin, gaping holes where anything of value—lights, doors, even mantels—had been stripped by thieves.

Now when you looked over the cane fields, a mass of green breathed back at you. The swamp healed its scars faster than any human body. The river was swollen and surged so close to the house I could watch herons picking their delicate way through the shallows that had once been the lawn. I slept on the porch to avoid the heat and the fingers of mold and mildew crawling unchecked across every surface inside. Not to mention the roaches and the rats. I got enough of those back in New Orleans.

Jasper came in the first night, cheeks flushed red in the lamplight. He was from Chicago, thick-blooded and not used to the constant, unrelenting humidity of the swamp. I had a hard time coming from the Tennessee mountains, so I imagined he must feel like he was roasting alive.

I lay on a mattress we'd pulled out onto the balcony, fanning myself and trying unsuccessfully to keep my white nightgown from sticking to my body.

"We found the well house," he said. "There are markings on the stones . . ." He pulled a damp notebook from his pocket and sketched with a pencil. Jasper was an artist. He'd come to New Orleans to draw the Mississippi, the cake slice houses, each layer a different color, the explosions of flowers in the Garden District.

I met him on one of my long walks at night, when it was finally cool enough to move. He stumbled out of a bar on Canal Street and knocked into me, sending us both flying. Later, when he grabbed my hips so hard he left bruises when I moved on top of him, I let him stay until morning, our bodies close but not touching, gleaming and breathless in the gray quiet of first light.

"She was real," he said. "She was here. Ava, this is really going to happen."

I pulled him down to me, kissed him. He tasted like bitter wormwood and licorice. "I told you to stop drinking so much of that with Caleb," I whispered. "It makes you talk too much."

He pushed me down on the mattress, kneeling above me and undoing his belt. I pulled my nightgown over my head, tossing it over the railing. It drifted out of sight like a dove shot on the wing, falling fast out of sight. "I don't need to talk anymore," he mumbled against my ear, nudging my knees apart. He pushed into me hard enough to make me gasp and sink my nails into his shoulder.

Talking with Caleb always made him rough and quick and aggressive. It was one of the few things that made hanging around Caleb tolerable.

"We're not men anymore, darling," he said a few minutes later, when our breathing was ragged and his cock twitched insistently, making me squirm and wish he'd just shut up and fuck me like Caleb did.

I wasn't proud of what Caleb and I were doing to Jasper, but his moods and his drinking and the days upon days where he wouldn't sleep or come out of the rattrap attic he called a studio ground me down. I was all right with being alone—growing up on the mountain had taught me the value of silence, of being peaceful with just your own company—but being ignored wasn't the same. It made me feel slight and worthless next to Jasper's books and paintings, made an ugly voice whisper I was just a stupid hillbilly he was wasting time with until he went back to where he came from.

Then there were the nights when he did come over, and he'd already gotten so angry at everything else in the world that he hit me until I backed into the corner of my sitting room and sobbed, tears washing the blood off my face and down into my collar. The next morning, when he washed the pink stains out of my favorite dress and brought me a cold bottle of beer from the corner store to hold against my swollen face, I always told him I understood.

And then I went to Caleb's apartment on Frenchmen Street and fucked him silently until I was so tired I couldn't move. He'd sit up, light a cigarette, and tell me to go home. I liked the pain when I struggled to pull on my stockings and underwear. I liked the sting where my thighs touched when I limped to the streetcar. I liked that Jasper had no idea, because Caleb's bruises were hidden by the ones he'd already inflicted.

"We're not men," Jasper whispered again. "When this is over, we'll be gods."

He slammed into me, hip bones jarring my thighs, and I finally came, letting myself yell. We were the only ones awake, and the hum of insects and night critters in the swamp didn't care if I joined in. Jasper moaned and came as well, rolling off me and panting on the mattress. "I can't wait," he whispered. "I am so done with this paltry existence."

"You have no idea how much I want this," I whispered. I'd finally be free to tell Jasper the truth. He couldn't hurt me once we'd found the ground where the *bokor* woman had spilled blood almost sixty years ago, once we'd taken it into ourselves.

It wasn't until the next day, climbing out of the boat, feeling mud squish in my shoes, stepping onto the tiny island and almost reaching the summit of that high place in the swamp, that I realized Caleb was staring at me, not the surroundings. That I was alone, Jasper and the others standing behind me. Around me.

As they grabbed me, tearing my dress and stockings, one of my shoes flying off, and carried me to the flat stone in the center of the clearing I screamed, ten times louder than I had in the night.

Nobody who might have helped me heard my screams. Nothing in the swamp cared if I joined in.

I jerked awake, head thick as if I'd polished off the rest of Leo's cheap vodka. I dreamed about Jasper periodically, of the time before we'd gone south from New Orleans looking for the plantation where the blood of innocent people soaked the earth. I dreamed about the after far less frequently. Usually it was that night, on the porch, nothing but my own sweat on my skin. Thinking that just maybe, things would be all right.

The memories of when Jasper would beat me out of sheer rage at being a colossal failure of a human being were much sharper, but I tried not to think about him any more than once every twenty years. The prick didn't deserve even that much, and I didn't expect the dream to show up tonight of all nights. I had so many other nightmares competing for space I was usually safe from that particular unfortunate life choice.

So I really didn't expect him to still be standing in the corner of the sad little room in Rapid City, three thousand miles from the sweltering bayou where I'd last seen his face. He stood in the corner by the dresser, his face stark white in the streetlight. Snow covered the lower half of the window, turning my room pale as moonlight. I'd slept for a long time—it was full night, the blizzard turning the world into the inside of a snow globe.

"Holy shit," I whispered, rocketing upright on the mattress. I had no weapon, nothing to defend myself with. I jumped out of bed, feet barely touching the boards before I ran. When it came to fight or flight, there was no shame in choosing flight.

"Come back, darling," Jasper called, his voice somehow echoing through the entire house. "You and I never did say a proper good-bye."

I skidded down the steps, catching my foot on a loose board and sprawling on the floor at the bottom. Except it wasn't floor, it was sucking mud, and the walls were trees, and Spanish moss floated down from the ceiling to brush my face.

"Up," I whispered as I struggled in the murky water. "Get your ass up."

If I'd had the new Ava in my head, the hound rather than the foolish, arrogant girl who was too stupid and horny, too desperate for power to realize she was going to die, I might have actually survived that night out in the bayou.

I ran now, hearing Jasper splash through the shallows behind me. A gator hissed and slid off a log to my left, and I stopped in front of an impenetrable tangle of cypress roots and undergrowth.

"Darling," Jasper singsonged amid the trees. "Your sacrifice will be remembered. Your blood will propel the rest of us into eternity. Now stop running and face your fate."

"You should do what he says, Ava." Lilith uncoiled from her spot, leaned against a tree trunk, and stepped forward, looking me up and down.

I backed up against another tree, fingers digging into the bark at the sight of her. She wore black pants and a jacket, a white shirt so bright it hurt my eyes unbuttoned to just above her cleavage, showing a delicate gold chain. Her hair was swept back, one twisting strand framing each side of her face.

She regarded me with those unblinking shark's eyes. "Don't have a heart attack. You're still useful to me."

"I don't know where Clint Hicks is," I blurted. That was the technical truth—I had no idea where Clint Hicks, dumbass warlock that Azrael had murdered—was at.

"See, I don't think that's entirely accurate," Lilith said. She examined the nails on her left hand. The manicure was so sharp it looked like it could carve through my flesh and bone, and I felt sweat roll down my thighs and back in the all-consuming humidity of the swamp. "I think he's so close he'd probably come running if you screamed."

"I'm not lying," I whispered.

"I know he left Wyoming," Lilith said evenly. "I paid a visit to that piss-scented dog park Billy's shifters laughingly call their territory. And now I find you here, in a place crawling with blood conjuring and demon nets *just* keeping me from seeing what's going on through your eyes."

I stayed quiet. She wasn't looking for a response, unless it was peeing myself from sheer terror.

"When Hellspawn sleep, you can page through their dreams, and if you're lucky you find an entry about whatever it is you're looking for," she said. "You, Ava, are not a very difficult book. More like Dick and Jane than *Anna Karenina*."

Lilith's lips parted for a moment, and I prayed she wouldn't actually try to smile. That would easily rank as the most horrifying thing I'd ever seen. "I don't know where your backbone came from all of a sudden, but I don't like it. You're on thin fucking ice and it's cracking."

She didn't really move. She was just *there,* in front of me, grabbing me by the neck and pushing down until I felt my voice box creak, a hair away from being crushed. "You lie to me again, Ava, and you'll see firsthand just how unpleasant existence can be on my shit list. I didn't give you Gary's book so you'd turn crusading avenger for every stray soul in the pages."

"Then why did you?" I croaked. "I'm not a reaper. I can't help you."

. Lilith gave me a little shake. "No, you're not, but since you ripped his throat out you're going to have to do. I *will* get Azrael on the end of my claws and you *will* help me put him there. One hellhound with delusions of grandeur is not keeping me from the light. Not when I've waited for this long. You understand?"

She let go and I fell on my knees, gasping. I was shaking uncontrollably, and I wanted to rake Lilith across her face, destroy the waxen perfection staring down at me like I was a stubborn stain. I didn't, of course. I stayed on my knees, watching her pointed shoes turn and walk away.

"I'll see you in the daylight soon enough," she said. "Now wake up. Your dreams are so fucking depressing I don't know how you can stand it."

The swamp was gone, but I continued to shake and cough. A door banged open and hands grabbed me by the shoulders. I snarled, but they didn't let go. "Ava!" Leo snapped. He pulled me to my feet, and then scooped me up like I didn't weigh any more than the overstuffed garbage bags in the alley where I'd been standing calf-deep in snow.

I was shaking because my fingers and feet had started to turn blue, coughing because it was so cold that breathing felt like taking a bat to the chest. Leo was wearing boots, jeans, and a too-long, too-loose flannel shirt, signifying it belonged to Wallace.

"What the hell were you thinking?" he demanded, carrying me straight past Veronica and a staring gaggle of hookers and up the stairs. "Were you *trying* to kill yourself?"

I finally managed to stop coughing. I must have been out there for at least an hour, to be this cold. The sharp needles driving through all my exposed skin told me hypothermia had finished setting in and was unpacking boxes and picking out curtains.

"It was an accident," I rasped. My throat was still destroyed from crying. I sounded like the evil old woman in every bad horror movie.

Leo didn't seem to care, he just knocked into my room and

grabbed the blanket off my bed, wrapping me in it and rubbing my hands aggressively between his own palms. "Everyone on this block heard you screaming. What happened out there?"

The shaking was just getting worse. I tried to curl in on myself so I didn't strain my muscles or break a tooth like I had one night in the forties when I'd chased a warlock across a frozen pond in Indiana. The ice held his three-hundred-pound ass, then promptly collapsed under my four feet, sending me into the freezing, crushing black below.

I managed to turn two-legged and pull myself out, and then I chased that fucker three more miles through the cornfields outside of Terre Haute before I finally put the bite on him.

I stumbled into a Mennonite couple's farmhouse and almost died, my heart not able to stand the strain of the unbearable cold and the flat-out sprint through subzero temperatures. The couple was nice to me right up until my blackened skin and labored breathing started to clear up, then it went pretty much like it always did when I showed religious folks the hound—lots of praying, yelling about Satan, and a quick getaway on my part.

"Ava!" Leo snapped his fingers in front of my face and I realized I'd drifted.

"I just had a nightmare," I mumbled. Nothing was working right, but at least the stinging in my frostbitten fingers had stopped hurting.

Veronica poked her head in. She was wearing sweatpants and a South Dakota State hoodie, looking completely different with clothes and no makeup. "She okay?" she said cautiously. "What did she take?"

"Run a bath," Leo said. "*Not* hot. We need to get her warmed up."

"Leo, if she's going off the rails she cannot be here," Veronica said. "I feel bad for her and all, but I've got my girls to think of."

"Jesus fucking Christ, Veronica. Run the goddamn bathwater and save the speeches for somebody who gives a shit," Leo snapped.

He picked me up, still wrapped in the blanket, and carried me into the bathroom. There was barely enough room for one person, never mind three, and Veronica stepped back, watching me from the door. She didn't look worried or upset, but I knew I'd worn out my welcome with this little near-death adventure.

Leo stripped off my T-shirt and lowered me into the bath. "Sorry," he said as I screamed at the touch of the water. It felt like I was boiling alive. "Trust me," he said. "It'll stop hurting in a minute."

The door to Clint's room banged open and he stared at Leo and me for a split second before he grabbed a towel and shoved Leo out of the way, covering me with sodden, stained terry cloth. "What do you think you're doing?" he growled at Leo, eyes narrowing.

"I'm saving her fingers and her feet from dropping off like the top of an ice-cream cone," Leo said. "The fuck are *you* doing? She almost dies and you're tumbling off to dreamland fifteen fucking feet away?"

"Can both of you just shut up?" I whispered. "I feel bad enough." The screaming had destroyed my voice, but the rest of me no longer felt like I was dying. As the pain ebbed away, Clint stood.

"I'll be right outside," he said, giving Leo a stare that Leo completely ignored, lifting one of my hands and examining the navy blue beds of my nails.

"You're doing fine," he said. "Once you stop looking like a Smurf you can have a real bath." He levered himself up. "I'll be back. You all right to stay by yourself?"

I nodded. Leo stepped out, then something occurred to him and he stepped back in. "*Were* you trying to kill yourself?" he asked.

"No," I said. My life might be a pile of shit, but I'd never considered ending it myself. Mostly because I couldn't, as far as I knew, actually die from most anything that would off a human.

"Okay," Leo said. "Good to know."

His footsteps faded and I sank down in the murky, rust-colored water. I could see how Leo got to "suicidal" from finding me in the snow. From the outside, I must look pathetic.

I drained the water and waited for it to run clear and steaming hot before I filled the tub again. Leo came back and stuck a handful of clothes through the door. "Veronica wanted you to have these."

"She must really want us gone," I whispered.

Leo shrugged. "You can't blame her. She's got her own to look after, and Clarence in there does have a bull's-eye painted on his perfectly manscaped chest."

He left me alone and I stayed in the tub until the water was cool again, and my skin had resumed a color that was close to normal. In the mirror, I looked merely corpselike, rather than like some kind of freakish, frozen zombie.

Veronica's sweatpants swam on me, but they were clean. I stepped out to find Leo sitting on the bed, tapping his pack of cigarettes against the bedpost in an arrhythmic clatter.

"I promise I am not going to hang myself from the closet bar," I said. "You don't have to babysit me."

Leo stood, perhaps sensing I intended to flop on the bed whether he got out of the way or not. "Not to be nosy, but either you're a hell of a sleepwalker or something is wrong. You were screaming. Really screaming, like you were in agony."

I put an arm over my eyes. Even the dim bare bulb hanging from the ceiling was too much. "I've been hunting down rogue souls for a hundred years. I have some crazy nightmares."

"I get those too," Leo said. "I don't end up almost frozen to death in my underwear."

His shadow moved to block the light, and when I looked up he was standing over me with his arms folded. I had the feeling this view was the last thing a fair number of Leo's enemies saw. "It was Lilith," he said, with no question at the end.

"So what if it is?" I said. "You're not involved in this. You can just go. Or I can. You and Veronica seem to have a pretty good arrangement."

"Look, last night was bullshit on my part," Leo said. He sat down on the end of the bed, his weight making the mattress cave in so I rolled toward him. "Veronica is somebody I've known for a long time. I trust her, and yeah, we're friends. But I was married for most of the time I knew her, so it doesn't go beyond what you saw. I don't have feelings for her and she sure as hell doesn't feel anything for me."

"I don't care." I sighed. "You and she could elope tomorrow. I just don't want you to feel like you owe me something."

"You saved my life," Leo said. "So I do, in fact, owe you a little something."

I could argue he'd done the same when he kept Gary off me long enough for me to tear his throat out, but I let it pass.

"It was my fault," I said. "Lilith got inside my head and she coaxed me outside. She was trying to find out if Clint was with me. She can't see past Veronica's demon nets, but if she doesn't know he's here she will soon."

Leo held up his hand. "Whoa, got inside your head how? Are you broadcasting right now?"

I shook my head. "Apparently any time I sleep, I'm a walking, talking video camera." A residual shiver worked its way up and down my spine. I did my best to ignore it. "I thought I was running. In the dream."

"Running from what?" Leo clicked his lighter, the gold lid flashing.

"Doesn't matter," I said. "But I think we should probably not be here when I pass out again."

"I know a couple guys in Denver," Leo said. "Low level. They mostly run the fights and do some trade with the Asians to bring oxy down from Canada. They aren't connected enough to rat us out to my father." He sighed and rubbed his forehead. "I think we're probably safest with regular people for a while."

"A human would say that," Clint said, coming in and sitting on the room's single chair like he paid rent.

"The human didn't ask you," Leo said. "You're not handcuffed to me, Clarence. You go right ahead and fly free."

I rolled into a sitting position and grabbed up my clothes from the floor. "Enough," I said. "Leo's right. You can come with us or not, but I'm not staying here waiting to get picked off by Hell's very own bitch on wheels."

I started shoving my things into a plaid suitcase I'd found in the closet. There was a drawer full of cheap bulk-rate toiletries in the bathroom and I swiped a handful of those too. At least I was once again the proud owner of a toothbrush.

Once we'd helped Clint push his truck out of the snowdrift kicked up by the plows and were grumbling down the road again, I turned around and rubbed the frost off the back window. I watched silently until the lights of Rapid City disappeared into the dim gray dawn, and only then did I feel safe.

CHAPTER

18

||||||||||||||||||||||||||||||||||||||||||||||||||||||||||||||||||||||||||||||||||||||||||||

Clint drove south, the snow fading away to the black and tan landscape of the Badlands. There was nobody else on the roads except for a few truckers blowing past us at eighty miles an hour.

The sun was all the way up, glinting softly off the tops of the Rockies, when Leo sat up. "Pull over at the next exit, Clarence. I need to piss."

"I thought you were all hot to get to Denver," Clint said.

"That's how it is?" Leo muttered, reaching for his fly. "Okay. You want your floor mats smelling like the bathrooms at Yankee Stadium, fine by me."

"Jesus, pull over!" I shouted. I jumped out of the cab when Clint rolled to a stop by a roadside diner. My legs were cramped, and I was going to choke at least one of them if I had to be in the truck for another second.

"Hey," Clint said, catching up with me. "What's gotten into you?"

"I swear to everything in the Pit," I said. "If I have to be a spectator at one more event in the Dick-Measuring Olympics, I'm going to wring both your necks."

"I'm sorry," Clint said. "All right? I don't want to fight either of you. We have problems other than a warlock with a tiny bladder."

I folded my arms. I felt like somebody had hit me with a car, backed up, run over me three or four times, and then clog-danced on my head for good measure. My head was fuzzy, my reflexes were dull, and I didn't think I could handle another visit from Lilith's brute squad just yet.

Clint moved his chin in the direction of a black Lexus that pulled up and parked at the low, red-roofed motel across the street. "That car's been with us since Rapid City."

"And you didn't say something?" I hissed. Clint spread his hands.

"What would you have done, exactly? Gotten out and chased it while barking?"

"Fuck you, Clarence," I said, rolling my eyes.

"Why didn't Lilith kill you?" Clint asked me. "You disobeyed her, since I'm still breathing. All she had to do was leave you outside a little longer to freeze. But she didn't."

I kept my arms folded to avoid making a fist. Punching a Fallen angel in the neck wasn't a mistake I was going to add to my exhaustive list of poor life choices. "I don't know," I said. "If you're dancing around something, Clint, quit with the jazz hands and just say it."

"If you're still here, you're still useful to her," Clint said, stepping forward so his body blocked the view of our conversation from the occupants of the Lexus. "In what way?"

"Because she thinks I'll fuck up and lead her to you," I said quietly. "And because she has a hate-on for you the likes of which I've never seen in a century of working for a man who held grudges as his profession."

"That doesn't explain why we're being followed," Clint snapped.

I turned away from him and strode across the dusty parking lot toward the car. "I'll find out."

The motel was a little mom-and-pop operation, flowers in front of every room, wagon wheels lining the brick sidewalk, little gnome statues peering at you around the spokes.

I picked up the nearest one as I passed and kept walking toward the Lexus. Through the tinted windows, I saw the shadow of a driver scrambling to put the car in gear, but I got there first, hefted the gnome, and smashed it hat-first through the glass.

"Morning." I lowered my face to see two tattooed, pissed-off heavies with the same taste in suits as Leo staring furiously back at me. "Mind telling me why you're following us?"

The driver yanked a gun from the shoulder holster inside his jacket. I grabbed the barrel as it swung at me and yanked with all my strength. The driver's body jerked forward, his nose smashing against the steering wheel. He slumped, and I pulled the pistol from his limp fingers, glaring at the passenger. "Let's try this again," I said, aiming at him over the groaning driver.

"This doesn't concern you, lady," the passenger snapped. "Just back off if you know what's good for you and let us take Karpov in."

I reached across the driver and grabbed the guy by his shiny lapel, dragging him through the window until he landed on his ass in the dirt. "I guess I don't know what's good for me," I said. "Possibly because I'm not a lady."

I ejected the clip from the pistol and worked the slide to pop out the bullet in the chamber. I pulled the firing pin for good measure and tossed the gun next to the thug. "Take your buddy and get lost," I said.

The guy squirmed through the dirt toward the gun, and I put my boot down on his hand. After the shitty morning so far, the pop of his first and second knuckle was more than a little satisfying. "I don't know if you're deaf or dumb or both, asshole."

He mumbled out a scream and I bore down with the ball of my foot. "Pack up your pal here, go out to the interstate, and stick out your thumb." I lifted my foot away as a show of good faith. "We clear?"

The guy jumped up and got his buddy up with his good hand. "Bitch," he spat over his shoulder as they limped away.

I got into the Lexus and pushed the button to move the seat forward. The driver had a good six or seven inches on me.

Hurting him felt good. I usually didn't stomp all over humans like that unless I was working. I certainly didn't go tossing around gangsters twice my size. I could still throw out my back or rip a tendon, but I didn't care right now. I pulled into the parking lot of the diner. Gravel sprayed from under the car's wheels. The interior smelled like leather and cigarettes and musty Russian aftershave.

I decided I liked the driver's seat of one of these a lot better than the trunk.

Clint stared at me as I climbed out. "What did you do?"

"Got us a new car," I said, shoving the keys into my pocket. "I was tired of our thighs touching. No offense."

I climbed the creaky steps to the diner and pushed open the metal door. It was oval and coated in riveted chrome, like the hatch of a spaceship. Clint followed me, narrowly ducking the door as it swung back. I was a tiny bit disappointed it didn't smack him in the face, but maybe it was just the mood I was in.

Leo was sitting in the last booth, nursing a chipped brown mug. I slid into the booth next to him. "Your dad sent two guys to give you a ride back to his place."

He started to jump up, but I shook my head. "I took care of it."

"For the record, I did not ask you to do that," Clint said, sitting down across from us. "I especially didn't ask you to commit grand theft auto."

"Instinctively, I sensed that you wanted me to," I said. "We have that kind of relationship."

Leo massaged a point between his eyes. "Jesus Christ. I knew Sergei was pissed off, but I didn't think he'd send a crew."

"Wasn't much of a crew," Clint admitted. "They ran off pretty quick."

"You shouldn't have," Leo said to me. "For all you know, he might have sent a couple of guys to throw blood conjuring around and you'd be dead."

I shrugged as the waitress approached with coffee. "You had blood conjuring on your side and I still kicked your ass."

"I didn't use it on you," Leo muttered. "And at most it was a mutual ass-kicking."

"You're grumpy before you've finished your coffee," I said, smiling at him. Even though I still hurt, bone-deep aches all through me, the mental fog of Lilith's nightmare was starting to lift. I almost felt like it wasn't a hardship just to be breathing, which was something I hadn't felt in a handful of decades.

Leo smiled back over the rim of his mug as our waitress put two more down and poured coffee. She'd washed her pink uniform so many times it was almost white, and the name tag was as chipped as the mugs on our table. It said her name was Naomi. She was young but worn-out, just like her uniform and her off-white corrective shoes. Her hair was bleached until the blond hit an abrupt DMZ of dishwater brown about two inches from her scalp.

She smiled, though, and it reached her eyes. "What can I get you folks?"

Leo lifted his mug. "Just a refill, hon."

"Eggs," Clint said. "Sunny side up, and some plain wheat toast."

Naomi scribbled away and then turned to me. I tried to smile at her, but the adrenaline of beating on the Russians was gone, and what occurred to me was to curl up and sleep in the booth for a few hours.

"Just coffee," I said quietly.

"Be right back with all that," Naomi said, pouring and walking away. I sipped the coffee and winced. It wasn't so much coffee as mop water that had at one point in its storied history come in contact with coffee grounds.

I spit it back into the cup. "This is shit. Being tailed by a couple of stone killers is actually preferable."

"How did those men find us?" Clint demanded of Leo. "What did they want?"

Leo shrugged. "No fuckin' clue. I'm guessing they were going to practice some light bondage on me and drive me back to Vegas to have a conversation with my father."

"Veronica," I said quietly. Leo shot me a sharp glare.

"She wouldn't. She and I have an understanding."

He'd also said she had her own girls and house to protect, but I let it go. It wasn't my business. I didn't get involved with humans. Leo would see eventually there was no point in sticking with Clint and me if he wanted to keep breathing.

I hoped he'd land on his feet. I imagined he was good at disappearing, and I hoped he found a place where he could forget about how wrong things had gone for him since we'd collided in that alley behind the strip club. I always hoped that people like Leo got away clean, although more likely he'd end up in the foundation of a new casino on the Strip about the time Lilith was peeling me like a grape.

Naomi set down Clint's plate and placed a hand on his shoulder. "Give me a holler if you need anything else, okay?"

He gave her a radiant smile and she blushed as she walked back to the counter. Aside from a couple of ancient truckers as weather-beaten as the tires on their rigs, we were the only people in the diner.

"So are your friends in Denver going to sell us out as well?" Clint said to Leo, shoveling eggs into his mouth.

"Veronica isn't your problem," Leo growled. "Worry about Lilith and let me worry about my old man, all right, Clarence?"

"Speaking of that particular devil, Ava never did answer my question," Clint said, turning to me. "Lilith spared you."

"Lilith *tortured* her," Leo said. "Sent her out into the snow to freeze. Let it go, for fuck's sake. She could have dimed your ass out anytime. You should be thanking her, not complaining."

"Torture, I have no doubt. Lilith excels at extracting every last drop of misery from a person, body and soul. Yet Ava's alive," Clint said. "So the question remains: why?"

The horrible coffee soured in my stomach. I didn't care that Clint didn't trust me—hell, I sure wouldn't trust me if I was sitting on his side of the table—but all I could think of was the expression on Lilith's face, the thin-lipped determination that reminded me of the warlocks I chased. Across ice, down the polished halls of mansions, through dingy Hell's Kitchen alleys that reeked of piss and day-old garbage. That face was always the same. They still thought they could win, and they were more than willing to go through me to cling to a few more minutes of life.

Sooner or later, they realized they couldn't cheat Death. The ones who never did were dangerous.

I slid out of the booth, boots thumping on the lumpy vinyl floor. "Excuse me," I muttered, making a run for the bathroom.

Naomi stared at me until I slammed the door in her face. A light clicked on above me, filling the tiny space with the kind of harsh light that makes you look two steps from dead even if you're not on the wrong end of twenty-four hours with no sleep and a demon rooting around inside your head. I sat on the lid of the toilet and pressed the heels of my hands into my burning eyes. After a minute, Leo knocked on the door. I grabbed a wad of tissue and swiped at the dampness on my face.

"Go away."

"Come on, Ava," he said. "He was being a jackass. Don't let it get to you."

I reached up and flicked the lock off. Leo stepped in and shut the door behind him. There was barely room for the two of us in the tiny space, even when he leaned against the wall.

"We can't keep this up," I said quietly. "She'll find us sooner or later."

"I told you to just give up the parakeet out there," Leo said. "You don't deserve this. Whatever he did, let him suffer for it. Why should we have to be involved in a slap fight between Lilith and some Fallen?"

"Because if I hand him over, Lilith will have no use for me, and she'll kill me," I grumbled. "I don't like the guy either, but me being a line on Clint is the only assurance I have Lilith won't skin me for what I did to Gary."

"If he was such a big loss, trust me, Lilith would have already snapped your head off like a Pez dispenser," Leo said. "Maybe we do turn him over, and we both walk. That's what a smart deal would be for Lilith."

"Lilith's smart," I agreed, "but she's also clinically insane. Sticking with the angel is the right thing to do."

Leo sighed, but then nodded. "Okay. You're the one who hangs around Hellspawn. I'll stick with you, but if he gives me one more side-eye I'm going to stick him in the throat and watch him drown in his own blood."

"Fair enough," I said. I stood up and opened the door. Naomi eyed us but was smart enough to keep her opinions to herself. Clint watched me carefully as I came back and sat in the booth. "I apologize. I was out of line."

"Yeah, you were." I rolled the bundled napkin/silverware back and forth with my index finger. Clint looked like he wanted to say something else, then sighed.

"I appreciate what you did, more than you know. Lilith has a talent for getting under your skin and digging around until you're just a broken pile of flesh. I should have remembered that."

"She's pretty pissed at you," I muttered. "What'd you do, break up with her in a text?"

Leo snorted, and Clint's mouth turned down. "It's a long story. I'm sorry she threatened you, and I'm sorry she made you dream-walk. Demons aren't as powerful here as they are in Hell and they like to piggyback on those who can more easily move across barriers and conjuring."

"She didn't threaten me, exactly," I said. The sensation of Lilith in my head was still there, like I had an empty spot behind my eye socket that was slowly filling up with poison, drop by drop. I didn't know if I'd be able to forget her face as she'd dug her nails into the skin of my neck. I was sporting a crop of scratches this morning like I'd tried on a tie made of barbed wire.

"She doesn't have to say much to terrify people," Clint muttered. "She's got Hell's most impressive set of crazy eyes."

"All she said was she'd worked too long to let me and Gary keep her from the spotlight," I said. "I have a feeling she'll say more to you."

Clint's fork dropped from his fingers and clattered against his plate before it flipped off the table onto the floor. Naomi hurried over to pick it up, and he shooed her away. "It's fine," he said tightly. "I'm not hungry anymore."

Leo watched Clint like he'd just jumped up on the table and

started singing selections from *West Side Story*. "What is your problem, man?"

Clint ignored him and leaned across the table until he was close enough that I could see the tiny lines around the black holes of his eyes and the two days' worth of stubble sprinkling his jaw. "Tell me exactly what she said to you," he growled. "Word for word. Don't leave anything out."

I tried to draw back, but Clint grabbed my wrist. Leo jumped up, but I shook my head. Clint would hurt him, and I didn't want Leo to be hurt. Especially not because of me.

"She said that she had worked too long for a hellhound with delusions of grandeur to keep her out of the light," I said quietly, trying not to squirm at the pressure of his fingers on my wrist. "And she said she'd get what she wanted from you one way or another. Then she told me my dreams were depressing her and I woke up because Leo was yelling at me."

"I was yelling because she was screaming in agony, for the record," Leo said. "Let go of her, Clint. Now."

Clint released me, flopping back against his seat and shoving his hands through his hair. "That bitch," he whispered. "That crazy, crazy bitch."

He leaned forward again, scrubbing at the skin on his temples. I realized I was sitting tensed up, waiting for him to hit me or explode. I wouldn't put money on either. I'd said something that I didn't understand the significance of, and that usually meant Gary was about to smack me around until he was less frustrated with his own shortcomings.

I also realized, almost as an afterthought, that I wouldn't let him. Maybe it was having Leo there, maybe I just didn't care anymore. But as Clint buried his face in his hands, I curled my fists and waited for the slap. I didn't know how I'd respond, but I was done covering my head and praying for it to be over.

Clint moved his hands after a time, but he didn't reach for me. He shut his eyes and then took a deep breath. "Lilith was the first," he said.

"The first what?" Leo asked. "What is going on here, Clarence? Why are you lying to us?"

"I'm not lying," Clint said. "I just don't feel the need to share every little thing with a criminal I barely know." He looked to me. "You know how I told you the Fallen were scattered to the four corners of Earth?"

I nodded. Naomi and the line cook were at the other end of the diner, chatting, and the two truckers paid up and left. We were as private as we were going to get.

"We didn't go willingly." Clint sighed. "When we left the King- dom, Hell was a barren place. No life, no light, nothing. It was a penal colony. There weren't many of us, not compared to the ranks who still believed."

"If you're going to tell me that a big angry sky man with a beard threw you into jail," Leo said, "please spare me. I don't believe and before that I was mostly raised by my very Jewish mother, so you're barking up the wrong tree."

"The Host rule the Kingdom," Clint said, narrowing his eyes. "Nine generals who give the orders. There's nothing higher than them, so you can relax."

"Okay, so you and your buddies had an argument with your bosses and you quit," Leo said. "Great. Why does this matter to Lilith?"

"Because we made them," Clint said quietly. "All of them."

"Demons?" I said. He nodded. He looked ashamed, like I'd just gotten him to admit Lilith was after him because he'd run her over and just kept driving.

"We needed help. Labor, companionship, a real chance at having a life, even if it wasn't the one we'd left in the Kingdom. So we each put our blood and our bone into a vessel. We mixed it with the earth of Hell and pooled our magic."

His words faltered, and Leo offered him a fifth of vodka from inside his jacket. I was starting to think Leo's ability to procure booze was his true magical skill.

Clint took a pull, screwing the cap back on with shaking fingers. A tanker rumbled by on the road outside and he practically flew out of the booth. Whatever he was telling us had him spooked, and that got *me* spooked. Leo had probably been right—I should have washed my hands of Clint back in Wyoming.

Too late for regrets now. I'd tried to jettison most of them when I died. If I didn't, they'd weigh me down until they crushed me.

Clint swallowed the vodka, made a face, and propped his elbow on the cracked plastic tabletop. "Lilith was the first. Then there were others. We intermarried, gave rise to hybrids, and then the demons bred with one another. Eventually . . . eventually there were hundreds of them for every one of us. There was violence . . . horrible things done to the Fallen, and to the demons as retribution. There were some Fallen who could never reconcile what we'd done to survive who believed they should be exterminated, and as for the demons . . ."

His voice was so low I could barely hear him, and his hands shook until he put them flat on the table. I waited, trying to be patient, but I felt like I'd leap out of my skin at the slightest sound. "They resented their very creation, and they attempted to crush us entirely. We Fallen found the deepest part of Hell. We decided we had to confine the demons there, for our own safety. But we'd been betrayed."

He went silent, and I traded a look with Leo. Clint had to see how creating a slave race and then shoving them into a hole in the ground when they got troublesome wasn't going to work out in his favor. I'd thought Hellspawn were arrogant, but the Fallen had them beat by a mile.

"They came for us," Clint said. "They tore us from our home. They created their own abominations, the reapers and the . . ." He trailed off, not looking at me.

"It's okay," I said. "I know I'm an abomination."

"When they took over, they used the Pit to contain the damned, the human souls the reapers collected," Clint said. "Hellspawn can't enter, and the damned can't leave. The spokes of Hell turn on the axle of the Pit, the power the damned emanate when they cross into Hell. The only place in Hell with light." He drew a deep breath. "The Fallen call it Tartarus."

"All right," Leo said, holding up his hands. "Look, story time is fun and all, but the fact that Lilith is pissed you people enslaved her is so far from mine or Ava's problem, it's in the next fucking state."

"I'm not finished," Clint growled. "Tartarus is sealed. Only a human soul can pass through the gates. If the gates ever opened, there would be chaos. And chaos is what Lilith loves more than life itself."

I expected Leo to roll his eyes or maybe just start laughing, but he'd gone silent. I looked between them. I knew enough to keep quiet and see which way the wind was blowing.

"Long after I was run out of Dodge, I started hearing rumors about human souls being recalled. Maybe two or three in all my time here. Necromancers who somehow found a way to breach the wall of Tartarus and bring dead people back."

Leo grunted. "Now I know this is bullshit. We don't bring souls back. Just bodies. A deadhead with a soul would be . . . well, it would be a real fuckin' freak, among other things."

I flinched. He wasn't talking about me, but he might as well have been. Aside from the fact that I had a pulse and breathed oxygen, that was me. I was a dead person with a soul hanging on to my body by a few tattered threads, just enough to give me the illusion of humanity until the hound came out.

I wanted to let it out just then, claw my way across Leo's lap, and take off across the scraggly forest of cottonwoods and long grasses that backed up to the diner. With the clarity that only the very wrong and the extremely screwed possess, I saw how stupid I'd been to think we had anything. Leaving aside his thing for redheads, I'd let myself think he was on my side, that we'd gotten along as well as the profoundly damaged could ever get along with anyone.

But fact was, I didn't like people and they didn't like me. That had worked for me for a hundred years, and just because a guy was tall and tattooed was no reason to chuck it in the trash.

"I imagine that reaper of Lilith's was helping her breach Tartarus," Clint said. "She always had a way of collecting the top shelf in psychopathic toadies around her." He'd stopped shaking, and his face looked less drawn. "How she'd do it, I don't know, but she sure seems to think it's possible."

"No wonder she came after me," I said. Abruptly, Leo jumped

up from his seat and ran out of the diner. Clint rubbed the back of his neck.

"What now?"

I followed Leo outside, trying to figure that out. He'd yanked my bag out of the cab and dumped the contents on the ground. "You okay?" I said, standing over him.

Leo held up Gary's ledger. "If your reaper really was hunting for necromancers who could bring a human soul out of Hell, then don't you think it'd be in here?"

"Why give it to me, then?" I said. Leo shrugged.

"She didn't think you were smart enough to figure it out. That's what happens when you start thinking you're too much of a badass to ever have anyone turn on you."

I leaned on the truck next to him. The sun was up and my skin warmed up for the first time in days. "Speaking from experience?"

"Never mistreat a man who has a reciprocating saw, bleach, and access to a junkyard," Leo said, flipping through the ledger. "All I'm saying."

I looked over at the Lexus. It was dusty, but even with a shattered window, ten times nicer than any car I'd ever owned. Five times nicer than most of the cars I stole. I thought about my Harley, how some crackhead was probably breaking it down for parts as I stood here, and sighed.

"You could just go, you know," Leo said. He didn't look up from the ledger. I shifted my weight so he couldn't see my face if he did.

"I get that you don't want me around, but I'm sticking with Clint. You can go. Take the car. I won't stop you."

Leo shut the book then, folding it into his arms. "That's not what I meant."

"Why?" I spat. "I'm just a freak with a soul stuffed inside a dead body. You think I don't know that?"

"Oh, Jesus." Leo sighed and tossed the ledger back on the passenger seat. I looked at the toes of my boots. It was better than looking at Leo. If I actually made eye contact I was pretty sure I'd slap him. Or burst into tears. Neither would do wonders for my image as an inhuman, soulless freak badass.

Leo's hands slid over my shoulders, his fingers squeezing gently through my shirt. "Ava," he said softly. "What happened to you wasn't your fault. You might not be human anymore, but your soul isn't tainted like what Clarence was babbling about. You're still you."

He lifted my chin with the tips of his fingers. "You're strong."

I bit out a laugh, but it sounded like a bark. That was fitting. My throat was tight and my skin was hot, from more now than the steadily warming sun. My heart pounded against my ribs, and I felt my pulse race against the spot where Leo touched me. "I am so far from strong, Leo," I whispered. "You really know nothing about me."

"I know because I know myself," he said. "You think I don't know the signs? I grew up with a father who beat us so badly that one time I lied and told the social worker the hospital called that I got clipped by a cab playing in the street. When I was fourteen I walked in on my uncles cutting up a prostitute who'd OD'ed in their car with meat cleavers. They offered me twenty bucks to mop the blood off the floor of the cooler and I did it. My dad was only around once in a blue moon, and he used our apartment to stash suitcases full of cash in the bedroom closet. We were still constantly having our power cut off. I gave the twenty to my mom so she could buy groceries." He straightened up, working the kinks out of his spine like he was gearing up for a boxing match.

"I went back to my uncle's restaurant the next day, and kept going back. A couple years later a Mexican Mafia soldier named Pablo Cruz beat one of our girls when she was out in Bushwick buying coke. Nobody wanted to deal with him, so I loaded up a syringe with my mom's insulin and followed him onto an F train around rush hour. I even made sure to jab him in one of his tattoos to hide the injection mark."

Hearing Leo describe murdering something like he was ordering a pizza didn't bother me. I was sure Pablo Cruz, whatever his redeeming qualities, had it coming. After my time with Gary, I could say that people who ended up in the crosshairs of someone like Leo, or something like me, almost always had it coming.

Leo spread his hands. "I had a talent for it. I found out I could call conjuring out of blood when I touched a guy my uncles did in with a hammer. Blood everywhere, and the next thing I know half of the restaurant kitchen is on fire. I was seventeen. My father was a lot more interested in me after that, even if I was just one of seven bastards scattered all over the Triboroughs. He taught me how to make deadheads, conjure, set demon nets to keep Hellspawn out. I never wanted to be a warlock. I was happier being a cleaner, driving junkers out to the scrapyards in Jersey, putting the screws on guys when they wouldn't do what Sergei told them. But if I'd tried to back out, he'd have made sure I ended up in the trunk with those schmucks, so I dove in, and I was good at that too." He lit a cigarette and exhaled slowly. "Point is, I see the same look in your eyes I know is in mine. You do what you have to do to survive, and that's all anyone can do."

"I don't want to go," I lied. "I know Clint needs my help."

"Clint needs to grow a spine and stop pouting about some hair-pulling that went on a thousand years ago," Leo muttered. "You could get in that car right now and drive out of here. I wish you would. Knowing you made it out would make me happy."

I shook my head. "I can't leave," I said. That was only half true, I realized as I turned away from the Lexus and back to Clint's beater truck. But *I can't leave because I don't want to leave you* was a real conversation killer.

"I wouldn't know about anyone he deliberately conned into making a deal," I said, pointing at the ledger. "All we get is a name and a past-due date."

Leo flipped open the ledger to a page he'd dog-eared. The twisting scrawl of Gary's handwriting made my head hurt. "This guy might be a candidate," he said. "Gregor Grayson. Killed twenty-three women in an abandoned hospital on Long Island and raised them. Dead-heads wandering the halls, attacking people out on the road . . ."

"He was mine," I said. I remembered how cold it had been that day, too cold to even snow. Frozen grass crunched under my paws. "He wasn't afraid of me," I murmured. "Most of them are."

"Or a woman named Henritte LaSalle," Leo read from another page. "Necromancer who specialized in bringing back dead children for grieving parents . . . or robbing paupers' graves for corpses when the actual kid was too decomposed. She sounds like a real charmer. Collected June 1953 in—"

"Kansas City," I finished. She'd been a little woman whose neighbors called her Birdie when they gave me directions to her house. She'd filed her teeth and she bit the fuck out of my shoulder when I came for her. I still had a scar there, so faint you could only see it if I spent an hour or two in the sun. The poison in her soul had seeped into my skin, just enough to burn a faint impression that never faded away.

I cornered her in her spare bedroom, dressed up to look like a nursery. The little girl lying on the canopy bed was very dead, probably a couple of weeks gone, judging by the bloat and the black and green splotches on her skin.

I'd actually enjoyed collecting on Birdie LaSalle. She'd laughed at me, spat something in French I didn't quite get, and gurgled as she died, still trying to laugh at me.

"So we have two who apparently managed to raise an obscene number of deadheads, and it sure does sound like Birdie got the real deal back for those parents," Leo said. "I mean, if I went in expecting little Timmy and got *Dawn of the Dead,* I sure as hell would demand a refund."

"Okay, but it's a long way from there to opening the floodgates of Tartarus and releasing Grayson and Henritte and all the millions of other people the reapers sent there," I said. "I mean, Clint lived in the woods for thirty years. It only took Jack Torrance six months to lose his shit, and he had a wife and kid to keep him company."

"Lilith sure has a hard-on for him," Leo said. "If this is what she's doing, it makes sense. Off the one person you know who knows your secret."

"Also professional advice?" I said. Leo smiled.

"Someday we should have a few drinks and compare notes. I'll tell you about the government witness and the Serbian death squad leader. You can tell me how you handled working for Gary all those decades."

"Drinking, mostly," I said. I made a note to avoid telling Leo anything about my time as a hound if I could help it. Depressing the shit out of him wouldn't do either of us any good.

Leo paused on a fresh page. "Caleb Whitman," he said. "In 1922, New Orleans. A necromancer who bargained for the knowledge to contact Baron Samedi, the *loa* of the Underworld. Some bullshit about the blood moon, unhallowed ground, human sacrifice yada yada . . ."

He stopped talking, which I assumed was because the blood had drained from my face and I was white as any of the dead-heads called by the witches in Gary's ledger. "Ava, what's wrong?" he said, frowning at me.

I felt hands around my neck, or maybe it was just my air choking off, the heavy pressure that builds on your chest as you drown in your own blood. The dull pain you're glad for because it fades out the sharp, unbearable ache of a six-inch skinning knife between your third and fourth rib. The blackness came with it, crawling from the edges of my eyes like the world was burning, curling up at the edges and disintegrating into ash.

Leo gave me a hard shake. "Ava!" he snapped. "Stay with me."

I fell to the ground without realizing it. There was a terrible wheezing sound loud in my ears, and something slamming against my ribs from the inside as the weight got heavier and heavier, choking off my air entirely.

"You're having a panic attack," Leo said from down a long, twisting tunnel, his voice echoing tinnily above the blood rushing through my ears. "You need to breathe deep. Listen to my voice and don't think about anything else. I want you to look at me."

I tried, Leo's face hovering large as the moon in my limited tunnel of sight. His tattoos started to squirm across his skin, the stylized trio of skulls on his neck turning their empty eyes and rictus grins to stare at me.

I pitched violently away from Leo and threw up, mostly bile and the few sips of the horrible coffee. It burned my throat like I was vomiting bleach, but after a few seconds my heartbeat stopped punching me in the chest and the bands around my lungs let go.

"You're okay," Leo said. His voice was still faint, but no longer so far away I had no hope of reaching it. "You're okay," he repeated. He kept saying it like a mantra, lapsing into Russian. *"Ya zdes'. Ty v poryadke."*

I swiped the back of my hand across my face, and Leo ran his palm between my shoulder blades, the kind of slow stroke you used to calm a cat or a small child. "What was that?" he asked softly.

"Caleb Whitman," I whispered, suddenly as cold as if I was still out in the snow. I started to shake and couldn't stop, not even when I curled myself into a tight ball, knees pressing into my ribs so hard I was amazed they didn't crack. "Caleb Whitman is the man who murdered me."

⌐eo stared at me. I sighed, looking down at the page of Gary's
└─scrawl. "I don't like saying this, but Clint might be right," I said.

"You know something about this Caleb guy?" Leo said.

I bit my lip, bearing down until I tasted blood. It went against
everything I'd taught myself during my time as the hound. Don't
talk, don't tell secrets. Don't trust anyone, especially a human.
Never, ever let on you remembered your life before.

"The other hounds are lucky," I said. "They don't remember.
That's the way it should be."

I hit my fist against the side of the truck. A few flakes of rust
drifted to the ground but otherwise I didn't make much of a dent.
"He's who I was dreaming about," I whispered. "Caleb. He's always
what I dream about when I have a nightmare."

I paced a few steps away from Leo. It was easier to talk looking out at the broken-down stretch of road than into his face. "Caleb cut out my heart before the ritual even started. I was the pure soul he offered up. Except I guess I wasn't the right vintage for Baron Samedi, because the only Hellspawn who showed up was Gary."

"That's a letdown," Leo said.

"I always wondered why he picked me," I murmured. I ran my toe through the dust, drawing a jagged circle. I wished I could just keep walking until the diner was behind me. "I guess he was never there for me in the first place." Caleb had gone less than five years after I died. It seemed so anticlimactic.

I faced Leo again. He unlatched the tailgate of the pickup and sat down, gesturing at me. "Come here. You look pale."

He was being polite—I was sure I looked like shit, but my legs were starting to feel kind of watery talking about all of this crap again, so I levered myself onto the tailgate, letting my legs swing.

"I met him through a boy named Jasper James. They were best friends. Caleb was mixed, but nobody in our circle cared. In New Orleans back then, people looked the other way if you could halfway pass. Point is, Caleb's great-grandmother, Hepzibah Whitman, was a slave on a sugarcane plantation south of New Orleans. She was a *mambo*—a voodoo priestess. She healed people, delivered babies. She got them through all of the misery that their lives entailed."

I was shivering again, like I always did when I thought about the tale of Hepzibah. Caleb had told it to me at least a dozen times as we lay under the lazy fan bolted to the ceiling of his single room. It always made me feel cold, even when I was alive, and I'd curl closer to him no matter how hot it was outside, even at midnight. I thought he told it in the first place to get me closer. I didn't realize I was wrong until his blade was already between my ribs, tight and snug as part of my own body.

I dug my fingers into the tailgate until the beds of my nails turned white. "There was another woman on the plantation, Mama Eugenie. She was big and jolly and kind, but people whispered if you crossed her, she'd make you sick, make you hurt. Mama was a *bokor*, a priestess who works with both hands."

"Black voodoo is nasty shit," Leo said. "I've run into a few *bokors*. Nobody's idea of a good time."

"Animals started disappearing," I said. I could practically hear the echo of Caleb's voice. It always got soft at this part, like pressure building in a steam valve. "The master's prize horse, a stud he brought from Kentucky, disappeared into the swamp. Nobody cared in particular, because, you know, fuck those slave-owning assholes."

"Until it wasn't just animals disappearing," Leo said quietly. "It was children."

"Mama affected an exchange," I said. "A pure soul for access to the land the Baron guarded. I don't know what she was really dealing with—Hellspawn, probably. But Caleb was convinced he could open a door to the Underworld and all the Hellspawn's power would be his for the taking if he could just find the spot where Mama worked her voodoo."

"Moron," Leo muttered, lighting another smoke.

"Hepzibah told her daughter the story," I said. "The daughter was a freewoman and she wrote it all down. Caleb had the journal, with the words and everything else he needed. All he needed from Gary was the spot. He was never very good at negotiating, but he was real good at stabbing people in the back. Just his bad luck Gary collected before Caleb could finish what he was up to."

"Ava, in your opinion," Leo said, exhaling a cloud of blue smoke, "do you think Lilith is really capable?"

"Absolutely," I said, without even needing to think about it. Gary had almost certainly been helping her, the two of them snickering behind their hands at their plans to start an industrial-level panic both in Hell and here on Earth.

I started to tell Leo this, but the whine of engines up the highway drowned me out. I saw three black SUVs turn into the parking lot, tires fishtailing on the gravel and kicking up plumes of dust three times as high as the diner roof.

Leo threw down his cigarette and jumped to his feet. "Get inside," he said, grabbing me by the hand and yanking me along. The first SUV careened to a halt and the passenger door flew open, disgorging a tall man in a tracksuit and wraparound sunglasses. He held a machine gun low at his hip like an outlaw gunfighter.

Leo cleared the steps of the diner in one leap and bashed open the door with his shoulder. I threw myself after him. Naomi stared at us, frozen with a silver canister of milk shake mix in her hand.

"Get down!" I screamed as I flattened myself out on the sticky linoleum. Naomi ducked, the milk shake splashing on the floor. Clint dove out of our booth and Leo dropped down next to me. As he landed, the world above my head exploded.

The grimy row of windows looking out on the parking lot shattered. Glass rained down, stinging my hands and the back of my neck. Bullets passed straight over the counter and thudded into the metal wall in the kitchen, punching neat circles into the greasy refrigerator unit and the pantry shelves loaded with napkins, sacks of pancake mix, and industrial-size vats of lard.

Naomi was screaming. I could see her lying behind the cash register, her mouth a round black O of panic, holding her hands over her ears. Tears sent her mascara cutting sharp black rivers down her cheeks.

The hail of gunfire stopped for a few seconds and I craned my neck around the still-flapping front door. There were six men standing about ten feet away from the diner. The two I'd smashed up plus their friends. They had given up pretty easily, and clearly felt bad about how the situation had played out.

The four new guests to the party carried short machine guns, with folding stocks that let them sling easily under their zippered satin jackets. Two of them ejected their banana clips and slammed new ones home. I started to go up, make a run for the kitchen, where we had more cover, but Leo clamped his hand on my arm and shook his head. In another split second, the firing started again.

The noise wasn't so much sound anymore as it was a rumble where my body touched the floor. I covered my head and waited, trying to keep my breathing steady. I'd been shot at before, enough times that it didn't exactly shock me when it happened, but a hunting rifle was a lot different from a Kalashnikov. The good news was that the things carried only thirty rounds, and Sergei Karpov's attack dogs didn't act like they'd invested a lot of hours at the range.

When the bullets finally stopped flowing again, Leo nodded at me and we belly-crawled through the glass, shattered dishes, and puffs of stuffing from the inside of the booth cushions. Clint joined us behind the counter and I grabbed Naomi by the arm, pulling her along with me to the kitchen.

"Oh my god," she whispered, her voice blown out from screaming. "Oh my god, oh my god . . ."

"Listen," I said, squeezing her arm hard enough to leave a mark. "Those guys outside aren't here for you, but they'll kill everyone in here to avoid witnesses. In thirty seconds they're going to come in and mop up anyone left alive, so you don't want to be here, all right?"

Naomi nodded, trembling. "I've got a son," she choked out. "I just want to see him—"

"You have a car?" I said. She shook her head.

"Marcus has the car."

"Who's Marcus?" I said. She pointed past Leo and Clint to the line cook, lying on his side in a pool of blood. Two giant holes had been punched in his stained apron, spinning him around and knocking him to the ground.

"Take his keys and go into the walk-in," I said. "When we tell you it's safe, run to the car. After you run, go pick up your son. Get back on the road, drive until you run out of gas, and don't come back here. You'll be safe that way."

She was already shaking her head, so I gave her arm a yank. "This is the only way you live past the next few minutes, Naomi," I said. "Go get his keys."

The door to the diner banged open, and I heard the tentative crunch of glass under slow, careful footsteps. Naomi scrambled over and yanked a fob from Marcus's back pocket, scuttling to the walk-in and slamming the door.

Clint looked at Leo and me. "What the hell are we supposed to do?" he hissed.

Leo's tongue flicked in, out, like he was a serpent scenting the air. I saw the Leo Karpov I'd first met, the one with no expression and no emotion. The guy who'd shoot a banger full of insulin on the F train and mop up blood without letting it worry him any more than a spilled glass of wine.

I was glad. I needed that Leo right now. Clint's pupils were huge, and I could see his pulse throbbing in his neck. Fallen weren't bulletproof any more than I was, and for all I knew he didn't even heal quicker than the average human.

"Leonid, stand up and we don't gotta hurt anyone else," a voice called from over the counter. From the congested, nasally overtone I was guessing it was the guy I'd bounced off his steering wheel. "Your father just wants to talk with you. It was your decision to involve the monster."

"Is that you, Illya?" Leo called. A moment of silence and he shot me a look, gathering his legs under him. I cast around, looking for anything that I could use against a pissed-off thug with a machine gun.

"For some reason, Illya, I don't believe you," Leo called. "Probably because you still owe me fifty bucks from that Jets game." He climbed to his feet in one graceful motion, hands up. "That was three years ago, Illya. You should pay your debts."

Illya raised the machine gun. "Only reason you're alive is because you're the old man's son. Now you've pissed him off and that doesn't matter anymore. About fucking time, if you ask me."

Leo's mouth slid up on the left side into a bitter smile. "Nobody asked you."

I grabbed the pot out of the coffee machine and swung it as I stood up, smashing it into the side of Illya's head while he stared at Leo. The carafe didn't break, but scalding coffee went all over

Illya's face and neck, turning his shirt brown like he was covered in old blood. Illya screamed and swiped at his face as blisters broke out, and Leo lunged for his machine gun, using the strap to yank Illya in and slam his face once, twice, three times into the counter. Illya collapsed, and Leo pulled him over the counter, taking his pistol from his waistband and tossing the machine gun aside.

"It'll be all five now," he said. He checked the pistol's clip. "Four bullets. Illya is such a fucking sack."

"We're rats in a trap," Clint said. "This is a firing corridor, and we have no way out."

"Chill out," Leo snapped. "I'm sorry if this reminds you of your time on the beaches of Normandy or whatever, but we're going to be fine."

I heard the door swing open again and looked over my head. The windows were completely punched out from the bullets. The frames were mouths of jagged glass shards, but I could make it. Adrenaline made everything slow and almost methodical. Against things like Lilith I was an ant, sure. Against a group of guys with guns and bad haircuts was another story.

"How many can you get?" I whispered to Leo. He thought for a second and then yanked a propane tank attached to the cook top away from its mount. I heard the gentle hiss of gas as he spun the valve open.

"Duck," I said to Clint, and stood up.

Leo rolled the tank out from behind the counter as I ran for the broken window. A bullet passed so close I felt it tear a furrow out of my jacket, cool air kissing the back of my neck and ruffling my hair.

I gathered my legs and leaped, letting go of my hold on the hound. I'd been crawling out of my skin ever since the shooting started, desperate to be in the form where I knew I was strongest and most vicious.

Glass slashed my palm, but by the time I landed on the gravel it was nothing, just a cut between my front toes that stung but didn't stop me.

Leo fired into the propane tank, which exploded and flung two of the thugs backward into the wall of the diner. The three who'd been outside the door still fell backward. One lost his grip on his gun, so I lunged for the one who was still armed, clamping my teeth around his wrist and bit down until I felt bone crack.

Screaming, he swatted at me with his free hand, but I didn't let go, shaking his arm back and forth until the joint moved freely, broken and useless.

The other guy scrabbled in the dirt for his pistol, but I planted my front paw on it, bared my teeth, and growled, "I don't fucking think so."

He backed up, hightailed it to one of the SUVs, and sped out of the lot, swerving over the center line of the highway. In ten seconds, the SUV was a black dot in the distance.

I padded over to the other two thugs and nudged them with my nose. One was alive—he smelled like sweat and I tasted the sour penny tang of blood when I inhaled. There was a deep gash in his neck from the exploding propane tank and he gurgled when he breathed. I stepped over him. There wasn't anything I could do. The other was dead already, cold and still, cloudy eyes staring back into the diner, where Leo tossed Illya's gun aside and Clint cautiously stood up from behind the counter. He stared at me, not blinking. I wanted to ask him what he was looking at—it wasn't like he'd never seen a hellhound before, surely.

"Can you change back?" he said. "I don't think Naomi needs to see this."

I felt stupid letting the thrill of attacking the three men subsume the human side of me, and I inhaled and opened my eyes to color and an eye line that roughly matched up with the bullet holes in the kitchen walls.

Clint knocked on the walk-in and got Naomi out the back door. "Don't look behind you," he said in a soothing tone. "That wouldn't be good news for anyone."

"Look who's the white knight all of a sudden," Leo muttered to me. Clint turned back to us.

"Just because I abhor violence doesn't mean I'm some kind of inferior species," he said. "I've seen a lot more of it than you have, and after a while you lose your taste for it." He reached down and gently rolled Marcus onto his back, closing his eyes. "Unless you're a psychopath, of course."

Leo, conversely, patted down Illya for his car keys and twirled them around his finger. "We need to go. Even in Bumfuck, Nowhere, the cops will eventually show up for a shootout, explosion, and animal attack."

Clint hesitated, and Leo snapped his fingers. "Hey. Unless you want to explain all of this from a jail cell, alone, and then sit back and wait for Lilith, get moving, Clarence."

Clint did as he was told, and Leo followed him, but stopped by the guy with the broken arm. He looked at me and tilted his head. "Give me a hand?"

I grabbed the guy by his good arm and helped Leo haul him to his feet. Clint watched us like he thought we might just dump the Russian headfirst into the fryolator, but Leo popped the trunk and dumped him in. The guy landed on his broken arm and let out a hoarse scream.

He'd landed next to a black canvas bag and Leo rooted around in it, pulling out a roll of duct tape and a handful of zip ties. "What's your name?" he asked the guy.

Tears squeezed from the Russian's eyes, and his chest rose and fell rapidly. His eyes were glassy and unfocused. I sighed and took the tape and the ties out of Leo's hands.

"Hey," he said. "I don't know if you've been paying attention but this is kind of my wheelhouse."

"He's in shock," I said. I snapped my fingers in the thug's face and he flinched. "I'm going to tie you up and tape your mouth. If you behave I'll be a good Girl Scout and make sure you live long enough to get that arm reset. It'll probably always hurt when it's cold and the steel pins will set off metal detectors, but you won't bleed out in the back of a car or go septic on your way to the ER. Sound good?"

He blinked once. His breathing was shallow, but his arm wasn't bleeding too badly. Deep punctures hurt like a bitch, but unless I'd hit a major vein he'd live. I tied his hand in front to take pressure off his arm, doubled up the ties on his feet, and pressed tape over his mouth. I turned to Leo. "See if you can find a blanket."

He came back with a rough furniture blanket from the other SUV, and I wrapped the Russian in it. "Let's go," Leo said. "I could do without getting arrested in the beautiful heartland of our great country."

I let Leo drive without any arguments. My palm had a long gash in it, and thin rivulets of blood ran down my wrist and soaked the cuff of my shirt. I found some napkins in the glove compartment and pressed them into the cut. I ran my tongue over the inside of my teeth. The taste of blood starts off as metallic, almost sickeningly so, like chewing on a handful of dirty pennies, but then it starts to taste stale and a little rotten, like a bad cut of meat. I rooted in the glove box more, hoping the previous owners had stashed some mints or even a flask, but there was nothing.

"Do we need to be worried about your father?" Clint asked from the backseat. "I mean, that was not a proportionate response to us figuring out we had a tail."

"That was just Illya being a shit stain," Leo said. "He got pissed Ava humiliated him and he came back swinging. It won't happen again."

We drove for another twenty miles or so in silence. Normally I was good with silence. I'd gotten used to it over the years. Silence meant nobody was paying attention to me, trying to pry into my business or my secrets.

Now, though, my hand wouldn't stop bleeding and I could feel Clint's eyes on the back of my neck. A rest stop sign flashed on the left and I tapped Leo on the arm. "Pull over."

"I don't think . . ." Clint started, and I growled at him.

"I said pull over."

Leo parked under a tree at the rest stop and I got out, pacing away from them to a picnic table set down a slope by a small stream almost choked off with weeds. The leaves were starting to turn, giving the barest hint of the frozen tundra that this place would be in a few months. I tossed the wad of bloody napkins into a trash can and put my elbows on my knees. It always took me a few hours to come back to myself after the hound. Last time I'd been so beat up and exhausted I'd just passed out while Leo drove us through Nevada, but I didn't have that luxury now.

Clint sat down next to me and looked at my hand, hissing between his teeth. "That needs to be stitched."

"I'll be fine in an hour or so," I said. "Hell builds us tough."

Clint looked down at the river. "Sorry I can't just heal you. Laying on of hands was never my thing."

"It's not really anyone's thing," I said. "Collected more than a few faith healers for Gary."

"I used to do something like what you did," Clint murmured. "I'd track down the wicked and return them to the Kingdom."

"So you were an angelic assassin," I said. "Having your mojo gone must be a serious case of blue balls."

Clint coughed, and I hoped he'd just go away, contemplate the beauty of a blade of grass or whatever it was ex-angels did with their free time.

"It was hard to accept, yes," he said. "I'll never age or change, but that doesn't do much good against bullets. I can't snatch them out of the air or stop time. I can't even heal myself."

"How'd you do it?" I said. "When everything imploded and your life became a steaming pile of shit? How'd you pick up and go on?"

"I joined what I thought were worthy causes but in retrospect were just a series of pointless, bloody wars," he said. "Then I picked out a new hiding place every twenty years or so. At first there were a lot of Hellspawn after me and the others. They wanted to do to us what we tried to do to them. Lilith is just the most tenacious."

Leo came striding from the car, looking pissed. If I were him I'd want to be moving too, but this was it. I'd come as far as I knew how to go. Nobody was going to give me an order, send me off to my next job. I could choose any road I wanted for the first time in a century and I was so overwhelmed all I could do was sit on a splintery picnic table carved with teenage couples' initials and no less than six crude interpretations of somebody's penis. If there was a level ten stories below ground from pathetic, I was probably there.

"We should keep driving," he said. "If we're moving it'll at least be harder for my father to figure out where we're going."

"Nowhere," Clint said. "We can keep trying to run from your father—who, I'd point out, is a powerful and well-connected head of a major crime outfit—but that doesn't change the fact that Lilith is probably pointing her broomstick at me this very second."

Leo's jaw ticked. "Fine. Sit here and wait to die if you want. I'm going."

"Those are the choices, yes," Clint muttered.

I stood up, walking toward the river. Up close, it was filthy, full of rusty beer cans and tattered plastic bags, the detritus of people who had come and then moved on in a handful of minutes. I'd have sat here on my Harley and not given the river or any of this a second thought. Just a pause, a small pinprick in the map between one collection and the next. Gary always in my ear, telling me where to go and who to kill.

Leo and Clint were still bickering. I could tell from their body language, torsos bending toward each other, Leo's arms tight while Clint was gesturing at himself, at me. I turned and walked back up the hill to them.

"Listen, you do what you like," Leo was saying. "Stay here, set up a tent, run for your life, whatever. But I'm moving on. It's the only option."

"It's not," I said. My palm, covered in dried blood, itched, but the bleeding had stopped. Soon the skin would knit and it would be like it had never happened. A few days ago, I would have been happy to forget. I liked that things blurred together like ink from a cheap pen. It made it easier to forget what I'd have to do again, and again, and again, every time Gary or someone like him snapped their fingers.

"Fine," Clint said. "We're all ears."

I curled my fingers over my palm, hiding the blood and the healing gash. "There's something we can do besides lie down and die here, or run from Sergei's boys and die later."

Leo raised one eyebrow. "And what's that?"

I drew in a deep breath, then let it out. I wasn't moving to the next spot down the road. This was it. There was no voice in my head except my own. I tried hard not to let that fact terrify me when I spoke.

"We can kill Lilith."

CHAPTER

20

|||||||||||||||||||||||||||||||||||||||||||||||||||||||||||||||||||||||||||||

Leo and Clint both gave me a long stare. "How do you propose we do that?" Clint said finally. "The Fallen had a hard time exterminating demons when they turned on us, and we certainly weren't powerless in Hell."

"Gary's Scythe," I said, mostly to Leo. He looked back at the dusty SUV.

"My father is not going to give it to you as a loaner."

"I didn't think so," I said. "A reaper's Scythe can kill anyone. Anything. If I get it and get close to Lilith, I'll put it right into her heart."

"How are you going to make Sergei give it to you?" Leo said. "Neither of us are his favorite person right now."

I hadn't really gotten that far with the idea yet. I was still back on the part where I stabbed Lilith repeatedly with the Scythe for what she'd put me through.

"Never mind my father, Lilith's not going to let you anywhere near her," Leo said. "She's clearly not stupid."

"Neither am I," I said, chafing a little at his skepticism. I'd expected pushback from Clint. Leo was supposed to stick with me. "She's not stupid, but she's greedy. I'll offer myself and the Scythe up. If she thinks she can get something from me—or even torment me—then I have a chance."

"Pretending for a second I don't think this is bullshit," Leo said, "how would Lilith even go about opening Tartarus from here? I've seen enough dumb warlocks have conjuring explode in their faces to know the wall between us is unbreakable."

Clint sighed, and I sincerely hoped he wasn't about to tell us another creepy story about demon eugenics. "When the Fallen were banished, many died in the crossing from Hell. Reapers and hellhounds and the like can cross over easily, Fallen less so. Imagine jumping from one roof to the next. If you slip and fall, you crash into the alley and snap your neck. Hellspawn have the hardest time crossing over. That's why they mostly stay down in Hell and let people like you do their grunt work."

"That or they're just lazy," I grumbled. "Gary sure didn't stir himself unless he had to."

"There was talk when we were banished from the Kingdom of conduits between our worlds," Clint said. "Crossroads spanning Hell, here, everywhere. But no one has been able to find them again. That's why demons needed emissaries with one foot planted here, to enable them to slip in and out of the cracks."

"Interesting as these fantasies of yours are," Leo interrupted, "if Lilith does somehow find a crossroads back to Tartarus and we show up for the party, it won't be with a reaper's Scythe. My father is even less warm and fuzzy than she is."

"If you want to live beyond the next few days you need your father out of commission," I told Leo quietly. "Otherwise you'll never stop looking over your shoulder, no matter where you go."

"I can't just kill my father," Leo grumbled. "Not only is he guarded better than a head of state, the other *vor* will ice me as fast as they can to swoop in on his territory. Russians clean house—no spouses, no kids, no family who could interfere left standing."

"I'm not talking about killing him," I said. "That's your deal. I just want him to give back what he stole from you."

Leo gave a bitter laugh. "Good luck with that."

"You're a tough guy, Leo," I said. "A scary guy. I don't get the feeling there's much on this earth that can rattle you. So why are you so afraid of your father?"

Leo pointed at me. "You want to be careful what you say right now. Just because we're road trip buddies doesn't mean you know me."

I took him by the elbow. Touching him was risky—he could haul off and slap me, like all the other macho gangsters I'd known, or just flatten me with a hex, like most of the alpha male warlocks I'd spent more than a few minutes with.

Leo grunted but didn't pull away. "You gave me a gift, Leo," I said quietly. "You set me free. Let me do the same thing for you." I tugged him back to me when he turned away. "When are you ever going to have a hellhound on your side again?"

"Sergei's survived a long time, and if you think I'm bad, he's ten times worse," Leo said. "He taught me everything I know, Ava.

Just because you turn into a big scary dog on command doesn't mean you can toe up to him."

"Let me worry about that," I said, and patted him on the shoulder. I walked to the SUV and opened the back, sitting next to the guy we'd grabbed. "If I take that tape off are you going to scream?"

He shook his head wearily, and I ripped it off. He yelped and then groaned, his forehead creasing. "You bitch. My arm hurts like hell."

"What's your name?" I said. He was young, without the gun and the tape on his face. He barely even had any smile lines, and I didn't see any ink on his neck or his hands. That was good. I could work with that.

"Tom," he said.

"Tom, really?" I leaned in. "Not Alexi or Nikolai or something?"

"If you're going to kill me I wish you'd just shut up and do it," he muttered. I shook my head.

"I need you to call Sergei Karpov and tell him his son wants to meet."

Tom laughed. It was more of a cough and a groan mingled together, but I took it in the spirit in which it was intended. "The only way Sergei wants his son is in a bunch of pieces in a bunch of different garbage bags, scattered randomly in landfills across the greater Reno-Sparks area."

"I get it," I said. "But I want you to call anyway."

He started to object and I reached out and flicked his wounded arm with my index finger. "Humor me, Tom. We've both had a long day."

Tom let out a soft scream. Sweat beaded on his forehead, but he nodded at his chest. "Cell phone's in my pocket."

I pressed the number in Tom's contacts and listened to him speak Russian for a few seconds. Leo was going to be pissed at me, but this was the only way I could think of to get Sergei out of his hidey-hole in Vegas and to a spot where I'd actually have a chance if things went bad.

Tom listened. There was a lot of yelling coming out of the phone, and he flinched. "He wants to talk to Leonid."

I put the phone to my ear. "Is that you, Sergei?"

"I don't know who you think you are . . ." he growled.

"I'm the girl who's saving your ass," I said. "You want to meet with us, Sergei, trust me. Leave the hardware at home and hear what we have to say. This doesn't have to be a war for you, Sergei. Hell, you might even end up with all your fingers and toes and earlobes right where they belong."

"I'm going to find you, dog, and I'm going to skin you," he hissed. "You're going to be a rug in my walk-in closet when I'm done."

I swallowed. My throat was dry, not because I was afraid for myself but because I didn't want to fuck Leo over if Sergei didn't go for this. "Wouldn't you rather have me alive and willing to do you a favor?"

There was a long silence on the other end. "I'm listening," he ground out at last.

"You've got other warlocks," I said. "Other cleaners. It's a simple trade. Me for Leonid."

Another period of quiet while the line hissed. "You fuck me, and I'll fuck you so hard your ancestors will be walking funny," Sergei said.

Leo came up the hill, and I punched MUTE. "Text me a location,"

I told Sergei. "A public place with a crowd. And speaking of fucking, if I walk into an ambush I'm taking every one of you vodka-scented bastards down to Hell with me. You know I can." Leo was almost in earshot, and I held the phone up to my mouth. "This is not a bluff. Ignore me and get fucked right in the ass."

I pressed END and tossed the phone back in the SUV with Tom. Leo cocked his head.

"What was that?"

"Don't flip your shit," I said, "but I got a meet with Sergei."

Leo proceeded to do exactly the opposite of what I'd asked, punching the car so hard a dent blossomed. "Are you fucking kidding me?" he shouted. "Who asked you to do that?"

"I know it's a lot, but I'm asking you to trust me," I said. "Just for a few more hours." I waited. He could hit me or choke me, or decide he'd had enough and shoot me. I'd gotten all of those reactions from various humans at various times. Would I get the reasonable Leo, the one who'd carefully stitched up my arm in that horrible motel? Or would I get the Leo who'd tried to torture me into doing what he wanted, the one Sergei had worked so hard to create in his own image?

"I don't want to hear another fucking word about my father," Leo growled finally. Minus the accent, he and Sergei sounded a lot alike. "Let's just get busy killing ourselves, because that's all this is. A fucking suicide pact with you, me, and Speedy over there."

"You don't have to do this," I said again. Leo sighed.

"I do. Because if I don't stick with you two, I'm just gonna be another set of spare parts in the Clark County landfill. Always kind of figured that's how I'd end up, but you went and convinced me I might be wrong, so this is your fault."

Tom's phone buzzed with a text and I picked it up. An unlisted number said:

PROMENADE, RENO. 11 PM.

"You want to drive?" I asked Leo. He pointed at Tom.

"We should probably offload the extra bags first," he said. Tom started whipping his head back and forth.

"Hey, I helped you! She said I'd be okay if I helped you! I know what you do, man. I don't want any part of that."

"Then here's a tip," Leo said, grabbing him by his jacket and yanking him out of the SUV. "Stop role-playing that you're a tough guy and go back to your job at the Circle K. You are not cut out for a life beyond a name tag and a polo shirt."

Leo pulled out his pocketknife and cut the zip ties on Tom's feet, then set him upright. He dialed 911 on the cell and dropped it on the pavement. "If I see you again, I'll cut your fucking eyes out," he said, and got into the driver's seat.

I climbed in as Leo laid on the horn for Clint, and we peeled out of the rest stop, getting back on the interstate and moving into the west once again.

CHAPTER

21

Leo and I traded off driving through the day and beyond sunset, following the red streaks in the sky. We were on the downswing of the mountains that led us through Sparks and into the city center of Reno. In another few minutes we'd see the neon of the casinos spiking off the desert floor like enormous plants that only flowered at night.

Clint had mostly stayed quiet, as had I. If I'd wanted to be chatty I could roll out the anecdotes about remember when Reno was just a faded boom town, barely a bump in the horizon. It was flat and brown and the Truckee River put off a distinctive aroma in whichever direction the wind was blowing.

I could talk about going to places like the Bank Club and Harrah's, sitting at one of the bars and watching people come and go. I could put on a dress and pumps and tease my hair higher than any of them, but there was still a wall of glass between myself and humanity. Only the bad ones seemed able to see through to me, while most people's eyes glided right past.

I could tell Leo about Sal Peretti, the man who'd taught me most everything I knew about dealing with men like him. Sal was probably as bad as they came, Leo with better manners and a nicer suit. He was handsome according to the criteria back then, which ran more to a thick head of hair and a fancy watch than symmetrical features or quality dentistry.

Sal wasn't ugly or missing teeth, though. He was an ex-boxer with a nose that broke well, making his face crooked but not ruined. The slightly jarred bones of his face made you want to keep looking, not avoid it. He had warm, honest brown eyes and a radiant, perfect smile that could melt the panties right off most any woman who crossed his path.

It was total bullshit. Sal had gone from boxer to fight promoter to crooked fight promoter who bullied black and Mexican fighters into taking a dive against whatever mediocre prospect his friends were betting on, with sidelines in loan-sharking and whoring. His management style ran to torched buildings and broken bones, and he'd never met a friend he wouldn't put a bullet in to make another dollar. A lot of people would have liked to see Sal cold on a slab, but he was too mean to die.

He drank and he screamed, but he didn't hit me. He would talk to me when he was feeling small and maudlin, and explain in excruciating detail how he did his business.

I asked him how he knew I wouldn't roll on him the minute I got pinched by the local cops, most of whom were either so old they remembered when gambling was illegal or guys who'd just gotten back from the war in Europe and were looking to crack skulls or make a few bucks turning the other cheek.

Sal told me he knew when to trust people by their eyes. People who looked at you straight on didn't have any fear. If they weren't afraid of him, Sal reasoned, they sure as hell weren't going to be afraid of the cops.

Sal's mom got sick, and suddenly his small-time grifts weren't enough to pay her bills and keep him in twenty-dollar shirts, a Cadillac, and steak dinners every night of the week. The money he was supposed to kick back up the chain stopped getting kicked anywhere except his habits. Two cars caught him on the road outside Sparks and punched enough holes in the Caddy that you could have turned it on its end and called it a cheese grater. Sal's friend's bosses, the men from the outfit in Detroit or Chicago—I never did find out which—knew what to do with desert-rat thieves.

In the end Sal's most valuable lesson was the one I got when I saw him lying quietly on the white table in the morgue, a sheet covering him to his neck. One of the bullets had gone in under his cheekbone and exited behind his ear. The hole was puckered and blackened from the heat of the bullet. No matter how smart you were and how little fear you had, there was always somebody out there waiting to put you down if you stepped out of line.

The next time Gary called on me, I didn't try to avoid him. I pawned all the stuff Sal had given me, bought a bus ticket to Omaha, and went back to work.

I didn't stop seeing Sal's face for a long time when I shut my eyes.

"I think I should be the one to talk to your father," I told Leo. He gripped the wheel until his knuckles were white.

"I think you're absolutely fucking nuts to suggest that."

I fell back on something Sal had told me. "You and he have a past. We don't have guys, so we need him off balance. If he sees just me, he won't know what's going on."

"Sergei tends to shoot at things he doesn't understand," Leo said. "Fair warning."

We parked in one of the garages at Circus Circus and left Clint with the car in case we needed to bolt quickly. Leo and I cut through the casinos, his eyes sweeping every face we passed. I kept a watch behind us, but nobody seemed to be taking any notice of me, which was normal. About every third woman and a few men gave Leo a smile or a wink, which also seemed pretty normal. Even after close to seventy years, the tang of stale smoke and the clank of the machines in the main casino were exactly the same as I remembered from my nights with Sal. All of those old casinos were gone, of course. The monoliths you could see from the highway were built on their corpses.

Leo stopped me with a hand on my arm and pointed toward a bathroom when we reached the lobby. "Come with me a second," he said. I raised one eyebrow.

"Is this some cheap line, Karpov?"

"My lines are never cheap, and I never need them," he said. "I just want to ask you something, in case I don't get the chance again."

The bathroom was quiet, dimly lit, almost like they wanted people getting up to no good in there. Leo and I stepped into the handicapped stall and he turned the lock. "I'm trusting you not to fuck this up," he said. He took his pocketknife from his jeans and flipped the blade open. "You trust me?"

Of course I shouldn't trust him. Not to put a blade against my skin. I'd learned a long time ago that trusting anyone with your life just made you that much more likely to lose it.

I nodded, and Leo took my arm and laid the blade against it. "Don't get freaked out."

I held still, against every instinct and bit of experience I'd collected in my time as a hound. Much like when I'd seen Veronica smile down at Leo in her bed, it was like everything I relied on to keep me going, help me survive, just switched off and something I didn't recognize took control.

Leo turned the blade so the point rested against my skin. "I don't know if this will work on you. I've never tried it on Hell-spawn before."

I barely felt it when the blade parted my skin and a thick line of dark blood welled. Leo let it dribble into his cupped palm. "Take your shirt off."

I raised an eyebrow. "This is not how I imagined this going."

Leo's mouth lifted on one side. "So you have imagined it."

I pulled off my jacket and overshirt and stood there in just my bra, feeling like I really was naked in the dim light. All of my scars and bruises showed up in sharp relief, and I tried not to cross my arms over my torso. I must look like Frankenstein's monster to a guy who was probably used to high-end Soviet Bloc hookers. Or at the very least, women who didn't look like they'd been cage fighting.

Leo didn't say anything or even look at my body. He dipped his fingers in my blood, then traced a quick mark on my breastbone over my heart. Warmth radiated from it, like the last vestiges of a sunburn, and I watched it fade until my skin was plain and pale once again.

"It's not foolproof, but it should keep your ass out of the line of fire if Sergei tries anything with blood conjuring. Bullets and blades, you're on your own."

"I've never had a warlock try to help me," I muttered. "Usually they just sling conjuring when they're running for their lives."

"As I no doubt will if I piss you off," Leo said. "You sure you want to do this? You look wrecked."

I tried not to take it personally. I wasn't pretty, because I wasn't human, and it didn't matter if I looked like a movie actress or a street corner bag lady. Leo didn't think of me in those terms. "I'm fine," I said. "Let's get this over with so we can both hopefully get to the next sunrise."

"I'll be watching," Leo said.

I stepped out into the night by myself. It was chilly—Reno in October wasn't exactly a desert paradise—but that didn't stop a parade of scantily clad women from stumbling along the sidewalk, or a trio of guys with ugly shirts open to their navels from checking them out.

I turned right and walked up the promenade, under the neon arch, the one all the tourists ran into the street to take pictures of, proclaiming that Reno was THE BIGGEST LITTLE CITY IN THE WORLD. The light changed at the intersection, and as I stopped in a crowd of early drunks stumbling back to their hotels and late partiers just heading out, someone gripped my elbow.

"Don't turn your head," a young voice instructed. "Walk forward." He pushed me into the street as the stoplight went from green to yellow. A cab swerved and laid on its horn. I slid my eyes up to the guy's profile. He was stocky and lumpy, head shaved close like a professional fighter. Once he was satisfied I wasn't being tailed, he let go of my arm and pointed up the block. "Mr. Karpov is waiting."

I saw the short figure smoking under the marquee of the Eldorado, the same intense gaze as Leo watching me over the burning end of his cigarette. I stopped next to him, putting my back to the dingy cement wall under the marquee. Above us, neon triangles of red and pink and gold flashed, the sparkling letters of the casino signs lighting and blinking, always leaving Sergei's face in shadow.

"You cost me a couple of good men," he said at last. Even though the street was loud, cars and people and music combining into a roar of white noise, I heard him perfectly.

"I don't like being shot at," I said, shrugging. Sergei flicked his butt into the street and glared at me.

"You should have let me take my useless son. Where is he? I don't deal with women or dogs."

"You're gonna deal with both if you want to keep sucking air," I said. Sal would have already bounced this guy's head off the brick, but I made myself act calm.

Sergei chuckled. "Little puppy, I live in a mansion. State-of-the-art security. I have a man with me at all times with a Heckler and Koch machine gun in his hands. I sleep with a six-inch blade in my hand. Tell me how exactly you are a threat to me."

"You came and met me on the street, for starters," I said. I took one step closer to him, got in his personal space to let him know I wasn't afraid. "Your boy didn't search me. I could have a blade of my own. I could cut your femoral artery and walk away. You'd be dead in thirty seconds, right here on this sidewalk."

Sergei laughed harder. It turned into a wet cough, and he dabbed at his lips with a handkerchief. "There is a rifle trained on you right now. If you move any closer you will get a bullet between your eyes. I pay for the best—ex-FSB snipers and soldiers."

I took a respectful step back. I didn't need to get a shot between the eyes before I'd even made my pitch. "That doesn't mean jack shit to Lilith."

Sergei cocked his head. "Who is this?"

"You know who she is," I said. "That Scythe you stole? Belonged to her reaper. She already made a promise to me to deal with you."

Sergei spread his hands. "So where is she? Why am I not speaking to her?"

"Because if she was this close to you she'd have already ripped your jaw off," I said. "I didn't kill Gary just to get another Hellspawn boss. You give me the Scythe and I'll get rid of her. What you do with it after that is none of my business."

Sergei sighed. "You're funny, puppy. I should just turn the Scythe over to you? Maybe I already sold it to the highest bidder."

"You're a small-timer who had to leave the East Coast," I said flatly. "I'm guessing you pissed somebody in Brighton Beach off good. You got the Scythe to put yourself on top," I continued. "I'm guessing you have it on you, because you know the kinds of things after it aren't flustered by guards and wall safes." I held out my hand. "Give it to me and both of our problems go away. You can dress up like Marlon Brando and act out *The Godfather* for all I care. I want Lilith dead, and if you had any brains you would too. I'm guessing you don't, though. Leo seems like he's the one who can actually think things through."

His lip drew back and I stood very still. He'd either kill me or agree. There was nothing more to say.

"So I give you my Scythe—and what will you do for me?" He stepped in, smiling at me. His teeth were straight but brown, stained from decades of cigarettes and strong Russian tea. "I'm not about bestiality, so you better have something to offer me beside your whore's body."

"I can't imagine why your son has a problem with you," I said. "I told you on the phone—if you help me, I'll help you. Hellhounds are useful. More useful than pissing off a demon, that's for sure."

"You have no reaper," Sergei sneered. "No power, and neither does my useless bastard son. If he did, I would be dead, not dealing with my son's woman."

"I'm not your son's anything," I said. "I'm trying to avoid a fight, Sergei. I'm going to get the Scythe from you. You haven't been able to kill me yet and you're not going to. How many hellhounds have you put down?"

He grunted. My heart was thudding. Sergei scared me, of course. Violent, unpredictable humans were frightening, and if a Hellspawn like me didn't admit that, then she was lying. But that didn't mean I'd show it.

"You know how many warlocks just like you I've delivered to my reaper?" I said. "So many I've lost count, Sergei. If I put my mind to it, you'll be dead and I'll still get the Scythe. I'm doing this so Leo doesn't have to spend his life looking over his shoulder."

I took another step back. "You have ten seconds to make a choice and then I'm walking." I counted to ten while he stared at me, the skin around his nostrils going white with rage, and then I turned and started back to the corner, the marquee lighting up the night around me. I waited for a bullet in the back, but it didn't come.

"Wait," Sergei said. He gestured back at the casino. "Let's have a drink, you and I."

Leo would be furious I'd gone somewhere alone with Sergei, but I just nodded and followed him into the Eldorado, past the craps tables, through a plain door marked EMPLOYEES ONLY, down a flight of stairs to a drab corporate office. Sergei sat behind the desk and extracted a bottle of good whiskey from a drawer.

"Why do you not sit down?" He glared at me as he poured. "We are doing business."

"No offense, but I don't trust you further than my hand in front of my face," I said. Sergei grunted.

"Drink," he said.

"Show me the Scythe," I said. He took a flat pouch from inside his jacket and held it out. I accept it, recognizing the weight of the Scythe immediately. It prickled the skin over my whole body, the Hellspawn magic radiating like plutonium into the night air.

Sergei snatched it back, sticking it back inside his jacket. "You will do what I ask, no questions. You will come when I call, you will never tell me no. Like a good dog. Or I will put you down."

"Fair enough," I said. I had no intention of honoring my agreement with Sergei. I was just saying whatever I had to so he'd give me the Scythe. I thought he might suspect, but we both had too much to lose by not going along. Even the possibility of having his very own hellhound had to be getting Sergei hard. Me, I just wanted to survive, and I wasn't above lying my ass off to do it.

Sergei shoved the glass at me. "No deal unless we toast. It's the Russian way."

Every part of me was screaming I needed this drink, and I knocked it back in one swallow. Sergei watched me, fingers resting on the rim of his own glass.

As soon as the cold fire hit my stomach I knew I'd made a mistake. It didn't taste warm and woody like it should—it was bitter and thick, like the laudanum Jasper used to keep around for what ailed him, or when he just wanted to get good and fucked up.

Sergei stood up as I started to go down, the floor dropping out of the crappy office and spinning me sideways. "You fucker," I tried to say, but my tongue was thick and motionless.

"Don't worry," Sergei soothed, coming around the desk. "I will not kill you immediately. You will stand in for punishing my worthless son. After you've bled and screamed for him, perhaps you and I can renegotiate."

He reached out to stroke my face, and I thanked my lucky stars that I fell over before he could touch me, my limbs going every which way. Before my vision narrowed to a pinpoint and the lights blinked out, I saw Sergei laugh once, humorlessly. "Stupid bitch."

CHAPTER

22

|||||||||||||||||||||||||||||||||||||||||||||||||||||||||||||||||||||||||||||||||||||||||

I came to on the floor, staring at the spindly legs of an iron bed. A rag rug dug into my cheek, leaving deep furrows, and I smelled tobacco and turned earth and frying bacon.

"This isn't right," I groaned, or tried to. My mouth and throat were dry and sticky from the effects of whatever Sergei had dosed me with.

"Sure isn't," someone drawled from over my shoulder, in a voice as crispy as the hog fat I could hear sizzling in the pan.

I sat bolt upright, a skirt from a dress I hadn't owned in over a century twisting around my legs. "Maw-Maw?"

My grandmother hmphed, rocking in her squeaky chair as she lit a long black cigarillo. "Sure, honey. Who else would it be?"

A quick look around told me I was right; I was back in the cabin clinging to the side of the mountain above Bear Hollow. My hands were rough from pulling weeds and chopping wood, my legs were still skinny but tan instead of deathbed pale, and my hair was the long, wavy cloud it had been before I'd bobbed it to look more like a New Orleans lady and less like a hillbilly who was afraid of soap.

"You best get yourself right before Hattie or Uncle Joe sees you," my grandmother told me. "They knew you were out all night, you'd be hauled off to some snake-fucking preacher before you could say boo."

I held up my hands. "Wait a minute." This wasn't like any of my nightmares. I was myself, the Ava I'd left when I'd passed out in the casino. I was just stuck back in my old life, and apparently talking to my dead grandmother, who smirked as she looked me over.

I'd taken plenty of drugs, voluntarily or not, and some could sure make you see things, but not like this. Unless Sergei had put a heaping helping of peyote into that glass along with whatever knockout cocktail he'd used, this wasn't from the drugging.

"You got something to say to me?" my grandmother said, and something flat and black slithered across the surface of her gaze, like a pebble landing in a pond.

"Not to you," I said, levering myself up using the rusty bed frame. There used to be a razor in the bedside drawer, left by my father, kept like a tiny grave marker by my mother after he was gone. I grabbed it, yanking the blade open and turning in the same motion, grabbing my grandmother's faded housecoat and pressing the razor against her wrinkled neck.

"Stop trying to skullfuck me, *Lilith,*" I snarled. "It didn't work out so hot for you last time."

Whatever was using my memory of Maw-Maw's likeness as a

mask didn't flinch, didn't even blink. "You hear me?" I shouted, giving it a shake. The blade nicked the skin, and a dark trickle of blood started, filling my nostrils with the scent of dirty pennies.

"I'm not Lilith," it said. It put its hand against my chest, almost a tender gesture, and the next thing I knew I was across the room, the razor clattering to the floorboards beside me.

"What are you?" I wheezed, my chest burning. My ribs, just recently healed from the beating I'd taken at the hands of the shifters, went tender again where I'd hit the wall.

"I want to help," the thing said, standing and wiping at the cut on its neck with Maw-Maw's favorite rag, the blue flowered one she kept wrapped around her silver hair or tucked in her dress pocket. "The Scythe is only part of it, Ava. You need to do what you were put in Hell to do."

"I couldn't have less of a clue what you mean, and could not give less of a shit," I grumbled, feeling my ribs.

"Forget about revenge," the thing said. "Lilith has already found the crossroads. You need to find her."

It came toward me, and I scrambled back. Its eyes were all black now, and shadows crawled across the floor and up the walls, shadows that hissed and cried and blocked out the light so all I could see were those black pits of eyes.

"You need to stop hiding, Ava. Stop denying." It grabbed me by the chin and pulled us together, so close I could smell the sour tobacco on its breath, feel the furnace blast of it against my cheeks and chin. "And you need to wake up."

It pressed our lips together, and the shadows sprung from its body washed over us both, drowning me in darkness black and vast as the deepest ocean.

I felt myself fly back to waking and sat up, slamming my head hard into metal. Everything was still black, but now it smelled like motor oil and burning metal, and I could taste sweet plastic-y duct tape over my mouth.

Next to me, in the tiny confined space, another warm body rested. I felt the limits of our confinement. My hands were also taped. The space was just slightly bigger than I was. Corrugated metal walls, a rubber seal just above my head.

I prodded at the form next to me, and it groaned. First things first, I ripped the tape off my mouth and then off the body next to me. "Leo?" My voice was hoarse, like I'd been screaming. I didn't feel like I'd been tortured or beaten, but being stuffed in here certainly didn't bode well.

"You're alive," he said, also hoarse.

"Same to you," I said. I worked on getting my hands free, biting at the edges of the tape until it tore, leaving me covered in sticky residue.

"I thought for sure you were done," Leo whispered. In the dark, pressed against him, I felt calmer than I had any right to, although that could have just been the drug still doing its dance on my brain.

"Me too," I whispered. Everything was loud and close in here. I got my hands free, pressed against the lid of whatever we were entombed in—an old chest freezer, I guessed, from the metal walls and the stale smell of freon. Nothing budged. I pressed harder, then hit.

"Forget it." Leo groaned. "They chain it shut and take it to the crusher or the landfill. If you're not dead from what they did to you before you went in or from suffocation, you sure as hell will be after that."

I dropped my arms. The haze was lifting from the inner land-scape of my mind and my skull was throbbing. "Your father is a real asshole."

"I've been telling you," Leo said. "I came looking and Sergei said we could talk, that I could work off my debt. He had a clean-ing job." His breath hitched a little against my back. "He showed me you, then . . ." He sighed. "Spoiler alert: I ended up in here with you."

"He gave me something," I said, feeling along the rubber seal. All I got was a shredded fingernail or two. "Felt like taking a ham-mer to the head."

"Etorphine," Leo muttered. "Street name's M99. Sergei's bud-dies back home use it on the girls they import to keep 'em quiet in the containers. I always had a girl or two who stroked out or choked on her own vomit to get rid of when the shipments ar-rived."

He must have sensed my intake of breath because he pressed his fingers into my back. "I'm not a saint, but I didn't deal with the whores. I stuck with what I was good at."

"Stop using the past tense," I said.

"You think I'm going back after what he did?" Leo growled. "Fuck him. He'll be lucky if I don't mount his dick on my living room wall."

"We won't be doing anything if we don't get out of here before the air runs out," I told him. "I'm not strong enough to bust this thing open, so if you've got an idea let's hear it."

Leo sighed. The air was getting thin and sour—I could feel it starting to make my head spin. If I hadn't had that dream, had never been jolted back, I'd never have come to at all.

"I could try some blood conjuring," he said. "I used to be pretty good at getting in and out of places that were locked."

"But you need human blood," I said. Leo coughed.

"No, this'll work with any kind. It's just . . . I don't know how much. Or what'll happen if there's blowback. We could get pulverized."

"That's gonna happen anyway," I said. I found a sharp metal latch sticking out from the lid of the freezer, and dug it deep into the flesh of my arm before pulling down. The blood was hot and fast flowing, and Leo wrapped his fingers around my arm, smearing it. He began to murmur in Russian, the words running together. I'd picked up a few languages over the century—Spanish, French, a smattering of German during the war—but Russian just sounded like water over stones to me.

Power, though—I could feel that, no matter what language it came in. It wrapped me up, cotton wool and thorns all across my exposed skin. Leo's whispers increased in urgency, his grip on me tightened, and stars spun in front of my eyes from the burning that engulfed me, radiating from the cut on my arm up to my skull and back down to my belly.

I cried out, and then there was a heavy, jagged clanking from outside and the lid of the cooler popped open, just an inch or two. I shoved it the rest of the way, gasping cool, recycled air flowing from a bare HVAC vent above us.

We were on the loading dock of the casino, wedged out of sight next to a Dumpster. I helped Leo saw the tape off his hands, and we both climbed out. Leo grabbed my hand. "Come on. We need to get out of here before he realizes we're gone."

"No," I said, pulling away from his grip and heading back toward the inside door. "I need the Scythe."

"Ava, forget it," Leo hissed. "We need to be out of Reno yesterday."

I just kept walking. I remembered what that thing in my dream had said, how I needed to forget about revenge, but revenge was all I could see. I wanted to hurt Sergei, for what he'd done to me and to Leo, for Leo's whole life, for the misery he wore on his face just under that expressionless mask.

"Ava," Leo said quietly. "If we don't go now, I'm going to die. You might survive, but my father is going to make sure I don't get another chance to screw him."

I stopped, the loading dock spinning again under my feet. He was right. I could get my own back on Sergei or I could go. It wasn't a hard choice.

Leo's shoulders went slack when I turned around, and I could see his relief as we hopped off the dock and jogged down the alley behind the Eldorado. "Wonder if Clarence took flight or if he's still waiting," Leo panted. He was pale, and we stopped in the shadows to get our bearings. No one behind us was yelling or shooting, and I figured Sergei must think I was good and dead. I wasn't keen to disabuse him of that notion. Clint better not have bolted on me.

The temperature was dropping rapidly in the hours before dawn, and I shivered as we hurried away from the promenade and into the wasteland of twenty-four-hour minimarts and faded, scuzzy motels.

I popped the door on an old Chevelle with dinged paint and Utah plates, and we drove back to Circus Circus. I felt something give a little in my chest when I saw Clint waiting, leaning against the SUV's bumper and tapping his foot. He glared when he saw us drive up.

"Grand theft auto is just a fun hobby for you two, isn't it?"

"Just get in," I snapped. Clint got his bag and climbed into the backseat.

"Mind telling me where we're going?"

"I have no fucking idea, beyond 'away,'" I said. Maw-Maw's tobacco rasp floated up in my mind again. *Lilith has found the crossroads. You need to find her.*

"Even with the Scythe, Lilith is way ahead," I said. "She knows where the crossroads are to reach Tartarus."

Clint gaped at me. All I could see in the rearview mirror was his teeth. "How the hell do you know this?"

"I just do, okay?" I said. I could tell from his startled glance that Leo was also wondering, but he had the sense to button his lip in front of Clint.

"How could she have found out?" I asked Clint. "If the Fallen knew the locations, it had to be one of you, right?"

"None of us would do such a thing," Clint said, way too fast.

"Don't hand us that crap, Clarence." Leo sighed as I merged onto the interstate. I'd never been so glad to leave a town in my dust. "Everyone has their breaking point, and everyone has their price."

"If I *did* guess," Clint said, "she would *not* have betrayed us. She was one of the few Fallen to speak against our treatment of the demons, in point of fact."

"Spit it out," I said as an interchange loomed ahead in the gray, greasy dawn. "North or south?"

"South," Clint said after a long moment. I merged over. A trucker laid on his horn and flipped me off. I returned the gesture with my blood-soaked hand, in no mood.

"A state and town would also be helpful," I said. Behind us, over Reno, the same iron-bellied clouds from Rapid City were gathering. Lilith was here, breathing down my neck. I was running out of highway.

"Bayou St. Charles," Clint said. "Louisiana. I'll know it when we get there."

I almost swerved into the oncoming lane. "Is that really the only place we can go?"

"If you want to speak to a Fallen who knows these things, it is," Clint said. He examined my face in the oncoming headlights. "Problem?"

"No," I said, speeding up as we left the city traffic behind us. "I can't think of one fucking place I'd rather be heading for than the town where I died."

23

The drive to Louisiana was mostly a blur of bad food and knotted-up muscles from sitting in the Chevelle. The seats managed to simultaneously sag and be entirely full of springs. By the time we stopped for gas in Shreveport, more than thirty hours after leaving Reno, I thought I might have a permanent curve in my spine.

Bayou St. Charles was a tiny map speck on the Mississippi Delta close enough to the Gulf that you could smell salt and mud when I opened the car door. Most of the houses we passed were on stilts, once we got off the main drag, which consisted of a post office, a diner, a liquor store, and a Piggly Wiggly. In rural Louisiana, you didn't need much else.

I didn't try to find out if the plantation was still there, out in the swamps, far from the clean salty air. I didn't want to know. I hoped that dump burned to the ground long ago, and the ashes got eaten by the bayou so you'd never even know it existed. I pulled into the gas station and filled up the tank, trying to ignore how familiar all of it felt. Nothing lasted long around here—everything changed with the seasons, with the creep of the modern world, even here in the back of beyond—and what progress didn't wipe out, Katrina had finished off.

There was nothing left of Jasper and Caleb. Fate willing, even their bones had been ground to dust in the Louisiana mud. There was nothing here to hurt me any longer.

Leo went to take a leak, but Clint stayed in the car so long I tapped on the window. "You're gonna get a blood clot you stay in there much longer."

He stepped out and looked at the little stilt houses across the highway. Some of the others we'd passed still had signs of FEMA building materials, or were clearly newer construction to replace a home that had been washed away. "Don't like it here much," he said.

I slammed the gas pump back into its cradle, glad to see Leo approaching from the back of the gas station. "You and me both."

I drove on, following Clint's foggy directions, until I thought we'd drive into the delta. Just before the road turned to water, he told me to turn off, and I pulled to a stop in front of another stilt house. This one was so old the corrugated roof was a deep orange rust, and the posts of the wraparound porch were entirely silver, looking no sturdier than toothpicks. I could hear the ocean from the driveway, even if I couldn't quite see it. The sky was that bleached blue-white that you only get near the ocean, when the land flattens out to sand and scrub. It was like being under a scrubbed blue bowl, and I worked the knots out of my back, relishing the heat trapped under the bowl's dome. Back in Nevada, winter had started setting in, but here it felt like the last of the chill from when I'd woken up in the snow worked its way out of my bones.

Clint climbed out of the car and flinched. "Jesus, it's humid."

"This is nothing," I said. "Air's moving. You want humid, try Canal Street in July in the days before central air."

The windows of the little house were open, but nothing moved behind the faded cotton curtains. There was no car in the driveway, though I saw a little dock across the way with a small powerboat tied at the end. "I don't think your friend is home," I said to Clint.

He shifted from foot to foot, and I wondered what was making him so nervous. "Not a friend?" I said. "If we're not welcome here, I wish you'd told me."

The first hint I had we weren't alone, and somebody was in fact home, was the sound of a shotgun racking up a few feet behind me. "Not him," a voice said. "Just you."

I turned around very slowly, putting my hands up and splaying my fingers so there would really, truly, be no misunderstanding. I don't care who or what you are, nobody wants to take a spray from a Winchester Model 12 at close range.

"I'm sorry," I said carefully. "Let's just chalk this up to wrong place, wrong time."

The woman holding the shotgun sneered. "Yeah, that's not happening, baby girl. Turn that happy ass around, tuck your tail, and get the hell off my property."

"Raphael," Clint said. "This isn't necessary."

She swung the shotgun to Clint. "I told you that's not my name anymore."

I looked at Leo. He was watching the whole exchange with mild amusement, hands half-assedly in the air. I glared at him. He could be taking our imminent shotgunning a little more seriously.

"I'm sorry. Annabelle," Clint said. "I wouldn't have brought Ava here if I didn't trust her."

"And the necrophile?" she snapped, moving the shotgun barrel to Leo.

"More or less." Clint shrugged. "For a human he's not that bad."

"Thanks, man," Leo muttered. "You're a true friend."

"You trust everyone," Raphael—or possibly Annabelle—snapped. "That was always your whole damn problem, *Azrael.*"

Clint spread his hands. "That name doesn't bother me. I accept what I am."

"And that includes running with hounds?" Annabelle shook her head. The swath of braids at her neck swished. "Uh-uh. You can get the hell out of here, all three of you."

"Lilith is planning to open Tartarus," I said. She swung the gun back to me and I tried not to flinch. "Clint said you'd know which crossroads she was planning to use. Tell us and we'll be on our way. Or just shoot me. Either way, my arms are getting tired, so decide fast."

We stared at each other, a long, unpleasant stare that held for an equally long moment. Like Clint, Annabelle had black hair and black eyes. Hers were tapered, like a cat's, and her skin was deeper and more tanned than Clint's. They had the same long limbs and sharp features, the same liquid way of moving. Definitely members of the same species.

Annabelle put the shotgun up, propping it on her shoulder. "Tartarus?" she said to me. I nodded.

"She's pretty serious."

"'Course she's serious," Annabelle snorted. "The bitch is crazy." She looked at Clint. "I told you to put her in that Pit with the others when you had the chance, but *somebody* thought that she could change, that she could be taught."

She climbed the steps to the porch and opened the door. "Well, come on," she called to us. "Y'all look rode hard and put up wet. Get in here and cool off."

Stepping into Raphael's house was like stepping into the home of every kindly southern grandmother I'd ever known—excepting my own, of course—if the grandmother was also really into skulls, heavy metal, and the Second Amendment. A plaid living room set crowded around a rabbit-ear television in one half of the front room. The other half was a kitchen with matching avocado appliances and a copper-veined Formica counter that sparkled under the imitation Tiffany lamp. Braided rugs covered the floor two or three thick, muffling our footsteps. Then you looked at the walls, saw the playbills from everything from Lilith Fair to Metallica, the collection of skulls and saints' candles crowded on a low bookcase under the window, and the rack in the kitchen that was filled not with granny-appropriate preserves but cloudy jars and burlap sacks full of all the trappings of a well-versed root healer.

A rack of guns hung above the TV, and Annabelle hung the Model 12 in the top slot. The gun was old, the walnut stock polished to a high sheen, and above it was an even older Spencer repeating rifle. The guns were roughly chronological, ending with a brand-new matte black Bushmaster in the bottom slot. Leo eyed them, but thankfully kept his hands to himself.

"She loves guns even more than you," I muttered to Clint. He glowered.

"I hate guns. They're a necessary evil."

Annabelle brought us glasses of sweet tea, and I glanced at Clint before I raised the glass to my lips. I wasn't in a real big hurry to repeat my experience with Sergei.

"It's not poisoned," she said. "Trust me, honey, if I wanted you dead I wouldn't be all passive-aggressive about it."

Clint leaned toward her. "You know I wouldn't be here if it wasn't a grave situation."

Annabelle rubbed the back of her neck. "What makes you think I know where Crazy Eyes is goin'? You suggesting I sold you out?"

"Of course not!" Clint said. "Even your best guess. This cannot be allowed to happen."

"Shit, Azrael, I know that better than you do." Raphael sighed. "I was there, you know. I saw every last nasty bit of it."

"Nobody's accusing you of anything," I said. "But Lilith is gonna do this, and she's gonna kill Clint as soon as she gets her hands on him."

"Oh, I doubt she's gonna kill him right off the bat, even if she might want to," Annabelle said with a thin smile. She got up and went to a bookshelf that was nailed together out of driftwood and scrap, pulling down a clothbound book. "You ever read the Gnostic Gospels, honey? *Can* you read?"

"I still have a human brain," I snapped. "I'm not just walking on my hind legs."

"My apologies," Annabelle said, flipping through the book at light speed. "Lots of hounds, they were raised up so long ago people didn't learn to read and write real regular like they do now. Run across a couple who couldn't tell you the specials at Bojangles', never mind read a book."

I stayed quiet. My grandmother taught me to read with her Bible, picking chapters largely at random and letting me stumble through them until I got it. I didn't want Annabelle knowing I remembered my old life. I didn't trust her, the way her eyes kept darting to Clint, me, and Leo, to the door, to her gun rack. She'd gotten within a few feet of me and I hadn't even smelled her, never mind sensed her coming. Until I knew how she did that, she didn't get to know my life story.

"The book of Enoch makes mention of Tartarus," she said. "Gets a little bit right here and there too—a prison to hold the worst Hell has to offer. Then you got the myths, say Tartarus was a place where they chained up one of the Titans when the gods of Olympus turned on him. But what Tartarus really does is act as the prison within a prison. Hell is minimum security and Tartarus is a supermax. Ever since the Hellspawn figured out they could juice human souls long after death, it's been stuffed to the gills with the damned, fast as the reapers can send 'em south."

"She knows all this," Clint interrupted. "I know this too. Come on, Annabelle—stop jerking us around."

Annabelle rolled her eyes at me. "Men are always so impatient to get to the main event. Foreplay has its place, honey," she said to Clint. "I'm telling you this so you realize Lilith can't just snap her fingers and open the prison gates. It's like cracking open Alcatraz—you gotta get your boat and your crew and your equipment. It's a process."

I nodded. "I just want to know where she's most likely to be. I plan to kill her."

Annabelle sat back, and I thought for a second I'd offended her, but then she started to laugh, a deep belly sound that shook her impressive cleavage under her tank top. "I changed my mind, dog. I like you all right," she said. She leaned forward and took her own glass of iced tea. "Only three angels know what closed Tartarus. Those three were all murdered by Hellspawn before we hauled ass outta Hell, so this is secondhand information. I making myself clear?"

Clint and I both nodded, and Annabelle set her glass down with a thud. "Right then. Lilith needs the three things that sealed the Pit to unseal it. That's blood, just like everything to do with black magic and Hellspawn fuckery." She shot Leo a look, and he raised his glass of sweet tea. Annabelle snorted. "Specifically she'll need the blood of three creatures—the Fallen, the innocent, and the damned."

Annabelle leveled her finger at Clint. "That'd be why girlfriend has the hots for you."

I looked at Clint, who drew back into the orange-green plaid of the sofa cushions. "Why me?"

"Why not you?" Annabelle scoffed. "Ain't like you've exactly done a lot to keep the Hellspawn from chewing you a new asshole."

"You *know* why I don't like to fight them face-to-face," Clint growled. "So I'm the Fallen. So what? Lilith still needs two more."

"She's got the power of Hell behind her, Azrael," Annabelle said. "How long do you *really* think it'll be until she finds what she's looking for?"

"What do you mean by an innocent?" I interrupted. How innocent could most people be in this day and age? Unless we were talking about a virginal nun in one of those countries where they didn't routinely have Wi-Fi or electricity, the chances seemed pretty slim.

"Someone without blackness on their soul," Annabelle said, as if I were a particularly dumb toy poodle. "Somebody who's actually done some good. Probably lives in a nice little house and does things like take in the neighbor's mail when they go out of town." She stood up and put the book back on the shelf. "Probably had a stint or two in the nuthouse too. Be somebody sensitive, but too much of a beautiful little average human to think the voices they're hearin' aren't some chemicals going screwy in their brain. If you told 'em they had magical powers they'd laugh at you."

"And the damned?" I said. Annabelle gave me a sad smile.

"Rest assured Lilith's already got her hands on that unfortunate soul, sweetheart, plucked straight from the reaper's grasp. There's nothing you can do except try to beat her to the other two."

Clint stood as well, brushing his hands down his pants. "It's decided. I'll offer myself to Lilith and draw her out."

Annabelle and I both started talking at once, and I jumped to my feet. "Bullshit it's decided," I said. "That's a horrible idea."

"Not to mention dumber than me going outside and digging a basement for this place," Annabelle grumbled. "Seriously, Clint, you never did have more than two brain cells to rub together."

"We have no way of finding this so-called innocent before Lilith does," Clint snapped. "I'm the only factor we can control, so let me do it."

Annabelle put her hands on her hips. Her cheeks had darkened with anger and her lips pressed together in a thin line. She looked like she was about to haul off and smack Clint, and I took a step back to give her room. If I was being honest, I was kind of hoping she would hit him. It wasn't anything I hadn't wanted to do since practically the second I met him.

"You know she's only picking on you because of your condition, Azrael," she said.

Clint glared at her. "I don't want to discuss it. I'm doing it, so, Ava, you better be there when she swoops in on her broomstick."

"You expect this little doggie to go against Lilith all by herself?" Annabelle said. "You're even dumber than you look, boy."

"She hasn't managed to kill me yet," I grumbled. Annabelle raised one thin black eyebrow at me.

"Then she hasn't been tryin' to kill you, baby doll, because if there's one thing Lilith excels at, it's homicidal intent."

"There needs to be a way to get to her without using Clint as bait," I said. "I won't let him take that chance."

Annabelle collected our glasses and went to the sink, slamming a basin around while she ran soapy water. "You should listen to her, Azrael," she called to Clint. "She makes a lot more sense than you do most days."

I went to stand beside her at the sink and picked up a blue-and-pink-flowered dish towel, drying the glasses as they came my way. "Anything else useful you can tell me about Tartarus?" I said quietly.

"Yeah. It's a nasty place and you should do everything in your power to stop Lilith from unleashing it on the poor unsuspecting people of this world," Annabelle said flatly. "I wish you hadn't mixed up in this, doggie. You're tangling with the demonic equivalent of Charles Manson."

I shrugged. "Wouldn't be the first time somebody really wanted me dead."

"You can gossip about me all you want," Clint said loudly. "I'm still going to go to Lilith."

"We haven't even started talkin' about you," Annabelle said, drying her hands on another dish towel, this one yellow and printed with huge palm fronds. "But now that you mention it, Lilith picking on a defective Fallen angel doesn't seem very sporting, does it?"

Clint hit his fist into the side of the bookcase. "I am not defective. Just because I don't show off . . ."

"Azrael, you spend days with this girl, let her think you're some bad man Fallen, and you wonder why I'm picking on you?" Annabelle turned to me. "He's broken, hurt at the crossroads when we fled from Hell, and now he can't get it up. Angelically speaking."

"Shut up," Clint warned.

"See, most of us kept at least a few of our talents from the Kingdom," Annabelle told me. "Me, I'm fast. Really fast. I can get you anywhere you want to go. Then there's the healing, the basic offensive conjuring, the affinity for weapons, and the fact that the Kingdom makes you really, really efficient at killing and maiming."

"I'm not gonna tell you again!" Clint shouted. Annabelle ignored him, and I was just trying to keep up with her.

"Unless, of course, you almost don't make it through the crossroads and fall out with all your talents stripped away, just a guy who doesn't age very fast and knows a few parlor tricks. I imagine you'd be mortified, right, honey? You'd go hide among humans, then when you find out you're still a good killer, if not a tough one, you get a shame hangover and go hide in the forest for fifty god-damned years." She turned those coal eyes back to Clint. "Use what-ever trailer-park wild bunch you can get your hands on as a human shield, play up the peace-loving, ray-of-light angel angle, stick your head in the sand, and wait for someone to fuck you in the ass. How'm I doing so far?" She was smirking right up until Clint grabbed the Winchester from the gun rack and squeezed the trigger.

Plaster and wood splinters rained down around Annabelle and me as the blast echoed through the little cabin. My ears rang like somebody had tapped a hammer against my head. Leo covered his head with his hands against the shrapnel and shouted. "Fuck is your problem, asshole!"

Clint pointed the barrel of the shotgun at the ground. "I said shut up," he repeated quietly.

Annabelle stormed over and yanked the gun out of his hands. "We all had problems, Clint. Some of us flat-out didn't make it. Remember Barnabas? Camael? They're dead now, thanks to the crossroads. So the least you can do is stop moping around and just be grateful you're still here."

"I don't know if I am grateful," Clint said, sitting down on the edge of the sofa. He put his head in his hands. "It's gone, Anna-belle. Almost everything I knew from the Kingdom. Even most of Hell. The crossing ripped it out of me. I don't know who I was. Just who I am. And that Azrael isn't afraid to die."

"Maybe you're not," I said, feeling a swell of anger like a pebble in my throat. "But I am. And I'm stuck with you, so pull your head out and think of a way to get Lilith here that doesn't involve being the juicy steak dangling in front of the Doberman."

Clint shook his head. "I'm sorry, Ava."

I opened Annabelle's screen door and stepped onto the porch.

"Then so am I," I said. I let the door slam and walked across the gravel of Annabelle's drive to the dock. I wasn't sure where I was going. I just had to get away from Clint and his sad, vacant stare where a fiery angel should be.

The dock extended far enough into the water that I could see other boats moving farther out, small white hulls stark against the water. Shrimp boats, mostly—people in the small delta towns didn't usually boat for pleasure. Leo came out onto the porch, but I waved him off, and he listened to me, thankfully. He was just human, but he was so much more useful than Clint right now.

The first time I saw the Gulf, I took off my shoes and stockings and stuck my toes in the sand. A wave sloshed over my knees and soaked the bottom of my dress. Women and men alike gave me dirty looks, but I didn't care. It was warm and vast, and it was the first time I felt like I'd really left home.

I'd helped my grandmother during the week after I came here from Tennessee. She taught me how to drive her coughing Model A, and we kept an eye out for revenuers when her still was running. My grandmother brewed real homemade corn whiskey, not the poisonous crap that most bootleggers passed off as booze, and soon I had enough money to move into New Orleans. It had been a happy few months before I met Jasper and Caleb.

And then things were bad, and they never got good again.

"You gonna come inside, or what?" Annabelle was behind me again. I hated that she moved so quietly. I didn't like people who could get that close to me without warning. She grinned. "Relax, honey. If I was gonna do you harm it'd have happened already."

She had a point there. "I just need a minute," I said. "This has been a long couple of days."

Annabelle followed my gaze out to the water. "Hell is loud," she said. "Noise all the time, even if it's just the wind blowing around the corners of everything. Here is quiet. I like it here better." She folded her arms. "I don't blame the demons for what they did. I was against it, which is probably why they've left me alone so far. But Lilith was never one of the ones I felt for. She's bad. You best watch your ass."

"I figured that out fast," I muttered. "Believe me."

Annabelle laughed. "You're not really a hound, are you?" She stepped close enough that she was in my personal space, but if I backed up I'd fall into the water.

"I'm a hound," I said, aware of the hound itself, waiting just behind my eyes to flash tooth and fang, *make* Annabelle back off me. Fast as I thought of it, Annabelle reached out and grabbed me by the chin. My fangs sprouted of their own accord and sliced into my lip, blood trickling down my chin. Annabelle whistled at the sight. "Those sure are some pig stickers you've got, girl."

"Let me go," I said, fighting the urge to snap my jaw closed on her fingers. If the jolt I'd gotten from Clint was any warning, Annabelle would fry me like a squirrel on a high tension wire.

"It's still in you," she murmured, staring me in the face. "Hell's still in you. Even without a reaper, you could still take a soul easy as breathing." I tried to tell her she was wrong, but before I could say anything she let go of me, taking a black blade from a nylon holster strapped to her calf, under her canvas pants.

Electricity flowed across the backs of my hands, up my arms, trickling down my spine. The hound recognized the tool of a reaper, even if this Scythe was rough and old—as far from the graceful curved blade Gary had used as an ax from a fine chef's knife.

"How . . ." I started, but Annabelle turned the blade in her hand, then faster than I could see pulled me to her by the arm and stuck the blade against the notch between my third and fourth rib. If she applied a little pressure, it would slide up and into my heart. I knew how sharp it was. Gary had demonstrated plenty of times with his.

"You here to kill me, hellhound?" she whispered in my ear. I tried to stay absolutely still, which wasn't easy with the crackle of the Scythe crawling over my skin and a pissed-off Fallen huffing in my ear.

The screen door creaked and slapped the frame as Clint came outside. He gave us a wave and started down the steps. Annabelle waved back. From a distance, it'd look like we were gossiping, the best of friends. "I smelled this Hellspawn magic on you the minute you rolled up to my house," Annabelle continued. "Give me a good reason not to gut you from crotch to neck."

I breathed in, out. It felt like a rock was sitting on my chest. "I remember what it was to be human. I killed my reaper and I'm planning to kill Lilith. I didn't know you existed until Clint brought us here, and I don't give a shit. I also don't have any Hellspawn magic. I'm powerless without Gary."

Clint was at the end of the dock, about twenty feet away. I shot a glance at him, and back at Annabelle. She was still staring at me, calculating something. "Not all of us lost our groove like Azrael over there," she whispered to me. "If you're lying to me, I know."

"I'm not," I said evenly. If Clint got between us, I had no doubt she'd cut him, and then I'd be back to square one finding Lilith, because her prize Fallen would be bleeding out like a fish on this dock.

"No, you're not," Annabelle agreed. "But you are damned, little girl, even more than you realize."

"I don't care," I muttered as Clint approached. "Please let me go."

"You should care," Annabelle whispered, removing the Scythe from my ribs and sticking it back in her boot. "Clint may have gone native, but I know what you are."

I blinked at her. I was dizzy from the pain of the Scythe and just wanted to curl up in a ball until she went away. "I'm one of my reaper's mistakes. I never should have been a hellhound."

"You're right," Annabelle said. "Because you're the black dog. Death's hound."

"Hey," Clint said as Annabelle stepped back and gave him a radiant smile. "Can I talk to Ava for a second?"

"Sure thing, honey," she said, starting to back away and head inside.

I grabbed her by the arm. She showed me her teeth, but I didn't reconsider the move. "Just what the fuck is that supposed to mean?"

"It means that once upon a time, when the demons had their shit on lockdown instead of the cage fight for control of Hell it is now, they had a single reaper to oversee all the damned. That reaper got pretty popular among the meat puppets. Usually rode a pale horse, and Hell followed with him." She jerked her arm from my grasp, brushing at the spot where we'd touched. "And that's you."

She walked away, and I stared after her, at a loss. Clint waited until he saw the inside door shut and then looked down at the gray, splintery boards of the dock.

"I'm sorry."

I sat down hard on a battered metal cooler at the end of the dock, grabbing my knees so my hands would stop shaking. "It's fine," I muttered. "I just . . ." I didn't know what I wanted. Annabelle didn't have a reason to fuck with me that I could see, but she could have plenty of reasons I didn't know about, the chief being that she was really with Lilith and this was all an elaborate con to throw me off and send me to ground. Make me so scared and desperate I'd give up.

Or maybe the blood conjuring I'd done with Leo had messed up her Fallen radar, made me seem more juiced with black magic than I really was.

Or maybe the fact I remembered being human and dying, the fact I'd been able to take out Gary, meant something after all.

That scared the shit out of me so much I couldn't even give it voice. "Can we please go?" I said to Clint. My voice was so low I could barely hear it over the waves brushing against the dock. "I don't care where. I just need to be away."

Clint frowned, and then sat down next to me. "Just because I can't toe up against Hellspawn doesn't mean we can't still do this," he said. "I should have told you. I figured between you and Karpov I'd be safe. You're both pretty scary individuals. That's why I stuck around."

"Is it?" I whispered. I didn't scare easily, but Annabelle had rattled me. I could write off what she'd said as a Fallen batting around a low-level hellhound for the fun of it, but she hadn't seemed like she was joking. I was pretty sure I'd escaped being stabbed by a heartbeat or two.

"Of course!" Clint said. "I saved you to save myself, really. Listen . . ." He rubbed his hands over his thighs like we were on a date, and he was working up to copping a feel. "When I came through the crossroads something happened to me. I can't do what Anna-belle can do, but more than that . . . I don't even remember much of who I was before. I remember Hell, snapshots of the Kingdom, but about myself?" He shook his head. "Blank. Like somebody took an eraser and swiped it across my memory."

I stayed quiet. I was still trying to calm down and I didn't trust myself to say the right thing. Not that I ever really did. I would never fill out a dating profile with "People say I'm a great listener."

"So I feel a lot of empathy with hellhounds," Clint said. "I know what a torment that is, to have who you really are ripped right out of you by the root." He laughed once, lowering his head. "Not that I was such a prize, I'm sure. I enforced the laws of the Kingdom. If the ruling council saw a worthy soul to join the ranks, I went and collected it. Whether the person was happy about it or not."

"If Annabelle is an example of how the Fallen really act, I think I prefer you this way," I said. Clint rubbed his hands together and then stood up, toes hanging over the edge of the dock like he was about to lift up and float across the water.

"She's not bad. She has compassion for life, at least. In the King-dom she wasn't a combatant. She was a diplomat, a scholar. That's how she knows so much about Tartarus."

"She knows a lot about a lot of things," I said. Clint was too preoccupied to catch the bite in my tone.

"I'm sorry I can't do what she does. Fallen can read minds, they're strong and fast, they can get from place to place using the crossroads. I'm sorry you have to look out for me." He turned back to me and smiled. Even to my eyes, it looked forced. "But it'll be worth it."

"When we kill Lilith," I said. Clint nodded. He was having a hard time sitting still. I bet if he'd had the room, he'd be pacing.

"Then I'll be free," I said. "We can go our separate ways."

Clint nodded, his eyes darting back toward Annabelle's house. "Right."

I stood up, kicking over the cooler. "You are so full of shit."

Clint blinked. "Excuse me?"

"You knew I was coming for you," I said. "Back in Wyoming. Annabelle said you knew something."

Clint held up his hands. "Whoa. Annabelle says a lot of things. What did she tell you?"

"It doesn't even matter," I said. I turned and stomped back to the car. Clint ran after me, grabbing on to the window frame of my door as I gunned the engine. Leo was already waiting in the backseat, and he touched my shoulder.

"Ava?"

"Don't," I snarled, so viciously he jerked his hand away and actually pulled in on himself, like I'd scared him. That fit. I was scared as shit myself right now.

"Stop!" Clint shouted, reaching in the window and grabbing the wheel as I started to put the car in gear. I growled, low and hot in my chest.

"Ava!" he said. "Tell me what I'm supposed to know!"

"I told you I knew who I was before I died," I said. "You acted like that was normal. But it's not, and I know it's not. I'm certainly not special, I'm not the Harry Potter of hellhounds, so what is it? What's wrong with me?"

"Turn off the car and I'll tell you," Clint said. "I don't want you to go running off on me."

"Jesus." I hit the steering wheel, feeling the impact vibrate up my arm. "It's that bad?"

"You were right about Lilith and me." Clint sighed. "We were close. She was my personal valet. It's an intimate relationship."

Leo snorted. "You mean she was your personal slave? You created her out of the mud and then made her do your dirty work? No wonder the bitch resents you."

"Lilith resents existing," Clint said. "She hid her hate well. The first inkling I had anything was wrong was when she started trying to ferret out how she'd been made."

"So she could pull the same trick?" I guessed. Clint nodded.

"Demons were the first, but not the only. We realized we needed beings that could easily navigate the crossroads. Just a few, not more than you have fingers on your hand, to keep tabs on the rest of existence. Warn us if the Kingdom was making a move to wipe us out for good. One of them was Raphael's favorite. He began to see things at the crossroads—lost human souls, lingering on long after death. Raphael took pity on them and ushered them into Hell."

"How sweet of her," I said. Clint folded his arms.

"I'm trying to give you the whole picture. Hell wasn't always a terrible place. Dark and harsh, certainly, but also a place of life. All of those who had no place in the Kingdom or on earth could find a refuge." He looked back toward the house again. "Human souls ruined it. Lilith figured out pretty quickly she could drain them dry and draw the other things, the things that skulked around the crossroads, into Hell to do her bidding. They killed one of our couriers outright, and we gave Raphael's creation protection, since he was out and about the most. His own hound."

He paused for a moment, and I chewed over what he'd just said. "This 'courier,' as you so euphemistically call him . . ."

"A reaper," Clint said. "The first reaper. A Prometheus that Lilith and the other demons would pervert into their own image. She got to him, finally. Spilled his blood and gave rise to that insect race your reaper was a part of." A smile flickered across his face. "Raphael had the last laugh, though. She gave the reaper and his hound the one thing that Lilith—and us, for that matter—could never have. She gave him a human soul."

I held my breath. I knew what was coming, but somehow I thought if I shut my eyes and didn't watch the freight train barreling forward, it wouldn't flatten me.

"The soul was released, and it was supposed to find a new body, wait for that body to die, and return to us. But Lilith was stronger than I realized and the demons banded together and banished us before it happened. Raphael has been waiting for a very long time to meet her creation again. You remember your life because it's not your first one. You've been waiting to meet your real reaper again."

"No." I shook my head, and everything blurred around me. "No, you're wrong."

"'And I looked, and behold a pale horse: and his name that sat on him was Death,'" Clint whispered. "'And Hell followed with him.'"

"Shut up," I ground out. I knew the Bible. I didn't need Clint using it to prove some bullshit theory.

"'And power was given unto them over the fourth part of the earth,'" Clint continued. "'To kill with sword, and with hunger, and with death, and with the beasts of the earth.'"

"Did you not hear me?" I shouted, hitting the steering wheel.

"This isn't true! I have nothing to do with you or any of the Fallen. I've never even been to Hell!"

"Not yet," Clint said quietly. "I was pretty sure when I saw you that night in the state forest. When I met Leo, I was sure. He lives by the sword. He's a necromancer—a warlock who destroys life, twists it, and gives it back in death." Clint leaned forward, and I turned my face away, partly because I was crying and embarrassed and partly because I didn't want to see this new, strange gleam in his eye. It scared me, and I'd had enough of feeling afraid for one lifetime. "He *is* the rider on the pale horse, Ava," Clint said. "And the beast of the wild? The Hell that follows with him? That's you."

24

grabbed the steering wheel of the Chevelle until it creaked so I wouldn't reach out and hurt Clint. I wanted to lash out at him, break things, spend my rage on fragile, breakable flesh and bone. A week ago, I wouldn't have hesitated to wrap my fingers around his windpipe, pressing my thumb in until it cracked under the pressure.

I didn't do any of that. I just sat there and stared straight ahead at the white, stretched skin of my knuckles.

It was Leo, finally, who leaned forward. He spoke softly into my ear, although I could tell from the whites of his knuckles where he gripped the seat he was as thrown off as I was. "We can just go," he said. "Fuck this guy. I always said he belonged in a mental ward."

I squeezed my eyes shut and breathed in, out. I wasn't going to have another panic attack, not because of two Fallen playing a head game. "No," I said. "Let him talk."

"Ava," Clint said. "Please understand, I wasn't manipulating you. I wasn't using you. I just didn't think you were ready."

I stayed quiet. Breathed. Stared straight ahead. I'd never wanted to hurt anyone as badly as I wanted to hurt him in that moment.

Leo wasn't this thing, this puppet Raphael had drummed up because she was bored. And I wasn't a hound first and human second. Clint was wrong. Or lying. I didn't care.

"Ava," he said again.

"Get away from me," I whispered.

"Ava, I'm sorry," he said. "But sooner or later, Leo is going to die. When he does, his soul will return to Hell and he'll remember his life there. His creation. He'll be defenseless against the demons in the Pit unless he has you."

"GET AWAY FROM MY CAR, CLINT!" I screamed, loud enough that the windshield rattled. Clint jumped back a full two steps, his eyes going wide as silver dollars.

"I know it wasn't what you wanted to hear," he babbled. "I know you think you're human and you resent what was done to you, but I'd hoped knowing this was always your fate would be some small comfort . . ."

I put the car in gear and sped toward him, spraying gravel and hitting the brake a few inches from his legs. Clint tumbled back, landing on his ass in the dirt.

"It isn't," I told him, getting out and stalking back to Anna-belle's shitty little swamp house. She was sipping her own glass of tea, watching us all out her front window. She narrowed her eyes when I banged her screen door open.

"Help you, doggie?"

"Give me your Scythe," I said, pointing at her boot. "Give it to me now or I swear I will use all this almighty reaper power I have to drag you straight back to Hell to be Lilith's punching bag for the next thousand years."

Annabelle rolled her eyes, then reached down and took out the Scythe, flipping it in her hand and holding it out to me grip first. "Take it. Belongs to my reaper anyway."

"Leo is *not* yours," I told her, resisting the urge to jam the black blade right back into her skinny neck.

"Girl, please." Annabelle flipped a hand. "How you think you two got together in the first place? The reaper knows his hound, and you know him. You couldn't have stayed away if you tried."

Rather than acknowledge that she was right, that Leo and I meeting and sticking together was improbable at best, I did what I did best, and ran. I shoved the Scythe in my jacket and ran straight back to the car, forcing myself to stop shaking before I jammed it into gear.

"Ava," Clint shouted as I turned the Chevelle in a large circle and pointed it to the road. "Ava, wait! I'm sorry!"

I peeled out, spraying him with flecks of gravel as I went. In the rearview, I saw the door of the house open and Annabelle come running. She also started screaming at me, but I turned back to the road just in time to see a shape loom in front of me. I only caught that it was big and black and smack over the center line before I jerked the wheel. The Chevelle shuddered and the front wheels jumped onto the shoulder, the soft sand sending me skidding out of control. A thick, twisted pine tree loomed up in the side window and the impact snapped me sideways, my skull cracking the driver's side window in a halo shape. Leo slammed first into one side of the backseat, then the other, his body going limp. A perfect circle of red blood glistened at the center of the driver's window where my skull had hit, the last thing I saw before my senses were taken over by the sound of screaming cylinders and shattering glass. The car shuddered to a stop after the impact, and I was whipped the other way, and then even the chaos of the crash faded to black.

I woke up staring at a rabbit. It was dead and stuffed and had a pair of small plastic antlers tied to its head. "What the fuck?" I said. The rabbit didn't have any answers.

I tried to sit up and found my head swimming, and one of my arms tied. After a few seconds of frantic reactive thrashing, I realized the tie was just a cheap nylon sling, and the feeling of being wrapped in cotton wool soaked in high-grade painkillers was because I was, in fact, pumped full of high-grade painkillers.

A small orange bottle on the nightstand, guarded by the jackalope, announced that somebody named Norma Ethridge had been prescribed thirty Percocet by a doctor in Henderson, Nevada.

That cleared a few of the cobwebs from my head, and I sat up again, fighting against a pile of faded sheets and comforters to get my feet on the floor.

"Whoa whoa whoa!" A figure rushed in and gently held me still. "Don't try to get up just yet. Your head was pretty bashed up when you got here."

I hit the figure in the throat with my good hand. He stumbled back, choking, tripped over a stack of nudie mags, and fell on the ground. I stood up, swaying from the pills as I yanked off the sling. "What are you doing here, Marty?"

Marty scrambled to his feet, pressing himself against the wall. "You crazy bitch!" he rasped. "This is my house, is what I'm doing. I took your sorry ass in."

There was a small window over Marty's shoulder, clothed by some drab, sun-faded curtains. Through the gap I could see a familiar low, slouched building and cheap plywood sign. I blinked for a long moment. My eyes felt like somebody had taken sandpaper to them. "Marty," I said, "where am I?"

"Las Vegas," Marty grumbled, bending to restack his magazines. "Where do you think?"

I sat back on the bed. My arm was stiff from being immobilized. In point, my whole body was stiff, my muscles hung over from the impact of running the Chevelle into a tree.

Swerving to miss someone and smashing into a tree. . .

"How did I get here?" I said abruptly. Marty glared at me, holding the Christmas issue of *Naughty Neighborhood Nymphos* protectively against his chest.

"You sure ask a lot of questions for some bitch who put a cap in me."

"It's a fair question, Marty." I sighed. The left side of my skull was throbbing, and when I touched it, the tips of my fingers found a patch of sticky, blood-encrusted hair.

"I got no fuckin' idea," he said. "I came to open up the office this morning and you were passed out on my welcome mat, beat to shit and muttering about black dogs."

Leo. Leo slamming hard into the Chevelle's door, body a tangled mass of limbs as we swerved up the sand dune and met the scrubby pine tree headfirst . . .

"Where's Leo?" I demanded.

"Leo Karpov? Don't know and don't care. Aren't you even a little curious about how I survived your crazy ass?" Marty said. I looked back at the jackalope, wondering if it would be an effective weapon to beat him to death with.

"No," I said. "I literally cannot think of anything I care less about at this moment in time."

"I can move my brain stem to any part of my body," Marty said triumphantly. "I shifted the important parts out of the path of that totally uncalled-for bullet you put in my brain."

"You sure about that?" I muttered as I let my eyes roam and saw more porn, more sad faded furniture, and more weird taxidermy, including an armadillo smoking a cigar. It glared at me from the top of Marty's TV set.

"Whoever dumped you left you flying solo," Marty said. "And a bloody mess."

"And yet you fixed my arm and put me to bed," I said. "Is this going to be one of those things where you try to chain me up and make me your wife? Because I can spoil it and say it will not end well for you."

Marty snorted. "Are you kidding? I hate you. I hate Hellspawn. I'm just waiting to see who'll pay me the most cold hard cash to torture you to death." He flipped open a laptop that, judging by its relative cleanliness and heavy load of boy band stickers, was stolen, and scrolled through a series of messages. "Soon," he said. "I figure after what you put me through, it's karma."

He rolled a tattered chair over to the laptop and wagged a finger at me. "Don't get any bright ideas, either. I'm hard to kill, and you have enough drugs in you to knock down a horse."

I watched him hammer away at the keyboard, humming and

smiling. "I don't suppose you'd be interested in doing something for me instead."

Marty sucked on his small, nicotine-stained teeth as he considered. "You got money?"

"Think of it as a public service," I said. Marty shook his head.

"Sorry, kid. It's ass, cash, or grass in this establishment. Besides, I don't generally do the bidding of some reaper's purse dog."

I sighed, testing out my bad arm. My rotator cuff was definitely torn and I was sore, but nothing felt broken. "You're not very bright," I told Marty.

He smirked at me. "Is that so? In what way?"

"Because when you have a dangerous dog in your house," I said, standing up and grabbing him by the front of his shirt with my good arm, "you chain that fucking mutt up before it bites you."

Marty yelped as I tossed him face-first onto the bed and got on top of him, pressing my knee into the small of his back and the Scythe into the nape of his neck. Whoever had brought me back to Nevada hadn't taken it. Either they'd been even dumber than Marty or they weren't working for Lilith. I could spend all the time I wanted pondering that mystery once I'd found Leo.

"You feel that?" I growled. Marty mumbled something into the comforter and I pushed the very tip of the Scythe into his neck. "Yes or no, Marty."

"Yes," he gasped. "Jesus, I can't breathe."

"This is a reaper's blade," I said. Marty wriggled in a panic, and I flicked him on the ear with my free hand. "This will slice your spinal cord like twine, and nothing you shapeshift into is gonna be a cure for that. So do you want to help me, or do you want to be an asshole?"

Marty mumbled something, and I grabbed a shock of his ginger hair, lifting his head an inch so he could talk. "Help," Marty gurgled. "I'll help."

I let him go, hopping off his chunky torso and trying not to let the floor roll under me as I did. "What do you know," I said, keeping the Scythe in view as he struggled off the mattress. "You were right. You are smart after all."

Marty gaped at me, twin spots of color flaming in his cheeks. "Look, just go," he said. "I don't want any part of whatever it is you're into."

"I need you to find Leo, and someone else for me too," I said. "You may be a sleazy little weasel, but you're good with that hacker crap, so get to it."

Marty swallowed hard. "Okay. I need to go over to the motel where all the servers are . . ."

I pointed at the door. "Get moving." I followed Marty across a sad expanse of gravel and through the back door of the Mushroom Cloud's office. The mess from the fight had been cleaned up, but there were big bleach spots in his carpet from my blood, and I saw some crime scene tape flapping sadly from the porch posts at the front of the motel.

"I love what you've done with the place," I told Marty. He pulled up his chair to his computer rig and glared at me.

"I'm gonna need something specific for a search. Computers aren't magic, you know. It's not like in the movies."

"Leo first," I said. "Last I remember we were in a car accident in southern Louisiana."

Marty typed, and before I could blink, the police report from Terrabone Parish was on the screen. "Says the car was empty when the cops got there," Marty said. He clacked some more. "There's a John Doe in the Las Vegas hospital that matches your asshole boyfriend's description. I figured whoever dumped you here might've ditched him too."

I looked at the clock on Marty's computer. Only about twelve hours had passed since the accident. I'd crossed thousands of miles in what sounded like minutes.

Any other day, I'd be freaked out and looking over my shoulder, but now I just shoved it into the back of my mind with all the other problematic crap I tried to ignore on a daily basis.

"Lilith is looking for a human," I said. "One called 'the innocent' in this ritual she wants to do. I'm guessing he or she is somewhere between Wyoming and northern Louisiana."

"Oh, that's helpful," Marty snorted. "I'll just Google it for you."

I whapped him on the back of the head. "I can still stab you. You haven't been very useful just yet."

Marty waved me off like I was an annoying fly and started typing. "Lilith got me collectin' names of people who brushed up against demons and reapers but didn't deal. Crazy types mostly, little bit of psychic blood or a dash of the old warlock DNA, generations back. She said it was to keep them from being used against her."

"You hate Hellspawn so much that you troll the entire Web keeping a database of pathetic souls who have run-ins with demons?" I said, cocking one eyebrow. Marty glared at me.

"Hey, just because your boss is a cunt doesn't mean you don't do what she says if you like your job. And your arms. And being alive." He looked up at me, his homemade database scrolling past. There were thousands of names, from the time widespread records started being kept.

Lilith had been planning this for a *long* time.

"I still need a clue beyond sweet and innocent," Marty said. "A location, a gender, whether they wear boxers or briefs . . ."

I thought of the marquee on Father Colin's church in Rapid City. *And I saw an angel come down from heaven, having the key to the bottomless pit . . .*

"Revelation," I said. "In Revelation there's a chapter about the two witnesses to the Apocalypse. One of them sees the angel blow his trumpet and open the seven seals." Unleashing the pale horse, among others, but every time I thought about Clint I wanted to cry, so I shoved it down.

"The witnesses were given the ability to prophesy the end of the world," I said. "And a bunch of weird stuff about fire flowing out of their mouths that I'm guessing is just creative license. But they definitely went out and killed a bunch of the enemies of God." I never thought my apathetic Bible study back in Bear Hollow would come in handy, but there's a first time for everything.

Marty stopped typing. "Got her," he said.

I blinked. "Seriously?"

Marty made the screen larger. "Yeah. She has a blog."

The Web page was bare, glaring green text on a black background, proclaiming SATAN WALKS AMONG YOU. The picture next to the headline was a cropped shot of a serious, brown-haired young woman who had what I would charitably describe as a serious case of crazy eyes.

"Kayla Stillman," Marty announced. Another monitor popped up her file from the Oklahoma DMV. "Proud owner of one of the ugliest Web pages I've ever seen and a criminal record in the great state of Oklahoma."

He started a bunch of files scrolling. "She was a specialist in Iraq until 2009, when she was injured by an IED. Came home on a medical discharge and ended up shooting her CO outside the hospital where she went for PT."

Marty whistled under his breath. "Kayla here claimed that she'd been given the gift to see demons and that they were here, right this second. Her little satanic panic got her off of the murder charge. She was diagnosed with psychosis brought on by severe PTSD and sent to a state hospital. Attacked other inmates three times, released last year . . ." He scrolled rapidly through screens. "Due to budget cuts. Couple of run-ins with the law since then for disorderly conduct, screaming about being a witness to the end of days. Direct quote from the police report. Here's her address."

I memorized it, along with Kayla Stillman's face.

"Here's the real thing," Marty said. He had what looked like police records, and I decided I should go soon, before the FBI showed up. Marty didn't strike me as the most detail-oriented hacker.

"That guy she shot? They found evidence in his house from a couple of cold cases in the area. Missing kids going back about ten years. Lots of paraphernalia in these crime scene photos. Guy was a warlock."

So Kayla was off the chain mentally, but she was right. She could see what I saw—the taint of magic on a soul, the true face of something like Lilith.

I stepped back. "Stay out of trouble, Marty. You get a new car yet?"

"No, thanks to you," he grumbled. "You don't have to jack me again, anyway. Your bike is out back."

I raised one eyebrow. "You didn't sell it to a chop shop?"

"Hell no," Marty said, leaning back in his creaky chair. "You have any idea what a pussy magnet that thing is? I've been riding it. Seemed like that was only fair."

I thought about what could have happened on the seat of my poor Softail and tried not to get nauseated. "You better not have rubbed your parts on it," I told Marty. I grabbed the keys, still on my fob, off his desk and ran out. I was going to have to push it if I wanted to pick up Leo and get to Oklahoma before Lilith got to Kayla Stillman. I had the sinking feeling as I gunned my bike toward downtown Vegas that I might already be too late.

CHAPTER

25

|||||||||||||||||||||||||||||||||||||||||||||||||||||||||||||||||||||||

Erick, Oklahoma, wasn't a depressed little flyspeck, although it was still small enough that most maps didn't show it. I'd stored my bike in Henderson and Leo and I had picked up a car, legally this time, with some cash I'd convinced Marty, with a little cajoling and a lot of threats, to wire over to Leo. We got off I-40 at Texola and spent time on an old stretch of Route 66, which eventually lead me to Erick. Signs everywhere pointed me to a museum commemorating Roger Miller, the country singer who I swore was in literally every jukebox in America when "King of the Road" was a hit.

There were also downed telephone poles and power lines everywhere, trees smashed up, and even a few houses that had their roofs ripped off and deposited in pieces all over their yard.

An old guy walking his dog saw me looking and pointed at the house. "Tornado!" he yelled over the idle of our decidedly temperamental ride. "Don't usually come this time of year. Folks over there weren't prepared."

I tipped my head at him and drove on. Leo shifted in the passenger seat. "I don't imagine you could be very prepared for a tornado spawned by a demon."

He'd been pale and bandaged when we'd walked out of the hospital, nursing bruised ribs and a concussion, but really, it was miraculous he hadn't been smashed to bits in the wreck. He hadn't even been wearing a seat belt, and he was in better shape than I was. My arm throbbed nonstop from the hours on the road, and I still had a thick cluster of bruises in my hairline from where I'd smacked the Chevelle's window. We should both be dead, when you got right down to it. But maybe the universe was saving us for Lilith, one last cosmic fucking over before I finally died for good.

If Kayla Stillman was dead, I was fucked. That was all there was to it. Lilith would find Clint, Tartarus would crack open, and soon Oklahoma would be beachfront property in Hell. I wound my way through the small side streets of Erick until I found the address Marty had pulled. The house was a cute Craftsman with a sharply sloped roof, but the paint was peeling, the yard was a jungle, and at least a month's worth of mail made a snowdrift against the front door. The windows were muffled with the thick blackout curtains that got used only by vamp nests or the truly paranoid. Staked in the front lawn amid the weeds was a piece of plywood spray-painted in thick, wavering letters.

FOR THERE STOOD BY ME THIS NIGHT THE ANGEL OF GOD, WHOSE I AM, AND WHOM I SERVE

I put the car in park. Leo whistled between his teeth. "We are definitely in the right place."

It was just after sunset, gray-blue light filtering down and turning everything into shades of shadow. Perfect for checking to see if Kayla was home, and alive. I wasn't going to go up and ring her bell—I figured one look at me, and if she wasn't already around the bend, I'd push her.

I moved down the side of her house, covered by overgrown bushes that snatched at my jeans and jacket. There were no lights on that I could see, and I caught my shin on a pile of rusted lawn furniture and fell flat on my face, tasting mud.

I cursed, but compared to where I'd been before, with Gary, I'd take breaking into the house of an armed, psychotic, possibly violent hoarder any day of the week.

The windows at the back of the house were covered in a rusted screen that crumbled in my hands, but they were low enough that I could hoist myself in. I found an empty metal bucket lying in the weeds to stand on and ran my hand along the sill, feeling for a gap.

"Don't do that."

I yelped and fell on my ass for the second time in as many minutes. Leo crouched down and helped me sit up. "Sorry," he whispered. "But you really don't want to break into this place."

"I really do," I hissed back.

Leo pointed to a thin wire running across the windowpane, so transparent it could have been a spiderweb. "Window's rigged," he said softly. "They're all like that. I did a job in New York setting trip wires on the door of a guy's boathouse out on Long Island. Wired Semtex and a propane tank so it'd look like an accident. I think our little friend in there probably just rigged up a spare claymore mine inside the window, though. That's what I'd do."

I breathed out, sitting down on the bucket. "Is she in there?"

Leo shrugged. "No idea. I've been here just long enough to discover this house has more booby traps in it than the Branch Davidian compound. On the bright side, if this place hasn't turned into a smoking crater, there's a chance Lilith hasn't found it yet."

We retreated to the car, a black Buick that looked like something Bonnie and Clyde would have stolen for a joyride. I could wait. I was a hunter, not a mindless killer. I could dig in and be patient, more patient than some jumpy head case like Kayla Stillman. She had to leave the house eventually.

Leo turned to look at me, the springs of the seat creaking under his weight. "So are we gonna talk about this wreck, and us being here, and how this is all Clint's fault?"

"He just . . ." I sighed. "After Caleb, you'd think I wouldn't exactly be surprised when guys lie to me, right?"

"He didn't sound like he was lying," Leo said.

I was saved from the You're a reaper/I'm your hellhound debate and whether or not Clint was full of shit when a short figure hurried around the corner and scurried up Kayla Stillman's walk, shoving a key in the front door like she was pissed off at it. I started to get out of the car, but Leo shook his head. "She's got her hand on whatever is wired inside that front door. If you startle her you'll both be fertilizing that lawn."

I sighed. "What if Lilith is in there? We need to get her to come with us. And if she won't come, we need to knock her out and kidnap her crazy ass."

Leo smirked. "Lilith's not getting in there. I put up a barrier around the whole house." He settled back in his seat. "She's safe for now, and when Lilith shows up, we'll get our chance." He looked over at me. "You still have the Scythe, right?"

"I can't wait to use it and get rid of this thing," I said, setting it on the seat between us. "It's been giving me hives."

"Why is the bullshit the God squad is spouting bothering you so much?" Leo said. "The likelihood I have some larger purpose in Hell is minuscule, and even if it's true, you know me, Ava. You didn't change when you died. I won't either."

The words ripped out of me in one breath. "But then you'd be dead, and I was never human to begin with. I'm *just* as bad as I've thought all this time. If I've been born and dying and becoming a hound for thousands of years, I've always been a monster, just like Lilith."

Leo blinked at me. "That fucker. I'm going to knock his teeth in when I see him again. Making you think these things about yourself."

"It all fits," I whispered, tears coming, even though I squeezed my eyes shut. I scrubbed them away with the heels of my hands. "It's why I remember being human—because I'm not. You and I both were made by the Fallen and recycled over and over again. Clint said this time when we die we'll end up back in Hell. You'll be a reaper and I'll be your hound." I shuddered. "And if we've found each other, it'll be soon. We're not going to make it through this. After everything I've suffered, and you, it's not fucking fair. We should have gotten a chance to have some semblance of the lives that got stolen."

Leo pulled me close by the shoulders, looking into my eyes. "The Fallen can say what they want. Do you think you were human? Before those men murdered you?"

I managed to nod, the tears so thick now Leo's face started to blur. "It's the only thing that kept me from just . . . ending it," I whispered. "If this is what my life has always been—"

"It's not," Leo cut me off. "Clint is wrong, you were human once, and Ava . . ." He moved my damp hair out of my eyes. "I'm not going anywhere."

I jumped across the space between us, grabbing him by the shirt front and kissing him so hard I split my lip. Leo moaned and pulled me into his lap, his fingers digging into my hip bones as mine dug into his shoulders. He tasted hot and sweet, like vodka and tobacco, and we didn't break apart until he grabbed my shirt and yanked it over my head.

I pulled at the tail of his shirt as well. His tattoos were stark in the dark car. There were no streetlights on this quiet block and his skin was almost luminescent in the shadows. We paused for a second, foreheads pressed together, our ragged breath heating each other's bare skin.

"Yeah?" Leo said, his hands moving up and down my sides, almost like he was trying to memorize the shape of my naked body. I put my hands on his chest in turn. He felt so solid and alive that the weight of what Clint and Annabelle had said dropped off me.

"Yeah," I said. Leo let out a long sigh, like he'd been waiting for weeks to hear the simple word, and kissed me again, sliding his hands under my ass and moving me to lie down on the lumpy car seat. I broke off the kiss.

"Wait." I slid off his lap and reached for his belt, undoing his jeans and jerking at the waistband. I felt like I was in a car picking up speed, hurtling down the side of a mountain, waiting until the last second to hit the brakes. I was being reckless for sure, probably stupid, but I didn't care. I could pick up the pieces from the crash when this was over.

Leo gave a sharp moan when I pulled his cock out of his pants, and dropped back bonelessly against the car seat as I took the tip in my mouth. "Jesus fucking Christ, Ava," he rasped. He was big enough that I couldn't swallow all of him, and already hard, but I did my best. Leo cursed again and wrapped a handful of my hair in his fist, urging me down farther.

I groaned when he did, feeling heat crawl all over my skin like I was standing naked under the afternoon sun. I used my free hand to unzip my jeans, needing to crawl back into his lap.

Leo stopped me after another minute. His hand in my hair was shaking. "I need you," he said, his voice shaking. "That's too much. I need to fuck you."

He didn't pull me to straddle him, though. Instead, he grabbed me under the knees and pulled until I flopped back on the seat. Leo rolled my jeans down and yanked at my panties so hard that one side tore. He licked his middle and index finger and shoved them between my legs, rubbing me roughly, so I whimpered. He slipped his fingers inside me, inhaling in surprise. "You must really want me." He grinned.

I could only nod. His fingers were good, so good, but I needed more and I thought I might start screaming out of frustration if I didn't get it.

Leo surprised me by ducking his head between my legs, kissing the dip in my stomach, my pelvic bone, and then lowering his tongue against me. He gave me a long slow lick, then another, working his tongue over my clit, licking and moaning until lights started exploding in the corners of my vision.

I pushed on his shoulder. "Leo," I whimpered. "Please . . ."

Abruptly, Leo lifted his head and pushed my thighs back so my knees pressed into my chest. I felt the tip of his cock press in, and gasped at the sharp pinch as he pushed his hips forward. I bit down on my lip to stifle a scream. I was on the small side, and Leo definitely was not.

He paused for a moment, hesitating to see if he'd hurt me, but I lifted my hips into his, begging him to keep going. He let out a slow pant, thrusting again and stopping. "Can you get pregnant?" he asked me abruptly.

I blinked. "What? No!"

Leo nodded. There was a sheen of sweat on his cheeks and chest, and he bent and pressed his lips into my forehead. "Sorry. Force of habit."

He thrust into me again before I could say anything, pushing me into the seat with each movement of his hips. I wrapped my legs around his waist and held on, digging my nails into his arms as he fucked me insistently, harder and harder, until just when I was sure I was going to split in two, I felt my muscles tighten and I came hard enough that I bit into Leo's shoulder to muffle a scream, tasting the salt on his skin.

"Oh, fuck," Leo mumbled against my neck, giving another ragged thrust or two before he came, collapsing with his face buried in my neck.

"Jesus Christ," he muttered after a few seconds of me silently trying to catch my breath. "I haven't come like that since I was sixteen."

He pulled away from me, sitting up and pulling up his jeans. I stayed where I was, my heart thudding like I'd just sprinted ten miles. I could already tell I was going to feel like I'd spent the night doing the splits come morning, but I couldn't have cared less.

Leo lit a cigarette. "Next time we do this in a bed. I need the space to fuck you senseless."

"You think there's gonna be a next time?" I said. I fished my shirt off the car floor and slid it back on, shimmying back into my jeans.

Leo exhaled and grinned, passing me the smoke. I took it, watching the pale cloud drift up to the ceiling.

"There is," he said. "And a time after that, and after that." He rubbed his shoulder and laughed. "You bit me. Am I going to turn into a hellhound now?"

"That's lycanthropes, ass," I said, not able to help the smile on my face. "You're not—"

Something rattled the car, and I fell silent, sitting upright with a jolt. It felt like we'd been rear-ended, but there was nobody else on the street. No other cars had passed the entire time we'd been parked by the tree-lined curb.

Leo stubbed out his cigarette. "The fuck was that?"

The car rattled again. Whatever it was acted like a heavy wind, shaking the Buick on its suspension, but none of the tree branches stirred outside.

Leo reached under the seat and came up with a gun, a brushed steel Colt automatic with ivory grips. "Is that Kayla woman doing this?" he muttered to me.

I shook my head, my eyes searching the darkened street outside. The only faint glow came from the moon and the golden light spilling out of the houses on either side of Kayla Stillman's, light that cast long shadows across her lawn.

As I watched, one of the shadows peeled away from the overgrowth and flew toward the car, moving so fast it shimmered.

"Watch out!" I screamed, pulling Leo down as it passed through the glass and over our heads. A bitter cold washed over my bare skin, frosting my breath and turning the tips of my fingers blue. The glass where the shadow had touched was now a halo of frost, so cold the pane cracked beneath it.

More of the shadows started moving outside, breaking away from the shapes of trees and mailboxes and streetlamps. It was so cold now my fingers were numb, and every breath burned my lungs.

"Shit," Leo whispered. I peered out the car window, watching them mass and move toward the Buick.

"What's happening?" I said.

"Revenants," Leo muttered, shoving his gun into his waistband. "Soul fragments," he said when I stared at him. "By-product of the magic necromancers use to raise deadheads. If they touch you, they'll burn the soul right out of you."

He pointed at Kayla Stillman's porch. "We're going to have to run for it. *Do not* let those things touch you."

He put his hand on the car door and looked at me. "You understand?"

I nodded silently. I hadn't run into many ghosts. Usually I was the one creating them. The few necromancers I'd pulled in before Leo had run more to the traditional deadhead army. These things, which looked like vaguely human forms draped in black sheets made of mist, were something new.

Usually ghosts were just loops of leftover humanity, sad little scraps that couldn't do much more than appear, cry, and fade away again. To find a truly malignant ghost was rare, and they were usually so entrenched into a place they were impossible to remove. I'd never seen any that roamed, or vibrated with so much black magic.

Leo tripped the latch and shoved the door open, and I dropped out, rolling on the pavement and coming to my feet already running. The revenants swirled to look at me, and even though they didn't have eyes—or faces—that I could see, I had the profound sense that I was the sole focus of their gazes.

I almost made it to the sidewalk on the other side of the street when one of them rose out of a pool of shadow in front of me. I came up short, staring into the shimmering black column, and felt a heaviness in all my limbs as the mist began to part. I saw a pointed chin made of bone, a mouth full of piranha teeth, and the gaping eye sockets of a skull where the eyes should be.

Something exploded next to my left ear, and splinters of wood flew off one of Kayla Stillman's porch post. Leo grabbed me and pulled me out of the path of the revenant, his gun in his other hand. We took the steps of Kayla's porch three at a time and Leo pounded on her door.

"Kayla!" he shouted. "Open the door!"

The revenants hissed but seemed hesitant to come much farther than the lawn. "They draw you in," Leo said. "Like rattlesnakes." He pounded on the door again, and I joined him.

A porch light flicked on. "Go away!" Kayla shouted from behind the door.

"Kayla, you need to let us in!" Leo shouted. "We're here to help you!"

Kayla's voice sounded high and strained. "I seriously doubt that!"

Leo rolled his eyes. "I'm kicking this door down in two seconds, so you better shut down any traps you've got hooked up to it." He waited a split second, then reared back and planted his foot in the doorframe. The door was old and solid oak, and it took a few kicks before Leo managed to bash it in.

We piled inside, Leo slamming the ruined door again. When I looked in front of us, Kayla was holding a shotgun. It wasn't an antique like Annabelle's Winchester, it was the cheap kind you could get at Walmart for less than a good bottle of scotch would run you.

Kayla racked the gun, her skinny fingers shaking with the effort. "I'll blow you straight to Hell!" she screamed. "You're God's mistake! Get out of my house!"

I grabbed the barrel of the shotgun, pointing it at the floor and stepping inside the firing radius before I sock Kayla hard in the eye. She yelped and went down, drawing her knees in and clutching at them as she glared at me. "I am a warrior of the Lord. I don't fear you, demon."

"Good for you," I said. "I'm not a demon. If demons don't scare you shitless, you're even crazier than I realized."

"I'm not crazy!" Kayla spat with surprising ferocity. "I see your face right now—the real face, the black dog with the red eyes. Demon!"

I smacked the top of her head again. "Stop that!"

I handed off the shotgun to Leo, who peered through Kayla's thick Lone Gunmen curtains. "The barrier will hold for a while. They won't try to come in until it starts to wear off." He emptied the shells from the gun and leaned it against the wall. "Where did they come from?"

I raised an eyebrow. "Where do you think?"

"I've seen one or two when there's two necromancers churning out deadheads in a turf war," Leo said. "But a whole pack of them isn't normal."

Kayla tried to jump up again, reaching for a small holdout pistol in an ankle holster. I grabbed her by the shirt and swung her into the wall hard enough to crack the plaster. "Bitch, slow your roll," I ordered her. "If we wanted to kill you, you would have been dead hours ago."

Kayla went limp under my hand, and Leo sighed, shoving his hands through his hair. "Then again," he said, "what about this is normal?"

"Who *are* you?" Kayla demanded. "I want you out of my house."

"I'm a hellhound, this is Leonid," I told Kayla, letting go of her so she'd trust me enough to quit thinking I was here to ax murder her. I drew the Scythe from its pouch. Kayla stared at it, her pupils dilating.

"You know what this is?" I asked, and she nodded, her thin lips slightly parted.

"The Grim Reaper's Scythe . . ." she breathed.

"Yeah, whatever," I said, putting it away quickly. Her doe-eyed fixation was creepier than any of the revenants outside. "The Scythe can kill anything," I said. "I'm going to use it on Lilith. And if you're smart, you'll help me stick her before she sticks you."

Kayla swallowed a lump in her throat, staring at me from under her long dark lashes. "I know Lilith. I know every word of the Bible. Chapter and verse."

"I don't doubt it," I said. "And sorry to tell you that the Lilith who putters around Eden and messes with Adam's head? She's a polite fiction. The real demon is much worse."

Kayla sighed and leaned against the wall again. A lot of the taut intensity endemic to people who seriously need to up their meds drained out of her. "I'm not crazy," she muttered again. "They said I was, and they took my rifle. I had to shoot him," she said sadly. "I had to stop him from hurting anyone else."

"That's me in a nutshell," I said. "Just trying to help."

"Lilith wants me because of what I see, huh?" Kayla said. She kicked one toe against a deep gouge in the hall floor.

"That's the short version," I said. "Trust me, you're better off just seeing the highlight reel."

The light in the hall flickered, and in the few seconds of darkness a silken voice slithered into my ear. "Couldn't agree with you more."

When the lights blazed back to life Lilith stood in the front hall smiling at me. Her hair was down, long golden ringlets that gleamed under the bare bulb in Kayla's ceiling.

Kayla let out a yelp and hid her face, curling into a tight ball. Lilith gave her a benevolent smile and then turned to me. "Hello, Ava. Thank you for all your help."

"I didn't help you," I said, frozen to the spot. Lilith never blinked. Her eyes were that flawless crystal blue, but she was like a snake—beautiful right up until she pumped you full of venom.

"You did, actually," she said, tapping the side of her own head. She was wearing slim blue pants and a fawn jacket, like she'd just stepped out of the country club to talk to us. "You remember anything after that little accident of yours?"

I squeezed my eyes shut. The thing in the road. The thing that came out of nowhere.

"You didn't make it easy to find you." She sighed. "But I knew

sooner or later Azrael and Raphael would get the band back together. So really, all I had to do was wait. Very bad form to leave
the scene of an accident, by the way. I almost lost you after you
managed to crawl away. When I've got you on my special steel table in Hell and we're playing with all of my favorite toys, you'll
have to tell me how you managed that."

So I really did have a mysterious taxi service that had saved me
from Lilith back in Louisiana. Just like the voice in my head had
saved me from dying in a cooler in Reno, and sharpened my instincts in Wyoming, where I'd avoided Billy's hit squad by inches.

That was interesting. When I wasn't facing a pissed-off demon
it'd be a good mystery to solve.

"How did you get past the barrier?" Leo spoke up. He was also
standing perfectly still, switching his gaze between Lilith and the
revenants outside like clockwork.

"You're not such hot shit as you think you are," Lilith told him.
"In a little bit of a hurry, maybe?" She turned back to me, tapping
her nails against the arm of her coat. "In the beginning I wondered
why Gary kept you around, but I see now. You're not the fastest
or strongest hound, certainly no great shakes when it comes to
brains, but you are tenacious. I didn't even have to look for the
innocent. I just had to stick with you."

"Ava doesn't belong to you," Leo said. "Or anyone else. So why
don't you just take what you came for and go."

"Leo!" I hissed while Lilith laughed, bubbly and genuine.

"I like you, Leonid Karpov. If I were a betting woman I'd see
great things in your future." Her smile dropped off and she sighed.
"Unfortunately I can't do that. You see, I need Ava around until I
get what I want."

"Why?" I said. Kayla was shaking as Lilith stood in front of her, and I didn't feel great about letting Lilith take her out from under my nose, but it was better to be alive and guilty than noble and in six separate Dumpsters along the interstate. "I'm never going to obey you. Why do you keep trying to get your claws in me?"

"Because I need a damned soul to spill their blood on the doors of Tartarus," Lilith said flatly. "And I can't think of one whose throat I'd like to slit more than yours."

"Not going to happen," Leo said, starting toward Lilith. I opened my mouth to scream at him to stay back, but it was too late. The snake struck and Lilith grabbed him by the windpipe, turning so her forearm was pressed against his throat. She forced Leo to his knees in front of her. I took a step, and she clicked her tongue.

"Don't," she said. "I don't have time for games, Ava. You get that girl up and walk out this door with me or I kill him."

I hesitated, staring at Leo. I was frozen with a panic I thought I'd left behind me a long time ago. All I could think was that it was all my fault, I'd let Lilith manipulate me, and that everything Clint said was true.

"Clint won't let you do this," I said. Lilith tossed her head back, laughing again.

"Ava, *Azrael* gave himself to me willingly when I found you in the swamp. He pleaded with me to save your life and not simply kill you outright, and because I am not, as you so classily insisted, a monster, I agreed." She stroked Leo's throat with her sharp nails and he flinched. "Seeing Azrael squirm after all he did to me . . . I admit, that's something I'll remember happily for the rest of my days." Her expression twisted and she pointed with her free hand. "Drop the Scythe on the floor."

I did as she said, watching the black holster hit Kayla's stained carpet with a sense of sinking down into something I could never hope to escape. My chest was tight and my vision was blurring, like I really was drowning.

"Good girl," Lilith said, saccharine creeping into her voice. "Now tuck your little tail and go kill the girl."

"No!" Kayla moaned, struggling to get away from me.

All I saw in that moment was Leo, and I strode over to Kayla and grabbed her by the back of her shirt.

"Not as yourself!" Lilith snapped. "Honestly, you try to do a simple thing like force a hellhound to kill an innocent stranger to teach them that they're *not* human and they never were and you still manage to screw it up. Tear her throat out. I need the blood, idiot."

Kayla looked up at me, tears streaking her face. "Please . . ." she whimpered. "I know I haven't lived a righteous life but I tried . . . I tried . . ."

I straightened up. It would be easy, I'd done it a thousand times. And then I'd turn myself over, and Leo would be safe. Nobody else would get hurt, especially not him. Whatever Lilith wanted to do to this miserable, dirty, angry pile of shit that humanity stood on top of and called a world, I didn't care anymore.

"Ava." Leo looked up at me. His pulse throbbed in his neck, but his voice was calm. "Don't," he said to me. "It's not worth it for me."

"Shut up." Lilith sighed. "You're not in charge here. You never were."

"I'm not talking to you, bitch," Leo growled. He looked back at me. "Ava, if you kill her you will never be able to live with yourself. Leave that girl alone and tell this whore to go sit on a flagpole."

Lilith's arm clamped tight around his throat. "I told you to stop talking. Do you want to lose your tongue along with your testicles?"

I started shaking, pressing my hands over my face and wishing it would all go away. Kayla scrambled away from me, but Lilith cut her eyes to the door, and it slammed shut of its own volition, locking.

"I'm sorry, Leo," I whispered as Kayla sobbed and Lilith shouted something at me. "I'm sorry."

"Kill that damn woman this instant or I am going to actually get angry!" Lilith bellowed. Glass shattered and the light overhead fizzed. The floor under my feet vibrated as I looked at Leo. He gave me a nod. I knew he was right. If I gave in to Lilith I wouldn't get away from her. I'd be shackled to her for the rest of my existence, bullied into cold-blooded murder on her say-so. I hadn't been thinking when I killed Gary, but I'd had time since, and I realized, almost calmly amid the screaming and sobbing, that I could be a dog on a leash or I could be a hound.

"Ava!" Lilith shouted. "Do what I say!"

I moved my eyes to Lilith's. "No."

Lilith's nostrils flared. "Fine." She plunged her fingers deep into Leo's back. Bone cracked, and he screamed as Lilith gave a twist and dropped him to the carpet, where he landed face-first.

I thought it was strange that he kept screaming when he was so still, blood slowly pooling under him, more blood trickling from his mouth and nostrils as he coughed. Then I realized it was me, and I fell on my knees, blood from the carpet soaking into my jeans. I cradled Leo as Lilith looked on.

"It's okay," Leo whispered. "Really. You did what you had to do."

I dropped my head to put it against his, and I felt Leo shoving something under my folded legs, our bodies hiding the action from Lilith's eyes. I pulled away a little, recognizing the thin, flat shape of the Scythe. The pouch was still half under Leo's torso, soaked with his blood, but the blade was within reach.

"You're going to be fine, Ava," Leo whispered, squeezing my hand. "Kill the bitch first chance you get."

He let out one more horrible, rattling cough. The last breaths leaving the body are startlingly loud and heart-squeezingly ragged. Leo shuddered once and went still, his glassy eyes staring at the carpet.

Lilith used one of Kayla's coats to wipe the blood off her hands as I knelt there, trying to make myself put the Scythe in my boot and stand up. I couldn't stop looking at Leo, and even when I squeezed my eyes shut, I knew I'd always be able to see him lying still and cold whenever I closed my eyes from now on. Forget Caleb and Jasper—this was the death that would be in my nightmares.

"Now that you've learned from that little object lesson," Lilith said, grabbing Kayla off the floor, "get your ass up and get moving."

I got to my feet slowly, one leg at a time. After the body blow of seeing Leo fall, I didn't feel anything. Everything was slow and remote, and I could see exactly what I needed to do like I was sitting high above, controlling the Ava standing in the hall with blood on her hands and her legs via remote control.

Kayla was in the way—if I tried to use the Scythe on Lilith now, she had a built-in human shield.

"Don't you pull another stunt like that again," Lilith snapped as I descended the porch steps, the revenants parting like mist before the prow of a boat.

"I won't," I said quietly. I meant it too—I wasn't going to defy Lilith again. I was going to play my part as a hound until she dropped her guard and I could jam the Scythe directly into her heart. That was the only thing that kept me moving as I followed Lilith away from Kayla's house and into the darkness of the street.

26

Lilith stopped in the center of the street, holding Kayla firmly by the neck, and beckoned to me. I looked back at the open door of Kayla's house. I could still see the outline of Leo's body. I shuddered and looked away.

"Don't cry, Ava," Lilith said. "Soon you'll be far away and this will just be the part before the time you spend in Hell."

"You don't scare me, witch," I said, looking at the cracked pavement so I wouldn't have to see Lilith smirking.

Lilith huffed a sigh and then turned away from me, facing the intersection. I felt a shimmer of electricity around me, the same feeling I got when I felt the unwrapped Scythe against my skin. When I looked up the intersection had vanished and the road stretched away into the invisible distance. Fog crowded the shoulders, and only a faint glow of a distant, invisible streetlight gave any sense that we were still in a place hemmed by space and time.

Kayla blinked rapidly, her chest rising and falling in short pants. Lilith pinched her neck a little tighter. "Don't pass out on me now, Kayla. Fun's just getting started." She inhaled the cool air deeply and grinned at me. "First time's a kick in the ass, isn't it?"

I shivered involuntarily, trying to shake off the spider-crawling feeling of whatever made this place run. "Where are we?"

"Between point A and point B," Lilith said. "That empty stretch of road on your way to the crossroads." She shoved Kayla forward, her heels clicking on the asphalt. "Welcome to the Lost Highway."

We walked for a long way, Kayla whimpering softly. Lilith whistled a snippet of a song I couldn't quite place. "I'm guessing Annabelle didn't tell you the nitty-gritty details. Just that this place was Bad and Wrong and Scary."

"She just told me you were dangerous and I should stay away from you," I muttered. I recognized the numbness of shock setting in. When Caleb had sacrificed me and I'd woken up, knowing I was dead but walking all the same, it had taken days for me to accept what was happening and have a breakdown. In the meantime I just moved around doing whatever Gary told me. This time, at least, I had a purpose. I kept the Scythe close. If I lost it, I'd have nothing.

We were closer to the light, and the fog started to peel away, revealing a barren stretch of desert between mountains, moon and stars high overhead, spilling down to the horizon like they only did when you were in pure emptiness far from anything man-made.

"The Lost Highway runs all over this realm," Lilith said. "It's how I kept getting the jump on you. Annabelle told me about it. Not recently—hundreds of years ago. Poor dear felt sorry for me." Lilith chuckled softly. "You really shouldn't trust the Fallen. You think I'm a survivor—those sons of bitches will sell their grandmother's kidney for beer money."

"Can we just get this over with?" I said. The Scythe itched at my leg, shoved into my boot. I tried to walk slowly and not give away any stiffness in my gait. I wasn't shocked that Annabelle had helped Lilith—she'd screwed me up good with her news that I might possibly be a single soul reborn over and over and that Leo and I meeting meant some dark thunderheads were gathering in the distant sky where both our lives entwined. She seemed like the type who loved to meddle. And who might be a psychopath to boot, always a winning combination.

"You may lack any direction but at least you're motivated," Lilith said, then wrapped her hand around Kayla's throat and jerked her head sideways. A sharp crack echoed in the still air and Kayla dropped in a heap.

I took in a breath and held it. I just had to pretend I was on the leash a little longer.

"You have a problem?" Lilith said. She pulled a soaked rag out of her jacket. I realized with a shudder it was soaked in blood. Clint's blood, judging by the clove-tinged aroma that thickened the air between us. Definitely not from a human.

"No," I said. "Just some confusion."

Lilith knelt in the crusty brown dirt and carefully placed the rag. "Such as?"

I stared at her, and she sighed. "Ava, if the two of us are going to be spending time together you can't be standing there like you're growing out of the ground."

"Why are you doing this?" I said. "I get it, you hate the Fallen, but why open Tartarus? Human souls running rampant won't exactly be a picnic. I put some of the worst people in there away. I know what kind of vindictive assholes are coming after you if they get out."

"That's the problem with reapers and mud dogs like you." Lilith stood up and brushed off her hands. "You're loyal as fuck but you fall far short on imagination." She spread out her arms and spun in a slow circle. "Where do you think we are?"

"The desert?" I said. Lilith smiled.

"That's exactly what I'm talking about. You were created by Hellspawn, you've lived your life ever since in one's shadow, and yet you know nothing about Hell. Yes, we're in the desert. But this desert is special."

I sighed. "Are we in Nazareth or something? Are we camping in the same manger as the baby Jesus?"

"We're in Nevada, smart-ass," Lilith said. "About ninety miles from Las Vegas." She bent down and rolled Kayla's body onto its back, tearing the front of her shirt open to the top of Kayla's bra. "The crossroads are conduits between here and Hell and the Kingdom, yes, but what creates them is destruction, suffering. Natural disasters, wars, death camps."

Murders of innocent women betrayed by the men they were stupid enough to love . . .

I saw a low row of dilapidated buildings in the distance, lit by the glow of Las Vegas along the horizon, a permanent sunrise from dusk to dawn. Even in the half-light glow, there was something oddly familiar about the row of little clapboard bungalows and rusty, war-era cars and trucks.

Lilith swept her arm at the little fake movie-set of a town and the barren, browned earth around it. "Dozens of atomic bombs exploded less than a mile from here. Makes for one hell of a cross-roads."

That was why all this was familiar. We were standing on one of the unused test sites, from the time when people in Las Vegas would sit on their roofs and watch the flash, the mushroom cloud blossoming in the distance, knowing nothing about the poison wind that swept across the desert floor toward their waiting flesh. Even as a hellhound, I felt my skin crawl being this close.

I tried to jerk away from Lilith when her hand shot out, but she grabbed my hand and sliced her nail across my palm, so deep I felt my fingers go numb as the nerves went dead. My blood spattered into the dirt, and Lilith reached down and stuck her bloody fingers into Kayla's rib cage. I heard bone crack as she pushed the breast-bone aside. Kayla's heart broke free with a rubbery snap.

My head started spinning. I had to do it now, while she was distracted. Lilith held out her hands parallel with the earth and started to murmur in the hissing, ebb-and-flow language of Hell. The blood droplets rose from the ground, from the rag and poor Kayla and what was pouring out of my hand, like raindrops flow-ing backward. The dust around us started to rise as well, and I wondered how many radioactive particles I was inhaling as the wind whipped my hair slick against my head.

I reached down and pulled the Scythe from my boot. In another ten seconds, none of it would matter.

Lilith's hair flowed around her head like a halo, in stark contrast to the body at her feet and the dust storm rising around us. I felt the breathlessness of the air, like the seconds just before a tornado hits. I'd ridden out a few back when I settled in Kansas and Nebraska after the war, sometimes lucky enough to make it to a shelter and sometimes not. The scream is unlike anything else on earth, a sound and a sensation so complete you'd swear the world had ended and the only thing that existed was the wind, drawing up all the sound and air around you.

My hand didn't shake when I turned the Scythe in my grip. I was within arm's length of Lilith. It was done.

At least it was until she spun around, grabbing my arm and snapping my wrist in one smooth movement. The Scythe fell to the dirt and I followed it, my hand hanging uselessly.

"Naughty," Lilith scolded. "I've come way too far to have some misguided attack of your conscience throw me off track, Ava."

"You just want the world to burn," I said. "I have to live in it. I can't let you."

Lilith crouched down. The dust and blood turned around us slowly, and I saw that Kayla's body had vanished. I was totally alone, totally at Lilith's mercy. "If you're gonna kill me can you just do it?" I said. "No monologue about how Hell rules and angels suck cocks in it?"

"I'm not going to waste time killing you," Lilith said. "Here's a little history lesson, Ava. I was born into slavery. Azrael was my master, and he was the worst piece of shit to ever fall from the Kingdom. He abused me in ways you can't fathom, and when we finally got the courage to fight back, those piss-ants tried to throw us into Tartarus."

She breathed in. The air had changed. I could smell the faint, sweet scent of decay, like a funeral home with the heat turned too high. "Do you know how I learned to fight back?" Lilith whispered. "I met someone, just like you did. Someone who made me believe I didn't have to live under the heel of the Fallen anymore. And they condemned him for that. They put him in that place, and I'm free, which is so far from how it should be. We lost our ability to enter Tartarus when we expelled the Fallen. Gary and I spent almost a thousand years waiting for this night, and then you came along. You almost ruined everything."

The earth fell back to ground, and I felt a jolt, as if I'd been riding in a car that had just run over a curb. "I didn't know," I said. "Clint told me . . ."

"Clint tells the story he remembers, and it's the one that makes him look good," Lilith snapped. "Him losing everything in the crossroads may seem like payback, but it's not. It's not even close. He gets to forget what he did to me and I live with it every day. I see the face of the one who saved me every day, knowing he's in Tartarus, enduring torture, paying for helping me escape Azrael's abuses and try to stand on my own."

As the dust settled, I realized we were no longer in the cool, clear air of the Mojave. Things were smoking, and the ground under my feet was a powdery gray mix of ash and lava sand that shifted when I tried to stand up, making me stumble. The stars had blinked out, and all I could hear was the screaming of wind across a vast, empty expanse.

"You of all people should know what you do to reapers and hounds is fucked up," I told Lilith, coughing as the dust invaded my lungs. "You enslaved me just like Azrael did to you."

"Reapers and hounds are the Fallen's bastard creation," Lilith spat. "You are nothing to me but fodder for the machine of the damned that turns the gears of my home."

She pointed ahead of us, and through the blowing sand I saw a pair of blank metal doors. They were old, riveted like hatches on a submarine, twice as tall as I was and about five times as wide.

"Welcome to the darkest part of Hell," Lilith murmured, almost reverently. "The place where I was born, and the place I was condemned to when the Fallen had no more use for me."

Lilith walked to the doors and placed her hands flat against the metal. I just stood, watching the Scythe in the dirt between us. I wasn't stupid enough to think she wouldn't snap me in half just like Kayla if I tried to stab her again. A dog that bites gets put down—Gary had sure drilled that into me.

"You're breaking open Tartarus to pay them back," I said. "I get it. But you have to understand that we're not on the same side and I had to do what I did to try and protect what *I* care about."

"I do understand that," Lilith said as the wheel locks on the doors started to rotate, creaking with a screeching so loud it ground my teeth. "But you don't understand me at all, Ava."

"Probably not," I muttered. Lilith stepped back as the long metal rods holding the doors in place started to rumble back into their sockets, shedding flakes of rust as big as my palm.

"I don't care about the damned in there," she said. "I don't care about Tartarus at all. I'm just here for the Fallen who showed the demons how to be free. He's suffered for a thousand years for what he did. I think that's enough."

"This Fallen is pretty special, then," I whispered, transfixed by the heaving, shifting darkness contained by the doors. Faint screams, constant and endless as an ocean tide, issued from inside the depths. I saw fences, spotlights, chain link, and barbed wire. I'd seen similar things in Europe after the war, places seemingly designed to contain the whole of human suffering, and then some.

This was worse than any of them.

"He's the only thing that matters," Lilith said, twin tears sliding down her face as she stepped toward the open doors of Tartarus. "The only one of the Host brave enough to leave the Kingdom. Brave enough after he left to stand with us." She stretched out her arms to the darkness. "Lucifer," she said softly. "It's been so long, but I came for you, just like I said."

Like a creature spurred to life by a clap of thunder, lights snapped on along block after block after block of cells inside Tartarus, more lights than any city back on the other side of the crossroads. I stood rooted to the spot, watching the shadows massing on the other side of the fence, which bent and sagged under their weight. Far away, in the depths of the Fallen's massive prison, sirens began to scream.

As the crowd at the fence broke it, tumbling over the ragged links and stretching the barbed wire beyond, I tried to make myself move. It wasn't easy. There was a shift in the gravity of Hell, a heaviness not present back on earth that kept me rooted to the spot.

"Lucifer," I whispered, trying to get myself used to the idea enough to do something about this clusterfuck. A Fallen. *The* Fallen. Bad enough that Azrael and the others had banished him to Tartarus right along with the demons. According to Clint, anyway. If I went by Lilith, then Clint was definitely the asshole in that equation. Still, Lucifer had been the one to get them all tossed out, if you listened to the human version of things. Odds are, he wasn't a real people person.

The shadow started to rush past us, and I saw they were people, washed out and bedraggled as any deadhead. Some screamed, or sobbed, or bled from the fatal wounds that had damned them to Tartarus in the first place. The damned were flowing free, a tidal wave building to fill the entire space of the door.

I made myself move, one foot at a time, pick up the Scythe, and got to Lilith's shoulder. "I get it!" I shouted in her ear, trying to make myself heard over the howling of the damned and the droning wail of the klaxons. "I understand this a lot more than just sowing chaos! But this is insane! If you need the damned, what will you do when Tartarus is empty and the world is so overrun there's no one to repopulate?"

Lilith bared her teeth. "If you haven't figured out that my millennium of partying with Azrael drove me a little crazy, you're a lot dumber than I thought."

"You love Lucifer, I get it!" I shouted. "But maybe he's in here for a reason!"

"Oh, most definitely," Lilith purred. "And when he gets out, he and I are going to clean house in Hell. Then I figure a nice little honeymoon to earth to clear out the dregs of the Fallen. Then, who knows. I heard the Kingdom is ripe for a takeover."

"Just take Lucifer and go," I shouted. "You got what you wanted! Take him, close this nuthouse up, and go live your lives together!" I let the Scythe dangle from my fingers, showing I meant her no harm. "I won't try to stop you."

"Ava." Lilith dropped her head to her chest. "Ava, Ava, Ava. I've spent a thousand years letting your miserable little realm exist. Letting Hell dissolve into a petty dictatorship without its true leader. Letting you worthless little insects live your worthless little lives. The way I see it . . ." She jerked me close, so I could feel her breath on my face. "The world owes me a favor or two."

We stood like that, an island in a stream of the damned spewing forth from Tartarus, running past us into the crossroads. I saw things that weren't human too, things with scales, things that crawled or leaped.

Where are the guards? I thought. What kind of a prison didn't have a warden?

"No guards," Lilith said, and smirked at me. "We're in Hell, Ava. I'm not running on half power anymore. Tartarus governs itself. No one but the inmates has ever gotten in or out until now."

Ahead of us, the stampede parted and I saw a tall, slim figure, turned into a shadow imprint by the klieg lights burning their bright spots into the ground all around us. Lilith let go of me, rushing forward. A pack of the damned slammed into me and knocked me to the ground. I curled in a ball and tried to protect my head and ribs. I didn't think they'd be very kindly inclined toward a hellhound in their midst. I wondered how many of these souls I'd sent to Tartarus myself, never knowing or caring what happened once Gary took them to Hell.

Lilith ran to the figure and embraced him, and he pulled her to him, lifting her off the ground. From my vantage he looked like he was ten feet tall, but when he stepped into the light he wasn't anything so amazing—just a pale platinum blond with the same piercing eyes as Lilith. Honestly, they looked more like brother and sister than anything, which just made the whole thing creepy.

"Who's this?" Lucifer asked, looking down at me. I uncurled my body as the damned gave him a wide berth, getting to my feet unsteadily. The Scythe was gone, scattered by the gang that had bowled me over. Worst of all, I wasn't useful to Lilith anymore.

"This is Ava, the hellhound who almost screwed everything for us," Lilith said. "But she's redeemed herself. Mostly."

"Ah." Lucifer smiled at me. "Allow me to thank her, then." He wasn't handsome in the way humans understand it, but there was something about his face that made it impossible to look away. I didn't have any illusions about what was going on. He was the snake and I was the mouse.

Rather that collapsing like I would have done a few weeks ago I felt angry, my gut churning at the trouble I'd gotten myself into. "Don't mention it," I gritted.

Lucifer laughed. "You're too modest. If I don't owe you thanks, I at least owe you payback for conspiring to keep me locked up in here."

He reached for me and I jumped backward. My feet tangled, and I went down hard on the arm I'd torn up in the car wreck. A scream wrenched from my mouth, and that made me even angrier. I'd had enough of looking weak. "You served your purpose," Lucifer said, standing over me and cocking his head like he was trying to figure out what I could possibly be useful for. "But I think it's time you were put down."

A shadow fell over me from the other direction, and Lucifer looked away from me, his jaw tightening at the sight of whoever stood there.

Over the sirens and the yelling, a voice I never thought I'd hear again spoke. "Leave her alone, asshole."

Leo reached his hand down and lifted me to my feet. I stared at him. "How are you here?" I whispered.

Leo smiled at me. "Don't worry about it, Ava." The Scythe gleamed in his other hand, and Lucifer frowned.

"This isn't possible. Lilith got rid of you. And . . ."

His lips pulled back from his teeth as he looked at me. "Well. I guess you're not just *another* hellhound, are you?"

I sagged a little. When the ultimate badass of Hell tells you you're an immortal hellhound, you sort of have to believe it.

"He doesn't matter," Lilith said urgently, plucking at Lucifer's arm. "He's just a man."

"He's *not*," Lucifer snarled. "You know what he is, and it's on you that you didn't hunt him down."

"Gary killed every warlock who could possibly be his human host!" Lilith shouted. Her voice sounded like gravel on a chalkboard, and her eyes were so wide I could see white all the way around. In a moment of almost detached amusement, I realized that Lilith was scared shitless. Not of me or Leo, but of what her charming boyfriend was gonna do to her.

"Clearly that incompetent sack of incubus cum *missed one*," Lucifer growled. He shoved Lilith away hard, so she landed on her ass in the dirt, ruining her perfect suit pants. "Get away from me. Centuries I wait and this is the best you can do? I expected better."

"Hey."

Leo raised the Scythe. "Doesn't matter who I am. I'm the guy who's going to put you back where you belong."

"How frightening," Lucifer said. He shimmered, like a zephyr of heat had sprung up from the desert floor, and I choked as his hands went around my throat. He'd appeared behind me, and clamped an arm firmly across my windpipe. I clawed at his arm, digging deep furrows out of his skin with my nails, but he simply grunted in pain.

"Stop that," he said, giving me a shake that made black circles spin in front of my eyes as he compressed my windpipe. "And the both of you—I defeated the Fallen's puppets before and I will have no trouble doing so again. As many times as it takes. You can become the Grim Reaper in a dozen bodies and I will always win."

"This isn't a fight," Leo said, but his voice had lost a lot of its conviction. Lilith watched us from the ground, a smile still playing around her lips.

"That's so cute. I send you to Hell and you show up for a reunion with Ava. She was so sad after I dropped you. She cried, like a sad little toddler."

"This isn't a reunion either," Leo said. "This is an execution." He still didn't move, though, and he clearly didn't know what to do, now that Lucifer had his hands on me.

"How about this," Lucifer said. His voice rumbled against my back. We were touching the entire length of my body. "You put down that blade and walk in the opposite direction, and I'll let you go with all your bits." He didn't feel warm—his skin was the temperature of the air, but his grip was rock solid. I could shift, I reasoned, and that might give me enough time to get away.

But then he'd hurt Leo. Leo was dead, sure, but there were plenty of things worse than dying once your soul ended up in Hell.

Leo looked at me, at Lilith, back at me. The Scythe turned in his grip, and he shifted from foot to foot. I knew he wasn't used to being the vulnerable one, the one not in control, and he didn't know what to do. I could see the long row of cell blocks inside the gates of Tartarus from where I stood, and as I watched the damned stream out of the gates around us I knew exactly what to do.

I looked back at Leo. "Just kill him," I said. "Put the Scythe in him. Right now."

Leo blinked at me. "Ava . . ."

"Are you mad?" Lucifer barked. "You'll kill her right along with me!"

"Leo," I said, never breaking eye contact. "It's okay. Just like you told me it was okay before, in Kayla's house." I'd die, sure. It wouldn't be the first time, but this time I got to make it count for something. In the end, that was always what I'd come back to when I thought about Caleb and what he'd done. How pointless the whole thing had been, how little I'd made my life mean.

I was older now. It was different. Even if I spent eternity in Tartarus, at least Lucifer would be right there with me, and Leo and I could be together.

There were worse deaths.

Leo hesitated, the Scythe poised, and I leaned forward against Lucifer's grasp even as he tried to pull me tighter. "Leo, do *not* let him leave this place," I said. "You know what you have to do, so do it."

"He won't," Lucifer said, his lip curling. "He doesn't have the stones."

"You're not great at reading people," I told Lucifer. "Probably why you spent a thousand years as a demon's cell block bitch."

Lucifer let out an angry snarl, but Leo stepped forward and stuck the Scythe into my gut just under my ribs, angling it up. I felt the red hot blade slice through me, and the thud as it went into Lucifer, deep enough to pierce his heart.

Leo shut his eyes. "I'm sorry, Ava," he whispered.

The pain was indescribable, the worst I'd ever felt. I could feel

325

every cell in my body lighting up as the Scythe took hold of the hound inside of me and ripped it back into Tartarus.

There was screaming, a lot of screaming, and darkness. Some of it sounded like Lilith, some of it like Leo, most of it from me.

I was dead, that much I knew, and my soul was burning. Hit something that's already damned with the Scythe and it goes up like flash paper. I waited for everything to stop, that last period on the page that I'd longed for so many times over the century I'd been a hound.

Instead, I opened my eyes and saw a sky full of thick gray clouds, lit by the spotlights of Tartarus in a dizzying pattern of roaming circles. A little bit of sooty rain fell, washing the dirt and blood from my skin.

It wasn't my blood, I realized, feeling myself over. I had a stab wound in my side that felt like I'd been stuck with a hot poker, but I didn't have that nauseating pain that comes with a gut wound leaking poison from my intestines into my blood. The blade had gone through the cords of my abdominal muscles and into Lucifer, who lay beside me. A vast pool of red spread around him as he lay facedown in the mud, not moving.

I got to my knees and forced myself to touch him, rolling him over onto his back. The Scythe had gone up and into his heart, a fatal blow delivered by an expert. Leo had done the good work I would have expected of him.

Finding out I was still alive was oddly anticlimactic. I'd been prepared to die for so long that actually going through with it, and then finding out I'd avoided the end by a few centimeters of blade, mostly just felt like a letdown.

But Lucifer was contained, and when I looked up I saw the doors of Tartarus were shut tight. No sign of Lilith. No Leo.

I wasn't alone, though, and before I could really freak out about what had happened I realized I had a much bigger problem than a dead Fallen at my feet.

The damned surrounded me, watching me, none of them ready to get close yet. That would change as soon as they realized Lucifer was dead. I shivered as the rain soaked me. That sidestep from dying might have been shorter and narrower than I thought. These assholes were going to tear me apart.

"Hey, girlie," one of the closest said, a barefoot human dressed in ragged gray pants and a shirt, every inch of him smeared with soot. "You don't look so hot."

I cast around. Stay calm, assess your surroundings, find a way out. The things I'd done a million times, only now I was stabbed, trapped in Tartarus, and there was no way out. That was the whole point.

We were in the main corridor of cell blocks by the gates, and farther in I could see a low spread of buildings, surrounded by barbed wire and topped off with the twin chimneys of a crematory that was the source of the oily jet-black soot that clung to everything and permeated the air with cloying smoke.

"Hey," the man said again. "I'm talkin' to you." He came close enough to touch and looked down at me, at the gaping knife wound in my side. "Looks like you might need fixing," he said.

"Fix-it!" another of the crowd echoed, and the surrounding damned took up the chant. The man and others reached out and grabbed me. I swatted and clawed at them, trying to fight them off, but there were just too many.

"Fix-it, fix-it," the crowd chanted, lifting me off the ground and propelling me toward a ramshackle shed leaning at the end of one cell block. A bare bulb dangled inside, and I could see a work bench and a metal table, covered with crusty dried blood.

I snarled as the inmates holding me laid me down on the table, a dozen hands holding me in place. Overhead, hooks dripped slow, coagulated blood onto the cement floor. I caught sight of an oil drum out of the corner of my eye overflowing with a rotting sludge of skin and fat that made my eyes water. The whole shed was rampant with flies and the smell of rotting meat.

"Mr. Fix-it will make you right as rain, girlie," the damned who'd spotted me said, then smiled. I decided right then that I did not want to meet Mr. Fix-it, and I'd risk exposing myself rather than take my chances with this mob.

I wasn't even sure I *could* shift in Tartarus, but when I shut my eyes I felt the familiar exchange between the hound and me, and when I opened them the damned were in a frothing panic. I leaped off the table, hitting the dirt and running for my life. There was a lot of yelling behind me, and the sight of a hellhound agitated all the damned in my path. They converged on me, and soon I realized that I was hemmed in, even my smaller size and a mouth full of wounding teeth not doing a whole fuck-ton of good against hundreds of damned souls looking to take their fate out of my hide.

Hands started to grab at me, and I snapped down on a few fingers and palms. The circle was narrowing, though, and it was getting harder and harder to dodge the grasping hands of the damned.

A rock bounced off my back, then another. Just as I realized I was going to go down under a hail of stones and broken bricks, a blinding blue light washed over the open yard.

The damned fell back, and I was temporarily blinded by the spot. When the sparklers cleared from my vision, I saw two figures approaching. They were taller than the damned, somehow more solid, and the damned fell back and knotted up far out of range of them.

I also backed up as they came toward me with no sign of slowing, but one grabbed me by the skin between my shoulder blades and the other thrust a black cotton bag over my head. I was lifted, struggling, and then something struck the back of my skull, turning everything soft and cottony and blank.

27

Ava," a voice said, soft and firm. A hand touched my shoulder. "Ava, come back to us."

I jolted up, and my head let me know how pissed off it was by sending a wave of nausea through me.

I was on two legs again, lying on a white leather sofa inside an office done in muted tones of white and gray. The only color in the room came from the tie of the man sitting across from me, behind a white desk carved from a single block of marble.

"You're all right," he said, standing and coming over to me. He wore a black suit and a white shirt that started my head throbbing even harder than it already was, it was so bright.

I sat up, my boots leaving streaks on the white leather. Inexplicably, I felt terrible about that and tried to wipe them away with my sooty sleeve, which only made things worse.

"Don't worry about it," the man said. "Happens all the time."

He was beautiful up close. It was an odd way to think of a man, but I didn't have a better word for it. His skin was that same golden tan as Clint's and Annabelle's, and his hair was lighter, soft brown streaked with a few sun-kissed strands here and there. His eyes were a bright gemstone green that dazzled in the soft light, and I got a close-up look as he leaned in and examined my pupils. "You're fine," he pronounced. "You feel all right?"

I touched my side, but beyond the blood crusted on my T-shirt, my side had already started to knit back together. The incision was red and sore, and if my arm was anything to go on, would be for weeks, but I didn't even feel all that queasy from the knock on the head. "I think so," I said, baffled. "Where am I?"

"Tartarus," the man said. He went to a window of long white panels and flipped a switch. They rolled back to show a view of the prison, from high up near one of the crematory chimneys. My heart sank.

"Not to make a bad joke," I said, "but what fresh Hell am I in now?" The office was basically bare except for the cube-y white furniture, nothing on the desk or the walls I could use to fight with. Even the floor was polished white cement, a high sheen that the cynical part of my mind figured would be easy to hose off when blood got spilled.

This guy definitely had the upper hand, so I stayed where I was, trying to stop the waves of dizziness so I could run if I had to.

"You're in the administrative building," the guy said. "Rest assured, none of the damned are allowed here. No Hellspawn at all.

You can't even turn into a hound within these four walls. I have barriers that prevent anything of that nature all around my office." He turned and gave me a chagrined smile. "When you're the warden you don't take a lot of positive meetings."

I felt my breath catch. According to Lilith, Tartarus didn't have a warden. It was just a dumping ground for the damned, the kind of wasteland where things like laws and decency came to die, caught under the wheels of basic survival.

Then again, what did Lilith know?

The guy came around the desk and stuck out his hand. "Sorry, I'm being rude. I'm Uriel. It's good to finally meet you in person."

I didn't take his hand, instead staring up at his square-jawed, perfectly tanned face. "I thought the only Fallen in here was Lucifer."

"Lucifer is the only Fallen," Uriel said, withdrawing his hand. He went to a small indent in the wall and revealed a bar behind a sliding panel. He poured me a glass of water out of a decanter shaped like a teardrop and brought it back. "Here. I know how parched you get down in the yards."

I took the glass cautiously. My throat was dry and felt like I'd chewed on sand, and I figured he wouldn't try to poison me, since he could have killed me when I was passed out.

"I'm an angel," Uriel said. "Not a Fallen. I came from the Kingdom to administer things here, but I am not like those animals you met. Especially not Lucifer."

I choked on my water, sending a flood down the front of my shirt. Uriel got a bar towel and handed it to me, frowning as I dabbed at my filthy shirt. "Sorry to be so blunt, but we need to talk honestly, and I don't have a lot of time."

"Angels only live in the Kingdom," I said dumbly, like I was five years old and telling somebody what sound the cow made.

"Some do," Uriel said. "Some live on Earth. We just know how to actually live, not run around fucking everything up and making a spectacle of ourselves like the Fallen and the Hellspawn." He accepted the towel back and put it down a laundry chute behind another soundless wall panel.

"Clint said . . ." I started, then stopped. Uriel cocked his head. He was tall, probably at least six and a half feet, but he carried himself well, his tailored suit fitting his lanky limbs like a carapace.

"Clint? Oh, right. That's what Azrael is calling himself these days." He tapped a drawer in his desk. "I've got a file on all of them. All of the Fallen who survived the exodus to Earth. All of the demons out there in Hell too."

"I'm really confused," I blurted, and Uriel laughed. When he laughed his entire face lit up, and if I'd met him anywhere else— if I was anyone else—I'd have a hard time speaking and not just staring.

"You're unique, Ava. I assume Azrael told you something to wet your whistle—mind if I ask how much?"

I nodded, seizing on the fact that he seemed pleasant and reasonable on the surface. I was pretty sure it was an act, but maybe I could get something. "If I can ask you something too."

"Anything." Uriel spread his hands. "Shoot."

"How are you here?" I said. "I mean, I don't know much, but I understand how the crossroads work."

"The Kingdom commands a lot of power, more than anything Hell has to offer," Uriel said. "When the Fallen built this place it didn't go unnoticed. We reacted late, but we did what we could."

He sat down in his desk chair, leaning back and crossing one shiny black shoe across the knee of his suit. "Azrael tell you the demons sealed him out of Tartarus?"

I nodded. Uriel grinned wider. "They had a little help. All we could do was close it up and make sure only the damned and the condemned came in and nothing ever, ever came out. The demons use the damned, and as long as they have souls on tap they don't ask many questions."

"Until Lilith," I said. Uriel sighed.

"That nutcase has caused me more problems than any other Hellspawn combined. Her and Lucifer's little homicidal love story is a pain right in my ass."

"He's dead," I said quietly. "Leo killed him."

Uriel didn't ask how or who Leo was, so I figured he must be poking around inside my skull like Lilith had. "Ava," he said aloud. "What did Azrael say?"

I knew what he was asking about, so I took a deep breath and let it out. "He said I'm not human, that I have the soul of a hound only. That he and the other Fallen created four couriers to travel the crossroads and that one of them started bringing lost souls to Hell. Me and Leo are those souls, dying over and over because there's no Fallen in Hell anymore to use us."

"Use is an accurate description," Uriel said. "Ava, you were human once. Azrael stole two human souls himself and twisted them, destroyed them to create the reapers and the hellhounds. He's a bastard of the highest order and always was."

I didn't mean to, but I teared up and a long gasp came out of my throat without my bidding. Uriel gave me a sad smile, then handed me a pristine white box of tissues from his desk drawer.

"The Fallen lied to you, Ava. They have as much of a stake in opening Tartarus as Lilith did. Actually, they're worse, because she did it for Lucifer and the Fallen are just waiting to pounce on the damned and use them for their own ends. With that many souls at their disposal they could reenter Hell, and then we're all bent over a table being fucked."

I sniffed. "Are angels supposed to cuss?"

Uriel chuckled. "I do. But I'm not very polite by angelic standards, or any others." He leaned across his desk, and I braced myself for what was coming.

"We knew Lilith was up to something, but she's slippery, so when Leonid Karpov came to our attention, we . . . arranged protection for the two of you."

I pulled in on myself. "What?"

"Think of what's happened since you two met," Uriel said. "Your souls are drawn together, true, but did you ever think it was odd how Lilith could never quite lay hands on you? How Raphael helped you, even though she hates Hellspawn *and* Fallen and probably adorable fluffy puppies too?"

Something he'd said clicked together in my exhausted, battered brain and I snapped my gaze up. "You said you'd never met me *in person.*"

Uriel grinned. "I prefer talking to you like this, rather than digging around for a trusted memory and showing up in your head as your grandmother."

"Oh, fuck . . ." I moaned, burying my head in my hands. Uriel leaned against his desk.

"Others were skeptical about letting this play out the way it did, but I knew you'd figure out what Lilith was doing and I knew you'd stop her. Now Lucifer is gone, Lilith is outed, and no one in Hell is any wiser that the Kingdom has a presence here."

"I could have died," I snarled at him. "A *bunch* of times. You should have told me what was happening, that you were . . . I don't know . . . riding shotgun in my mind this whole time?"

"Just visiting occasionally," Uriel said. "Lilith and her reapers have done a good job of killing off either the reaper or their hound before they could find each other. This was the first time in a very long time both of you were born and survived long enough to meet."

I shivered uncontrollably, Uriel's words worse than any truth bomb Lilith could dump on me. He leaned forward and I braced myself for the other shoe to drop and explode my world even more. "I'm going to give you a choice, Ava, because I'm not just in it for myself. There's no upside to me letting you and Leonid continue to exist. I can blink your souls out of existence and that'll be that. The thousand-year cycle will be over. But . . ." He held up a finger. "Hell's been languishing for a long time without a leader. It's weak. And the Kingdom doesn't like weakness. The realms coexist, and if one of them collapses, it'll be like beads falling off a broken necklace."

He stood up again and gestured to me to do the same. I had to crane my neck to meet his eyes.

"That's the physics," Uriel said. "The practical side is that you're a lot better at killing Fallen and Hellspawn that most of us in the Kingdom. Real-world experience and all that." He opened the drawer he'd pointed to and handed me a black accordion folder. "That's every Fallen that survived the exodus. Leo takes up the mantle of Grim Reaper, you become his hound as you were meant to. The pair of you hunt down and destroy every last one of said Fallen, and you and Leo can go about your business of reaping souls until the heat death of the universe for all I care. You'll be together, and more important, you'll have our gratitude."

I swallowed. It was going to be harder to keep my cool than it had ever been when my life was actively in danger. Uriel was still smiling, but it wasn't reaching his eyes anymore. He was waiting for me to say no, and I had no doubt if I did it'd be my blood getting hosed off the floor.

"Clint—Azrael—doesn't remember anything about his time in Hell," I said. "I think as far as he's concerned what he told me was the truth."

"I really don't care about Azrael's feelings," Uriel said. "He did terrible things, Ava. He manipulated you and he enabled Lilith to set herself up as the queen bee in Hell, and by extension, he's responsible for you being a hound this time around. It was her reaper, right?"

I looked at my feet and nodded. "I'm just not sure how I feel about genocide."

"Genocide?" Uriel raised an eyebrow. "Ava, you're not wiping out something as precious and worthwhile as life. Think of it as correcting nature's mistake. Angels stay in the Kingdom, the Hellspawn in Hell, humans and the things born from them on Earth. There's no place in that picture for the Fallen."

I met his eyes again. "What happens if I say no?"

Uriel's face hardened. "I'm cleaning up Lucifer's and Azrael's mistakes one way or the other. Technically, you're one of them. I'm being generous here, Ava. I suggest you pull your head out of your ass and work for me. You keep breathing, the Fallen are gone, and

your buddy Leonid even gets to live on as the head of the reapers."
He gestured at the window. "He's going to be plenty busy rounding
up all the escapees from Tartarus, so it's probably best to just keep
this little side job on the Fallen between us."

I folded my arms. "You're pretty confident I'm going to say yes."

Uriel reached out and patted me on the shoulder. "You stick
with me, Ava, and you'll find out I always get what I want." He
went to his office and opened the door. "One way or another."

I hurried to the threshold, looking out into nothing but blank
white hall. "I haven't said yes."

Uriel pointed to the pair of doors at the end of the hall. "You
don't have to say it. Just don't try and cross me."

I thought about it. Not for very long. It wasn't a hard choice,
even if it was a shitty one. I wasn't going to toe up against an angel
for some principled stand. "How do I get out of this place?" I demanded. "I can't use the crossroads."

"You can," Uriel said. "You don't give yourself enough credit,
Ava. You're capable of things you can't even imagine yet." He smiled
and patted me on my sore arm. The ache and the throbbing in my
shoulder vanished, and I felt warm and relaxed, as if I'd just spent
an hour in the sun. Fucking angels. Always with the Dr. Feelgood
routine.

"Take the elevator all the way to the top," Uriel said. "It will
deposit you where you're supposed to go."

"And Leo?" I persisted. Uriel pointed at the elevator.

"He's already free."

I went to the door and pressed the black button set into the
featureless wall. I didn't think the Fallen deserved to be wiped
out wholesale, but I also didn't think somebody who lied to me

and told me I was always going to be a slave deserved my undying loyalty, either. Who was responsible for what happened to me in Bayou St. Charles a century ago, and the time before that, and the time before that, even if he didn't remember.

If getting out alive took agreeing to be Uriel's personal Fallen hit squad, then I'd do it. I'd do anything to survive. That wasn't the hound. That was me. The person I'd been all those millennia ago when Azrael had snatched me up and twisted me into the hound of Hell.

"Ava," Uriel called as the elevator doors rolled back. I turned. Shadowed as he was by the light of his office, he looked downright spooky, like a bird of prey watching me from a high wire.

"Yeah?" I whispered.

"If you try and fuck me over, there won't be a place in Hell or on Earth you can hide from me," Uriel said cheerfully. "I'll find you and I'll make you suffer."

The doors rolled shut before I could respond and I jabbed the top button, collapsing against the wall with my heart pounding. In the last twelve hours I'd been kidnapped by Lilith, traveled to Hell for the first time, almost been stranded in the Hellspawn equivalent of a supermax, and met an angel who would probably peel my skin like a grape if I crossed him.

And I was going to have to. Because scary as Uriel was, I was through being somebody's bitch. Nobody got to tell me to kill on command, ever again.

The doors rolled back and the lights flickered as I stepped out, and I winced as bright desert sun hit my eyes. I was standing on the side of the highway, the brown and red rolling hills of the Mojave spread out as far as the eye could see. The tall chain fences of the Nevada Proving Ground stood far away down a hill, but I was free of Tartarus. The crossroads had brought me back.

The air was hot and dusty and full of diesel fumes from the trucks rumbling in the distance as they headed down the mountain grade toward Vegas, and it had never smelled better.

I lifted my face and felt the hot sun.

I was alive. I'd never let myself think of it like that, not since that night so many years ago. It might not be the way I'd wanted it, but I was alive and that was beautiful and I kind of wanted to scream.

I opened my eyes when a car rumbled to a stop on the shoulder of the highway. It was low and black, classic muscle that grumbled like it was alive, white exhaust snorting from the tailpipe. The headlights were crimson, and as the window lowered I leaned down to tell the driver I didn't need a ride. I gasped instead.

"Hey," Leo said. "You look a little lost."

I yanked open the door and dove across the seat, wrapping my arms around him and squeezing. Leo grunted but put his arm around me in return. "If somebody had told me being dead would be this sweet I wouldn't have tried so hard to stay alive."

I sat back, looking at him. "Leo, you know—"

"I know," he cut me off.

"And Lucifer and Lilith . . ."

"Lilith went through the gate right along with you and her boyfriend and she didn't come back out," Leo said coldly. "I made sure of it." He reached over and opened the glove box. The interior of the car was as black as the outside, the glove box lined with satin. A small leather-bound black notebook sat inside. I picked it up and paged through it. The pages were blank, but as I looked, a name floated into view on the first page, followed by another, and another, so many that they crowded together in dizzying, indecipherable text.

"As far as anyone on this earth might care," Leo said, putting the car in gear but not releasing the brake, "I died back there in Oklahoma. Now it's just you and me."

"And a whole bunch of reapers with no leader who probably want your balls on a nice silver tray for sending Lilith to Tartarus," I said.

Leo looked at me. "Hey, if you don't want this, you can walk away."

I should have told him. Right there in the car, I should have told him the truth about Uriel and what I'd agreed to do. I should have told him everything.

But I didn't. I was alive. I had time, time to figure out what I was going to do about Uriel's ultimatum and about Clint's death sentence and about what Leo and I were supposed to do with this new ledger, weighted with the names of all those who had escaped from Tartarus.

Not to mention I had Leo. I'd never met anyone like him, and I didn't talk because I wanted to stay there, right there in the car with him, for as long as was humanly possible. I'd felt invisible until I met him, because he was who I was meant to stand beside, our souls irretrievably linked by Azrael.

Azrael was probably going to be sorry he'd ever brought us to Hell in the first place.

"I'm ready," I told Leo. "Where are we going?"

He accelerated onto the highway, heading east. "Got an address in that book for a place called Head Office. It's in Minneapolis. Figured that's as good a place to start as any."

I was quiet for a moment, and he looked at me as the road unfurled outside. "Ava?"

"What are we going to do?" I said quietly. "If it's the same as before, and we just keep running into problems like Lilith? Nothing ever ends well for me, Leo. Ever."

Leo shrugged. "Then we do what we were made for. We send the problem back to Hell, and we keep on going. It's not like either of us was ever going to have a happy ending, Ava. But we're together, and as far as I'm concerned that's not all bad."

"For me either," I said. Leo smiled and opened up the car's throttle. "Hey," I said, looking through the glove compartment and finding nothing but gum and an antique highway map. "Where's the Scythe?"

Leo gestured around himself. "You're sitting in it."

I felt my eyebrow go up. "I guess when you're created by the Fallen you get the VIP reaper treatment."

Leo pulled the familiar black pouch out of his jacket and handed it to me. "Doesn't have much juice anymore. I think icing Lucifer took the sting out of it. It's yours to do what you want with it."

I took the Scythe and turned it over in my hands. I shivered a little as I remembered the pain when Leo had stabbed me. When Annabelle had used a Scythe on me and when Gary had used his the time before that.

I rolled down the window and chucked the Scythe out as we went around a curve. It flashed once in the sun and disappeared into a ravine. "Minneapolis, huh?" I said. "I hate the cold."

"Doesn't bother me," Leo said. "I'm built for it. I'm Russian. Was," he corrected himself. "I'm gonna have a hard time getting used to that."

343

"It gets easier," I said. Leo reached over and patted my leg.

"I'm glad I have you to show me the ropes."

"I'm glad we made it long enough for me to show you," I said, and really meant it. Leo went quiet after that, but I didn't mind. I didn't mind what was waiting for us in Minneapolis, that our time could be cut short if one Hellspawn took it into his head he didn't like the changeover. I didn't even mind that Uriel was expecting me to become his executioner or that I still didn't really know anything about Hell and its obviously FUBAR politics beyond the tiny slice I'd been shown by Lilith.

Those were problems for tomorrow. Right now, today, I was alive, and I could sit here forever with Leo, driving into the rising sun and watching the road slip away, mile after mile, under my wheels.

ABOUT THE AUTHOR

Caitlin Kittredge has written fifteen novels for adults and teens, including the award-winning Iron Codex trilogy. She also writes the horror comic *Coffin Hill* for DC/Vertigo. Caitlin lives in Massachusetts with several spoiled cats and a vast collection of geeky ephemera. When she's not working she enjoys fixing up her 1881 Victorian house and reading extremely nerdy nonfiction books about serial killers, the cold war, fringe science, and anything else that strikes her fancy.